1836—1848:

The Saga Continues...

White House builder Jeremy Brand is gone, but his heritage lives on in Circumstance, his half-Indian daughter, who now risks her life to help run the Underground Railroad...in Bravo, love-child of Jeremy and Rebecca, discovering his illicit parentage, finding love and enduring terrible tragedy, and inheriting his father's wondrous gifts...and always in Rebecca, Jeremy's first love, advising presidents, ruling Washington's social life, and bearing the undying hatred of the aristocratic Connaughts, still thirsting for revenge on all the Brands.

Now the first locomotives shriek across the vast wilderness and the nation trembles on the brink of a new age. Andrew Jackson, Samuel F. B. Morse, Ulysses S. Grant, Presidents Van Buren and Tyler and Polk all will play a vital role in the story of the Brands...as that dynasty will, in turn, firmly take history into its own hands...

A DISTANT DREAM is their story, it is our story, and it is one of the most powerful stories ever told...

THE AMERICAN PALACE ★ BOOK 4

1836   1848

A DISTANT DREAM

Evan H. Rhodes

BERKLEY BOOKS, NEW YORK

A DISTANT DREAM

A Berkley Book/published by arrangement with
the author

PRINTING HISTORY
Berkley edition/June 1984

ISBN: 0-425-06592-8

For Beverly Lewis

"It is our Manifest Destiny to overspread the continent allotted by Providence for the free development of our yearly multiplying millions."

John L. O'Sullivan
1845

Preface

THE WHITE HOUSE...the most powerful office on earth. To Americans, it's the most visible symbol of our democracy. To the downtrodden of the world, it stands as a shining beacon of man's eternal quest for freedom.

In October 1792, when the cornerstone was laid, the building was called the American Palace, and in 1810 a new name, the White House, came into popular use. But no matter what the name, legend surrounds it, for in this house that belongs to all the American people, lives the one man they've chosen to lead them through times of peace and war, adversity and triumph.

As the White House rose, and the tiny village that was Washington, D.C., grew, so too did Rebecca Breech grow, becoming a woman of extraordinary intelligence and beauty. The Brand brothers, Zebulon and Jeremy, loved her, and she was fated to marry one but to love another. Through the tempestuous years of the young nation's emergence, Rebecca, right at the center of power, became the conscience of the country.

Dishonor and death stalked her, for she was a woman whose passions constantly put her in harm's way. But she survived, and became the matriarch of the Brand dynasty, a family destined to serve the nation and the White House. She herself became the confidante of Presidents, often their gadfly, and numbered among her intimate friends the great and near-great in the executive office, the Supreme Court, and Congress.

Rebecca imbued her children, Suzannah, Gunning, and Bravo, with her own consuming idealism for the United States, the greatest experiment in democracy that the world has ever known. Her children and grandchildren also came to serve the White House and the nation in various capacities, and in their zeal, learned to know the First Families not only as the general public perceives them, but as intimate friends privy to their innermost, darkest secrets. The Brands, and we, learn the answers to some intriguing questions:

Which President, though out of office for years, was still able to play kingmaker and have his protégé elected to the highest office in the land?

Which former President, subsequently elected to Congress, battled for eight years to repeal a Gag Rule that he believed was unconstitutional, and during this struggle was threatened with violence and death by his fellow congressmen?

Which President created a national scandal when, after the death of his wife, he married an heiress thirty years his junior?

Which First Lady insisted on having a court of twelve ladies-in-waiting to attend her at White House functions?

Which President died in office a scant month after his election, lending credence to the curse leveled against the White House that said any President elected in a year ending in zero would die in office? In 1840, 1860, 1880, 1900, 1920, 1940, and 1960, that curse proved to be horribly true. Will it strike again for the President elected in 1980?

Which President set himself the goal of acquiring all the land from the Atlantic to the Pacific for the United States, and in the process went to war and had that unpopular conflict named after him?

As the generations of the Brand family become more important in the growth of the nation, and as their relationships with the White House grow ever more complex, more questions will be raised, and more answers revealed:

Which President participated in séances in the White House to contact his dead son?

Which First Lady, accused of being a spy for the enemy, had to be publicly defended by her husband?

Which President, though a great general, was one of the

most inept executive officers this nation has produced, presiding over a scandal-ridden administration?

Which First Lady, reputedly passionate in her lovemaking, had the most profound effect on her husband's policies?

All this and more will be revealed in this book and in *The American Palace* series.

Now Book Four, *A Distant Dream*, continues where Book Three ended, with Rebecca Brand journeying from Texas to Washington with her gravely injured grandson, Matty, while the Connaught family, archenemies of the Brands and traitors to America, plot to see that Rebecca and her grandson never reach Washington alive.

THE BREECH–BRAND FAMILY TREE

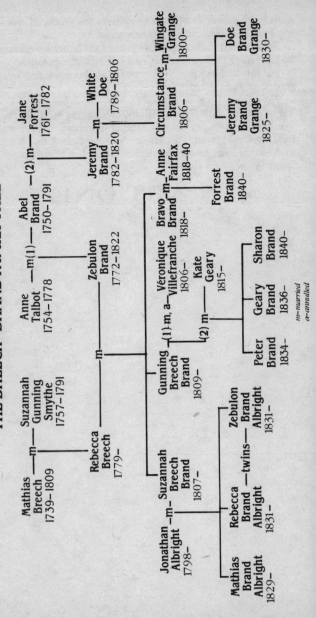

PART ONE

Chapter 1

"How is Matty?" Rebecca Breech Brand anxiously asked Enoch, her young black servant. She'd left the steamboat cabin for a few moments to find out when they'd be docking in Baltimore; the city should soon be visible in the gray dawn light. But for Rebecca, every minute she spent away from her grandson filled her with the fear that he'd slip away from her.

"He's pretty much the same," the freedman said. "Hasn't stirred at all. Just sleeping, peaceful and innocent."

If only it were just sleep, Rebecca thought. She gazed at her seven-year-old grandson, feeling a pain so profound that it was all she could do to keep from sobbing. White bandages wound around his head, stained red and brown along the line where his skull had been fractured.

"Oh Lord, Lord, why must it always be the innocent who suffer?" Rebecca murmured.

Enoch cleared his throat. "Mrs. Brand, it wouldn't hurt if you tried to sleep some more. I'll keep my eye on him, wake you if there's any change. You haven't hardly slept at all in the two weeks, since Galveston."

Enoch, the hired hand of Suzannah and Jonathan Albright, Rebecca's daughter and son-in-law, had come with Rebecca and Matty from Texas. Every doctor in the western territory had pronounced Matty's case hopeless. Most of them couldn't

3

understand why the boy was still alive. But Rebecca, refusing to give up hope, had persuaded Suzannah to let her take Matty back to Washington, D.C., with her. "I know Wingate can help him," she insisted. "You may think of him as just your cousin's husband, but he's the finest doctor in Washington. He's kept President Jackson alive all these years."

Suzannah agreed; Wingate Grange was their last hope. She'd wanted to go with Rebecca herself, but there were the twins, Zeb and Becky, to take care of and the ranch to rebuild, so she'd sent Enoch along as protection for her mother and son.

Rebecca propped herself in the corner of the bunk and passed her hand over her eyes, feeling all the weariness of her fifty-seven years. She was still an uncommonly attractive woman, though the events of the past months had etched anxiety deep into her face. Her once flamboyant auburn hair was fast turning white, and her huge, luminous hazel eyes alternately reflected pain and hope—pain for all that her grandson had been through, and the prayerful hope that his life could still be saved.

In November of 1835, little more than six months ago, Rebecca had journeyed from Washington to Texas to visit her estranged daughter, Suzannah, whom she hadn't seen in seven years. Rebecca decided that she had to bury all the old griev-ances she held against her son-in-law, Jonathan Albright, for that was the only way she would get to know her three grand-children.

When Andrew Jackson learned of her plan to go to Texas, he asked her to be his eyes and ears in that Mexican territory. Jackson had never given up the dream of the United States occupying all the land from sea to shining sea, and Texas played a crucial part in those dreams. As a young woman seeking an outlet for her driving intelligence, Rebecca had begun writing political pamphlets under the male pseudonym Rebel Thorne—in the young country, a woman's political viewpoints were rarely taken seriously. Through the years, Rebel Thorne's pen had championed the cause of freedom, notably in the War of 1812, and in Jackson's battle against the Second Bank of the United States. Though Rebel Thorne had sometimes erred in political assessments, the country recognized that this voice was on the side of the angels, and Thorne's reputation had grown.

When Rebecca's identity was finally discovered, President Jackson had flown into a rage and roundly excoriated her. But several years later, when the crisis in Texas developed, Jackson had hinted that Rebecca might wield her pen in the cause of Texas freedom. Rebecca had tentatively agreed, thinking she might do her country a small service.

But she hadn't been prepared for the maelstrom that engulfed her. American settlers in Texas had sought more equal representation in the Mexican government; failing that, they had rebelled. A few weeks after Rebecca arrived at the Albright ranch near San Antonio, General Antonio López de Santa Anna, president of Mexico—in reality dictator—swept into Texas with an army of five thousand men to quell the Texas rebellion.

Rebecca and Matty were in San Antonio when Santa Anna had entered the city, and she was forced to watch the fall of the Alamo, forced to watch all its gallant defenders butchered by Santa Anna, who'd ordered that no quarter be given. Rebecca also discovered, to her horror, that Devroe Connaught, the nemesis of the Brand family, was working as a secret British agent, helping Santa Anna. For decades, the lives of the Connaughts and the Brands had been threaded through with hatred and lust for revenge. Rebecca feared Devroe as she feared no other man, for this was not a man who could be reached with reason—this man was mad.

After the fall of the Alamo, General Santa Anna, realizing Rebecca's reputation as a reporter, released her with the admonition, "Go and tell your countrymen about the invincibility of the Mexican Army! All those who come to Texas to aid the rebellion will be slaughtered like these perfidious rebels!"

Rebecca didn't argue with Santa Anna; her principal concern was to get Matty back to the Albright ranch. But her fears about Devroe came to pass when he ambushed her on the road to the ranch. Only by some miracle had she and Matty escaped with their lives. Though in Matty's case, he now barely clung to life.

Then had come the ordeal of the Runaway Scrape. Thousands of Texans fled for the border of Louisiana before the dread scourge—General Santa Anna, the butcher of San Antonio and Goliad. Sam Houston—leading a handful of men, Jonathan Albright among them—tried to stem the might of the Mexican army, drawing it deeper and deeper into Texas. Each new atrocity perpetrated by Santa Anna forged the Texans into a more resolute fighting unit. Finally at the Battle of San Jacinto, spurred on by Houston's cry, "Remember the Alamo!"

the Texans avenged the deaths of their brothers, and crushed
the Mexican army.

Though Texas had achieved its independence, it mattered
little to Rebecca; nothing mattered unless Matty lived. For she
and she alone was responsible for his condition. If she had not
opposed Suzannah's marrying Jonathan Albright, they would
have remained in Washington, since Jonathan had been Andrew
Jackson's aide. And had she not come to Texas now, Devroe
Connaught's mad vengeance would never have touched the
innocent boy.

The blast of the ship's whistle rending the air caused Matty
to cry out. Rebecca instantly crouched beside him, stroking his
feverish forehead. "How are you?" she murmured.

He looked at her through wounded eyes. "Grandma, I still
hurt," he whispered.

"I know, my darling, but very soon you're going to be all
right. Did you hear that whistle? That means we're coming to
Baltimore, and soon we'll be in Washington. We're going to
see the best doctor there. Remember? I told you all about him—
your cousin Wingate."

Matty moved his head in a slight nod.

They heard the mate on deck sing out, "Baltimore! Baltimore dead ahead!"

"Can we go outside, Grandma?" Matty asked. "I want to
see it."

Rebecca debated for a moment, then gave in; perhaps the
fresh sea breeze would help him. She bundled him in a blanket,
then Enoch carried him outside. With the cool breezes of the
June morning on their faces, they stood at the rail, listening to
the piping of the gulls that followed in the steamboat's churning
wake. Ahead of them, the distant spires of Baltimore grew ever
larger.

As they entered Baltimore's harbor, Rebecca pointed out
the brick structure that stood guard on their right. "That's Fort
McHenry," she told Matty. "Do you know that's where your
father and I first met? He was only seventeen, acting as a
courier. General Jackson was fighting down in Alabama, and
had sent him with war communiqués for President Madison.
But when your father heard that the British were attacking
Baltimore, he came here to help. A huge British fleet sailed
into the harbor, more than fifty big ships. The British had just
burned Washington, D.C., and they knew that if they could

capture the big port of Baltimore, they would split the United States in two and win the War of 1812. I was watching from a farm on that hill over there, and your father, thinking that I was a spy, wanted to arrest me as a spy. I must say it made me rather angry, until he decided to let me go.

"Well, all night long they bombarded our fort. If they could breach its defenses, they knew they could invade Baltimore. The rockets and the cannons were enough to make you deaf. But in the light of the rockets, we could see that the flag was still flying over the fort. We had won! The only thing the British could do was pull their armada back and retreat.

"The next January your father was with General Jackson when he defeated the British at the Battle of New Orleans. We had won our Second War for Independence, and for the first time, we felt as if we really were a nation of one people."

As she told the story, Matty clutched her hand, his grip growing fiercer as the waves of pain washed over him. His other hand moved to his head and pressed against the bandage. Then his eyes closed and he drifted off into unconsciousness.

When the steamboat had docked, Rebecca learned to her dismay that heavy rains had washed out sections of the road to Washington, D.C. The stagecoach station master warned her that the ride would be bumpy.

"But you know, the Baltimore Railroad has just started a daily run to Washington," he said.

"You mean the railroad tracks have already been laid?" Rebecca was surprised, until she recalled that she'd been gone almost eight months. "How's the service on that?"

"Why, right fine," the station master said. "We've hardly had any derailments at all, maybe one or two every week or so. And the cows are learning to stay away from the tracks. Though the other day the engine did run one down, and the farmer went after the engineer with his shotgun. But outside of that, we're getting the passengers to Washington in one piece."

Rebecca shook her head. She couldn't risk a derailment. "Enough. Instead of taking the stage or the train to Washington, I think it's wiser for me to go by packetboat to Georgetown. I'm afraid a bumpy ride could do Matty serious injury."

"Maybe that is the best," Enoch agreed.

"But I want you to take the stage to Washington. You'll get there quicker than on the packet. Tell my son Bravo that I'm coming, and that he's to meet me at Georgetown with our carriage. Tell him that he must bring Wingate Grange with him."

"Don't you think I ought to stay with you?" Enoch asked. "I told Miss Suzannah I'd watch out for you and the boy."

Rebecca touched his arm. "Thank you, Enoch; you've been my rod and my staff on this trip. I don't know what I would have done without you. But this is the better way. I want everything ready when we get there tomorrow evening. And I want Wingate to start thinking of how he's going to help Matty."

"Whatever you say, ma'am."

Rebecca booked passage on the packet to Georgetown, which would leave with the tide. During her time onshore, she'd been so concerned with Matty, she'd paid scant attention to the people who haunted the quay. She would have been horrified to know that one of them was Sisley Urquhart, the aging servant of the Connaughts. He'd spend the past week scanning the passenger arrivals and departures, on the off chance that Rebecca Breech Brand would arrive in Baltimore.

When he saw her, his scarred, pitted face went white. He waited until he was sure which boat she was taking, and then mounted his horse. Soon he was galloping toward the Connaught plantation in the hills above Washington.

Chapter 2

VÉRONIQUE VILLEFRANCHE CONNAUGHT surveyed her elegant pine-paneled dining room with a critical eye. The crystal chandelier and the cut-glass goblets fairly sparkled in the last rays of afternoon sun, and the Queen Anne silver gleamed on the polished Chippendale dining table.

Though she and Devroe were dining alone this evening, Véronique prepared, as always, with the same exquisite attention to detail she would have given a state dinner. It never failed to impress her husband, whose entire life was shaped by rigid codes of form and usage.

She plucked a gardenia from the floral centerpiece and tucked it into the loose love knot lying on the nape of her neck. The flower was hidden from view, but its vaguely evocative scent surrounded her. Véronique delighted in such bits of feminine mystery; they appealed to the performer in her. In this fashion she'd once pleased and aroused audiences on both sides of the Atlantic, but now she had the infinitely more exacting task of perpetually pleasing and seducing her husband, Devroe. With his austere, frosty English manner, it was not an easy task.

Their marriage had been anything but a love match; it had been conceived as little more than a practical arrangement, with their shared hatred of the Brand family as a bond. "But hate can be just as potent a force as love," she murmured. She

9

opened the French doors leading to the formal boxwood gardens, fragrant with scent from beds of phlox and the last sprays of lilac. The Connaught plantation house was situated on top of a hill, and many miles in the distance, she caught a glimpse of the capital, a city of perhaps twenty-five thousand, nestled at the fork of two branches of the Potomac River.

Though she grudgingly admitted that the setting was pretty, Véronique detested Washington; she thought it provincial and stultifying in its quasi-Puritan morality.

"It will never compare to the great capitals of the world," she mused aloud. "Certainly not Rome, London, or Paris."

Yet she couldn't help but wonder at the strange workings of the fate that had made this city so important in her life. Perhaps it was because here she'd first experienced the abandon of love.

Gunning Brand . . . a man with as heroic a physique and appetite as a woman could hope to meet in this lifetime. She'd been a young toe dancer in her father Audubert Villefranche's troupe in those years, but she'd always had her eye on the main chance. She set her cap for Gunning, and despite his mother Rebecca's interference, Véronique snared and married him— only to discover that he was wanted by the army for being absent without leave. His reason was undeniably, and flatteringly, romantic—he'd deserted his duties in order to go to New York to be with her. Nevertheless, his rashness had jeopardized her and her father; the authorities threatened to deport them both. To protect herself, she did the only thing she could: she cooperated with the police to insure his capture. All this was engineered by the deft hand of Devroe Connaught, who long ago had sworn to bring the Brands to their knees.

Too late she learned that Devroe had been using her also. In fact, he had arranged to have Gunning catch her and himself *in flagrante*, leading to the duel in which Gunning had almost been killed. When Véronique's marriage to Gunning was annulled—by that bitch, Rebecca—Véronique suddenly found herself about to be abandoned by Devroe.

Playing a desperate gambit, she let Devroe know that she was privy to his secret—he was an intelligence agent working for the British government in the United States. She told Devroe that she'd given that information to her attorneys; if anything happened to her, the full story would be made public.

Nonetheless, Devroe had been on the verge of eliminating

her, when she proposed an alternative so shocking that he could only listen in awe. "Marriage. I will give you a social acceptance you could never gain by remaining a bachelor. Already Washington is rife with rumors about your exotic tastes. I will bear you heirs. I will be your helpmate in the destruction of the Brands."

Devroe listened, not immune to her logic—or to her driving ambition. To keep her under his power, he agreed to marry her, first having her sign a prenuptial agreement renouncing all claims to the Connaught fortune. He planned to discard her as soon as she'd produced an heir to continue the Connaught name in America. But the firstborn was a girl, named Romance. Using every bit of her feminine wiles, Véronique had gotten herself pregnant again. This time, it was a boy, named Sean, after Devroe's father. And then somehow she'd produced another son, a beautiful child named Carleton, whom the stupid slaves had immediately nicknamed Cotton.

She and Devroe settled into a prickly relationship, with Véronique constantly toiling to justify her position as mistress of the Connaught estate. Though her life was filled with tensions, she rarely regretted the choice she'd made. With each year, her position in Washington society grew stronger; she had a natural talent as a hostess, and the great and near-great of Washington supped at her table. She lacked for nothing in the way of clothes and jewelry, and she adored her children. How different from the life she'd led, dancing in scanty costumes before leering audiences, at the mercy of any man who could afford to buy her a meal. Now she called the tune, and people danced to that. Regrets? Never! . . . save in the dead of night, when she remembered Gunning's golden body, remembered his relentless passions which had transported her to . . .

"Ah, you are acting like a schoolgirl," she chastised herself. Then she grew alert at the sound of her husband coming downstairs. The moment Véronique saw his thin, pallid face, made even more bloodless by the tension of the moment, she knew that something was seriously wrong. He wore an elegant black silk evening suit cut by his tailors in Bond Street, with a white silk shirt with ruffles at the throat and cuffs. He kneaded his crippled right hand with his left, his habit when he was distressed.

"Urquhart came back this afternoon. What I've feared all along has happened," he said tersely. "Madam Brand has finally

reached Baltimore. Tomorrow evening, she should arrive at
Georgetown."

"What will you do?" Véronique heard her own fear in her
question.

"I may have to leave the country."

"But that's insane!" she gasped. "Uproot our lives? Jeopardize the children's health with a long voyage to the Continent?
All because of some woman who should be dead anyway? I
won't have it!"

Devroe poured himself a glass of whiskey and downed it
in one gulp. Véronique couldn't help but notice that his hand
shook when he lifted the glass, and this unnerved her even
more. "Devroe, tell me, from the most objective viewpoint,
just how serious can this really be?"

"Very serious indeed. The woman saw me participate in the
battle for the Alamo, heard me discussing military strategy
with General Santa Anna. She knows I've been working for
the downfall of Texas, and she'll accuse me of being a spy."

"But Texas is a thousand miles away," Véronique exclaimed. "It's her word against yours. And who is she? A
commoner, a woman whose father was a stone merchant! How
could she stand up against a Connaught? Surely you'd be able
to face her down."

"I've no doubt that I'd be able to do just that," Devroe said.
"But once the suspicion is planted, the damage is done. You
also forget that this misbegotten nation that calls itself a democracy likes nothing better than to turn everything upside
down. Here a commoner's word carries as much weight as an
aristocrat's. You also forget that Madam Brand is an intimate
of President Andrew Jackson's. She'll poison him against me.
Even if I should escape legal censure, my effectiveness as an
agent for His Majesty's government will be ended."

Véronique scrambled for a way out of this dilemma. "Would
it be so terrible for us if we went to England?"

"You know that I have invested heavily in western lands,
and have been forced to put up this plantation and the next
crop as security. If we leave now, we lose everything. In
America, I'm an outstanding member of the Washington community. In England, with our circumstances reduced, we'd be
little more than minor members of the Connaught clan. And
we'd be returning to England as failures. His Majesty's government won't look kindly on that, particularly since they've

invested so heavily on my mission in the United States."

"Well then, we can't let it happen," she said firmly. "We must stop this meddlesome woman."

"I thought I'd finished her in San Antonio," he said. "But the Brands lead charmed lives." He touched his cheek and temple, scarred by the murderous spines of a cactus that Rebecca Breech Brand had plunged into his face.

"When did you say that her boat will dock in Georgetown?" she asked.

"Tomorrow evening. She has her grandson with her, the one I . . . inadvertently injured. Doubtless she'll use the child to gain sympathy, and that can cause us grievous harm."

"Devroe, we've worked too hard to allow this woman to ruin our lives, and the lives of our children. *Something* must be done."

They worried the problem endlessly through dinner. Over a crème caramel topped with slivers of chocolate and crushed pecans, Véronique said, "There is only one solution." She waited until the butler left the room, and then began to outline a plan, a plan which seemed to grow more feasible as she spoke.

When she finished, Devroe said, "Your idea sounds promising, but there is one tiny flaw. If it were discovered, it would mean prosecution in the District of Columbia, and I doubt if my rather checkered career would withstand such scrutiny. The authorities might even make other connections, and conceivably unearth some evidence concerning the assassination attempt on President Jackson."

Véronique's eyes widened at that piece of information. She'd always suspected that Devroe was involved in that scandal, but this was the first time he'd ever mentioned it. A deranged English housepainter had tried to gun down the President on the steps of the Capitol, in January of 1835. President Jackson had insisted that the man had been part of a conspiracy. And now Devroe had confirmed Véronique's own suspicions. She filed away that bit of information in her mind, determined to use it if ever her position with Devroe was threatened.

"You're right, my husband," she said sweetly. "Nothing must be traced back to you. I'll take care of the entire matter myself."

"You can do this?"

"I can."

"What about the boy? If it goes as you suggest, he'll be killed also."

Véronique shrugged. "You say he's already little more than a vegetable. Of what value is such a life, measured against the lives and fortunes of our own children? Besides, he's the child of Suzannah Brand Albright, and it was through her that you lost the use of your arm. Surely this is poetic justice, *non?*"

Devroe kneaded the limp arm. He would carry this crippled, useless limb to the grave, but revenge on Suzannah and Jonathan Albright would make it an easier burden to bear.

"My dear, when do you plan to accomplish all this?" Devroe asked.

"I should leave for Washington this very night. I've many arrangements to make. Devroe, have a carriage waiting for me. No coachman, I'll drive myself. The fewer people who know of this the better. Oh, and it might be wise for you to be seen in public. Tomorrow evening, why not dine with friends in Washington? Daniel Webster, or Henry Clay, or both, would establish an unshakable alibi."

He leaned toward her, took her hand and raised it to his lips. He liked her plan. In fact, he'd drafted one on similar lines. But how much better if she were the one to take the risks! "If you accomplish this, you shall have earned my deepest gratitude."

"Thank you." It eased her heart to hear him say that, eased the feeling that she was continually balanced on a precipice, waiting for the slightest wind to topple her to destruction. Perhaps with this act she would convince him of her usefulness. But the truth was, that even without Devroe's gratitude as a spur, Véronique would have chosen this course of action herself. In no way would she permit Rebecca Breech Brand to jeopardize the future of her children.

She hurried upstairs and went to her dressing table. In a rear compartment, she still kept some of her old stage makeup. She'd never understood why she hung on to this remnant of her earlier, unhappy existence, but now she was glad of it.

Véronique was beautiful; she knew it, and so did most of Washington. Her flawless complexion, coquettish dark-brown eyes, lustrous dark hair, and piquant face were well known and widely recognized. "Therefore, I must do something to change that," she said to her reflection.

She labored for over an hour; first, a lump of putty on her

nose to broaden and lengthen it, which she then artfully covered
with greasepaint and then powder. Deep lines drawn at the
corners of her mouth disguised her almost perfect lips—lips
that had inflamed Gunning Brand, and had proved the salvation
of her romance with Devroe. She painstakingly drew myriad
crow's feet radiating out from her eyes, muting their passionate
luster. Finally, she dusted her hair with white powder so that
she no longer looked like the beauteous matron of thirty, but
rather like an old woman of sixty.

She chose a dark dress of linsey-woolsey, then donned a
nondescript hooded cloak. "My own father wouldn't know
me," she said, delighted with the transformation. She thought
for a moment, then slipped a loaded pistol into her reticule.

Making sure that none of the servants were about, she slipped
downstairs and out the front door. Horse and carriage were
waiting; she got in and drove off.

Night had fallen by the time she reached the darkened streets
of Washington. The streets were deserted. Only a few lanterns
were lit in front of major government buildings, and she avoided
those streets. She headed to the western sector of the city,
toward Foggy Bottom, and the dens of gambling and whoredom
that lined the riverfront. These were the haunts of the German
and Irish laborers imported to help build the capital. Here too
were the taverns filled with prostitutes and sailors who'd jumped
ship, the flotsam and jetsam of the New World. Among them,
she would find four men to do her bidding. For a price.

Curiously, along with her fear, she felt the vague stirrings
of excitement, that she could find herself in such a position of
power—of life and death, as it were. And that she would finally
be rid of Rebecca Breech Brand, a woman who'd thwarted her
at every possible turn.

Yes, Véronique thought, driving into Foggy Bottom, I do
understand Devroe's obsession with revenge. "There are times
when only revenge can soothe the spirit. And I shall have it."

Chapter 3

ENOCH RAPPED hard on the heavy paneled door; this was the address Miss Rebecca had given him, 18th Street and New York Avenue. All the polished brass sparkled in the morning light, the shutters on the elegant brick house glowed with fresh paint, and the white window boxes sported a riot of geraniums.

Enoch's journey from Baltimore to Washington had taken a long time. The stagecoach didn't start until noon, and the roads were pocked with potholes from the heavy spring rains. Some sections were washed out completely. Three miles from Bladensburg, the stagecoach broke an axle, so the passengers had to walk to that village. There Enoch had stayed overnight in a barn, since he would have quickly gotten lost in the dark in the strange city of Washington. He'd set out again on foot at dawn.

"Here I am at last," Enoch said, as he heard footsteps approaching inside the house. The door was opened by one of the prettiest, light-skinned mulatto girls he'd ever seen, and it was some moments before he found his voice. "Does Bravo Brand live here?"

Bittersweet wiped her hands on her gingham apron to get off the light film of flour. She'd been helping her grandmother Letitia bake bread, and as the tall black man continued to stare at her, she wished she'd had a chance to tidy up.

"Bravo Brand lives here," she said. "But he's working right now and doesn't want to be disturbed."

"This is important," Enoch said. "I have a message from his mother."

Bittersweet's hand flew to her mouth. "Is Miss Rebecca all right? Where is she?"

"She's fine, but I could tell you better if you'd let me in."

"Bittersweet, who's all at the door?" came the querulous voice of Letitia, the Negro maid who'd raised Rebecca and had been with her family all her life. "Anybody selling anything, we don't want any."

Bittersweet ushered the tall, strapping black man into the kitchen, where her grandmother sat at the table, carefully peeling and slicing apples for a pie. Letitia, close to seventy now, suffered from stiff joints, and milky cataracts blurred her vision. In contrast to Bittersweet, her skin was very dark. A blue bandanna covered her crisp white hair.

"This man's come to see Bravo, Grandma," Bittersweet said excitedly. "Says he has a message from Miss Rebecca."

The paring knife clattered from Letitia's gnarled fingers and she rose on shaky feet. "My Rebecca be all right?" she asked anxiously. "Oh my Lord, that woman be such a trial, going off everywhere without me. Never could take care of herself."

"She's all right," Enoch reassured her, curiously moved at the concern this woman had for Rebecca. "She ought to be here this evening. I've come from Texas with her."

"Texas?" Letitia cried. "Then what about my Suzannah?" She grabbed Enoch's arms. "Tell me she's all right."

"She's just fine." He wondered whether to say anything about Matty, then decided against it. "Could I see Mr. Bravo now?"

"This way," Letitia said, and led Enoch toward the basement door. "He's down there, fooling around with another invention. Like to blow the whole house up under us, he will, and that's all I got to say about the matter. Now I got to get the rooms ready, change the linen, everything fresh."

"Bravo?" Bittersweet called. "Somebody to see you. It's important."

"Send him down," Bravo shouted up the stairs. "I can't stop what I'm doing now."

Enoch followed Bittersweet down the stairs, ducking his head to keep from bumping it. He walked into a low-ceilinged basement that was set up with all sorts of machinery. A tall youth, no more than seventeen or eighteen years old, stood hunched over a drill press, which was attached to some sort of foot-pedal contraption with a huge stone flywheel.

"Hello, I'm Bravo Brand, and I'll be with you in a minute," the young man said.

Enoch watched as Bravo's deft hands guided a sharp drill that stripped away a spiral of metal from a long metal cylinder. The lad's shoulders were thin but quite broad; his rolled-up shirtsleeves displayed wiry biceps. Yet despite the waves of energy that emanated from him, there was something so gentle and naïve in his expression that Enoch couldn't help smiling. He liked Bravo at once.

Then Bravo finished, disconnected the drill, and turned to Enoch letting the flywheel coast to a stop. "Sorry to keep you waiting." Enoch thought he'd never seen a man with more startling coloring. His hair was flaxen, almost white, and his eyes were such a light, vivid blue that they looked like pieces of the sky set in his head.

Very quickly, Enoch told Bravo what had happened, assured him that Suzannah and her family were all right, and gave him Rebecca's instructions. "Matty is very sick," he finished softly. "I didn't say anything upstairs, because I didn't want to upset the old woman. But Miss Rebecca wants you to bring Dr. Grange when you pick her up in Georgetown."

Bravo paced the narrow aisle between his workbench and the machinery. "When is the boat due?"

"According to the schedule, late this afternoon."

"All right," Bravo said. "We'll get there early enough so there won't be any chance of missing her. Bittersweet, run and tell Circumstance and Wingate that Mother's coming home, and ask Wingate if he'll be good enough to come with me about three."

Bittersweet nodded, and then with a last fleeting look at Enoch, raced up the stairs and out the door, hurrying to Circumstance's house on the other side of the White House grounds.

While Bravo was cleaning up, Enoch looked around. "I've never seen a workshop like this before. Miss Suzannah talked about all the things you used to make, but I never . . . What's that you're doing now?"

"It's a very complicated project, harder than anything I've tried to do up to now. You see, a few months ago, a man named Sam Colt applied for a patent. I saw the application because I like to see the devices people want to patent—and when I'm old enough, I want to work at the Patent Office. Anyway, Colt's device could make a pistol shoot more than one bullet at a time. As a matter of fact, it could make a pistol shoot *five* bullets without reloading."

"Five?" Enoch repeated incredulously. "Without reloading?"

"It's true. The Patent Office granted Colt a patent. I'd been working on something similar—matter of fact, I've been corresponding with Eli Whitney about my ideas."

"Name sounds familiar."

"He's a gun manufacturer in Connecticut," Bravo said. "And he's the famous inventor of the cotton gin."

Enoch scratched his head. "Invented the cotton gin and makes guns? Funny combination."

"Well, Whitney encouraged me in what I was doing, but Sam Colt beat me out," Bravo said, smiling. "Colt calls his invention a revolver. There aren't any for sale yet—probably won't be for a couple of years." He handed his gun to Enoch. "That's what I was making when you came downstairs."

"You sure this thing will work?" Enoch asked dubiously. It was a cumbersome-looking gun, not at all sleek like a dueling pistol.

"No. I haven't tried it out yet," Bravo said. "But in theory it should work. You press the trigger to shoot the first bullet, then it makes the cylinder revolve—see?—moving the next bullet into position. It can do that five times in all before you have to reload."

"Why then, if Sam Houston had a few of these—these revolvers at San Jacinto, it would have made the fight that much easier. You could shoot down five enemies with this kind of thing while they were trying to reload."

"Exactly," Bravo said. "Whichever country perfects this kind of weapon first—well, you see the position they'd be in. One man would become equal to five."

"You say you've finished it?" Enoch asked.

"Just about. I was putting in a different kind of bore into the barrel. I think it will make the bullet's trajectory more accurate."

Enoch nodded. He didn't understand half of what this boy was saying, yet he somehow believed him.

"Bravo!" Letitia called down the stairs. "Bring that boy up and let him eat, you hear? He must be starved."

She had put out a cold platter: ham and cheese, generous slices of whole wheat bread and freshly churned butter, and a mug of cider. Enoch fell to with a will. Letitia kept feeding him, all the while questioning him about Suzannah and Jonathan and their children.

Letitia's son Tad, who worked as a stablehand and driver for the Brand family, came in with another jug of cider and refilled Enoch's mug, then stood in the corner listening.

When Enoch finally confessed that little Matty was ill, Letitia clutched her bosom. "I knew it! My heart told me that everything wasn't all right. But now that he's here, Letitia will get him well, you'll see."

"Tad, fix up a room over the carriage house," Bravo said. "We'll put Enoch up there."

Almost as soon as Tad went out, Wingate Grange and Circumstance arrived and pressed Enoch again for all the details. Circumstance, the half-breed daughter of Jeremy Brand and an Indian maiden he'd met while on the Lewis and Clark expedition in 1805, was now a striking woman of thirty. She had the tawny skin, prominent cheekbones, and almond-shaped eyes that spoke of her Indian heritage. But the color of her eyes, an aquamarine-blue, was a direct legacy from her father, Jeremy.

Her husband, Wingate, after struggling for several years as a young doctor, had risen to some prominence in Washington because he'd become one of Andrew Jackson's personal physicians. So far, Wingate had been successful in keeping that desperately ill man alive.

Bravo asked Wingate about Matty's condition. "What do you think? Will he get better?"

"It's impossible to tell anything until I've examined the boy," Wingate said. "But it sounds very serious. When I was young, I saw some such operations performed on the battlefield at New Orleans, but none of the men survived. Of course, that was more than twenty years ago, and medicine has advanced a great deal, but..." His gentle voice trailed off.

"But there is hope, isn't there?" Circumstance asked anxiously. "Oh my God, what poor Suzannah must be going through."

Bravo grasped Wingate's arm. "You saved Gunning's life

after Devroe tricked him into that duel. We can't let Suzannah's
son die; we—" He broke off, his voice choked with tears.

That afternoon, Bravo hitched two horses to the carriage
and he and Wingate set out. Tad and Enoch wanted to go along,
but Bravo said, "We don't know when the boat is actually
arriving, and there's a heck of a lot to do around the house to
get it ready for mother. You know how particular she is."

"I don't like you riding out without extra hands," Tad said,
and Letitia agreed. "The roads are bad," Tad continued, "and
there's been lots of robberies and things."

Bravo knew that Tad spoke the truth. Feverish land spec-
ulations and the battle between Jackson and the Second Bank
of the United States had brought ruinous inflation to the country. The perpetual malcontents and the petty criminals were
using this as an excuse for growing lawlessness.

"Thanks, Tad," Bravo said. "But Georgetown isn't that
far—only two miles. We'll be home well before dark. If we're
not here by dark, come and get us then."

Pennsylvania Avenue was the main thoroughfare between
Washington and Georgetown, its older sister city, which remained the port and principal market for the District of Columbia. Bravo turned onto M Street, Georgetown's main avenue,
where the shops bustled with activity. Though the harbor was
slowly silting over, ships still came into the port, though not
nearly in the numbers George Washington had hoped for. At
the waterfront, Bravo hitched up the carriage, then he and
Wingate paced the wharves, scanning the horizon, waiting for
the Baltimore packetboat.

As the evening approached and the boat still didn't appear,
Bravo grew more agitated. Wingate put his hand on the boy's
shoulder. "This is a time for steady nerves. I can't afford to
have two patients on my hands."

Bravo slumped. "Of course you're right. It's just that I feel
so helpless waiting. I wanted to go to Texas with mother, but
she wouldn't hear of it, said I had to finish my studies at the
university. And so I have, but what good is any of that if
Matty . . . I should have gone with mother!"

Another hour, and still no sign of the packetboat. Finally,
just around dusk, the ship maneuvered into the harbor and
docked.

"There's mother!" Bravo exclaimed, pointing to Rebecca,

standing at the rail. As soon as the gangplank was laid down, Bravo bounded on board, followed by Wingate. Bravo put his arms around his mother, feeling her trembling in his embrace.

"Thank you for coming," she whispered, resting her forehead on his chest. "It's been such a long trip. I feel as if I don't have another ounce of strength left in me."

"Forget everything," Bravo said. "We're here now, and you're safe."

At the far end of the wharf, half-hidden by crates and bales of merchandise, Véronique Villefranche Connaught, still in her disguise, nudged a huge mulatto she'd hired named Tortuga. "That's the woman," she said, "and the blond-haired boy is her son. Mark them well."

Tortuga grunted. "Better join the others at the bridge now. You said she'd be alone. This will take extra planning."

"He's only a boy," Véronique said sharply, "and you have four other men with you."

"Even boys can fight," he said obstinately.

Véronique set her jaw. "All right. There will be an extra fifty dollars in it for you all."

"Good, good," he grumbled.

"But no one in their carriage must reach Washington alive. Do you understand?"

"I understand."

Chapter 4

As Rebecca led Wingate and Bravo to her cabin, she missed her footing and Wingate grabbed her arm to steady her. He'd never seen her looking so weary and drawn, and with her history of fainting spells and palpitations, he was concerned for her.

Matty lay on the bunk and Wingate made a cursory examination. His color was bad, the discoloration around his eyes attested to a severe fracture. Wingate put his ear to the boy's chest, felt for a pulse, then pulled back his eyelids. The child's vital signs were all at a low ebb.

"How long has he been this way?"

Rebecca leaned against the cabin wall. "This morning just about dawn, he woke with a cry and said, 'Grandma, my head hurts so bad I can hardly see! It's all dark around my eyes.' Then he drifted off and hasn't stirred since."

Wingate lifted Matty gently. "Let's get him back to your house as fast as we can. I can do a much more thorough examination there." He carried Matty off the packetboat with Rebecca and Bravo following.

Bravo made arrangements to have Rebecca's trunks delivered to the house. He wished then that Enoch and Tad were there but he didn't want to wait for them, with Matty as bad as he was. It had gotten nearly dark, so Bravo lit the lamps on either side of the carriage. "That should help us see the ruts and potholes a little better," he said. Then the three of them climbed into the carriage. Wingate laid Matty carefully on the front seat, and he and Rebecca sat across from him. Bravo sat in the driver's seat; he flicked the reins and they started off, Rebecca cringing for Matty at every jolt.

"Go as slow as you can," Wingate told Bravo. Then he turned to Rebecca. "How long ago did this happen?" When she didn't respond, he said, "I know it's painful for you, but you must tell me everything. Don't leave out a detail. Anything you say may help me with the diagnosis."

This wasn't exactly true, but Wingate sensed that unless Rebecca unburdened herself, she might trigger a serious break-down of her own health.

Under his gentle urging, she began to speak in rambling sentences. "It happened a few days after the fall of the Alamo, so it was early March." Rebecca stared at her hands, remem-bering the horror of General Santa Anna's slaughter. "There were only a few survivors, among them William Travis's slave Joe, and a Mrs. Dickenson and her infant daughter. Santa Anna freed them, and decided to let me and Matty go also, though Devroe Connaught railed against that."

"Devroe Connaught?" Bravo exclaimed, turning in his seat.

Rebecca explained Devroe's involvement, then went on, "Mrs. Dickenson, Joe, the children, and I started walking. When we got to the crossroads some fifteen miles away from San Antonio, the others continued on toward Gonzalez, but Matty and I took the road that branched off to the Albright ranch. I knew Suzannah would be sick with worry."

"Where was Jonathan in all this?" Bravo asked.

"With Sam Houston, first at Washington-on-the-Brazos, where they were trying to form a provisional government, and then later they went to put down an Indian uprising that had been instigated by the Mexicans."

"You knew the country well enough to travel it alone?" Bravo asked.

"Not really, but Matty did. Though he's only seven, Jon-athan's trained him and the other children to be self-reliant. I knew he'd get us back to the ranch. We were traveling without food or water, but Matty knew which berries were edible, knew enough to cut open a barrel cactus and chew its pulp for water.

"We walked well into the night, then collapsed near a stunted tree; both of us were so exhausted that we fell asleep almost immediately. Well past sun-up, Matty shook me awake. 'Grandma, somebody's coming,' he whispered. I listened, but I couldn't hear anything. Matty motioned me to put my ear to the ground, and sure enough, I heard vibrations through the earth.

"Several minutes later I saw a rider approaching. Devroe Connaught had tracked us from San Antonio. I grabbed Matty and flattened against the ground. Devroe rode past us, only to come circling back, and he stopped not ten feet from where we were hiding.

"I heard him say, 'How charming to find you here, Mrs. Brand. I do believe that it's time for you to come out of hiding so that we may settle old scores.'"

"The bastard!" Bravo interrupted.

"Then I heard the click of a pistol," Rebecca continued. "'Why don't you run?' he called to us. 'That might provide me with some amusing sport.'"

"I'll kill him!" Bravo swore. "I should have killed him when he tried to murder Suzannah and Gunning!"

"Bravo, watch the road!" Wingate cautioned him as they hit a pothole.

Bravo clenched his jaw and listened as his mother went on.

"Devroe went on taunting us. 'You don't want to run? Would you prefer to beg? That too could be amusing. And your last moments on earth should be amusing, don't you agree?' I told him to do what he wanted with me, but to spare Matty. After all, the boy knew nothing of all the misery that had passed between our families.

"But Devroe spat at me, 'He's a Brand, and I'll see all the Brands wiped off the face of the earth before I'm through. Nothing less will ease my soul!' He raised his pistol and pointed it first at me, then at Matty, that sickening, insane sneer on his lips. 'Which shall it be? You first, my Rebecca? No, perhaps the boy, so that you'll feel the same exquisite pain that I felt when I learned that Jeremy Brand had killed my father. Yes, the boy first!'

"I threw myself in front of Matty, but Devroe circled his horse faster and faster, while I scrambled to keep him from getting a clear shot. Finally I fell to my knees from exhaustion. Then Matty sprang at him, yelling, 'You leave my grandma alone!' As Devroe aimed his pistol at me, Matty grabbed his leg and tried to yank him from the saddle. Devroe kicked at

him, but Matty hung on and the horse reared. Devroe fired,
but Matty had deflected his aim enough so that the bullet only
hit my upper arm and passed through the flesh.

"Devroe finally shook Matty off. Devroe couldn't reload
while he was in the saddle, so he dismounted and came after
Matty with his saber. Matty tried to scramble away, but Devroe
caught him. I'll never forget his words... 'By nightfall, the
buzzards will have eaten their fill of both of you.'

"Before I could reach them, Devroe brought his sword around
in a sideways swipe. Matty ducked, but the blade glanced off
his head, biting into the bone."

"How awful," Wingate muttered. "Clearly, he's a madman;
we'll have to bring him to justice. Have him put away in an
asylum."

"But mother, how did you get away?" Bravo asked.

"When he hit Matty, I came at him, I don't remember
exactly, but I think I tried to tear out his jugular vein. Though
he could only use one arm, he was still stronger than I, and
he knocked me to the ground. Then I saw a piece of the barrel
cactus that Matty had cut open the night before for its water.

"When Devroe saw that Matty was still alive, he raised his
sword to run him through. I grabbed the cactus... he turned
toward me just as I hit him in the face. The cactus spines
stabbed into his eyes and he screamed and dropped his sword.
I scooped it up, and went after him as he stumbled for his
horse. But I was weak from the gunshot wound and he managed
to mount up before I could reach him. He tried to run me down
but I darted behind the tree, and when he passed, I swung the
saber, tearing open the horse's flank.

"By now, Devroe was blinded by the blood in his eyes, and
frightened that I might cripple his mount, so he galloped off."

A long moment of silence passed, marked only by the rumble and creak of the carriage as they rolled through Georgetown's cobbled streets. At last, Rebecca continued with her
story. "After Devroe left, I picked up Matty and carried him
until we reached the ranch."

"How far was that?" Wingate asked softly.

"I don't know. Perhaps twenty miles."

"Mother, how awful!" Bravo breathed.

She shook her head wearily. "Whatever's happened to me,
I deserve it all for my own transgression in this world... When
I was a young girl, I loathed the Connaughts, envied them

because they were rich and privileged. I despised old Victoria Connaught because of the way she lorded it over all of us—commoners, she called us. Because she was a Tory, I condemned her as a traitor. Sean Connaught, Devroe's father, was one of the cruelest men I'd ever met . . . and I didn't grieve when Sean met his end on the battlefield of New Orleans. But now all my hatreds have come back to haunt me."

"But Rebecca," Wingate interrupted, "Victoria Connaught *was* a traitor, and Sean Connaught *was* a cruel, murdering madman. I know that from my own encounters with him."

Rebecca made a temple with her hands and leaned her forehead against it. "That's true, but my hatred went far beyond that. My hatred had at its heart . . . jealousy, because the Connaughts had all the things I foolishly believed were important. Wealth, social position, security . . ."

She looked at her unconscious grandson and her eyes welled with tears. "But Matty! He had nothing to do with any of this. Surely he's an innocent! Why, oh why—" her voice caught and she choked with tears. "Oh, Wingate, we must save him, we must!"

"You know I'll do everything in my power," Wingate said. "But you must also tell this entire story to President Jackson."

"Is he in Washington?"

"Not at the moment. He left some weeks ago, but he should be back in another week."

"I'll see him as soon as he returns."

Bravo carefully guided the carriage down M Street, then bore right onto Pennsylvania Avenue where the two streets intersected. He kept the horses on a tight rein as they approached the bridge over Rock Creek.

"The bridge can be treacherous in the dark," he said to the others, "and tonight especially, we don't want to risk any accidents."

Chapter 5

JUST BEYOND the bridge, hidden in a copse of trees, Véronique Villefranche Connaught spoke in hushed, urgent tones to her four hirelings. They were a disreputable lot of cutthroats: Gunther, a thick-witted German mercenary; Olaf, a Norwegian sailor who'd jumped his ship in Baltimore then drifted to Washington; Vervene, a rodent-faced man with a cast in one eye that made it impossible to tell where he was looking; and Tortuga, their leader.

Tortuga was a gap-toothed mulatto of monstrous proportions with mottled skin gathered around his body in folds, and red-brown crinkly hair. Legally, he was a free man of color; he was also heavily involved in the West Indian slave trade. He'd sold his last cargo of "black gold" in Washington, only to lose all his profits at the cockfights. When the cock he'd bet on lost its fight, Tortuga bit through its neck with his teeth, then flung the bird in the owner's face. Adrift in Washington, he'd become a bounty hunter, tracking down runaway slaves. He'd agreed to take this job for the quick cash.

Véronique feared Tortuga the most; his temper seemed as foul as his breath. Keeping her voice pitched low, she went over the plan for the final time. "The road is pitted and treacherous, so it won't be hard to run the carriage off the road. The drop down to Rock Creek is more than a hundred feet, and the carriage will be dashed to pieces. If anyone should survive the fall, snap their necks."

"You say there are other people in the carriage besides the woman," Tortuga growled.

"A boy will be driving, and there is a slight man in the back. I doubt that either of them will be armed, but take no chances. You all understand that the woman is most important. She must die. Naturally, it would be wisest for all of you if there were no witnesses."

Tortuga unsheathed his knife and ran his thumbnail over the razor-sharp blade. There was something strange about this woman; she was not who she appeared to be, of that he was certain. He said in his guttural voice, "You must hate this woman very much."

"She caused the death of my child," Véronique lied. "But that's of no matter to you. You're being well paid for a few minutes' work. Remember, avoid firearms. There aren't many houses nearby, but gunfire might alert any stray travelers."

They turned as they heard the hollow clatter of horses' hooves on the bridge. Then Véronique saw the twin twinkling carriage lights. "That's them," she whispered, feeling a thrill course through her body. "Do the deed with dispatch," she said, in the moment of high excitement, "and there'll be a bonus for each of you!"

As the carriage reached the Washington end of the bridge, Bravo stopped, got out, and took the horses' bridles. The gibbous moon emerged from the cloud cover and picked out the swollen currents of Rock Creek racing by below.

"Bravo, what are you doing?" Rebecca demanded.

"Part of the road along this stretch has washed out," he called over his shoulder. "It's safer if I lead the horses."

Rebecca fretted over the delay, but Wingate said, "That's a good idea, Bravo. It's a long drop down into that ravine."

Wingate had always noticed how impatient Rebecca acted toward her youngest son—demanding far more of him than of her other children. Over the years, as Bravo had matured, Wingate and Circumstance had guessed the reason for that impatience; and one day, they felt, Bravo would have to be told.

Bravo picked his way carefully along the road. The howl of a distant wolf made the hair on the back of his neck bristle. But it wasn't that kind of predator he was worried about. It wasn't wise to be out after dark on this deserted road. It was safe enough during the day, for usually a steady stream of traffic flowed between Washington and Georgetown. But at night, the highway became the domain of the thief and robber. He touched the pistol tucked into his belt, reassured by its feel.

He'd just about cleared the washed-out section of the road when the ground began to sound with the thunder of approaching horses. He couldn't make out how many there were, but certainly more than two.

"Wingate, do you have your pistol?" he demanded.

"No, I don't!"

"Damnation!" Bravo swore, as he quickly blew out the carriage lamps.

"Bravo, what's happening?" Rebecca cried. The rumble of horses drew closer, then suddenly there came the loud report of a pistol and the bullet thudded into the wood of the carriage. Instinctively, Rebecca moved to shield little Matty's body with her own.

"Highwaymen!" Bravo shouted. "Keep down!"

But Rebecca knew better. "They're Devroe Connaught's men, and they'll kill us all!"

Wingate struggled to get past Rebecca, all the while cursing himself for not carrying his pistol.

Tortuga, leading the charge of the four men, bore down on the carriage, shouting at the stupid drunk Norwegian who'd shot too soon and wasted his bullet. Tortuga made out the form of a lad crouched near the horses. Easy enough to dispatch. Then he saw another man standing up in the carriage. He had no weapon visible. The whole thing was almost too easy.

Gunther, the German, charged Bravo, swinging at his head with a club. Bravo ducked, but the horses spooked and bolted forward, throwing Bravo to the ground.

"Whoa!" Bravo yelled as he was dragged, but he clung with all his might to the reins. If he let go, the carriage might easily roll over him.

The bucking horses threw Wingate back into his seat. A jumble of impressions instantly crowded in on him—the bolting horses, the carriage swaying perilously closer to the edge of the ravine. Unless he stopped the runaways . . . He climbed over his seat, and with the rushing wind in his face, braced himself, and then with a desperate lunge leaped onto one of the horse's backs. Clinging to the traces, Wingate worked him-

self forward on the galloping beast, until he was able to grab
its long mane. Then he reached down and grabbed one end of
the dangling reins. He was aware of men on horseback charging
all about him, but he could only concentrate on stopping the
horses. He pulled back on the reins with all his strength, until
he brought the horses to a halt.

Bravo, dragged all this way, lay on the ground, not moving.
From the corner of his eye, Wingate saw a man with a sharp
face riding down on him, waving a sword. Vervene swung at
Wingate, but he rolled to the far side of the horse, and Vervene
missed.

Then Bravo stirred. He shook his head, trying to get his
bearings. Vervene turned his horse and charged back, bearing
down on Bravo. But the boy saw him coming and whipped his
gun from his belt. As Vervene swooped toward him, the sword
glinting in the moonlight, Bravo aimed—he hated shooting
the horse, but it was the only clear shot he had—and fired.
Bravo's bullet caught the stallion in the chest, and with a piteous
whinny it crumpled to the ground, crushing Vervene to death
under its weight.

Olaf swore in Norwegian, and swung at Bravo with the butt
of his pistol. Bravo fired a second time, and the bullet smashed
into the drunken sailor's lungs, killing him instantly.

In the shouting and confusion, the whinnying and rearing
of the horses, Gunther's curses sounded clear and sharp. He
shouted to Tortuga, "The boy's fired twice! Both his guns are
empty. Let's finish them off now!"

Tortuga heaved his horse closer to the carriage, crowding
it closer and closer to the edge of the precipice. Wingate tried
to fight him off, but the man bulled his way, like a mountain
of flesh. In the back of the carriage, Rebecca huddled on the
floor, Matty cradled in her arms.

Gunther dismounted and strode forward toward Bravo, his
eyes narrowed in the darkness. He fired and Bravo felt the
bullet whiz by his ear. Gunther took careful aim with his other
pistol just as Bravo raised his own gun. "Fool!" Gunther barked
with laughter. "You've already fired."

But Bravo squeezed the trigger of his repeating gun. At the
flash from its muzzle, surprise etched itself on Gunther's face,
turning to horror as the bullet tore through his neck and blood
fountained from his mouth. "How—?" he gurgled, and then
he toppled forward, dead.

With a cry of rage, Tortuga moved on Bravo, both pistols firing. The first bullet caught Bravo in the side and knocked him back against the wheel of the carriage. The second bullet missed, but Tortuga drew his knife, and went to slit the boy's throat. Wingate flung himself at the giant and managed to knock the knife from his hand.

"I'll kill you with my bare hands!" Tortuga roared. He grabbed Wingate in a bear hug and began to crush the breath out of him. Wingate struggled, but couldn't free himself from the viselike grip. He felt his lungs constricting, his eyes began to pop, and then with an effortless motion, Tortuga swung Wingate over his head, held him poised there for a moment, ready to throw him down into the ravine.

Bravo clutched the spokes of the wheel and pulled himself to his feet. He fired at Tortuga, catching him in the shoulder, and spinning him around. The giant stared at Bravo, a querulous frightened look on his face at the gun in the boy's hand that never ceased firing. Then he dropped Wingate and pitched forward, tumbling down into the ravine and disappearing in the darkness.

Bravo scrambled to Wingate. "Are you all right?"

Wingate heaved for breath, great tearing gasps, unable to speak. He pointed to the back of the carriage and managed to get out one word, "Matty . . ."

They stumbled to the rear and raised Rebecca up from the floor. "Mother, are you all right?" Bravo asked anxiously.

She was shaking so hard she could barely speak. Then she sobbed, "Quickly, oh quickly! There may be more of them around."

Almost in response to her fears, they heard another horse galloping off, and they heard confused shouting in the distance. "Oh please," Rebecca moaned, "let's get away from here."

With a painful effort, Bravo pulled himself back up into the driver's seat. Wingate, recovered sufficiently by now, climbed up alongside him. He saw the bloodstain spreading over Bravo's shirt.

"You've been hit."

"I think it's only a flesh wound."

Wingate jammed his handkerchief against the wound. "Hold it there, tight." He took the reins. "I'll drive."

The shouting grew closer, and finally they could make out

Tad's voice. "Mr. Bravo? Miss Rebecca! Is that you?" he called. "You been killed?"

Wingate shouted back, "No, Tad, we're alive, but Bravo's been shot!"

Tad and Enoch came up, barely visible in the dark. "We was just coming when we heard gunshots. I told you not to go without us!"

"I should have let you come, Tad," Bravo conceded. "But I just got a light wound, thank God."

"Bravo, are you sure you're all right?" Rebecca asked.

He nodded. Wingate flicked the reins, and moving as quickly as he dared, started back to the Brand house on New York Avenue. As they drove, he asked Bravo about the weapon he'd been using. Bravo explained it all. Wingate shook his head in wonder. "I always knew you were a genius, and tonight I'm really glad you are. If you hadn't had that gun with you, we'd all be dead."

The Brand house was all lit up, for everybody had anxiously been awaiting their return. When Bravo tried to get down, he pitched forward onto the ground and lay there.

"Oh, help him quickly, somebody!" Rebecca shouted.

Tad and Enoch lifted Bravo, and Bittersweet came running. "Carry him into the house," Wingate ordered the two men. He turned to Bittersweet. "Tell Letitia to bring clean linen. Start boiling water. Then have Tad take the carriage as fast as he can to my house to fetch Circumstance. Quickly now; I don't know how badly Bravo's hurt. And God only knows if Matty will survive this night."

Chapter 6

TAD AND ENOCH heaved Bravo's inert body onto the settee. Wingate shrugged off his jacket, rolled up his sleeves, and quickly examined the youth.

Rebecca came into the room, holding Matty; she gently laid him down on the love seat. He hadn't regained consciousness, but he was at least still breathing. Rebecca swept over to Wingate. "How is Bravo?" With both her son and her grandson so dangerously wounded, her entire world seemed to be crashing down around her.

"As far as I can tell, the bullet passed cleanly through Bravo's side," Wingate said. "No vital organs or blood vessels seem to have been touched. You see—" He pointed to the wound. "—The bleeding's almost stopped. I think he'll be fine."

"Thank God," Rebecca whispered.

Bittersweet hurried into the room with clean dishtowels and a kettle of hot water. In her two years in the Brand household, she'd come to idolize Bravo, and she was almost in tears seeing him unconscious and bleeding.

Wingate cleaned the wound, laved an ointment on it, then wrapped the bandages around Bravo's midsection. By the time Wingate was finished, Bravo began stirring, and then he opened his eyes.

34

He looked around him in a daze. Recognition came slowly and he said with a sheepish grin, "Sorry I passed out."

Wingate gripped Bravo's shoulder. "The way you handled yourself tonight, you deserve to sleep for a week."

Rebecca knelt beside her youngest son and kissed his cheek. "Thank you, darling."

The color rose to his face, as it did every time she praised him. "I couldn't let anything happen to you, could I, mother?" With a grimace, he hiked himself up on one shoulder. "How's Matty?"

"We're about to find out." After a more thorough examination, Wingate looked up at Rebecca. "I don't see any major change in his vital signs. But the pressure on his brain has got to be released, otherwise..."

She bit her lip. "That's what every doctor's said."

"I've never performed an operation like this before. There may be other doctors in Washington more qualified than I am."

Rebecca shook her head vehemently. "No, Suzannah and Jonathan both said that they were going to leave it in your hands. And in God's," she added with a sigh.

"And if I should fail?" he asked quietly. "You've got to understand that there's only the barest chance that Matty could survive such radical surgery."

She reached for his hands and gripped them, as if by the intensity of her pressure she could make him understand how she felt. "I know what we're asking you to do. I know that if Matty dies..." The words caught in her throat and she gulped, unable to go on. Wingate waited until she finally managed to say, "Jonathan, Suzannah, and I all know that Matty is slipping away from us. I suppose that in our hearts, we feel he's lost to us already. So don't you see?—you're our last resort. If there's the slimmest possibility that you can help him, even if it's only to ease his suffering, then we must all take that chance."

She broke down completely then. Wingate put his arm around her and held her until she stopped sobbing. "All right." Wingate's quavering voice sounded as if it came from a great distance. "I'll operate tomorrow."

Bravo stirred on the settee. "Where will you do it? At the hospital?"

Wingate shook his head. "Under ordinary circumstances, I probably would. But the wards are already filled with patients who've come down with Potomac fever. The last thing we can risk is to expose Matty to unnecessary disease. He's so weak now that anything could carry him off. Rebecca, if it's all right with you, I'd like to operate here."

"Of course. Just tell us what you want done, and we'll do it."

Wingate ran his fingers through his curly brown hair. His warm, mellow brown eyes, though blurred with fatigue, still sparked with intelligence. "Bravo, do you remember when Gunning was shot, and we needed light? You arranged some sort of mirror contraption that focused the candlelight on Gunning's chest, so that I could see to operate. Well, this operation will require even more delicacy. Could you tell me how to rig up something like that again?"

Bravo nodded. "Now that we've got a few hours, I can probably do something even more effective."

About ten minutes later, Circumstance came hurrying in, followed by Tad. She went to Matty and stared at him. She clenched her hands together until her knuckles were white. "He looks so much like Suzannah," she whispered. "Oh, how I feel her agony."

"Wingate, is there anything else you'll need?" Bravo asked. "Anything special?"

Wingate put his fists to his eyes, thinking, trying to calm his own roiling emotions. He understood now why doctors rarely operated on members of their own family; the strain was enough to render a man totally incompetent. With a glance at Rebecca, he said, "There are a few other things, Bravo, but we'll talk about them later."

Rebecca stepped forward. "I know you're trying to spare my feelings, Wingate, and I thank you for it. But believe me, the more I know of the truth, the less chance there is that my fears will rule me."

"All right, then," Wingate said. "Bravo, I'll need a brace and a quarter-inch auger. We'll try that size first, and pray that we don't have to use anything larger."

Wingate's intent slowly penetrated into Rebecca's mind and all the color drained from her face. "You mean that you're going to drill directly into his head?"

"I don't know of any other way. There's obviously a blood clot on his brain, and fragments of bone pressing into the brain. I've got to relieve the pressure that's causing his seizures, and his spells of unconsciousness."

Bravo had also turned pale as he listened. "But then what? Will Matty just walk around with a hole in his head?"

"What we do is fill the hole with a plug of wood, the hardest wood available."

"Ash," Bravo said without hesitation. "I'll cut some plugs for you."

"Good. Make sure they're tapered. If the operation is successful, and pray God it will be, then we'll plug the hole, and gradually ease the plug out as the skull begins to heal. Matty's skull is still growing, so that the hole should close itself up within a month or two."

A pall of silence fell over the room as each of them pondered the enormity of what they were about to undertake. Then Wingate said, "We'd all better get some sleep. I'll be here early in the morning, to start the preparations. I'd like to operate at noon, when the light's the brightest."

Then he and Circumstance left. The rest of the Brand household dragged themselves off to bed; Bittersweet curled up in the armchair in the drawing room, to be on hand in case Bravo needed anything during the night.

Rebecca had Tad carry Matty to her room and put him in her bed. She lay on her chaise lounge, feeling the anguish deep in her bones, yet nevertheless alert to any change in the boy. But all through the dark hours, Matty made no sound, and she knew in her heart that the next day would tell whether he lived or not.

Rebecca knelt by Matty's side, her clasped hands pressed to her forehead in prayer. "O Lord," she whispered, "you and you alone know of my many sins, and the hardness in my own vain and foolish heart that's brought misery to so many . . . misery and even death. I ask you only to remember that this child was an innocent; he had no part in the feud between the Connaughts and the Brands. He deserves to live. Whatever years remain for me on this earth, I will bear all torments that you deem fit to visit on me, and if there indeed be a hell, I will endure those fires till my sins be burned from me. Only let him live, Lord! O Lord, look on him with mercy."

At dawn the Brand household was already up and about. Bravo had gotten a few hours of fitful sleep and then roused himself. He paid little attention to his own fever, and began constructing a series of hinged mirrors. When properly placed, they reflected the lamplight with far greater intensity than could be achieved only by direct light. Done with that, he then commenced to sharpen several drill bits, from one-quarter inch to one-half inch in diameter.

"I hope we don't have to use the larger ones," he said to Enoch. The tall dark man was helping Bravo—supporting him more than anything else. Bravo had a number of dowels made of ash, from which he cut some plugs, carving them to a fine smoothness.

By the time Wingate and Circumstance arrived, Bravo had done all he could think of.

"I think it's best to operate in the dining room," Wingate said. He put a heavy blanket down on the table, and covered that with a clean muslin sheet. Tad brought Matty down from Rebecca's room and laid him on the table.

Wingate ran a length of cord over Matty's legs, tying him down to the table. "He's unconscious now," Wingate said to Circumstance, who was going to assist him. "But when I begin to drill, he may regain his senses, and the pain—well, he'd just better be secured." He ran a second strap over the boy's shoulders.

Rebecca came into the dining room, and Wingate shook his head. "It would be better if you weren't here."

"But—"

Circumstance took her by the shoulders and led her out. "This is the most delicate operation that Wingate's ever attempted. He must concentrate only on Matty. If he has to worry about what you're going through also, it might distract him."

Rebecca nodded dully. She and Letitia sat on the high-backed sofa in the hall outside the dining room. Both women sat in stunned silence while Bittersweet brought in the steaming pans of hot water and the linens that Letitia had washed, then dried in front of the kitchen fireplace.

While the preparations were going on, Rebecca stared at her hands. "Devroe," she muttered to Letitia.

"Don't even say that name, lest you bring his evil spirit into this room," the maid said.

For a moment, the passions of Rebecca's youth raced through her and she said, "If I had a gun I'd kill him! No, I'd kill him with my bare hands." Yet, as she visualized Matty, wounded, drained, close to death, she felt an overwhelming remorse about her thoughts of vengeance.

"Vengeance," she said sadly. "It's for that very reason that Matty's inside."

Letitia took her mistress's hand and clung to it for reassurance.

"Somewhere, somehow, there has to be a better answer than killing. Someday, we'll become civilized enough, human enough..." Then she straightened her shoulders. "But until that day, I've got to guard myself and my family against madmen like Devroe Connaught."

Letitia bobbed her head.

"When this is over, I'll go directly to Andrew Jackson and warn him," she said to Letitia. "He must be told that the British have a vested interest in Texas, that they'll do anything to keep it from becoming part of the United States."

Enoch helped Bravo carry the equipment up from the basement. Bravo gave the plugs, the brace, and the auger to Wingate, then set up the reflecting mirrors on the dining table. He placed a few lamps at strategic points, and the reflected light shone brilliantly on Matty's head. But Bravo's exertions, coming so soon after being wounded, exhausted him, and he leaned heavily against the table for support.

Wingate led Bravo back into the drawing room. "Lie down. I'll call you if I need you. If you pass out on me while I'm operating, it will only make it worse."

Bravo nodded and eased himself gingerly down onto the settee.

"I'll be starting very soon," Wingate said to Rebecca and Letitia. "It may go on for hours, so don't be upset, and try not to make any noise. Keep everybody away from the front door."

Letitia called for Tad. "You, Tad, stand out there by the front door, and shoo everybody away who comes calling. Don't matter who, even if it be the President of the United States."

Wingate closed the door of the dining room, and the click had such a sound of finality that it was all Rebecca could do to keep from hurling herself through the door, and clinging to her grandson, so that if he died, she would be drawn down into the underworld with him.

Chapter 7

CIRCUMSTANCE LAID out all of Wingate's instruments on the dining table: scalpel, stethoscope, suturing equipment, the ash plugs in varying sizes, clean linen and swabs, a small hammer, and the dreadful-looking auger and brace.

Wingate stripped to his shirtsleeves and put on a rubber apron, with a second apron of clean white linen on top of that. With a finely sharpened scissors, he cut off all of Matty's hair around the fracture. He then carefully shaved the area. Once the scalp was laid bare, he was able to see the full extent of the wound.

The indentation in the skull was clearly visible, a line running about two inches long, and markedly depressed. He looked at Circumstance. "It's a wonder the boy isn't dead. The fractured bone is pressing in on the brain. Fluid and foul humors have built up inside. But if we can relieve that pressure . . ."

He drew a large, U-shaped mark around the fracture, then picked up one of his scalpels. His eyes met Circumstance's, and love and reassurance flowed between them. Using a clean linen cloth, she blotted the beads of sweat forming on his forehead. He nodded his thanks, gripped the scalpel, and then cut the skin along the lines he'd drawn.

Almost immediately, the incision began to bleed; Circumstance kept blotting it with cloths wrapped around wads of cotton. Wingate lifted the flap of skin and laid the scalp bare to the bone. At once he saw that the bone of the skull was

40

chipped and crushed along the indentation. Using his forceps, and working with infinite patience, he carefully picked the fragments out. Those that were deeply imbedded, he pried out with pincers. Though the work was arduous, he tried to pace himself, for he knew that this was the simpler part of the operation.

The minutes ticked by until almost an hour had passed. Every so often, Wingate would become aware of a horse and carriage passing by in the street, or the cries of a vendor hawking his wares, or the distant laughter of children. Occasionally, Matty's face would twitch, but so far the boy hadn't regained consciousness.

At last, Wingate had removed all the bone fragments he could see, and he put down his probes and pincers. Anticipating his need, Circumstance handed him a glass of water and Wingate drained it. The sun slanting through the windows, the burning lamps and candles reflected in the mirrors, made the room uncomfortably hot, but he needed all the light he could get.

Now the moment of truth was upon him—he could delay it no longer. He picked up the small hammer, gripped it, and then holding the drill in his other hand, tapped it gently into Matty's skull. "I've got to get the point started," he explained to Circumstance.

But nothing happened.

"You must strike harder," Circumstance said softly. "Wingate, you must. It's the boy's only chance."

He straightened and took a deep breath, feeling a surge of anger at his own inadequacy. There was so much that doctors didn't know—so much in the mystery of the human body and mind that eluded all their attempts to discover the secrets of man, and of creation! It made his own efforts to heal seem puny and ineffective.

"Wingate," Circumstance said urgently.

He nodded, then taking his courage in his hands, rapped the hammer smartly against the end of the drill, and the tip bit into the bone. Matty's head shuddered, but Wingate pressed on. He began to turn the handle, and the auger bored deeper and deeper into the bone, blood spiraling up along the curves of the drill. The muscles in Matty's face twitched spasmodically, and Circumstance reached down and held the boy's head immobile between her hands.

The drilling continued and Wingate felt the pain with every revolution of the bit. Then he felt the slightest easing of pressure, and knew that he'd cut through the bone and was into the brainpan. Carefully, he reversed the drill and eased it out. The moment the drill was free, Wingate and Circumstance heard a hiss of released air, and then through the hole there came a welling up of all sorts of foul fluids.

Circumstance kept wiping it away, but each time she stopped it continued to ooze to the surface. It appeared that it would never end, but at last the flow diminished. Wingate applied a suction cup to the drilled hole and very gently began to draw the fluid out. Another hour passed while Wingate worked to bring out as much dead material from the brain pan as possible.

Once Matty moaned, and Wingate thought his own heart would stop at the boy's cry, but then he lapsed back into unconsciousness. Wingate put his ear to the boy's chest and listened. "Rapid and palpitating," he said to Circumstance. "Not as strong as it was."

"How much longer?" she asked. "I don't think he can stand much more."

Wingate applied the suction cup a few more times and felt relieved when the last remaining drops of fluid came out clear. He cleaned the wound, then put back the flap of skin, and cut a small hole in the skin to accommodate the plug of ash wood. From the various plugs Bravo had made, he chose one that fit perfectly. He tapped it gently into place, leaving perhaps a quarter of an inch extended.

Wingate sewed up the skin flap, using a fishhook needle threaded with catgut. Then he carefully wrapped Matty's head with bandages. "Done," he said.

With a sigh of relief, Circumstance blew out the candles and the oil lamps, opened the door to the entrance hall. Rebecca and Letitia, who'd kept the vigil there, rose to their feet, their expectant faces strained with apprehension.

Wingate came out of the room, his gait a weary shuffle. He took Rebecca's hands. "He's still alive."

Silent tears rolled down her face, and then she could restrain herself no longer; sobbing, she buried her face against his chest. Letitia pressed her clasped hands to her mouth to stifle her whimper.

At last Rebecca raised her head and looked at Wingate, her hazel eyes magnified by her tears. "Thank you. I'll never be able to repay you."

"Don't let your hopes get too high," he warned her. "The boy is still in fierce danger. It will be days, maybe weeks, before we know if he'll survive."

Rebecca ran the back of her hand under her red-rimmed eyes. "What are we going to do now?"

"Keep watch over him. I'll spend the night here, if that's all right with you. Somebody will have to stay with him every minute, night and day."

"We'll take turns," Circumstance said. "Me, and Bittersweet, and Rebecca."

"And me too," Letitia put in indignantly. "That's my Suzannah's child, and ain't nobody going to keep me away from him."

Matty didn't stir at all during the first night. After she'd gone home and fed her own children, Circumstance came back to Rebecca's and stayed with her husband. Every hour, Wingate checked Matty's heart and reflexes.

"They seem to be functioning all right," he said to Circumstance. "Truthfully, I wouldn't know what else to do now. I've done everything I know how, and the rest is in the hands of fate, or chance, or God. If only I knew more!" he said with a sudden burst of impotent anger. "There's so *much* we don't know."

He walked to the window and stared out at the darkened streets of Washington, washed by the pale moonlight. Circumstance went to his side, her angular features even more pronounced in the play of light and shadow.

"I can't get over the feeling that if Matty does survive, he's destined to do great things," she said quietly. "It's inconceivable that anybody could be asked to suffer this much, and yet still cling to life. There's got to be a reason. And you will have been instrumental in helping Matty fulfill his destiny."

Wingate ran his hands through his hair. "Sometimes, like this afternoon, I think I know less than a butcher."

"Don't say that," she said firmly. "You're the best doctor in Washington. Everybody says so."

"Not good enough. We must constantly push back the boundaries of darkness and superstition and ignorance that surround this profession. How many doctors do you know whose primary aim is to rise to a position of wealth and prominence? How many doctors have turned their backs on the oath that should lead them to the service of humanity?"

"But not you," she said quietly. "You have a calling. It shines in your eyes, shows itself in the steadiness of your hands. It's part of your spirit, my darling. Whether Matty lives or dies, you know yourself that you did everything you could, and more. You reached into your own healing soul to give him life."

He turned and stared at her eyes, ghostly in this light. As he touched her cheek she caught his hand and held it. "Thank God I married you," he whispered.

Rebecca, Circumstance, and Bittersweet spelled each other in caring for Matty; the days passed but still he remained unconscious. Letitia fussed around the room, though her failing eyesight and her age made her more hindrance than help. But Rebecca didn't have the heart to keep her out. When she wasn't in the sickroom, Letitia was in the kitchen, making jams and preserves, and baking batches of cookies that kept the house smelling of cinnamon and chocolate. "Matty'll be wanting these just as soon as he wakes up," she said emphatically. "Miss Suzannah, she always liked my cookies."

"So do I!" Bravo shouted to her as she passed his room. "But you've suddenly forgotten all about me."

"Hush you now," Letitia said irritably. But half an hour later she came into Bravo's room carrying a tole tray loaded with cold chicken, smoked meats, freshly baked whole-wheat bread, and mugs of apple cider and milk fresh from their cow.

Bravo hiked himself up on the bed. "You've brought enough for a platoon of men."

"Well, look at you. You lost a lot of blood. Got to get it back in your body, or you liable to slip through a crack."

Good food, rest, and Bravo's own natural health and youth made for a speedy recovery. Within the week he was out of bed and walking, albeit slowly.

One sultry afternoon, Bravo and Rebecca were out in the front garden, he lying on the grass, trying to decipher a technical manual about electricity, she busily pruning the rosebushes. Not many people were about, the day being too warm for unnecessary exertion.

"Oh Lord, look who's coming," Rebecca said. She tried to duck into the house, but it was too late.

Mr. and Mrs. Fairfax and their daughter Anne, who lived across the street, walked past the Brand garden. Mr. Fairfax

doffed his hat. Rebecca made the mistake of smiling back, and
the Fairfaxes stopped to chat.

Mr. Fairfax was a solid burgher of a man, with erect carriage
and imposing whiskers, which he constantly kept fluffing. Despite the heat, not an ounce of perspiration showed anywhere
on him. He liked nothing better than to pontificate on the evils
of the world, and particularly on the rapidly degenerating mor-
als of the younger generation—"They are all going to the dogs!"

Mrs. Fairfax, a devout woman, came perilously close to
being a religious fanatic, and even closer to being a bore on
the subject. She was just a shade more imposing than her
husband, no mean accomplishment. Her bust was so full it
should be described as a monobosom; an equally developed
derrière somehow kept her balanced.

Their daughter Anne was a timorous-looking creature. "Hello,
Bravo," she murmured in a lovely, melodious voice. Bravo
brightened and went to her.

Under ordinary circumstances, Rebecca wouldn't have
greeted the Fairfaxes. She had reason. In 1832, when Rebecca
had been forced to reveal her identity as the pamphleteer Rebel
Thorne, it had created a crisis in her life. The Fairfaxes were
part of a delegation of Washingtonians who'd sanctimoniously
suggested that Rebecca remove herself from the capital, the
better to hide her shame. "Somewhere in the distant countryside
would be preferable; after all, writing political tracts, and under
an assumed male name, is something that no decent Christian
woman would do," Mrs. Fairfax bleated. Rebecca told them
in no uncertain terms just what they could do with their petition,
which had alienated the Fairfaxes even further. But since Bravo
seemed to like Anne, Rebecca now held her peace.

Though Anne had lived in the neighborhood for almost a
decade, and Rebecca had seen her grow up, she'd never paid
too much attention to her. Now she gauged her very carefully.
She stood a bit too tall for a girl, with long arms and legs that
gave her body an ungainly appearance. She wore her hair, a
honey blond, parted in the center and pulled severely into two
buns at the nape of her neck. The style was more appropriate
for a matron of forty than a girl of seventeen. If only she would
free it from all those restraining pins! Rebecca resisted an urge
to pull them out right there, let the loosened hair give her thin,
angular face some softness. Her nose was a trifle too short and
snub for patrician beauty, and her lips were too full by far.

Rebecca found this Anne's most interesting feature, for it was a hint of sensuality otherwise missing in her plain face.

Rebecca became aware that Mrs. Fairfax was belaboring her with news of a religious meeting. "Week next. These are treacherous times for the Christian soul," she confided, "and we must do what we can to keep the commandments and Christian virtues uppermost in our lives."

"You must come," Mr. Fairfax insisted. "Anne will be playing the organ, and the child does it so well. Mrs. Fairfax taught her herself."

"It's about all the dear child has the strength to do," Mrs. Fairfax whispered to Rebecca, tapping her heart. "God has given Anne physical weaknesses so that her spirit and soul might soar."

After extracting a promise from Bravo that he would attend the service, the Fairfaxes left. Rebecca rolled her eyes. Bravo waved goodbye to Anne, who'd turned to sneak a glance at him, only to be propelled forward by Mrs. Fairfax.

"Mr. and Mrs. Fairfax are such good Christians that they make me feel like a heretic," Bravo said with a grin. "They can quote the Bible pages at a time! But Anne's very different from that."

"She seems to like you too," Rebecca said.

Bravo blushed furiously. "I know she's plain-looking, and she's so shy that sometimes it's painful to talk to her, but I think she's a very decent person."

"Well, I'm glad you've made a friend," Rebecca said. Puppy love, she thought, dismissing it.

From where Bravo stood he could see the South Portico of the White House. "Mother, when are you going to tell President Jackson about your trip to Texas?"

"I understand that he's due back in a few days. I'll tell him the first opportunity I get."

President Jackson had been in extremely poor health from the day he was elected. The strain of living in the White House and of shouldering the burdens of government for eight years had weakened him even more. The recent death of his beloved niece Emily Donelson had nearly finished him. She had been his official hostess and had kept the family together, but she'd died of tuberculosis. Convinced that he too suffered from the disease, Jackson had gone to the seashore to build up his strength, and to be alone with his anguish.

* * *

A week later, Jackson returned to Washington. The campaign for the upcoming Presidential election had taken an ugly turn, and Jackson thought it best to be on hand to maneuver his favorite, Vice-President Martin Van Buren, into the White House.

When Rebecca learned that Jackson was back, she sent a note to the executive mansion. Within the hour, Uncle Alfred, Jackson's slave and manservant, appeared at Rebecca's door with an invitation for her to dine that evening at the White House.

"The President, he didn't exactly order you to come," Uncle Alfred said, "but I think it's best that you be there."

Rebecca laughed, and Uncle Alfred grinned also. For when Jackson commanded, who dared disobey? She took extra pains getting dressed that evening. She sat before the oval mirror of her dressing table, brushing her long titian hair, now shot through with gray. Oddly enough, the gray hairs didn't make her look very much older, it only made her hair look lighter in color. She chose a cool summer gown of pale jonquil, edged in white cotton eyelet, and a white woolen stole that she'd crocheted in a pineapple pattern.

Letitia, who was helping her dress, grumbled occasionally. Rebecca bore it for a while then said, "Now what is it?"

"I know you going to see the President of the United States and all, but don't forget that you a grandmother, if you know what I mean."

"I don't know what you mean."

"Well then, make sure you come home tonight, and that's all I got to say about that matter."

Rebecca felt herself blushing; she didn't know whether to be embarrassed, amused, or angered. She gazed at herself thoughtfully in the mirror. Her visit was supposed to be an affair of state, yet she'd dressed as carefully as a young girl. Andrew Jackson had always affected her that way.

"Well," she sighed, "what once was . . . it's all a moot point anyway. Andrew's been so ill these past few years . . ." Nevertheless, when she walked out of her gate and headed toward the White House, her step was light, her body erect, and her heart filled with anticipation.

Chapter 8

REBECCA LIFTED her skirts to keep them from dragging in
the dust as she walked the few blocks to the President's house.
She did a quick calculation in her mind. She'd left to visit
Suzannah in Texas in November of 1835, so it was now eight
months since she had stepped foot inside the Executive Mansion. Yet the moment she climbed the steps leading to the
North Portico, she felt that she'd come home.

The oversize front door stood open to catch the evening
breezes; all the windows were open also. Rebecca entered the
Grand Entrance Hallway and was greeted by a black butler,
immaculately dressed in a dark uniform with shining brass
buttons. He led her to the Oval Room on the main floor.

"The President asked you to please wait here," he said.
"He'll join you as soon as he's free." The butler bowed his
way out of the room.

Rebecca wandered around the Oval Room. Many said it
was the most beautiful room in all America. In terms of its
shape and design, Rebecca thought so too; the gracefully curved
wall, the tall windows were all architecturally pleasing. But
she found the color scheme and the decor a little too demanding.
The fabric on the French Bellangé chairs and on the sofas was
a doublewarp crimson satin, complemented by two shades of
gold; an American eagle was woven into the center of a wreath

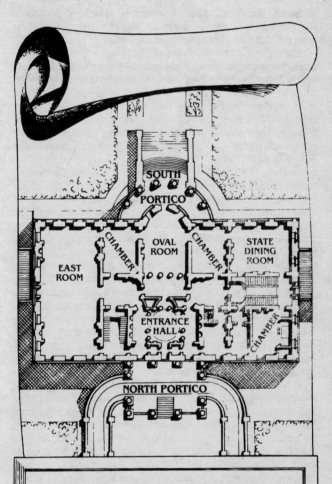

SOUTH
PORTICO

EAST
ROOM

CHAMBER

OVAL
ROOM

CHAMBER

STATE
DINING
ROOM

CHAMBER

ENTRANCE
HALL

NORTH PORTICO

GROUND FLOOR PLAN OF WHITE HOUSE

of laurel, the classic symbol of victory. The oval Aubusson rug, woven especially for the room, was of a deep green velvet with the national coat of arms in the center.

She moved to the window and stared out at the south lawn; a few hundred yards away, the muddy waters of the Potomac coursed by. To one side of the window, she saw the magnolia tree that President Jackson had planted in memory of his late wife, Rachel. Every spring the tree bloomed riotously, the creamy white flowers nestled among the large, thick dark-green leaves. "Some day, I must plant something on these grounds in memory of Jeremy," she said aloud. "Perhaps Circumstance will help me."

Jeremy . . . So much of Rebecca's own life was intertwined with this mansion. It was here that she'd first met the Brand brothers, Jeremy and Zebulon, oh so long ago—October of 1792, when the cornerstone of the American Palace was laid.

She was only thirteen then, but old enough to appreciate the dark brooding handsomeness of twenty-year-old Zebulon Brand. She knew that Zebulon had a passion for her; so did his half-brother, Jeremy, but he was only a lad of ten or eleven at most, and she scarcely paid any attention to him.

Jeremy had been sold by his brother as an indentured servant to Mathias Breech, Rebecca's father, but his indentureship was later bought by James Hoban, the architect for the White House, who had recognized the boy's talent. During the years, as work on the White House progressed, Rebecca watched Jeremy grow into a lean, attractive young man, while Zebulon descended deeper into a life of sensual excess.

It was in this very room that Rebecca had first met Abigail Adams, wife of the country's second President. That meeting had changed the course of Rebecca's life, for Abigail had fired her with the novel and frightening idea that a woman needn't be merely a plaything for a man, needn't be confined only to the drudgeries of the household. If a woman had a brain in her head, and the ambition, then she could make of herself anything she wanted in this new and wondrous land. The old order, which had heretofore imprisoned women, was ready to be changed, but it was up to the women of the new nation to change it.

Encouraged by Abigail Adams, Rebecca went about changing her own life. She knew she was intelligent, far more in-

telligent than most, and so she began writing political tracts
that reflected her own insights into the Washington scene. The
first half-dozen or so were rejected, but the subsequent ones
were printed in the Washington newspaper, the *National Intelligencer*. Rebecca wrote under the male pseudonym of Rebel
Thorne; the populace wasn't ready to accept a woman writing
about the political arena. During the War of 1812, Thorne's
articles proved to be a rallying point for the nation after the
British had burned Washington, D.C. Thorne's exhortations
also helped galvanize the citizens of Baltimore when the British
attempted to invade that important port city.

It was in this very room, back in 1803, that Rebecca realized
that she didn't love Zebulon Brand, but instead loved his half-
brother Jeremy. But she lost Jeremy to the siren call of the
Lewis and Clark Expedition of Northwest Discovery, and in a
fit of anger she married Zebulon.

Because the White House was not only the center of political
power in the nation, but also the center of social activities in
Washington, D.C., it was in this mansion that her prickly
relations with the Connaught family, notorious Tories, had
come to a disastrous head. The feud between the two families
had started back in 1792. This feud, brewed of the potent
poisons of politics, power, and passion, deeply affected not
only her life, but the lives of her children and grandchildren
as well.

In this mansion, she'd known the most horrifying moment
of her life, when Jeremy Brand, by then her lover, plunged to
his death while making repairs caused by the British burning
of the capital in 1814. Though Rebecca always suspected Zebulon was responsible for Jeremy's death—he believed that Bravo
wasn't his son, but the issue of Jeremy—Rebecca hadn't confided her suspicions to anybody. What good would it do? It
would only ruin the lives of her children, Suzannah, Gunning,
and Bravo, if their father was proven to be a murderer . . . And
then fate had given Zebulon his rightful due, a horrible death
by lockjaw.

As for the presidents who'd inhabited the mansion, Rebecca
had known them all: George Washington, who'd conceived the
idea of a White House, but who had never lived in it; John
Adams, vain and irascible, but totally incorruptible; and Thomas
Jefferson, one of her favorites. There was a man gifted in so

many areas that he was truly a Renaissance man. Yet even Jefferson had a dark side to his nature—and what a national scandal that had created!

"Little Jemmy" Madison came next—perhaps the most astute political thinker in the country, but woefully inadequate as President, rescued only by the indefatigable energy, quick wit, and buxom charms of the ebullient, ubiquitous Dolley Madison. Handsome, phlegmatic James Monroe, presided complacently over the Era of Good Feeling. But his wife, Elizabeth, with her high-and-mighty ways and aristocratic pretentions, came down with a severe case of Queen Fever. A three-year course of treatment by Rebecca and the best of Washington society had taught Mrs. Monroe that this was a democracy, and that royal pretentions had no place in the White House.

Brilliant statesmanship brought John Quincy Adams the presidency. A man from the eastern establishment, Adams suffered as the population of the nation shifted ever westward, and in 1828, he lost the election to the charismatic frontiersman, General Andrew Jackson.

Rebecca had first met Jackson in 1807, during Aaron Burr's trial for treason, and had immediately liked his honesty and forthrightness. Then she had renewed the acquaintance in 1818, when he was given a hero's welcome in Washington. Jeremy Brand had served under Jackson at the Battle of New Orleans and it was Jackson himself who urged Rebecca, by then separated from Zebulon, to seize a new chance at life with the man she loved.

Then Jeremy died, and twelve years were to pass before Rebecca experienced the touch of another man. How extraordinary that President Jackson . . . In their mutual grief, he mourning for the death of his beloved wife, Rachel, and she for Jeremy, they'd somehow managed to reach out and find comfort with each other. More than anything else, theirs was a spiritual communion, but in the calm maturity of her middle years, Rebecca discovered that such a love could be as sustaining as the tempestuous passions of her youth. Though no one could ever replace Jeremy, the compassionate, loving side of her nature had come to life again. I owe that to Andrew Jackson, she thought.

"Rebecca!" came the vibrant voice from the doorway, and she turned to face the President of the United States.

She gasped inwardly when she saw him, for he looked as wan and drawn as a cadaver. Whatever strength he had left seemed to reside in his voice. He noticed the look on her face and nodded.

"Yes, I know I look like a corpse. I don't know why the good Lord is keeping me alive."

"Why Andrew, it's to make sure that the Union is preserved."

He chuckled appreciatively. The preservation of the Union had been his overriding concern throughout his two terms in office.

Despite his ill health, Jackson managed to carry himself like a soldier, erect and commanding. His hair, a silver-white, stood on end as if shot through with electricity. His face was scored with deep lines, and his hand would occasionally clutch at his ribs, to alleviate a constant pain.

Years before, he'd fought a duel with Charles Dickinson, a Nashville dandy, to defend Rachel Jackson's honor. She had married Andrew, mistakenly thinking she was legally divorced from her first husband. The mistake was honest, but the scandal haunted the Jacksons throughtout their lives. Jackson killed Dickinson in the duel, but not before his adversary's bullet had smashed into his chest and lodged near his heart.

"Seven years ago, Wingate advised me to have this bullet removed," Jackson said. "I should have listened to him then."

"It's not too late; he could still do it."

"I'd die the minute he started operating."

They stood silently for a moment, gazing into each other's eyes, communicating more with their glance than words could ever convey. As gallant and courtly as ever, he took her hand and led her to the damask couch, where she sat, her pale yellow skirt flaring out over the crimson upholstery. He eased himself into a spindle-backed rocking chair opposite her.

She offered him her condolences on the death of his niece, and he nodded his thanks. Then he said, "I received all your letters, and of course, read all the articles you wrote—that Rebel Thorne wrote—about the conflict in Texas. It's a shocking, terrible tale, and one this country must never forget. But now I want to hear everything from your own lips," he said, his tone now that of the commander-in-chief of the United States armed forces. "Tell me of Texas."

Chapter 9

As SUCCINCTLY as possible, Rebecca told her story. When she got to the massacre at the Alamo, Jackson's face whitened. Rebecca's voice dropped to a tremulous whisper. "I'll never forget the haunting bugle call of the *degüello,* Santa Anna's signal that there would be no mercy. Each of our men fought like ten; again and again they turned back the Mexican charge, inflicting terrible casualties. But at last, sheer numbers over-whelmed them, and every last American was slaughtered. Never have I seen such wanton cruelty—boys of eleven and twelve bayoneted mercilessly; William Travis killed with a bullet be-tween his eyes; Jim Bowie bedridden, but hacked to pieces nevertheless; and Davy Crockett and his Tennesseeans muti-lated almost beyond recognition. Then all the bodies were piled up into a common funeral pyre and set ablaze."

Jackson angrily wiped away the tears coursing down his scored cheeks. "But Sam Houston, and my boy Jonathan, they beat Santa Anna at San Jacinto! They taught that pompous little dictator a lesson he'll never forget!"

She waited until his outburst subsided and then asked, "An-drew, what will you do about Texas? Their petition for state-hood is in Congress. Will you put pressure on our legislators?"

Jackson kneaded his long gnarled hands. "It's as delicate a situation as I've encountered in my years as President. Of *course* I want Texas as a state in our Union; it's what I've

always wanted. Just between you and me, Rebecca, I won't
be satisfied until we claim all the land from the Atlantic to the
Pacific. But for the moment, I must bide my time."

"But why?"

"Mexico has quietly let us know that if we move to admit
Texas as a state, or to annex the territory, she will consider
our action a declaration of war."

Rebecca blinked. "War . . . ?" Her voice trailed off. She felt
a clutch in her heart for Suzannah and her family. "That can
only mean that the Mexicans hope to reconquer Texas."

Jackson nodded. "They haven't given up, not by a long
shot. To complicate matters, Great Britain and France have
also intimated they feel annexation would create a serious im-
balance of power, and would support Mexico."

"But surely the Monroe Doctrine forbids their interference."

"Exactly!" Jackson responded. "If it was just the English
and the French, then I'd say, Damn 'em, we'll enforce the
Monroe Doctrine. But the question of Texas has divided our
own country. The North claims it's just another southern ploy
to increase the slave territory."

"Well, we both know that there's some truth in that."

Jackson let out a long sigh. "If John C. Calhoun and the
other southern nullifiers had their way, they'd secede and join
with Texas. No matter what happens, the issue of Texas must
not be allowed to split the Union asunder!"

His fierce blue eyes flashed with resolve. For the first time
Rebecca fully understood the dilemma that faced the nation.

"Andrew, tell me the truth. If war should come, are we
prepared?"

"We are not," he exclaimed. "I fear that the destiny of this
country is *never* to be prepared for war. It's one of the peculiarities of our democracy, and comes from our fear of a standing army. We fought to rid ourselves of the British army, and
I believe there's a fear that any army represents oppression."

"But then what are we to do?"

"Rely on volunteers, as we've done in the past."

Rebecca groaned. "Like the volunteer army in 1814, when
the British attacked Washington—valiant, but pathetic. They
had no training, no morale, nothing that could compete with
the British fighting machine."

Jackson nodded. "At least we have West Point."

"A sort of college for Army officers, isn't it?"

"Yes. And it turns out good officers. One is the son of an old Mississippi friend of mine, Joseph Davis—visited me at the Hermitage for three weeks when little Jeff was seven years old. In 1824, he was appointed to West Point, and became a lieutenant colonel in 1828. Jefferson Davis is a fine soldier, and if West Point can produce more like him, I have no fear for our fighting forces."

The light outside was fast failing, and the butler came in and lit the lamps. Since the breeze from the Potomac had quickened, he also closed the windows, for Jackson was notoriously vulnerable to drafts.

"Will you be dining in the State Dining Room?" the butler asked.

Before Jackson could say yes, Rebecca, sensitive to his abject weariness, interjected, "We're so comfortable, why don't we just have a tray right here?"

"Why, if that's agreeable to you, it would be a help," Jackson said with relief.

Rebecca picked up a folded afghan and placed it over Jackson's legs. She'd knitted it for him five years before, and it pleased her that he was still using it.

Jackson took out his corncob pipe and lit it. The sweetly pungent odor of Virginia tobacco filled the room. When Rebecca frowned at him, he said, "No use making faces, my dear. I know I shouldn't, but there are two things I'll never give up—coffee and tobacco. No use chastising me. After all, I am the President!"

Uncle Alfred brought in a dinner tray for Rebecca—Potomac trout, lightly sautéed, a decanter of white wine, and a variety of vegetables, including string beans and kohlrabi. Jackson had a bowl of warm milk with toast—the only food he could digest.

"How are Jonathan and your daughter, Suzannah? And my godson—Mathias Andrew, isn't that his name?"

Rebecca put down her fork. She hadn't mentioned her personal trial, she didn't want that tale to color the demands of state. But she could contain herself no longer. Voice trembling, she told him of Devroe Connaught's dealings with the Mexicans. When she recounted Devroe's attack on her and Matty, Jackson half-rose in his chair.

"By the eternal, I'll smash that coward!"

"Andrew, please—"

"Where is he?"

"I've tried to find out. If the Connaughts are in Washington, they're not showing themselves. I've heard that they've gone off to England for an extended stay with the English branch of the family."

Jackson's rage was awesome to behold, but at last he calmed down. The shrewd mind that had served him so well as a frontier lawyer now exerted its formidable influence. "Were there any witnesses?"

Rebecca shook her head.

"So it would be his word against yours?" When she nodded he said, "Rebecca, we're confronted with a grim situation. Since Texas isn't yet part of the Union, but an independent country, I doubt Connaught could be brought before a United States court of law."

"But Matty—" Rebecca began.

He leaned forward and took her hands in his. "I know, I know. Such injustice cries out to heaven for redress. Sooner or later we'll move against Connaught, bring him to trial, I promise you. He claims to be an American citizen, yet from what you tell me, he was aiding the Mexicans, and is probably still in the employ of Great Britian. He's a spy, no other word for it. We do have laws about treason. Don't worry, my dear, one way or another, he'll be made to pay."

With Jackson's assurances ringing in her ears, Rebecca felt a little easier. Of course she wanted to see Devroe Connaught punished. But more important, wanted it done legally. She was afraid Bravo would take it into his head to punish Devroe himself, and every time one of her children tangled with a Connaught, it turned out tragically.

After the dinner trays had been taken away, the talk turned to current happenings in Washington. "What of the upcoming election?" she asked. "I wish you'd reconsider and run for a third term. I know that Martin Van Buren would step aside for you, and the Democratic Party would be ecstatic."

The Democratic Party, under the sure guidance of Martin Van Buren, had held its election convention in Baltimore in May. Van Buren, with Jackson's full support, had been nominated handily.

"I could never survive another four years in this job," Jackson said. "It's enough to kill a man. But even if I were able to run, I wouldn't. George Washington set the example of only serving for two terms, and to my mind it's an excellent precedent."

"But nothing in the Constitution forbids a third term."

"There are other considerations. Limiting the presidency to two terms prevents a man from becoming too entrenched in the office, prevents him from taking on the aspects of a dictator." He smiled wryly. "Since my opponents have consistently called me King Andrew, you can see the difficulty."

"Oh, that's nonsense. Name-calling is one of our national pastimes. Besides, the common man is solidly behind you and your policies."

"That's just the point. It's the policies that are important, not the man. That's why I've been grooming men like Thomas Hart Benton, and Speaker of the House James Polk. And that's why in this election I've thrown my support to Martin Van Buren. He's promised to keep up all the programs I've started. The Whigs will run William Henry Harrison, hoping to capitalize on his ancient victory at Tippecanoe, back in 1811. The Southerners want Senator Hugh L. White. And of course, Senator Daniel Webster is eager to make his bid for the Presidency. All three Whigs have begun their slanderous attacks on Van Buren."

"Why do we tear at each other as if we were deadly enemies?" she asked. "After all, we are all Americans, presumably we all have the best interests of the country at heart."

"I wonder," Jackson mused. "Often I think there's an element in this country that would prefer an aristocracy based on wealth and position. Certainly, Nicholas Biddle with his Second Bank of the United States falls into that category, as do all the entire Eastern bankers. The only protection for the common man, the laborer, the farmer, is to broaden the base of the electorate."

"Oh?" Rebecca said softly, and arched her eyebrows. "Does your broadening of the electorate include giving the vote to women?"

"Now, now, Rebecca, let's not fight on your very first visit. I don't have the heart for that."

"All right, I'll grant you a truce—but only for this evening. Sooner or later this nation will have to address itself to the problem of equality of rights for women."

"Rebecca, your raspberry ice is melting."

She looked at him with such deep affection and humor that

he reached for her hand again and held it. "You've been a comfort to me these many years, and I thank you with all my heart."

They didn't speak for a long time, just sat there, listening to the quickened wind sighing through the branches outside. Then Jackson looked around the room. "You know, I view these past eight years as the most awesome experience of my life. The decisions made here—my God, they were far greater than any I had to make at the Battle of Horseshoe Bend, or even at the Battle of New Orleans."

She looked at him encouragingly, impelled by her curiosity both as a woman and as a reporter.

Jackson continued, "When I left Nashville eight years ago, I was considered a fairly prosperous planter, at least by Nashville standards. Oh, Rachel and I hadn't had an easy time; we started out living in a log cabin. It was years before we had any security at all. But if a man works hard, he can do anything in this great land.

"But now, after eight years in this White House, I find myself destitute. I have ninety dollars in my pocket, and that's about the extent of my resources."

"Andrew, that's awful! I had no idea—"

"When I first moved into the mansion, everybody assumed I was a barbarian. Even you, if I remember correctly," he said, smiling.

She blushed. "Well, that first inauguration almost wrecked the house, and you had to be spirited through an open window lest you be crushed to death. I'd say that we had ample reason."

He chuckled at the memory and she continued, "Whatever my early misguided notions, I've certainly changed. I've known every President who's lived here, and all I can say is that you've done the mansion proud."

"I had to uphold the honor of the country. To the diplomatic corps in Washington, and to our illustrious legislators, the way a President runs the White House is an important issue. They were all waiting to condemn me, and to condemn the office. I couldn't let that happen, even if it meant spending every last cent I had."

"You must let me lend you some money—whatever you need."

"Thank you, my dear Rebecca, but that won't be necessary. As soon as I get back to the Hermitage, begin planting the cotton fields again, I'm sure I can recoup my losses. But we must get Congress to appropriate enough money to run the White House. It's a great White Prison, that's what it is, and the man who gets elected is locked away in it for four years!"

"That may be, Andrew, but you know you wouldn't have missed it for the world. Every President who's elected knows he's a candidate for immortality." She smiled engagingly at him. "That's why you all run." Try as he might to remain stony-faced, he burst out laughing. "You always did have a way of pricking our balloons!"

"Seriously, though, who knows what would have happened without your firm hand during the nullification crisis? When South Carolina moved to secede from the Union, only your threat of invading that state with federal troops preserved the country. Surely generations of Americans will bless you for that."

Jackson's voice grew somber. "It's a terrible dilemma, and we haven't seen the last of it. If the southern states had their way, they'd form a new confederacy this very day, with Washington, D.C., as their capital."

"That's a shocking thought," Rebecca mused. "Yet, Washington is essentially a southern city."

"If this nation is ever split in two, we'll become prey to all the rapacious powers in Europe. They're just waiting with bared fang and claw for that to happen."

"They've never really given up their designs on us, have they?"

"No. And that's why it worries me so profoundly that foreign banks hold so many of our notes. That happened because of Nicholas Biddle and his damned Second Bank. We had to borrow from nations essentially antagonistic to us, and that makes us vulnerable. I hate to see it."

Jackson seemed to be tiring very rapidly, and so Rebecca rose to take her leave. He saw her to the front door, and they walked out onto the North Portico together. The busy sound of cicadas buzzed in the night air, occasionally punctuated by the tinkle of a cow's bell. A few lone gaslamps burned in front of government buildings, but other than that, Washington lay in darkness.

"Good night, my dear," he said. "It's always a joy to see you. You buoy me, remind me of younger, more vigorous days."

"Thank you, Andrew."

"Oh, one last thing, Rebecca. Now you know I've never been the sort of person to force anybody to do anything..."

Rebecca smiled to herself. If ever a man insisted on getting his own way, that was Andrew Jackson. But...

Jackson was saying, "This election won't be easy. The issue of Texas and slavery is bound to raise its ugly head. Biddle and his bankers will try to buy the election from the Democrats. I was hoping you'd see fit to use your considerable journalistic talents to help Van Buren. You know him, know he's a man of integrity."

Rebecca didn't feel that way at all about Van Buren. He was her idea of a consummate politician. He'd practically invented the political patronage system in New York State, and had successfully navigated a perilous course through the dangerous political shoals of Washington, without taking a stand on anything.

"You seem a trifle uncommitted," Jackson said softly.

"Andrew, have you heard the latest Van Buren anecdote making the rounds of the capital?" she asked. "The story goes that a senator accepted a bet he could trap Van Buren into actually committing himself on some positive belief. 'I say, Van Buren,' the senator said, 'it's been rumored that the sun rises in the East. Do you believe it?' Van Buren replied, 'Well, senator, I understand that's the common acceptance, but as I never get up until after dawn, I can't really say.'"

Jackson chuckled. "I've heard a few anecdotes about him myself." Then his long gaunt face grew even more somber. "But sometimes in a democracy the electorate must choose between the lesser of two evils, and that, I fear, is precisely what we're faced with now. Harrison is a pompous fool! As a soldier he wouldn't last two seconds in my command. Soldier? Bah! Old Granny is what he is!"

"I suppose you're right," she sighed. "If the choice is between brilliant but wily Van Buren and the rather lugubrious Harrison... well, Van Buren it is. Good night, Andrew. Thank you for a lovely evening."

She descended the steps of the North Portico and walked along the curving gravel path toward the front gates. She heard Jackson calling after her, "Stay in touch, Rebecca. Let me know how Matty fares."

Chapter 10

THE VIGIL at Matty's bedside continued. Wingate came every day at dawn to examine the boy, and then again at nightfall after he'd completed the rounds of his other patients. A week passed without any appreciable change in Matty's condition.

Late one afternoon, Circumstance relieved Rebecca. "Get some sleep," she said. "You won't do Matty any good if you collapse from exhaustion."

After Rebecca left the room, Circumstance took Matty's small hand in hers. She stared at him for a long time, trying to penetrate the veil that lay between them, almost willing the boy to open his eyes. She began to press his hand rhythmically, talking to him all the while. She kept it up throughout the entire time she sat with him, the fierce energy flowing from her body to his, imploring, cajoling, pleading with him to open his eyes, telling him that he was out of danger, that everything was all right, and with each sentence she kept pressing, then releasing his hand, then pressing again.

He still remained in a coma. Undaunted, Circumstance instructed Rebecca and Bittersweet to try the same technique, and the two women followed her pattern. Another two days passed without response. But one morning, while Letitia was sitting with him, singing some old spirituals, she thought she felt the slightest return pressure on her hand. She saw his eyelids flicker, and then the boy opened his glazed eyes, and tried to focus on her.

"Mama," Matty managed to say through cracked lips.

Letitia heaved herself out of her chair and ran through the corridor. "Miss Rebecca, Miss Rebecca! He opened his eyes. Squeezed my hand, he did. He talked!"

Rebecca, who'd been dozing fitfully in her room, wakened and flew to Matty's side. When she saw that his eyes were open, it was all she could do from bursting into tears.

Matty stared at her, his head twitching in tiny spasms as he tried to remember. "Mama," he said again.

"She's not here right now," Rebecca said softly, as she knelt by the side of his bed.

"Who might you be?" Matty whispered.

Rebecca felt a pang in her heart, but she said cheerfully, "Why, I'm your grandma, Rebecca. You taught me how to ride and everything while I stayed with you back in Texas. And you showed me the honeybees and their hives down along the river, and—"

"Grandma," he said weakly, recognition lighting his eyes.

Whatever anguish Rebecca had gone through disappeared with that one spoken word. Very gently she tried to explain that they were in Washington now, where they'd come to get him well, and that soon he'd be going back to Texas to his mother and father, sister and brother. She saw him struggling to comprehend it all, but finally it was too much for him and he closed his eyes. He slept for a bit, then woke again.

"Matty, how do you feel?" Rebecca asked.

"My head hurts," he said. His hand moved toward his bandaged head, but she held his fingers.

"Of course it hurts. But I promise you, it will get better. Are you hungry?"

"I'm not, but my stomach . . . it's growling like a hungry bear."

"Letitia, do we have any food?"

"Yes, ma'am! Been cooking and canning and baking for this moment, yes, ma'am, we got food!" And off she bustled to the kitchen.

Rebecca sent Tad racing off to fetch Wingate and Circumstance. They came quickly, and Wingate examined the boy very thoroughly, trying hard to act in a considered, professional manner. But after the examination he picked Rebecca up in his arms and hugged her.

"Not too much excitement now," he warned everybody.

"Letitia, clear broths only for the first few days." Seeing her disappointed expression, he added, "Matty will tell you when he's ready for substantial food." Bravo crowded into the room and Wingate pushed him back. "Only one visitor at a time. But whoever is here, keep talking to the boy. Try to make him remember everything he can."

Excitement and joy reigned at the dining table that night. Everybody was there—Rebecca and Bravo, Circumstance and Wingate and their two children, Jeremy and Doe, and Letitia, Bittersweet, Tad, and Enoch. Matty lay in the next room, sleeping peacefully.

Letitia outdid herself with the food, roast duckling, crabmeat cakes, a baked ham, stringbeans wrapped in lettuce leaves and steamed with strips of bacon which gave them a wonderful smoky taste, summer squash baked with butter and sprinkled with cinnamon, fresh whole-wheat bread, two cakes, and fresh fruits, berries, and cheeses for dessert. Rebecca broke out a vintage bottle of wine, and Bravo lifted his glass in a toast.

"To my sister Suzannah and her family—how I wish they were here with us this joyous night! To my brother Gunning, and his wife Kate, off in the Kansas Territory. But most of all to my nephew, Mathias Andrew Brand Albright!"

"It's like a wedding done took place in the family," Letitia said, "or more a birth, maybe."

Though Matty's recovery was still very slow, after a few months the worst was over, and Rebecca wrote to Suzannah and Jonathan:

"Every day he makes more progress. He's eating solid food now, and with a hearty appetite, as if to make up for lost time. Bravo has made him the most ingenious toys, things that require him to use his hands and brain, and Wingate encourages this, for he thinks it will help Matty get back the full use of his faculties.

"As you might expect, Matty's enslaved Letitia completely. When she's not cooking for him, or washing his clothes, she just stands in his doorway staring at him, remarking all the time how much he looks like her Suzannah.

"Everybody in Washington has come to call. Daniel Webster came, wearing his blue coat with the gold buttons, and his buff-colored vest and white cravat. Matty showed Webster the coonskin cap that Davy Crockett gave him shortly before he was killed at the Alamo. Henry Clay told Matty that if he stayed in Washington, he could work for him as a page boy. When Matty found out that Bravo had once been a page, that intrigued him all the more. Matty even got a smile out of 'Old Eloquent,' John Quincy Adams. I must say I'm overcome with everybody's kindness, yet I hope I don't sound too cynical if I casually mention that this is an election year, and that politicians especially tend to be kind during the election season. Everybody asks to be remembered to you and Jonathan, and our joy is their joy. Once again this family has Wingate and Circumstance to thank for our good fortune, first in saving Gunning's life, and now Matty's. When I think how badly I once treated Circumstance I'm filled with shame.

"I've saved the best for last. Autumn has been quite cold and rainy, especially October. (Thank God they're macadamizing another stretch of Pennsylvania Avenue. They estimate that in ten years, they'll have the entire length paved, so we'll be able to drive without breaking an axle in those damnable potholes.) I hadn't seen much of Andrew Jackson; he's had a constant chest cold. He's stayed pretty much to himself; ever since young Emily Donelson died of tuberculosis, Jackson's convinced he's got it too. Wingate keeps telling the President that the cough and spitting up of blood are caused by his old dueling wound, but you know Jackson, once he makes up his mind about something.

"At any rate, yesterday, who should show up at our door but Old Hickory himself! All wrapped in his fur-lined cloak against the chill, and leaning heavily on the arm of Uncle Alfred. 'I've come to see my godson before I die,' he said to me.

"Well, the household was agog! I've never seen Letitia speechless before, and Bittersweet ran to her room in the basement and wouldn't come out. Though in her case I think it's because she's so terrified of anybody who represents the law.

"Bravo wanted to take the President down to his workshop to see his inventions, but Andrew simply didn't have the strength to walk up and down those narrow steps. So Bravo brought up a few of the things he's been working on, including his repeating pistol. Andrew was amazed, said it would revolutionize war. Because the weapon was so deadly, so many men could be killed by one revolver, he thought that it might end wars once and for all. Men would have no recourse save to settle their differences peaceably, or face annihilation. A splendid thought—but the nature of man being what it is, I wonder.

"Well, the President went to Matty's room and said to the boy, 'Do you know that your father was once my ward?' Matty, who absolutely knows no fear, whether it be facing a panther down or chatting with the President of the United States, said, 'Yes sir. My pa told me all about it. That's why my middle name is Andrew.'

"'Right you are, lad, and I'm also your godfather,' Jackson boomed, so pleased with Matty that he fairly got some color back in his cheeks. Really, Andrew is so wonderful with children, so sensitive to the workings of their minds, that it's sometimes impossible for me to imagine him on the battlefield, commanding armies.

"Andrew had come with some presents, a roll of parchment with the official seal of the United States, and a small piece of wood that he said had been left over from the U.S.S. *Constitution*. You may remember that I told you they used the excess wood to build Jackson's carriage. Well, Matty couldn't have been more thrilled. He said to Jackson, 'My grandfather Zebulon fought in the Tripoli Wars and he and Stephen Decatur and the United States Navy beat up that mean old Pasha.' Then Matty thought for a moment, and said, 'Mr. President, I have a piece of wood that was important to me too, and I want you to have it.' He handed President Jackson the plug of ash that Wingate had recently removed from his skull, the wound having healed over so nicely.

"It was Jackson's turn to be delighted, and he said that he'd always keep it as a memento. Then he hugged Matty and told him he could come visit him anytime at the Hermitage, and to bring the whole family with him.

"Jackson plans to return to Nashville right after the election, whichever way that turns out. We're going through the usual campaign rhetoric, slander, and accusations; one would think from reading the papers that the men who run for our highest office were either fools or criminals, or both. I've begun writing an account of the campaign for the *National Intelligencer*.

"I'll keep you posted as to all events, and in the meantime, know that Matty daily grows better. Soon, though my heart will break, he'll be ready to go back to you in Texas. All my love to the twins, Becky and Zeb, to Jonathan, and to you, my dear Suzannah. Mother."

PART TWO

Chapter 11

THE PRESIDENTIAL election of 1836 was unusual in several respects. Rebel Thorne wrote about the new thrust in politics: "For the first time in the sixty-year history of our nation, a political party has chosen its presidential candidate by a national convention of delegates. Vice-President Martin Van Buren, whose idea this was, has been nominated by the Democratic National Convention.

"The Whigs, who consider themselves the more erudite and genteel of our two parties, disdained holding a convention, since they believe that each section of the country should have the opportunity to support a favorite son. But hark me, readers—There's a far more devious motive behind the Whigs' action.

"Daniel Webster, who's long entertained hopes of becoming President, has easily captured the loyalty of his native New England. In the West, General William Henry Harrison of Ohio has been selected; though heretofore not especially regarded as being of presidential caliber, the hero of Tippecanoe has his notoriety going for him. Southerners have thrown their support to Senator Hugh L. White. But what is the real reason behind the Whig strategy?

"Why, they plan to split the vote, and hope that no one candidate will get a clear majority. If that happens, the presidential contest would be thrown into the House of Representatives, where the Whigs and the Southern Democrats will join forces to deny Martin Van Buren the election. Is this the proper role of legislators who are supposed to be guardians of the public trust? How heinous if they resort to such patent trickery to deny the will of the people! Do they not believe then in the ideals of democracy, for which so many of our forefathers fought and died?"

Rebecca's outburst earned her the enmity of a great many legislators, among them Daniel Webster and Henry Clay, the principal leaders of the Whig Party. She paid little heed. She continued to write as she had always written, from her beliefs, from her intellect, and from the depths of her being. But she felt that she needed one telling issue with which to confront the Whigs, and finally she thought she'd finally found that issue.

"The monied establishment," she wrote, "the majority of the newspapers, the Southern Democrats, the men of extensive property holdings, all labor ceaselessly against Van Buren. What is behind the unbridled vehemence of their attack? Allow me to put the facts before you so that you may draw your own conclusions. Consider, then, the case of Nicholas Biddle. That worthy gentleman from Philadelphia was the president of the Second Bank of the United States, before it lost its charter with the government. According to his own admission, Biddle has poured a considerable amount of money into this campaign. For full well he knows that if Van Buren is elected, then Biddle's bank will never be rechartered. But if the Whigs win, Biddle will return to power as the most powerful financier in the country, and his eastern banking establishment will once more control the fiscal policies of the nation.

"You think me too extreme in my conjectures? Well, I can only remind you of this. One of the Whig candidates is in the employ of the Second Bank of the United States! He's fought legal battles for Biddle, and has always received a retainer from him, even while he was serving as a senator. I speak of none other than Daniel Webster! Am I so naïve—dear voter, are *you* so naïve—as not to recognize this as a monumental conflict of interest? If Webster was elected President, and had to decide on a case involving Biddle, or his bank, could we ever be sure that such a President would be acting from his conscience, rather than from his purse?"

Again a howl of protest from the Whigs and threats of lawsuits from Biddle and Webster, though none ever materialized. And one night a brick was thrown through Rebecca's window. But that didn't stop her, and she continued to excoriate the Whig candidates right up until the election.

The results were quite astonishing. The Whig master plan to split the vote failed miserably. With that party fielding three candidates, the final effect was to diffuse their own strength. When the electoral votes were tallied, General Harrison received seventy-three, Senator White twenty-six, and Daniel Webster fourteen. Martin Van Buren, the self-effacing but wily fox of Kinderhook, received one hundred and seventy votes, and was elected the eighth President of the United States.

But victory for the Democratic Party wasn't totally complete. Senator Richard M. Johnson, Van Buren's vice-presidential running mate, had received one hundred and forty-seven votes in the electoral college, a single vote short of the necessary majority. Consequently, that contest was to be thrown into the Senate and decided there. The Whigs controlled the Senate, so Johnson's chances were in extreme jeopardy.

Though President Andrew Jackson was still suffering from his persistent cough, he feted Van Buren with a victory celebration at the White House. Most of the members of Jackson's cabinet had been invited, along with half a dozen influential senators, including two uncommitted southerners. Francis Blair, a staunch supporter of Jackson and Van Buren, and the owner of the *Globe*, came. Richard Johnson also attended, but the handsome, gray-haired stalwart looked very subdued, if not glum. Both the *National Intelligencer* and the *Washington Telegraph* had hinted at dark secrets in Johnson's life that would make him suspect, perhaps unworthy of becoming Vice-President.

Rebecca, Circumstance, and Wingate had also been invited, Rebecca because of her efforts in behalf of the Democrats, Wingate because Jackson always felt easier when there was a doctor within reach, and Circumstance both because she was Wingate's wife and because Jackson had become quite fond of her. For the past several years, she'd been coming to the White House as often as she could. Armed with her sketch pad, she'd drawn the various rooms, both the public and private chambers, recording it all for a history of the mansion. She was writing it to honor the nation, the house, and her father Jeremy Brand, who'd helped build the White House.

President Jackson and Circumstance had had occasion to spend time together, and though Jackson had a reputation for being harsh with Indians, one could never discern that in his relationship with this half-breed. Circumstance had inherited the exotic beauty of her Indian mother, and the uncompromising honesty and talent for drawing of her father. On the surface, the young woman appeared placid, at times seeming to walk in sort of a reverie, but Jackson was a good enough judge of character to know that within this woman, fires smoldered.

As Rebecca surveyed the guests, she said to Jackson, who was escorting her into the State Dining Room, "Andrew, though I'm sure you mean this dinner as a celebration, I get the distinct impression that you have far more serious motives. A little campaigning, perhaps, for Richard Johnson?"

Jackson looked at her in mild surprise. "Why Rebecca, how can you think such a thing of me? Though now that you bring it up, it would be very awkward if Van Buren didn't have a Democratic Vice-President to help him in the trials that lie ahead."

The guests seated themselves at the dinner table. Outside a light snow was falling, turning the landscape into a glistening blue-white world. But the hearty fire crackling in the fireplace, the candles burning in the gilt sconces and girandoles, all imbued the room with a warm golden glow. The crystal carafes filled with Madeira and Tokay, the heavy cut-glass water tumblers, and the sparkling silver service gave evidence of Jackson's elegant, understated taste. Rebecca remembered when Jackson had fought with Congress over the appropriations for the White House, and had finally extracted fifty thousand dollars from them to refurnish the mansion. Now she saw Martin Van Buren gazing at it all—covetously, she thought. The look on his bewhiskered pink face with the bright blue eyes seemed to say, Soon I shall be master of all this!

What an extraordinary career the Little Magician has had, Rebecca thought. Van Buren was short in stature, unprepossessing, fastidious in dress and manner, but Rebecca knew that all that masked an intense ambition. Serving first as Jackson's secretary of state, Van Buren had locked horns with John C. Calhoun, Jackson's Vice-President during his first term. There had been a scandal in Washington concerning Peggy Eaton, the wife of Jackson's secretary of war. Considered a woman of loose virtue, she was shunned by the wives of Jackson's cabinet members. Jackson had defended her against Calhoun, and Van Buren, seizing his chance, had sided with Jackson. Thus he's successfully eased Calhoun out of favor, and indeed, had replaced him as Vice-President during Jackson's second term. Unquestionably, Van Buren was a politician without peer. Yet Rebecca couldn't quite overcome her uneasy feeling that it was one thing to be a good politician, and quite another to be a good leader. She remembered Jackson saying, "Sometimes it's necessary to vote for the lesser of two evils." But you're being unfair to Van Buren, she thought. Since you've worked so hard for his election, at least give him a chance to prove himself.

It didn't take long for the conversation to turn to the coming battle for the vice-presidency. Francis Blair, who was sitting next to Circumstance, paused in the midst of a mouthful of roast duck à l'orange, and said, "Mrs. Grange, if Johnson hadn't fallen short by that one vote, we wouldn't be having this crisis."

"But surely the Senate can do little else but confirm him," she answered. "He's clearly the choice of the voters."

Blair turned his thin, slight frame to her and murmured, "Ah, if only it were to be decided on those issues."

Circumstance looked at him quizzically, and Blair continued, "The Senate is a notoriously fickle body of men, often hypocritical. Johnson's created a great deal of resentment among some southern senators, and even among some northerners."

"I'm afraid I'm not up to date about political gossip," she said.

Blair, an inveterate newspaperman, leaned forward avidly. "Well you see, for years Johnson lived openly with a mulatto woman, had two daughters by her, raised and educated the girls, and not only acknowledged them as his, but also presented them socially. Such a breach of conduct is to a southerner— well, you can understand why they're up in arms against him."

Circumstance stiffened, and the startling aquamarine eyes in her tawny face widened. Blair was taken aback with the sudden change in her. He wasn't aware of her heritage. Her father, while on the Lewis and Clark expedition, had fallen in love with an Indian maiden named White Doe, and had married her. White Doe died shortly after giving birth to Circumstance, and Jeremy brought the child back to Washington. There he'd raised her, protecting her from the snide gossip of Washington society, whatever there was of it in those early years. Many a matron considered Circumstance a bastard . . . there'd been a time when even Rebecca felt that way. As long as Jeremy was alive, Circumstance had a defender, and nobody dared say anything to her face. But when he died, she was lacerated by the vicious teasing from the young bloods in the District. Such lies have an insidious way of working their way into a young girl's soul . . . and when she'd been knocked unconscious and raped, she'd refused to tell anybody about it, fearing that they'd say she'd brought it on herself. Only Wingate's compassion had sustained her. He insisted that they marry in spite of the horror of her rape, and from that moment on, their love had grown.

Circumstance was no longer a girl vulnerable to such slander; a decade of marriage, a loving husband, children, and a growing sense of her own value gave her uncommon strength. She fixed her gaze in turn on the two southern senators who sat across from her at the large table, and addressed them in a voice loud enough to be heard by everyone.

"You probably don't know this, but I'm working on a history of this mansion, and of all the Presidents and First Ladies who've lived here."

"Well, that's interesting," one of the senators said in his southern drawl, but his insouciant manner clearly indicated his boredom.

Rebecca and Wingate looked at each other, not quite knowing what to expect; Circumstance could be unpredictable. The other guests stopped their conversations to listen to her, for her tone was insistent.

"Do you realize that of our first seven Presidents, five were southerners?"

That seemed to pique the senator's interest, for he beamed and said, "Oh yes, we're very proud of the South's contribution."

"Would you consider Thomas Jefferson an exemplary President?" Circumstance asked.

"Certainly one of the greatest—and, incidentally, the founder of the Democratic Party!"

"How would you rate that other illustrious Virginian, Chief Justice John Marshall?"

"You said the word, my dear—illustrious." The senator was practically preening by now.

"Well, in my investigations, I've uncovered so many interesting facts," Circumstance went on.

By this time, Rebecca had an inkling of what Circumstance was doing, and she was beginning to feel anxious.

"Do you recall the scandal surrounding President Jefferson?" Circumstance asked the senator.

Down the table, Richard Johnson slowly began to flush. Rebecca flashed Circumstance a warning sign, but she plunged ahead.

"Did you know that there was a movement to impeach President Jefferson?"

"No!" one senator cried.

"It's true. All because he was accused of living with his mulatto slave, a woman who ultimately bore him five children—children who were considered bastards."

Richard Johnson squirmed in his chair and half-rose from his seat, but a curt motion from President Jackson stayed him. He slumped back, at once looking angry and miserable.

Circumstance kept her gaze fixed on the southern senators. "Some legislators brought their petition to Chief Justice John Marshall. They demanded that Jefferson be impeached on the grounds of conduct unbecoming a President. Well, Marshall hemmed and hawed, and finally said that he didn't think the charges would stick. Do you know why? Because Chief Justice John Marshall had a mulatto mistress of his own!"

"That can't be!" one senator said, while his confrere protested, "That's unsubstantiated slander!"

"It's true," Rebecca called with an air of absolute authority. "If you like, Senator, I'll send you copies of my articles when I covered that scandal for the *National Intelligencer*."

Circumstance smiled appreciatively at Rebecca, and then she addressed Richard Johnson for the first time. "Senator Johnson, from what I've heard of your conduct, I take you to be a man of extraordinary courage, one who places his personal ideals and responsibilities far above the shifting demands of political expediency. Surely such a man exhibits the same qualities of leadership so highly prized by the members of the Senate at this table. If there's any fairness at all in our democracy, then I'm sure that an enlightened Senate will confirm you as our next Vice-President."

Andrew Jackson, at the head of the table, cleared his throat.
"Well said, my girl!" The other members of the dinner party
were quick to take their cue from Jackson and heartily agreed
with Circumstance. The two southerners could only mumble
under their breaths, and bury their noses in their dessert of
frothy syllabub.

All of Washington turned out on the day that the Senate
cast its vote for Vice-President. Rebecca, Circumstance, and
Bravo pushed their way into the Senate chamber. It was jammed
with the young blades of Washington, and fair young maid-
ens—as well as some not so young nor fair—all bedecked in
their finery.

The southern diehards expressed themselves voluably on the
question of Johnson's credentials. "Unthinkable that a man who
openly consorted with a Negress, sired children—and *acknowledged* them; aye, that was the rub—unthinkable that such
a person should serve in the second highest office in the land.
Why, permit such a thing to happen, and then even a Catholic
or a divorced man might be elected!"

When the votes finally were tallied, a great cheer went up
in the chamber, for the Senate did confirm Johnson, giving
him thirty-three votes to his opponent's sixteen.

Rebecca squeezed Circumstance's arm. "Oh, isn't it grat-
ifying when it all works out on the side of the right?"

The three of them walked into the Hall of Representatives,
which was teeming with excited people. "You look bemused,"
Rebecca said to her son.

"I was just thinking about what the southerners said," he
replied. "Do you think we'll ever see a divorced man or a
Catholic elected President? I don't believe there's anything in
our Constitution that forbids it."

"As far as I remember, there isn't," Rebecca said. "The
stumbling block is not so much in our laws, but in the prejudices
of our own people." Then she halted suddenly, and blurted,
"What about a *woman* for President?"

Circumstance and Bravo looked at her as if she might be
deranged. "Mother, how can that be?" Bravo asked, twitting
her gently, for this wasn't the first time they'd had this discussion. "Women don't even have the right to vote!"

"You need hardly tell me that," Rebecca said, flaring with
irritation. "But one day we will, I promise you."

Circumstance shrugged. "Men will never give up their power of their own volition."

"That's true," Rebecca agreed. "But the fault lies more with the women of this country, who accept their servile positions without a murmur. They're so used to being downtrodden that they have neither the will nor the inclination to fight for what should be theirs. In a land of supposed freedom for all, the vote should be our inalienable right. I, for one, intend to dedicate the rest of my life for that cause."

"A hopeless task you've set for yourself," Bravo murmured.

"Perhaps," she said, and then her shoulders straightened imperceptibly, and her enormous hazel eyes glinted with a passion long banked. "I may not live to see a woman cast her ballot, but one day my daughter, or my granddaughter will, I swear it!"

Chapter 12

DECEMBER'S SHARP winds intensified to the howling blizzards of January, and then to the drifting snows of February. Great chunks of ice floated down the Potomac River, making ferry passage between Washington and Virginia hazardous.

At the Capitol, a large fire burned in the lobby of the Hall of Representatives, and the legislators huddled around the blaze, warming their hands, and backsides, only to return to the chilly Senate and House chambers to continue with the process of lawmaking.

The Brand household, snug against the weather, moved through the winter days with a certain sense of peace and contentment. Daily, Matty grew healthier, and there was talk of him returning to Texas, though how he would get there hadn't yet been decided.

"Why don't I take him, Mother?" Bravo said. "I haven't seen Suzannah in seven years. After that, I can swing north up into the Kansas Territory and see Gunning and Kate and their son. I'm sure that Sam Morse could do without me for a few months."

Months ago, the Brand family had received word from Gunning, who was stationed at Fort Leavenworth, that Kate had given birth to a baby boy named Peter. The news pleased Rebecca enormously. Deny it as she might, Gunning remained her favorite child, but he'd always been in so much trouble that she'd despaired of his amounting to anything. After a youth full of wanton excesses, he'd married Véronique Villefranche, a venal opportunist of the worst stripe. Fortunately, Véronique had abandoned him and their marriage had been annulled. Then Gunning met Kate Geary, who helped nurse him back to health after his duel with Devroe Connaught. The seventeen-year-old tavernkeeper's daughter fell desperately in love with her patient. After he recovered, Gunning went off to serve with the army in the Kansas Territory. The U.S. government was pushing the Indian tribes farther and farther west, and the army was overseeing their removal and eventual resettlement. After a few lonely months in the frontier, Gunning sent for Kate, and she joined him. Never underestimate the influence of a good woman, Rebecca thought, a little hopefully.

But as for Bravo's suggestion that he take Matty back to Texas, that would have to wait. She didn't exactly mistrust her youngest son, but Bravo always seemed so preoccupied that he was likely to forget Matty at a stagecoach station without realizing it.

On a sharp, biting day at the end of February, Bittersweet came running into the house clutching a letter. "Postman says it's all the way from Texas!"

The arrival of a letter made household activities cease. Letitia limped in from the kitchen, Bravo bounded up from the basement, and Rebecca hurried down from the sewing room. They crowded into Matty's room, where he was exercising on a complicated set of ropes, weights, and pulleys Bravo had designed.

"It's a letter from your mother," Rebecca told Matty excitedly, as she opened the envelope. Matty leaned against her chair as she read.

"'Dear Mother, First of all, how is my Matty? Oh, does he remember me? I'm enclosing a miniature which I had painted by a local artist in San Antonio. It's a fair likeness, I think. Please show it to Matty.'"

Rebecca handed the tiny portrait to her grandson and he studied it. The features were correct enough, Rebecca thought—dark-brown hair glistening with highlights of red, wide-set dark-brown eyes, finely chiseled nose—but the heart of Suzannah seemed to be missing. Only in the set of the determined mouth

had the artist really captured the resoluteness of Rebecca's
daughter.

"Yes," Matty whispered. "I think I remember now. That's
Mama!"

Rebecca crushed the boy to her fiercely. She released him
and went on reading. "'Every night I thank the Lord for Matty's
recovery, and I also thank Wingate and Circumstance. Jonathan
and the twins join me in my prayers.'"

Rebecca looked at her grandson. "Do you remember them?"
she asked softly. "Becky and Zeb? Your brother and sister.
They're about a year younger than you are."

His brow wrinkled as he strained his memory, but he shook
his head. "I don't remember." He seemed on the verge of
crying, and so Rebecca hurried on with the letter.

"'When the Mexican army retreated, they burned everything
in their path; our house, the outbuildings, and the barn were
all put to the torch. I'll never understand such wanton acts of
destruction, but since they've been going on since time im-
memorial, I can only wonder at the base nature of man. Jonathan suffered just as much as I did at our loss, but he never
complained and just started working. Becky and Zeb helped
all they could too. As Jonathan said, the secret is to keep at
it, day by day, and as the weeks and the months pass, somehow
it gets done. When Matty gets home, I think he'll find the
house very much the way it was.'"

Matty turned away from Rebecca as if he'd done something
wrong. "I try to remember, I really do. But nothing comes."

Rebecca put her arm around his frail shoulders. "You will.
As soon as you see the ranch, and your horse and your whole
family—why, it will all come back to you."

She continued reading. "'The euphoria we all felt at winning
our independence from Mexico has been tempered by harsher
realities. Our government is bankrupt; everything seems to be
in a swirling state of flux. I suppose we simply don't know
yet how to govern ourselves, and this fills me with awe at the
accomplishment of our founding fathers. They, after all, had
thirteen states to weld into a nation. What geniuses those men
must have been! And how fortunate you were, mother, to have
known so many of them.

"'We're hoping that we'll soon be annexed by the United
States, and not be left adrift; people talk of nothing else. But
I was distressed to learn in your last letter about the political

difficulties in the United States. I hope they'll be cleared up quickly. Doesn't everybody realize that we're really all one people? Some hotheads in our government are talking about wooing England, and perhaps becoming politically aligned with her. How quickly and conveniently those fools have forgotten about the arms and munitions England sent to the Mexican army.

"'Speaking of England, I suppose that sooner or later I must address my thoughts to Devroe Connaught.'"

Rebecca was about to skip this portion of the letter, fearing the effect it might have on Matty. But Bravo guessed her thoughts, and interrupted firmly. "Read it all, Mother. Let Matty make his peace with it. The sooner he does, the healthier he'll become."

Rebecca considered that for a moment and decided that Bravo was right. She read on, "'At first, my rage against Devroe was so consuming that, had it been in my power, I would have consigned him to hell. But Matty's recovery, and then the passage of the months, have enabled me to see things in a different perspective. The feud between our families goes back so many years—even before I was born. I remember that when I was a little girl, I heard whispers about Elizabeth Connaught going mad, and the death of her husband, and later, of the death of her daughter, Marianne. When Devroe's father Sean Connaught finally died at the hands of Uncle Jeremy, it must have seemed to Devroe that his entire family was being slaughtered by ours.'"

Rebecca broke off. "No, that's not true! Everything that happened to the Connaughts, they brought down on their own heads. But that's Suzannah for you, always seeing the other person's side."

She turned her attention to the pages again. "'All I can think of now is that the killing must stop. It's time for forgiveness, and I must make the first move. So, nightly, I pray for the Lord to give me the strength and the courage to forgive ... that's exactly what it takes, strength and courage. I hope at last that I'm being truthful when I say that I forgive Devroe and all the Connaughts. For I know in my heart that if I persist in this hatred, then I'll turn out exactly like them.'"

"Who's Devroe Connaught?" Matty interrupted. "What did he do?" He looked at Rebecca with his large dark brown eyes, and his hand moved jerkily to his forehead.

Rebecca hesitated, then said, "One day, I'll tell you all about it. Now listen to the last part of the letter. 'As soon as spring comes, I plan to come to Washington to see you all, and then to hold my dear son in my arms. We miss him, and all of you, more than we can say. Jonathan and the twins join me in sending our love. Suzannah'"

Rebecca folded the pages of the letter. Everybody in the room shifted and stirred. Rebecca placed her hand on Matty's shoulder. "You'll be going home soon, and that will be wonderful for you. But I'm afraid it will break my heart."

"Don't cry, Grandma. Even if I'm all the way far away in Texas, I'll still love you."

Everybody went back to his chores. Suzannah's coming back to Washington! Rebecca thought. She felt overjoyed with that prospect. But as she stared out the window hoary with frost, and at the glistening ice-blue icicles that wouldn't melt in the weak winter sun, she couldn't overcome an uneasiness in her heart.

Saturday afternoon, after Bravo had finished working at Samuel Morse's studio, he met his mother at the offices of the Breech-Brand stoneworks in Georgetown. Rebecca's father, Mathias Breech, had started the small business in the 1780s and had made a decent living from it. But when the capital of the country was to be moved from Philadelphia to the District of Columbia, there was a mighty surge in the stone-and-brick business. All the government buildings going up in Washington had required construction materials. Mathias had even supplied and dressed the Aquia sandstone that had been used for the White House, and he quickly became quite prosperous. Though the Breeches would never be as wealthy as the Tayloes, or the Custises, or the Van Nesses, Rebecca had been considered something of a catch not only for her beauty, but because of all she'd inherit.

After Mathias's death, Zebulon, by then Rebecca's husband, had taken over the business and almost ruined it. But when he died, Rebecca stepped in and not only saved it from bankruptcy, but gradually turned it back into a thriving concern. Rebecca had long ago given up any active involvement in the day-to-day running of the business, and left that to her competent foreman, an Irish immigrant named O'Shaughnessy. Enoch had opted to remain in Washington, instead of returning to Texas—

Rebecca thought that Bittersweet had something to do with
that—and so Rebecca saw to it that he got a job at the stone
works. Rebecca wondered what would happen to the business
when she died. Gunning had never been interested; his tem-
perament wasn't suited to such exacting details, and he chose
the army as a career. As for Bravo, his interests lay in a much
wider world. He was the first of the Brand children to have a
college education, and Rebecca felt intuitively that the stone
works might limit his horizons. Nevertheless, she also insisted
that he know just how the business worked.

As the afternoon light faded, she lit the oil lamps, and the
two of them sat at high desks, figuring the accounts. "How is
Samuel Morse?" she asked.

"He's fine, and asks after you all the time."

"What's he up to these days?"

"Well, he's working on an idea of how to transmit messages
across great distances. By wire."

"By wire?" she asked, looking up from the balance sheets.
"Is such a thing possible?"

Bravo nodded eagerly. "Wire is a conductor of electricity,
and if the wire is properly strung at intervals, with relay stations, then a message could be tapped out on the wire, received
at the next station, and sent on from there. Rather like sending
messages by semaphore from place to place in what they call
a telegraph arrangement, only the distances could be much
greater—you wouldn't be limited to the distance you could
see. According to Sam Morse, it would be possible to send a
message, say from Washington to Baltimore."

"In how long?"

"Almost instantly."

"I don't believe it!"

"But it's true. We're working on a series of sounds that will
be a code—one series of sounds for each letter of the alphabet."

"Bravo, really! What in heaven's name makes you think
that such a notion can work?"

"But I've already seen it work. Morse has such a system
rigged up between his house and his studio. That's how he
calls the servants when he needs them."

"I think he should stick to his paintings," Rebecca said.
She'd bought an etching of a Morse painting, "The Lighting
of the Lamps," done of the House of Representatives.

"Oh, he's a fine painter," Bravo said impatiently. "But what he's working on now will be much more important for this country. I can see these wires spanning the continent. Instead of news taking weeks to travel say from here to Texas, it could be done in a few minutes."

"Across the continent in a few *minutes?* You'd better not repeat that to many people, or you'll be locked away in an asylum!"

"That's what everybody keeps telling us," Bravo said, his jaw set. "People with small minds. Even Anne Fairfax looked at me kind of strangely. But Mother, I thought you'd be different."

Rebecca raised her eyebrows at her son's implicit criticism. Then Bravo said, "Morse has been trying to raise money to prove his theory, but as you say, everybody thinks he's mad. They thought Eli Whitney was mad, and Robert Fulton. Any time people don't understand what's new under the sun, they accuse the person of being mad. Well, I believe in him, and I'm working out his new code with him right now."

"Really? What do you call this magical thing?" Rebecca asked, her defenses up.

Bravo shrugged. "He hasn't named it yet, though to my mind, Morse's code is as good a name as any. Mother, I guess I should tell you—I've given Sam some of the money I've saved so he can continue his experiments."

"Bravo! That's really foolhardy."

"It wasn't foolhardy when you invested in the railroads, against the advice of Mr. Van Ness."

"Yes, but I have a great deal more experience in these matters than you do."

He looked at her earnestly, his blue eyes passionate with belief. "Mother, this is important. I think it's important enough for you to invest in it also. Though I doubt that you'd get any of your money back for years."

Rebecca put down her pen. Her son had challenged her. Has advancing age made me more cautious than necessary? she wondered. Whatever the truth, her innate conservatism in business gave her voice.

"This isn't the time to extend oneself in any investments. There's an unnatural euphoria in the air, the banks are lending money hand over fist for land purchases, small businesses are going wild in efforts to expand, money is loose. We've increased our debts to foreign banks at an alarming rate, and I just don't like it."

"But everybody says that with Van Buren about to be inaugurated, the boom will continue."

"That's what Mrs. Van Ness told me the other day, and she swears by it because that's what her husband told her, and since he's the president of the bank, who should know better? But when will people realize that anybody who speaks from a vested interest automatically supports his own point of view? Objectivity is the rarest thing to find in such circumstances. I'm cutting back our inventories of stone and brick. I'm calling in our debts, and I'm converting the paper money we have on hand into specie. There's nothing like solid silver and gold when times are hard."

"Mother, I don't pretend to know as much as you do about these affairs, but I think you're worrying needlessly. Lots of people I hear are taking advantage of this business crest to make their fortunes."

"Get-rich-quick money schemes never work," she said. "Oh, perhaps for a year or so. But Zebulon made and lost three fortunes, and when he died, we were almost destitute. I'm all for common sense in these things."

"All right, Mother. You're going to do what you want anyway, so there's no use my talking."

Bravo bent to continue his work on the balance sheets, and Rebecca, seeing his towhead and the crisp line of his profile, was struck with his resemblance to his father. Jeremy had sat like that over his sketchpads... the memory of that overwhelmed her with a rush of sadness. How different all our lives would have been if I'd followed my heart and married Jeremy, instead of marrying Zebulon in a fit of pique. It seemed to her that all their difficulties stemmed from her own stupidity. It would take a lifetime to assuage her guilt.

Suddenly Bravo looked up, his eyes concentrating on something other than the balance sheets. "Mother, what do you really think of Suzannah's letter? I mean the part about forgiving the Connaughts?"

Rebecca clasped her hands and placed them under her chin. "I think she's right. It's time for all of us to act like sane human beings again."

"That's a noble sentiment, I grant you, providing both families agree to it. But you know the Connaughts never will."

"With any luck, we'll never see them again. They've gone to England, and with everything that's happened here I doubt that Devroe would dare show his face in Washington."

Bravo shook his head slowly. "I don't trust him. Devroe's wealth is right here in this country. He's not about to give that up. He knows that as long as President Jackson wields power, he's in jeopardy. But the moment a new President's inaugurated, he'll come back."

Rebecca shrugged wearily. "You may be right. I don't know anymore. Frankly, there's nothing much we can do about it. I've talked to Jackson and he's explained all the legal complications. I don't have the strength to cope with them anymore. All I want is to be left in peace."

"But how can you live in peace?" he exploded in sheer exasperation. "How can anybody live in peace when there's a mad dog roaming the streets?"

Taken aback by his vehemence, Rebecca could only say, "I wish you wouldn't talk that way. Believe me, I have just as much anger about Devroe as you do, perhaps more. But what's our recourse?"

"Settle this man-to-man," Bravo said grimly. "When he tricked Gunning into that duel, and almost killed him, I swore that I'd avenge myself on him one day." He took a flattened bullet out of his pocket and let it lay in his palm.

"Throw it away!" she said sharply. "Bravo, if we take the law into our own hands, we're sure only to have another round of bloodshed."

"For an intelligent woman, Mother, sometimes you're very naïve. The Connaughts will never give up hating us. They feed on hate, grow on it; it gives them a reason to exist. They're like eaters of carrion, and revenge is their food. That Véronique Villefranche is a perfect match for Devroe. You know how she cuckolded Gunning, then betrayed him. We mustn't allow the Connaughts to choose the time and place for their next move against us. It puts us at such a disadvantage."

"Bravo, stop! For God's sake, and for the sake of reason and sanity, no more killings!"

Chapter 13

SATURDAY, MARCH 4, 1837, dawned clear and cold, with the temperature hovering in the twenties. Thousands of people had flocked to the capital for the double occasion—Van Buren's inauguration and Andrew Jackson's farewell. Canny hoteliers and tavernkeepers had the foresight to lay in huge supplies of victuals, and so food aplenty was to be had—provided one could afford the inflated prices. But that wasn't the case with beds; they weren't available at any price. A delegation from New York spent the night sleeping in barbers' chairs, a group from Virginia bedded down on pooltables, and others slept in barns, stables, and carriage houses. The hardiest pitched their tents on the Mall. Andrew Jackson had served for eight years under the most difficult of times, and now a grateful people had come to bid him farewell.

At the Brand house, Rebecca and Bravo were preparing to go to the inaugural ceremonies. Rebecca put on her miniverlined cape of a deep purple wool that harmonized pleasingly with her periwinkle dress.

In his blue greatcoat with its high stand-up collar, supple kneelength boots, and a top hat, nineteen-year-old Bravo looked adult enough even to impress his mother.

Wingate and Circumstance arrived with Jeremy and Doe,

and when the children joined Matty in his room, the house soon rang with the children's laughter.

"Why can't we go to the inauguration?" Matty asked.

Wingate shook his head emphatically. "It's a long ceremony and it's out in the open. The last thing you need is to catch cold."

Doe, who'd recently turned seven, looked at Matty from under her long, silken lashes. "When the wind blows, does it whistle through your head?"

Jeremy, an adult twelve-year-old, who daily looked more like his father with bright brown eyes and curly brown hair, said, "Don't pay any attention to her, Matty; she's silly."

But Doe had a mind of her own and insisted. "Will you show it to us later?"

"You can hardly see anything anymore," Matty told her. "It's all grown together." Doe pulled down the corners of her mouth.

Tad brought the carriage around, and Rebecca, Circumstance, Wingate, and Bravo climbed in. "You know who I wish were here with us?" Rebecca asked. "Dolley Madison. I wrote and invited her to stay with us, but she says there's still too much to be settled, with James's estate. She's staying on at Montpelier for a few more months. She did mention that a distant cousin of hers was coming to Washington for the inauguration, somebody named Angelica Singelton."

"Have you heard from her?" Circumstance asked.

Rebecca shook her head. "No word yet, nor was there a calling card. Perhaps she never made it."

"How old is she?" Circumstance asked.

Rebecca shrugged. "I've no idea. Dolley was never very good at details like that."

"Did Mr. Madison leave Dolley well off?" Wingate asked.

"Apparently he did, but Dolley put her affairs in the hands of her son, Payne Todd, which means she'll soon be penniless. A more profligate, self-centered wastrel I've never encountered. Isn't it amazing that parents can so rarely see the flaws in their own children?"

"You don't seem to have that problem with me," Bravo said innocently, and Rebecca slapped his arm in mock irritation.

"How old was Mr. Madison when he died?" Wingate asked.

"Eighty-five," Rebecca answered. "Amazing, isn't it? He was always so frail, and in such poor health that we never imagined he'd live another year. Without question, it was Dolley's devotion that added those years to his life."

"I don't remember her at all," Bravo said. "But you sound like you're fond of her."

"I'm more than fond of her—I love her. She had an enormous influence on my life, and she always acted like a second mother to me. She left Washington shortly before you were born, but when she visited the capital, she was very partial to you."

"She's a woman bursting with energy and love," Circumstance agreed, "and I adored her also. Now that she's alone, we've got to do something for her, make sure she's not lonely."

"Well, I'm going to do everything I can to persuade her to move back to Washington," Rebecca said. "The capital isn't the same without her and her levees, and her bustle, and her laughter. Do you remember when she started having Easter-egg rolls on the White House lawn?"

"I'm sure she'll go down in the history books for that," Bravo said under his breath.

Tad soon had them at the White House, where they joined the line of waiting carriages. They were to follow President Jackson's phaeton from the mansion to the Capitol.

"Look, there he is," Bravo pointed excitedly, as Andrew Jackson appeared on the North Portico.

The President, bundled in a calf-length great coat, leaned heavily on the arm of Uncle Alfred, while Martin Van Buren supported Jackson from behind. It took some doing for Jackson to negotiate his way into the phaeton.

Wingate shook his head in despair. "He shouldn't be venturing out today. I was called to the White House late last night—another of his attacks. After I examined him, I absolutely forbade him to go to today's ceremonies. He's that ill. He told me to save my breath. This is a day of triumph for him and for his policies, and he wants all of Washington to see that he absolutely supports Van Buren."

Rebecca nodded. "The Senate once refused to confirm Van Buren as minister to England, so it must give Andrew the greatest of pleasure to see his protégé sworn in as the President of the United States."

"And sworn in by Chief Justice Roger Taney, who was also once rejected by the Senate for a lesser position," Bravo added.

"So, on his last day in office, Jackson must be content that he's had his way again," Circumstance said.

"To my mind, he's one of the strongest Presidents we've ever had," Rebecca said. "No matter how you feel about him personally—and Circumstance, I know you're upset about his Indian policies—nevertheless, he's done everything he could to preserve the Union, and that must be our first priority."

"An amusing thing happened last night," Wingate said hurriedly, trying to smooth over the prickly moment. "After I put the President to bed, Uncle Alfred and I were talking. The old slave was complaining that the general was being highhanded, not listening to anybody about his health. So I said, 'Uncle Alfred, when the day comes, and the general goes to his Maker, do you think he'll get into Heaven?' Uncle Alfred looked at me and said, 'If the general wants to get into Heaven, who've they got up there who's going to stop him?'"

The burst of laughter eased the tension just as the President's carriage began to roll. Jackson's phaeton was constructed of very fine-grained highly polished oak, taken from the frigate *Constitution*. The carriage had been built for Jackson early in his term of office, and it was his pride and joy. Its one seat was just large enough for Jackson and Van Buren; the driver rode in a high box up front. Each coach door sported paintings of Old Ironsides in full sail. Four beautifully matched iron-gray horses drew the phaeton. Jackson had bred the horses himself, and in fact supplemented his income by breeding and selling racehorses.

The ride down Pennsylvania Avenue to the Capitol proceeded slowly. The crowds lining the avenue cheered the President and the President-elect as they passed. The men looked so different: Jackson, gaunt, old, and infirm, still projected a commanding presence; Van Buren, sitting short in his seat, tried to look dignified, but he appeared like a mischievous boy who'd gotten caught with his hand in the cookie jar—only this cookie was the Presidency of the United States.

The procession finally reached the Capitol. Jackson and Van Buren disappeared into the massive white building, crowned with Bullfinch's dome, and a short while later emerged on the inaugural platform on the East Portico. At the sight of the President, a great cheer rose from the shivering, assembled crowd.

A smile lit Jackson's craggy face. He leaned on his cane, his left hand clutching his white fur hat. Like a pillar he stood

in the gusting winds, acknowledging the ovations of the shouting mass of people, taking strength from their spontaneous roar
of approval.

"I think we're seeing an instance where the rising sun is
being eclipsed by the setting sun," Rebecca mused.

When the cheering subsided, Van Buren stepped close to
the front of the platform and in his clear, distinct voice, began
reading his inaugural address.

"Do any of you realize that Van Buren is the first President
to be born under the American flag?" Rebecca asked. "Every
other President was born in America while it was still a colony
of England's. How odd that Van Buren should have the distinction of being the first."

"You sound as if you don't like him very much," Wingate
said.

"Oh, I *like* him well enough," Rebecca answered. "But I
must confess that he doesn't inspire me. Frankly, I would prefer
inspiration to liking somebody." She sighed and said, "I sense
such a significant change in our leaders—that is, in the men
who aspire to be President. They seem to be turning into
such . . . politicians. You must admit that Van Buren does pale
in comparison to Jackson."

Van Buren, at fifty-four, stood five and a half feet tall, and
looked even shorter. His Dutch ancestry showed in his bright
blue eyes and pink-cheeked complexion. He wore muttonchops
that reached to his chin, and his blondish hair, what there was
of it, was fast graying. Though born the son of a tavernkeeper
in Kinderhook, New York, Van Buren had early adopted an
elegance in manner and dress, and even on this solemn occasion, looked rather dandified. Rebecca had always been struck
with Van Buren's uncanny resemblance to Aaron Burr; a rumor
that would never die insisted that Burr, who'd reputedly visited
his family's tavern in Kinderhook, was Van Buren's natural
father.

Van Buren had married his childhood sweetheart, Hannah
Hoes, and their marriage was apparently happy. She bore Van
Buren five sons, one of whom died in infancy; then, at the age
of thirty-five, she died of tuberculosis. Van Buren chose not
to remarry.

His inaugural address turned out to be a model of moder-
ation. He promised every American that his needs would be
looked after by the new government. Rebecca found the speech

intelligent enough—one could always count on Van Buren to
know his facts and figures—but it also illustrated the man's
infuriating love of straddling fences. "He's so cautious, so
anxious to please everybody, that you may be sure that *nobody*
will be satisfied," Rebecca whispered to Circumstance. "How
much better for the country if he could only be his own man."

At the conclusion of the address, Chief Justice Roger Taney
administered the oath of office, and Van Buren repeated, "I
do solemnly swear that I will faithfully execute the office of
President of the United States, and will, to the best of my
ability, preserve, protect, and defend the Constitution of the
United States."

Rebecca's heart soared as she heard the oath, and she leaned
toward Circumstance, "Can you imagine? With those thirty-
five fateful words, we've passed the power peacefully from
one elected official to another. We've done it without armies
forcing a despot to relinquish his office, we've done it without
bloodshed, we've done it because our people believe in this
Union of States. We're a young nation, but what an example
we're setting for the rest of the world. May this experiment in
democracy go on forever. Sometimes, my dear children, I just
want to sing hossanahs!"

The oath over, Van Buren kissed the Bible, and President
Jackson stepped forward then to congratulate him. Gun salutes
were fired by all the nearby military stations. The people cheered
themselves hoarse as the band played "Hail to the Chief."

Then President Van Buren and General Jackson returned to
the White House, where crowds swept through the mansion
for three hours to catch their first look at the new President,
and their last glimpse of the old.

Van Buren had let it be known that he planned to make this
inaugural ball the grandest ever. He'd chosen the assembly
rooms of Carusi's for the occasion, and by collecting old political debts and fat contributions from the party faithful, he'd
made sure that it would be done lavishly.

When Rebecca, Wingate, Circumstance, and Bravo got back
home, they made arrangements to meet that evening to attend
the ball. "I've been to so many of these things that I've lost
count," Rebecca said. "But I must say they're always exciting,
and this one should outdo them all. I can't wait!"

Chapter 14

REBECCA HELD onto the doorknob while Letitia laced her into her waist-cincher. For the formal inaugural ball she'd selected a peacock-blue satin gown with a demure square neckline, and a full, flaring skirt that accentuated her stately figure.

"I think it's something of a miracle that I can still fit into my old gowns," she said to Letitia, as she sucked in her breath.

"Proud of it too, ain't you?" Letitia grumbled.

"Why shouldn't I be? There's no reason for a woman not to be attractive even though she's getting on. I'm fifty-eight, and frankly I'm proud I've made it this far. Though how I did it I'll never know."

"Me either."

"Do you remember when I'd starve myself for an entire week to get into a costume that had a waist several sizes too small? How foolish we were in those years!"

"I wasn't," Letitia interrupted. "Just wore my old gingham in the summer, and my wool in the winter, and that did me just fine. 'Course, I was a slave then, so we didn't get much else."

"Well, you've been free for years now, and if you hadn't let yourself get so heavy, you could have worn all my old clothes. So stop complaining."

"I'm not complaining," Letitia said, suddenly feeling that

93

she'd gone too far with her mistress. "You know I thanks you with all my heart for freeing me, and for letting me keep my Tad. But every night when I closes my eyes, I wake up with a fright, worrying about Bittersweet." She looked at Rebecca with her cataract-clouded eyes. "Yesterday I heard that two bounty hunters caught another runaway slave. Came all the way from Georgia, those bounty hunters did. Seems there's no hiding from them anywhere. You know what happens to a runaway when they catches her, especially to a pretty thing like my Bittersweet."

"You're right," Rebecca said. "But your granddaughter came here more than two years ago, and so far there hasn't been a whisper of trouble. Why are you suddenly so concerned?"

"Can't rightly explain," she answered with a tiny shrug. "It's something the heart knows, and it's keeping me up nights, expecting to hear them come banging on my door."

When Letitia had first been a slave of Mathias Breech's, she'd been bred to provide additional slaves. All her children had been sold at auction, except for Tad; Rebecca insisted that her father allow Letitia to keep her son. One of Letitia's daughters had been sent to Mississippi. She bore a child to the plantation overseer, a white man; the daughter, Bittersweet, almost looked white. When Bittersweet was fourteen, her dying mother warned Bittersweet to run away, for she too was reaching breeding age. The moment her mother died, Bittersweet fled. She walked all the way to Washington, D.C., because during her childhood she'd heard tales of her grandmother Letitia there. When she finally arrived, more dead than alive, Rebecca didn't know what to do. The law was very strict about runaway slaves; if she hid Bittersweet she'd jeopardize not only herself but the rest of her family. But she and Bravo had decided that Letitia was really one of the family, and they had no choice but to accept Bittersweet into their home and lives.

Two years had passed, without arousing anybody's suspicions, but Rebecca knew the threat was always there. Washington, essentially a southern city, harbored vehement pro-slavery sentiments. If Bittersweet was caught, not only would she be branded and sent back to Mississippi, but Rebecca and her family faced the possibility of prison. Without question, Bittersweet would be safer in one of the northern states. Though the fugitive-slave laws still applied there, the people were less apt to turn a runaway over to bounty hunters.

I'll have to explain to Letitia that going north would be the best thing for Bittersweet, Rebecca thought. And I'll have to tell her soon.

Letitia finished hooking up the blue-green gown. "You sure were beautiful in those years," she said. "You still cut a mighty fine figure for a woman been a grandmother four times over."

"How is it that every time you compliment me, I feel damned with faint praise? Really!"

"Wear your amethysts; they'll go nice with this color." Letitia helped Rebecca fasten a wide choker of amethysts around her neck, and a broad bracelet of matched stones on her left wrist. "Who gave you these?" she asked.

"None of your business."

"I know who it was; don't think I forgot. Ought to be ashamed of himself—should be tending to his business in the White House."

"Oh, Letitia, for heaven's sake, don't make so much out of it. He gave them to me as a friendship gift."

"Staying out all night—I near worried myself sick to death."

"That was more than four years ago!"

Letitia recognized the sharpness of her mistress's voice and didn't pursue the subject. After a moment, Rebecca said, "You know, I think back on those early years and wonder, how did any of us survive? Why is it that when you're young, every little word, every little kiss, has such significance, as though the turning of the world depended on it."

"It's because you had a contrary mind. Nobody could say anything to you that you didn't take the opposite side."

"Oh, that's not exactly true."

"Almost exactly, and that's all I got to say about that matter." She smoothed the folds of Rebecca's gown, and then gave her a peck on the cheek. "My girl's still the prettiest in these parts. Now you have a good time, hear? Will he be there?"

Rebecca shook her head. "He's too ill. I don't know if he'll survive the year."

"Been saying that for eight years, since he got to Washington! Mark my words, that man will outlive us all. Have a good time, anyway."

Rebecca went downstairs and waited for Bravo. Matty came into the drawing room and gazed at her. "Gee, Grandma, you look so different."

"Not too different to smother you with kisses," she said,

and started to chase him around the settee. When she caught him she held his squirming body in her arms, feeling the very fiber of his young body renewing her own energy. That, after all, is one of the secrets of grandchildren, she thought. You see the world afresh from their eyes, and you yourself are renewed.

Bravo had agreed to escort his mother to the ball, even though he rarely enjoyed these functions. When he appeared, Rebecca was struck with how handsome he looked. Something had happened in the months since she'd returned from Texas, some change that had moved him from being a lad to the threshold of manhood. At nineteen, he'd almost achieved his full growth, and stood slightly under six feet tall. He didn't have Gunning's heroic, powerful physique; he was more leopard than lion—very much the way his father had been, she thought. His hair hadn't darkened at all since childhood, and remained so blond it looked almost white, with a healthy sheen that caught and reflected the light. He wore it long, just short of his shoulders, and he was always brushing it out of his eyes in a manner redolent of Jeremy. His eyes, a startling electric blue, were further testimony to his parentage: Jeremy's eyes had been that color. One day I'll have to tell him who his real father was, Rebecca thought. I owe him at least that much. Though to be perfectly truthful, she thought Bravo already suspected it.

He wore a navy frock coat cut to the new knee length, a buff-colored waistcoat, and a ruffled white shirt with blue silk cravat. The bones in his face were strong, a trifle craggier than Jeremy's, and the deep-set eyes were arched over by thick blond brows. Their expression was one of quick intelligence and an inquisitive turn of mind.

He'll meet somebody soon, and he'll be getting married, she thought with a start—and then wondered why that should upset her. Was she trying to hold onto him, the last of her children? No . . . it was simply that he reminded her so much of the love of her life that he always unnerved her. It's best that he marry and get out of the house, she told herself, for lately, she'd begun to notice how Bittersweet looked at him. The two youngsters had such an easy camaraderie; if left unchecked, sooner or later it would express itself physically, for that was the way of the world. And that would be tragic for everybody concerned.

Rebecca linked her arm through her son's. "Bravo, I have a distinct feeling that tonight you're going to fall in love."

"But Mother, I already am in love."

"Really?" she exclaimed, his answer catching her completely by surprise. "With whom?"

"Why, with Anne Fairfax." He straightened and stood taller when he said, "We're engaged."

"Engaged? When did all this happen?"

"Oh, the past couple of months."

"Have you talked to her parents?"

"No, not yet. You see, they're very protective of Anne. That's the reason she wouldn't go to the inaugural ball with me tonight. She didn't want to upset them."

"Bravo, I don't mean to demean your fondness for Anne, but surely what you're talking about is puppy love. That sort of thing passes quickly enough."

A look of disappointment crossed his face. "Don't you like her?"

"Of course I like her; from the little I know of her, she seems a very sweet girl. But she's so shy and retiring. And those parents—mercy!"

"Well, I'm not marrying her parents."

"In this case I think you would be. Bravo, listen to me. I'm talking about love, the kind that you know in the fiber of your being, the kind that blinds you. You haven't yet met that one very special person who'll sweep you off your feet."

"Honestly, Mother! Sometimes your ideas of romance are so mawkish that they're not to be borne. If you want my honest opinion, it's you who still want to be swept off your feet!"

"The very idea!" she exclaimed, and then, their voices twined in laughter, they were out into the clear, cold sharp March night.

Carusi's Assembly Rooms, at the corner of Eleventh and C streets, N.W., had already been the scene of three inaugural balls. Gaetano Carusi, the proprietor, met Bravo and Rebecca at the front door and kissed her hand. Speaking English with a blending of Italian, he exclaimed how beautiful she looked.

"Perhaps he's the man meant to sweep you off your feet," Bravo whispered to his mother.

"Lord, I've known Gaetano since he came to this country, thirty-five years ago. Now there's a story of success, the kind that could only happen in America. He was a musician of some renown in Sicily, and President Jefferson imported him to lend some style and musicianship to the Marine Band. The band was so bad Jefferson—himself an expert violinist—could barely tolerate it, but Gaetano whipped them into shape. Then he opened Carusi's Assembly Rooms. He and his sons not only run the place, but they play with whatever band they have."

Rebecca lifted her skirts as they ascended the elegant, crescent-shaped stairway to the grand ballroom. As they entered, Rebecca's eyes widened at the scene confronting her. A thousand candles burned in the crystal chandeliers and in the sconces on the walls, throwing a blazing light on the assembled crowd. Jewels of all sizes sparkled on the bodies of the beautifully-gowned women. The belles and matrons of Washington had outdone themselves; many wore the latest fashions from Philadelphia, Boston, and New York.

Martin Van Buren entered, to a great and prolonged cheer. The people in the Democratic Party's political machine had come not only to pay their respects to the new President, but to divide the fruits of their victory. As one of the party leaders had recently said, "To the victor belongs the spoils!" and the patronage-seekers had come to Washington with outstretched, avaricious hands.

"Who is there who will say them nay?" Rebecca wondered aloud. "Van Buren was elected on just such promises of patronage."

"You know, it's odd," Bravo mused. "We expect our President not only to be our political leader, but also to set the moral and ethical tone for the country."

"Is there anything wrong with that?"

"No, except that it's impossible. He's only human."

"Perhaps. But surely the elected leader should strive toward that, rather than immerse himself in patronage and other petty behavior."

"Ah, there's Anne and her parents," Bravo said. The Fairfaxes were wending their way toward them. Rebecca steeled herself. The greetings were stiff and formal, and this distressed Rebecca even further. Was there ever a more lugubrious couple? But it was Anne and the way she looked that broke Rebecca's heart.

Seventeen years old and got up to look like an old maid! Her acid-green gown made her look more sallow than she was, and did nothing to accentuate her good points. In fact, knowing

the Fairfaxes, and their predilection for seeing sin lurking in
every corner, Rebecca found it surprising that they hadn't
adorned their daughter in a voluminous black tent.

No, Rebecca thought, each feature taken separately didn't
do much to recommend Anne Fairfax. Yet why did she feel a
twinge of pity for her? Was it because the desperate look in
her brown eyes suggested that here was a sensitive plant which,
if nurtured, might bloom?

Though Rebecca had always been something of a snob about
appearances, it wasn't Anne's looks that so much unsettled her.
Rather it was the girl's unrelenting shyness, a voluntary with-
drawal from any social situation. Having been a woman who
was in the forefront of so many things, she had little patience
with this kind of person. No, and no again, Rebecca decided;
she'll never do for Bravo.

The Baltimore Band struck up a Viennese waltz, and Bravo
said, "Anne, may I have the honor of this dance?"

Anne looked inquiringly at her father, the wish and desire
momentarily lighting her face. Mr. Fairfax seemed about to
consent, but Mrs. Fairfax lifted her bulbous nose a bit higher
and sniffed, "The Fairfaxes don't believe in such un-Christian
displays." Mr. Fairfax added hurriedly, "Dancing—particularly these new dances where the partners *touch* each other—
is surely a tool of the devil, bound to lead young people astray.
Oh, I tell you, they are all going to the dogs!"

"Surely you jest, don't you?" Rebecca asked, feeling her
blood rising. "No? Well, then I must send you all the references
in the Bible to dancing, and their place in life."

Mrs. Fairfax's expression turned into one of icy disdain and
she grasped Anne's hand firmly. "Come along, my dear, there's
no need for us to be subjected to these free-thinking views."
She said the words as though they were a sort of a curse. The
Fairfaxes started off, and Anne looked back once, rather forlornly, and Bravo could only shrug. He mouthed the words,
"I'll see you later!"

"Thanks, Mother," Bravo said. "Now I'll have to do a fair
amount of crawling and eating crow before I can get back into
the good graces of the Fairfaxes."

"I hadn't noticed that they had any good graces," she said.
"They're so unbearably censorious. No dancing indeed! Then
why have they come here tonight at all?"

"Now, Mother, you might just as well make your peace

with them. After all, they're going to be your in-laws."

Rebecca gave a tiny shriek. "Do what you like! Marry
whoever you want, but I have no intention of being anybody
but myself, especially with those—antique pieces! How could
you even consider marrying somebody who won't even stand
up for herself?"

Daniel Webster and Henry Clay made their way over to
Rebecca, and soon the three of them were engaged in a spirited
conversation about the economy. Suddenly the band and the
entire assembly insisted that President Van Buren lead them in
a dance. He scanned the ballroom, and his gaze rested on
Rebecca. Oh, dear, no, she thought, but Van Buren was already
heading her way. "Had I known this would happen I would
have worn my flat-heeled shoes!" she whispered to Webster
and Clay.

Van Buren led her onto the dance floor, and the band struck
up a reel. Considering that she was taller than the President,
she thought the reel was going passably well.

"You do me justice again, madam," Van Buren said in his
courtly fashion. "We know what it's like to be without spouses,
don't we? Who is there to be my hostess at the White House?"

Rebecca couldn't believe what she was hearing. Had Van
Buren had something to drink? She was relieved when the dance
ended and Van Buren took her back to Webster and Clay, then
went on to pay his respects to other politicians and their wives.

Webster brushed back his coal-black hair, and his beetle
brows converged in a single line. "No question about it, that
man is a magician to have gained the presidency."

Clay, tall, formidably handsome, with a large, intelligent
brow, looked with disdain at Van Buren. "He doesn't even
look or act like a chief executive. The little ass-kisser!"

Rebecca suppressed a smile as she listened to the two giants
of Congress rip Van Buren to shreds. They're worse than gos-
siping females, she thought. Van Buren's term in office would
be far from tranquil; too many people were sharpening their
knives for him—particularly Clay and Webster, both of whom
had always coveted the presidency.

Wine and spirits flowed in abundance, and the food was
superb. It had been especially prepared by Carusi's three sons;
besides the typical hearty Chesapeake Bay fare, there were
some Sicilian delicacies that proved a sensation: mushroom
caps stuffed with snails and minced garlic, a pepper-hot tomato

sauce spread liberally over angel-hair spaghetti. The spicy items required a great deal of champagne to cool down the hot palates, and bottles popped without stop.

Bravo was standing near the punch table, sipping the icy wine and wondering what he could do to improve his situation with the Fairfaxes. As he turned, he collided with a young woman standing behind him, and he spilled his champagne all over her cream-colored satin gown.

"Oh you clumsy—!" the girl cried out, and Bravo turned to stare into the eyes of the most beautiful creature he'd ever seen in his life.

Chapter 15

BRAVO'S MOUTH fell open as he continued to stare at the young girl. How to describe perfection? Her lustrous dark-brown hair was parted in the center, with loose curls framing her delicate oval face. Her skin shone with the same sheen as the creamy satin gown she wore. Her shoulders were bare, and her head elegantly placed on her long neck. Her dark, expressive eyes hypnotized him as they blazed with anger.

"You've ruined me," she said to Bravo in a southern accent, at once mellow and barbed.

Still transfixed, he couldn't find the words to answer, but remained gazing at her as if she were the incarnation of something he'd once dreamed, but had never expected to see in reality.

"Dolt! Don't you have anything to say? Not even an apology?" she demanded, stamping her tiny foot.

At the sight of her exposed ankle, Bravo felt the blood rush to all the vital parts of his body. He managed to stammer, "I'm sorry. I didn't mean . . ." He snatched the handkerchief out of his breast pocket and dabbed at the champagne which had left an ugly stain across the bodice of the gown. "I didn't realize that you were behind me. I'm terribly—I hope it isn't hopelessly ruined. You'll—" He stumbled on, conscious that his words sounded leaden and inarticulate, those of a mere bumpkin. His tongue felt thick in his mouth, and his fingers burned from having touched her.

She turned to move away from him. He caught her arm. "Won't you tell me your name?"

"I see no reason for that!"

"So I might make the proper apologies."

"You've done and said quite enough, sir."

"Oh, but I insist. Please," he said.

More to get rid of him than anything else, she pursed her perfectly formed lips and said, "My name is Angelica Singleton."

His eyes lit in recognition. "Oh, that's wonderful!" he exclaimed. "My mother—you see, we've been waiting for you to get in touch with us. Your cousin Dolley Madison—she's my mother's best friend and—" He stumbled on, trying to build a bridge between them. In his pauses and hesitation he knew he was making a fool of himself, but it didn't matter. He kept staring into those dark eyes; in that brief moment, he'd fallen hopelessly and irresistibly in love with this creature.

He took her arm, and over her protests, drew her to Rebecca. She looked at her son's dazed expression and wondered how he had gotten drunk so quickly. "Mother, this is Angelica Singleton. You remember, Dolley Madison's relative."

"What a happy coincidence," Rebecca remarked, and then she saw the soiled gown. "Bravo—?"

He nodded shamefacedly.

Rebecca shook her head. "I must apologize for my son, he can be the clumsiest . . . Come, my dear, we'll go to the retiring room and see if we can't do something about that stain. Warm water should take it out, otherwise it will set in the fabric and the gown will be ruined."

"I'll buy her a new one!" Bravo called after them. He watched Angelica Singleton glide across the floor. Suddenly, he felt so weak that he had to sit down. "What's come over me?" he muttered. "I feel as if I'm coming down with Potomac fever!"

In his mind, he saw Angelica . . . slowly taking off her cream-colored gown, saw her in her white chemise, saw her soft shoulders and the delicate skin. Then he saw her standing naked before him, and knew that he would never be content with anything save that reality. His visions of her made him ashamed; she was too pure to be the object of such carnal thoughts. Yet they persisted on intruding, demanding, firing his body and making it impossible to stand. He sat there while the hot and cold flashes swept over him—hot when he thought of the consummation of his passionate visions, cold when he realized that he might never see her again.

"No," he said aloud, "I'll never allow that to happen. I won't!"

Anne Fairfax came over to him, and it was moments before he recognized her. "Bravo, I'm afraid that I'm leaving. I came to say goodnight. Shall I see you tomorrow?" When he just kept staring at her with glazed eyes she said, "Whatever is the matter with you? Are you ill?"

"Oh, God, yes I am," he said suddenly. "I'm not feeling well at all. I don't know about tomorrow. Perhaps we'd better not."

Anne waited a moment to see if she'd misheard him, or if he would say anything more. But he turned his head away from her. With a crushed, forlorn look, she walked off. She'd seen him talking to the beautiful young woman in the cream-colored gown, and correctly guessed what had happened. She lost the battle to fight back her welling tears.

Remorse overcame Bravo. He wanted to go to Anne, comfort her, tell her that they'd meet next week. But what if Angelica came out of the retiring room and he missed her? By the time he'd made up his mind to go after Anne, she'd left.

At long last, Angelica and Rebecca appeared. The two women were talking and laughing as if they'd known each other forever. Before he could talk to her, Angelica was swept off into a quadrille by a group of army lieutenants. Bravo's eyes followed her everywhere on the dance floor.

Rebecca looked at him ironically. "I see the young lady has made an impression on you," she said.

"She's the most beautiful, she's the most, she's... I can't find the words! Oh, God, did she say anything about me? Will she forgive me? Did you invite her to our house? You said you would, to please Dolley."

"If you promise not to be too clumsy, Angelica's promised to come to tea on Wednesday."

His hope sprang up, then was dashed down again. "Wednesday? But this is only Saturday! Wednesday is a lifetime away."

Bravo waited impatiently for the dance to be over and then he bombarded Angelica with plans. "The racetrack is open tomorrow. You must let me take you there."

She declined demurely. She did the same when he suggested that they go to the National Theater, where they were presenting a new production of *All's Well That Ends Well;* she was already going to see that with somebody else. And she declined when he proposed a ride along the banks of the Chesapeake and Ohio Canal to see the new locks they'd just put in.

"I'm afraid Wednesday is the earliest that I'm free," she insisted.

Once more she was surrounded by beaus, for Angelica Singleton was surely the loveliest young lady at Carusi's. She sensed that was the general opinion, and that knowledge fed on itself until she blazed with the recognition of her own beauty.

"Mother, I'm hopelessly in love with her," Bravo blurted.

"So, I would say, is every man in the room."

"No, no, this is different! I mean it. Suddenly, I understand what you meant when you talked about love. I must have her, I must win her! I can think of no greater happiness than to spend the rest of my life with this adorable creature!"

"Bravo, it usually takes two people to make that kind of pact. Don't you think you should consult her first?" She was trying to keep the conversation on a jocular level, but Bravo could hear nothing but his own heart.

"There's nothing in my life more important than being with her. I warn you, I won't rest until I make her my wife."

Rebecca didn't like the turn this outburst was taking. She'd never seen him like this; he was the last person in the world she'd ever thought would be obsessed by a woman. "What about Anne?" she asked.

"What? Oh . . ." He looked at her with a confused expression. "I don't know."

Suddenly there was a commotion in the front of the hall. Somebody had just entered, and it was creating quite a stir. It wasn't the President, who was still on the dance floor. Nor was it Richard Johnson, the Vice-President. Could it be Andrew? Rebecca thought for a hopeful moment, feeling her own pulse quicken.

Then she caught a glimpse of a brilliant red dress—Chinese red, the dressmakers called it, for that particular shade of expensive silk came only from the Orient. Rebecca could see the back of the woman's neck, and a portion of the dazzling river of diamonds she was wearing at her neck.

Rebecca felt her heart begin to thud. "No, it can't be," she whispered, feeling herself grow faint. "It mustn't be!"

Bravo sprang forward and shouted, "It's Véronique and Devroe Connaught!"

Chapter 16

"How DARE they show themselves?" Rebecca whispered. "How do they dare?" The horror of all that had happened swept over her, and yet, unbidden, came the note of sanity from Suzannah's letter: "It's time for the killing to stop."

Even in her distress, Rebecca couldn't help noticing that Véronique looked more ravishing than ever, the brilliant red dress highlighting her flawless skin, the rich black curls so artfully piled. Their sojourn in England had done the Connaughts a world of good. Even Devroe, in dark-green velvet, looked quite the aristocrat.

Bravo started forward, but Rebecca grabbed his arm. "Don't do anything foolish. Not here. Not now. It's the President's inauguration."

"I don't care what it is," he muttered, his face bloodless with anger. "He tried to kill you and Matty, and he's going to pay for it!"

Bravo tore himself from Rebecca's grasp and strode toward the Connaughts. Devroe's eyes narrowed when he recognized him, and Véronique's hand tightened on her husband's arm. Bravo took his gloves, and swinging hard, slapped Devroe across the face. Véronique's shrill scream tore through the room, and instantly silence fell, followed by a hubbub of voices asking "What happened?"

"As a gentleman, I demand satisfaction," Bravo said.

Devroe's good hand flew to his cheek. More than anything, he wanted to accept this child's challenge, show him the wrath of the Connaughts. But he and Véronique, already anticipating that this might happen, had devised a course of action to protect their reputations while at the same time bringing the Brands to ruin.

Devroe called out to the assembly, "I call upon everyone in this room to bear witness to this. I am being persecuted by these Brands. Not a word has passed between this young man and myself, and yet on this historic occasion, he's insulted me and my wife."

"You, sir, are a vile, villainous murderer, and you shall not go unpunished," Bravo said through clenched teeth.

"Again these rash accusations, again these persecutions," Devroe cried. "Shall there be no end to them? I consider myself a respected member of this community, a naturalized citizen who's chosen this country as his own. Am I not to be left in peace?"

A number of people previously alerted by the Connaughts lent their voices to Devroe's plea. Soon the entire assembly took up the call for Bravo to remove himself from the premises so that the festivities could continue without the interruption of these young hotheads.

"If you refuse to meet me on the dueling field, I'll seek you out," Bravo said, his voice rising above the shouts.

"Once more I ask you all to hear this," Devroe said. "I am being threatened, though I seek only peace, seek only to obey the law that forbids dueling. I am being coerced in this grievous thing. Is there no justice in the room?"

Bravo raised his fist, but a group of men crowded forward and restrained him. At the outbreak of the commotion, President Van Buren had retired to a far end of the room, and his cronies crowded around him to protect him from any harm.

Rebecca hurried over to Van Buren. "Martin, please, I beg your indulgence. I'm not here to argue right or wrong about the Connaughts, only to save this evening from disaster. You must arrest my son."

Van Buren looked at her incredulously, and she repeated her request. "Have the constable lock him up. Only overnight. Give his temper time to cool."

"All right, my dear, if that's what you think best."

Two Capitol policemen on duty at the ball were sent to arrest Bravo. He fought like a wildcat against them. The other men in the room, unable to resist the brawl, hurled themselves onto the struggling Bravo and subdued him. He was unceremoniously carried off to the local prison, a storefront affair on Pennsylvania Avenue, already overflowing with celebrants who'd had a little too much to drink.

The following day, Rebecca went to the jail and had Bravo released to her custody. The long hours had given Bravo an opportunity to think of all that had happened; he was crestfallen. "That Devroe—every time I think we have him in our grasp, he slips away like a jelly," he said.

"I know," Rebecca said. "Now there's not a chance in the world that anything you do would look right to the local authorities. Not after the scene you created last night."

"He's cleverer than I thought," he admitted. "But still, one day the scales will swing in our favor."

"That day is yet to come," she said. "Bravo, listen. I know this will hardly console you, but the world has a way of giving a man his due. Sooner or later, Devroe and Véronique will get their just reward. In the meantime, all we can do is lead our lives."

Bravo started to object, hesitated, and then turned beet red. "Mother, last night, did you happen to notice if Angelica . . ."

"She saw the entire thing, and was very distressed by it."

Bravo groaned. "Will she come to tea anyway?"

"I wouldn't blame her if she didn't."

"Oh, Lord, what am I going to do?"

"Nothing. Let it rest, Bravo, or you're sure to ruin any chance you have with her."

"I'll go mad until Wednesday!" he exclaimed.

High in the hills overlooking Washington, D.C., Devroe Connaught and Véronique were in the drawing room, having cocktails before dinner. The nurse, imported from England to tend to the three Connaught children, brought them in to say goodnight to their parents.

Devroe, an undemonstrative man, was a stern but sympathetic father. He was fond of his firstborn, an exquisite little girl named Romance. She had her mother's dark good looks, and an acquisitive nature. Already, she had claimed many toys of her brothers, spiriting them away into her own toy chest. At five, she was self-possessed, spoke English and French fluently, and could sew and do needlepoint. Véronique had enrolled her in Monsieur Generet's Dancing School in Washington, D.C., where the delighted dancemaster proclaimed to all who would listen that one day she would be a great dancer.

Sean Villefranche Connaught had just turned four, and was being groomed to be the heir of the vast Connaught fortune in the United States. Devroe expected a good deal from his elder son; he wanted to make sure that his upbringing in no way reflected the laxity of these stupid Americans, who let their children grow up wild. Weeds, those were the only things that grew wild, and they were meant to be rooted out, burned, or poisoned. He had great plans for Sean, and from his infancy, the boy had been made fully aware of that.

The third child, Carleton, was two years old, and though he'd been a colicky baby, crying at all hours of the night and day, he'd calmed down now, and it appeared he might yet develop into a decent member of the clan.

Romance curtsied to her parents, Sean bowed, and little Carleton, who could barely talk, tried to say a few words. Then the children were taken to their quarters, where nurse would read them a story first in English, and then in French.

"You're raising them well," Devroe said to Véronique in a rare moment of praise.

"Thank you. It pleases me that you're pleased."

"Is there nothing we can do with Carleton, though? He seems—well, how shall I say it?—a bit effete."

"*Mon dieu,* he is only two years old!" Véronique exclaimed. "How can one tell anything at such an age?"

Devroe shrugged. "Certain of his mannerisms, the way he mimics your father's gestures, for example. Perhaps it would be best for all concerned if Audubert didn't spend so much time with the children."

Véronique's cheeks burned. "These children are his life," she said. "Surely there is nothing wrong with a grandfather doting on his grandchildren."

"Nothing, providing that the influence is a good one. Attend me in this, Véronique, your father has become something of a laughingstock in Washington. His work at the National Theater as a stage manager . . . is that the sort of thing that you're proud of? Well, of course you're proud of it; there is your past as a toe dancer, and the rather nefarious life you led."

Véronique held her breath, not daring to answer. This was a daily torment that he put her through, always recounting her past, making sure that a sense of shame remained with her, that she would never forget who was master at the Connaught plantation.

"Your wishes in the matter will be obeyed," she said, acting the dutiful wife. But she would have killed him if she could. Still, this was the choice she'd made, and when she tallied the furniture, the magnificent fertile acreage, and the slaves, she convinced herself that she'd made the right choice. How then to explain her despair in the dark hours of the night, alone while her husband lay sleeping in his room, rarely venturing to share her bed? She was a passionate creature, and many was the night when she wished for the embrace of her first husband. In those dark hours, not even wealth and position could be an effective balm for her fevered flesh.

Devroe refilled her sherry glass, and she watched his long elegant fingers as they embraced the bottle. Can a woman live without love? she wondered. She knew that he'd married her purely as a convenience, to keep her mouth shut about his activities as a British agent in the United States, and also to use her as a breeding machine. Well, she had more than fulfilled that function. But not a day passed when she didn't wonder if this day would be her last as the mistress of the Connaught manor.

Her plan to do away with Rebecca had failed miserably, and Devroe, who didn't tolerate failure easily, made his disappointment and contempt known.

As mistress of the Connaught manor, Véronique had put aside her toe shoes and cloaked herself in the airs and graces of an aristocrat. She wasn't without a certain facility in playing the role. Her father had been a member of the petty nobility in France, and though she was born in 1806, long after the Revolution, he had instilled in her the qualities of her background. Added to this, her own beauty, and her touch of theatricality, had earned her the reputation of one of the finest hostesses in the District of Columbia.

In a city that responded to privilege and power, Véronique quickly made her mark. Legislators were eager to do the Connaughts' bidding, knowing they would receive their largesse. Devroe grudgingly appreciated his wife's ability in these matters; sometimes there were things a woman could do and say that would have been unconscionable for a man.

"You were absolutely right in your assessment about what the Brands would do when we made our appearance at the ball," Devroe said. "Now everybody knows that Bravo has a grudge against me. It shouldn't be too difficult to contrive a situation where I can act in self-defense."

"Exactly. Jackson is out of office now, and cannot harm us. Besides, if you plan to carry out your major ideas your presence here is absolutely required."

He nodded sagely. "If all goes well, in a matter of months we will bring this benighted country to its knees."

"You're sure of that?"

"There are many ways of making war. Sometimes I think the old ways, the caveman tactics, are all outmoded. Finesse, intelligence—those are the qualities that cause one nation to rise above another. Every day we see the British empire expanding her influence and domain."

"Devroe, your plan is one of exceptional brilliance," Véronique said. Oddly enough, she wasn't exaggerating. No matter what she thought personally about her husband, no matter what hell he put her through, still she knew he was an exceptional man.

"Those months in England and on the Continent weren't spent in vain."

"You're sure that the banks in Europe will follow your plan?"

Devroe nodded. "It took a bit of persuading, but after all, they're just as anxious as we are to see that this upstart nation is appropriately chastised. The consensus in Europe is that the United States—this trash bin for the criminals of the world— is acting too high and mighty. If that weren't enough, there's always the spur of money. Money is God in the banks of Europe; when they feel threatened by loss, they'll do anything. And the credit of the United States is stretched to the breaking point. Already some western banks have defaulted on one or two of their major notes. Without the Second Bank of the United States to act as a brake, credit has run rampant. Now all the English and European banks are prepared to call in their loans—simultaneously! It will wreck this country."

"Devroe, are we protected, ourselves?"

"I've seen to that. We'll have to make a show of losing a

great deal; otherwise we might incur the wrath of the locals. But rest assured, my dear, the bulk of the Connaught wealth is very adequately protected."

He raised his glass and toasted Véronique. "I drink to the economic disaster about to befall this country. From its ashes may a new monarchy arise. May this country be gathered back into the folds of the Empire, where it will take its rightful place beneath the British crown."

Chapter 17

"Is EVERYTHING READY?" Bravo asked for the hundredth
time. It was Wednesday afternoon, and he strode around the
drawing room, inspecting the arrangement of the china, checking the level of the wine and whiskey in their decanters, stoking
the fire so that it would be warm and welcoming when she
arrived.

"Why you fussing so?" Letitia asked, as she placed the tea
sandwiches on the sideboard. "This Angelica, or whoever she
be, she's only a girl. Ain't no angel."

"Oh, she's so much more than that," Bravo said as he picked
Letitia up and tried to whirl her around. "She's a goddess!"

"Plumb crazy," Letitia exclaimed. "Knew all that work in
the basement would cook his brain one day."

The tall mahogany grandfather clock in the foyer tolled five,
and Bravo looked at it anxiously. "Where can she be? Maybe
something's happened to her!"

"Bravo, relax!" Rebecca said. "I asked her to come between
five and five-thirty, so for the next half hour, she cannot even
be considered late."

Promptly as the clock struck the quarter hour, Angelica's
carriage pulled up to the front door. Bravo bounded forward
and let her in. She was even more beautiful than he'd remembered. The gusting March winds raised the color in her cheeks

and made her eyes sparkle. Her cloak was a burnt orange, to
match her dress. When she entered the drawing room, Bravo
felt that a burst of the sun's last rays had followed her.

Angelica Singleton curtsied to Rebecca, who was some-
what beguiled by this old-fashioned form of greeting. Really,
Rebecca thought, say what you will, young ladies raised in the
South usually had impeccable manners.

"I'm having the most wonderful visit." Angelica proceeded
to tell them in minutest detail what she'd done in Washington.
Bravo hung on every word, waiting for the moment when he
could add something to the conversation that would show her
just how thoughtful, intelligent, and brilliant he was. Somehow, that moment never presented itself.

She addressed him with fair regularity, but he sensed that
this was just good breeding, and he guessed rightly that he
could be anybody in the world. The realization was discon-
certing, but he was so completely in her thrall that he could
have gazed at her forever.

"This afternoon, I went for a delightful drive in the country,
and passed a most agreeable hour with Devroe and Véronique
Villefranche." She went on about the plantation, the superb
service, the kindness and consideration shown to her by the
Connaughts.

The drawing room became deathly quiet; Bravo's face hardened, and the color rose to Rebecca's cheeks. Angelica sensed
the change in mood and asked innocently, "Have I said something wrong?"

Bravo stood up and moved to the fireplace. He stared into
the flames, trying to collect his thoughts, then said soberly,
"Our families haven't been on the best of terms. It's something
that goes back for generations, and for reasons that have been
obscured in the fogs of the past. Perhaps when we know each
other better, I can tell you about it, but obviously, that moment
isn't now."

Rebecca was stunned with Bravo's statement. Not for a
moment had she thought he would stand up to this girl. Yet
he had, and done it as a gentleman. Never in her life had she
been more proud of him than now.

Curiously enough, Bravo's stand had much the same effect
on Angelica, for she lowered her eyes and said demurely, "Had
I known that mentioning the Connaughts would have caused

you such distress—oh, I'm a hopeless, insensitive fool."

Bravo immediately jumped into the breach and assured her that she was none of those things.

But Rebecca felt an uncomfortable edge of distress at what had happened. Surely Angelica had seen what transpired at the inaugural ball. Wouldn't common sense have dictated that she not mention the Connaughts? Yet she had . . . artlessly, to be sure, but there'd been a deliberateness in what she'd done. Was she testing Bravo, seeing what he was made of? His response had certainly caused Angelica to look upon him with a great deal more interest. It made Rebecca think that Angelica was far more complex than she seemed. Bravo was too straightforward, too innocent to be a match for that kind of woman.

Then Rebecca stopped short. What in the world are you doing? she asked herself. First you have objections to Anne Fairfax, and now you see hidden motives in Angelica? Anybody would think that you wanted to keep Bravo tied to your apron strings for the rest of his life.

The rest of teatime passed pleasantly enough. Angelica described her life in South Carolina with a mixture of good humor and forthrightness, the boredom relieved only by the gay plantation parties and the occasional shopping trips to Charleston. In the course of the description, she managed to intimate that there wasn't anybody special in her life, that she found the young beaus there all too provincial. Bravo's heart leaped up at that. At least she wasn't spoken for.

The clock struck six, and Angelica, with a tiny shudder of distress, put down her teacup. "My heavens, you've all been such wonderful company that I don't know where the time has gone. I promised Mrs. Cutts that I would be back at the house by six, promptly, so I must fly."

Loath to let her go without a private moment, Bravo said, "Mrs. Cutts's house in on the northeast corner of Lafayette Park, only half a dozen blocks from here. I'd be most pleased if you'd allow me to escort you there. If you've never seen the park and the White House at twilight, it's something you shouldn't miss."

"Oh, but I couldn't," Angelica said. "I never go anywhere without a chaperone, and . . ."

"That's silly," Bravo said, holding her cloak for her. "I assure you the streets are perfectly safe."

Angelica looked inquiringly at Rebecca; when she nodded, Angelica said, "All right, then. I know this is dreadfully daring of me . . ."

With another curtsey and the promise that she would write Dolley and tell her all about her *wonderful* tea with Rebecca, Angelica left.

She and Bravo strolled along New York Avenue to the White House grounds, Angelica's carriage following at a discreet distance.

The air was still crisp, but of a crystal, heady clarity. Twilight colored the sky with pastel shades. For a moment the White House was bathed in the roseate light, then turned the mysterious pale blue-gray that presages dusk.

"I love South Carolina," Angelica said, "but it has none of the excitement I sense here in Washington."

Bravo's hopes soared. "Can you imagine yourself living here?"

"Oh, definitely. Why, the ambassadors, and the legislators, and the diplomatic affairs—one would get to know the world in a way that couldn't happen on a plantation, don't you see?"

"Oh, I agree," he said emphatically.

"It seems to me that would be a splendid mansion to live in," Angelica said, pointing to the White House.

"An awful lot of responsibility goes with it," Bravo said. "You know, my Uncle Jeremy Brand helped build it."

"I didn't know that," Angelica said. "How exciting!" She made it sound even more thrilling than Bravo had ever imagined. "President Van Buren and his four sons were ever so kind to me at the inaugural ball. They even invited me to come to dinner as soon as they've completely moved in."

Bravo's heart plummeted.

"But of course, I'll be leaving before then."

"You're leaving? When?"

"Why, didn't I tell you? Tomorrow."

Bravo suppressed a groan. He felt a pain in the pit of his stomach, and thought he might be sick. They'd turned the corner of the White House grounds that gave them a view of the North Portico. "Angelica, I'm not very good with words, and I realize that we've only known each other a few days."

"Well, really only a few hours," she corrected him, "if you count the time we've actually spent together."

"All right, then, a few hours. But I believe . . . that the soul knows whom it must love." He saw the look of surprise and distress in her face and hurried on lest she stop him. "The soul knows, and that's what people call love at first sight. I knew from the moment I saw you that you were the one person I wanted to be with forever."

"But this is madness! You're making fun of me, saying things to hurt me."

He stopped and grasped her hands. "Oh, no, my dear Angelica; I wouldn't hurt you for anything in the world. It's just that I haven't been able to sleep for the past four days, tossing and turning with thoughts of you."

Her hands flew to her ears. "Stop! I won't listen to another word. What kind of person do you think I am?"

"The most wonderful girl in all the world," he said quietly. "One that I hope, when I'm worthy enough, to make my wife."

She stopped walking then, and searched his face. All she saw was the honesty reflected all over his golden, handsome features. "But it's insane to even talk about such things," she said.

"It's not," he insisted. "Those are the only things worth talking about."

"But I hardly know you! I don't know your values, your profession."

"I've just recently graduated from Georgetown University," he said. "I'm working in the studio of Samuel Morse; he's the most famous painter in Washington."

"Are you a painter, then?" she asked, appearing a little crestfallen.

He shook his head. "No, I'm...I guess you'd say I'm something of an inventor. Mr. Morse is developing a new way of communicating." He went on to explain about the electromagnetic telegraph, but could see that it wasn't making much of an impression on her.

"But how—I mean, can one earn enough to live on?"

"Not at first. But I've applied for a position as a junior inspector at the Patent Office. As soon as someone dies or leaves, I'll be hired. But Angelica, if you believed in me, why there isn't anything that I couldn't do. If you want, I'll move to South Carolina, work in the fields—anything, just to be near you."

"I don't want to stay in South Carolina," she said. "I want to travel, see the world. I want to meet and learn and do."

"Then we'll do that. Someday, Angelica, I know I'm going to do something valuable for this country, something valuable for the world. Share it with me."

He spoke with such urgency, that she could no longer consider it a joke. An aberration, perhaps, but she did find it flattering, almost irresistible. They'd reached the Cutts house and stood on the corner, talking faster and faster as the light failed, neither of them wanting to part in this magical moment of light and love, flooding over them yet fast fading. "I intend to marry you," he said quietly. "Nothing will stand in my way. I'll make you the happiest woman in all the world, or I'll die trying."

Tears started to her eyes and rolled down her cheeks, and she whispered, "You must stop. I'm only a poor young girl, not used to hearing such things. You say that the soul knows...Well, I can tell you this. When I first saw you that night, I too felt something. Perhaps that's why I was so angry with you when you spilled the champagne on my dress."

"You felt it too?" he cried, clutching her hands. "I knew it! Nothing that strong could be one-sided! Nothing. Oh, my darling!" He swept her into his arms and kissed her soundly on the mouth. He felt her warm sweet lips, felt her body tense with surprise, and then felt her lips part as they stood on the corner of H Street and clung to each other, both losing themselves in a moment of youthful ecstasy that swept all control from them.

Then with a gasp she broke free, ran into the house, and slammed the door. He shouted after her, "I'll write to you! I'll come to visit whenever you want! I'll wait! I love you, Angelica, I love you!"

He ran all the way home, flinging his arms out as though to make the joyous wind his carrier, to lift him to the heavens. He grabbed the limb of a tree and swung perilously from the branch, to and fro, calling out with each giant swing, "I'm in love! She loves me!"

When the branch snapped and he toppled to the ground, he didn't even feel his skinned knee. A passerby stared at him as if he might be deranged, and Bravo shouted, "I'm madly in love...I have an insane passion...I'm crazy about her!" The passerby ducked his head into the wind and hurried away. Bravo ran out of metaphors, but his heart pumped the knowledge through him with each rush of blood.

"I am in love! I'll never love another! The soul knows whom it must love. Knows what it must learn!" And in the deepening dusk fast turning to night, it seemed to him that with this insight, God had given him the most wondrous gift in the world.

When he reached his block, he'd calmed down considerably; now he was only singing. He never noticed Anne Fairfax standing at her window, watching him, a look of unutterable sadness on her face.

He barged through the door of his house. Rebecca took one look at his disheveled clothes and called, "How did you rip your pants?" He might not have heard her, for he bounded up the stairs, a look of wonderment on his face. She saw his expression, and felt her heart wrench. This moment dissolved to a time twenty years before, when Jeremy had looked at her that way. But the wrench in her heart was not only for memory's sake. Angelica Singleton . . . there was much more to that young lady than the honeyed accent and the beautiful, innocent eyes. Rebecca had a presentiment that this girl could hurt her son to the depths of his being, hurt him in a way that could twist his life . . .

And there's nothing I can do about it, she thought, already accepting the possibility as fact.

Chapter 18

DURING THOSE next weeks Bravo walked around as if hearing distant music, thinking strange thoughts, locked away in the isolation of the lover denied the sight of his love. He grew solemn and too thin, yet he filled the Brand household with his burgeoning masculinity.

"What *is* the matter with Bravo?" an exasperated Rebecca asked Letitia.

"Growing up is all," she replied as she stirred the soup. "He's a man now. Ain't nothing gonna change him back."

His manhood followed his falling in love, or perhaps it was vice versa, Rebecca thought—but in any case the result was the same.

He spent long hours writing to Angelica, detailing everything that had happened in Washington since she'd left. The workings of Congress, the start of a number of new government buildings, the lush new spring growth. "The gardens are a riot of color here, wildflowers dot the fields, each one prettying itself so that it may be plucked by you." Sometime he thought the sentiments so foolish that he'd rip the letters up, frustrated that he couldn't express himself in a way that would honor their love.

The day Angelica's first letter arrived, Bravo read and reread every word, pondering secret meanings, disturbed that the writing was so formal—yet had anyone ever written a finer hand? He kept the letter on the bedside table, and it was the last thing he touched before he went to sleep, and the first thing he saw on awakening. His work didn't suffer, his efforts were focused, for he had an immediate purpose now—he had to earn enough money so they could get married as quickly as possible.

He begged Angelica to allow him to visit her in South Carolina. She wrote back that he must not, under any circumstances! If he came, she would refuse to see him. She needed time to think; if he loved her truly, he would understand.

"He's turned into a stark, raving fool!" Rebecca said to Letitia while they were salting a side of bacon.

"He's like his father," Letitia said.

"Never!"

"You don't remember the day you went to Jeremy's studio and discovered all those drawings he did of you? Hundreds, you told me. That he'd been doing for years."

"Oh, but that was different!" she exclaimed.

Letitia snorted. "'Course it was, because it was *you*. No, that boy is like his father. There's some men, they can love lots of people—especially in the dark; it don't make much mind to them. But then there's other men, they love once in their lives, and never again the same way. That's Bravo. It's the most beautiful thing in the world, and the most painful, mixed up together so a person can hardly tell from one minute to the next how he's feeling. Oh, my, yes, my Bravo's in love, and nothing you or me or he can do about it."

Toward the end of April, Rebecca received a letter from Suzannah saying she was about to embark for Washington, and if her plans went well, she'd arrive in mid-May. That threw the Brand household into a frenzy of preparation. Letitia lived in a constant flurry of feathers as she plucked goose after goose, making a new comforter for her Suzannah, one she could take back to the wilderness with her. Preserves were put up, berries cooked in huge pots over a slow fire to make jams and jellies. The house was cleaned top to bottom. Rebecca got into the spirit and had everything painted—the trim, the shutters, the door. Bittersweet spent days polishing the brasses on the front of the house, doorknob, doorknocker, the finials on the gate.

Rebecca wanted to go and meet Suzannah in Baltimore, but reason prevailed—she had no idea when the boat would arrive: it could be a day early or a week late, depending on the cargo and weather conditions. She waited, she fretted, she grew sharp with Bittersweet, Tad, and Letitia. Finally, when she ran completely out of patience, Suzannah arrived.

Rebecca saw her first, from the window of her bedroom upstairs. She was coming up the street slowly, carrying a large portmanteau, and the weariness of the trip on her shoulders. Rebecca flew down the stairs and out the door, and reached the gate at the same time as her daughter.

"Oh, darling, darling," she whispered, holding Suzannah in her arms. Suzannah hugged her back, and it was difficult to tell who was doing the comforting. Questions tumbled from Rebecca's lips—the trip, the children, Jonathan.

But there was only one thing on Suzannah's mind. "Matty," she murmured.

Rebecca led her into the house, and Suzannah stared all around her, imprinting it on her mind. Letitia came shuffling in from the kitchen, her rheumy cataract-filmed eyes searching the dim face before her.

"Is it . . . my Suzannah?" she started to ask, and broke down and cried midway through the sentence. Suzannah came to her and hugged her fiercely.

"I prayed for such a long time," Letitia said. "Oh, I wouldn't let the Lord alone with my prayers, that he would send you here so I could look on your face one last time before I looked on his."

"Hush now, hush," Suzannah said softly. "I don't want to hear any talk like that. We live in each other's hearts."

"You're my baby," Letitia moaned, and burst out crying all over again. Suzannah held her until she calmed down.

Rebecca took her into Matty's room, where the boy was napping. Suzannah leaned over to the bed and stared at her son. Only then did she break down, sobbing softly with the relief of seeing him, this child that she'd given up for dead.

"It's all right, he's all right," Rebecca whispered over and over until Suzannah regained her composure.

"Mother, let me sit here beside him, until he wakens," Suzannah said as she dried her tears. "I haven't seen him in such a long time; my eyes must drink my fill of him."

Rebecca nodded, then closed the door softly. She came back once, with a pot of tea and some sandwiches, placed them before her daughter, and then was gone again. Suzannah sat there for almost an hour while the tea grew cold and the food remained untouched. Once she reached over and, gently as a breeze, ran her fingers over her son's face.

At last Matty stirred, and opened his eyes. He became aware of another presence in the room, and a look of confusion and fear made his face twitch.

"Hello, my darling Matty," Suzannah murmured. "It's me, Mama."

"Mama?" he repeated. "Oh, I must have fallen asleep while I was doing my chores. You won't tell Pa, will you?"

Matty sat up in the bed and stared at the room around him, stared at Suzannah, hopelessly confused in time and place until she said, "Matty, I've come all the way from Texas to see you. We're going home."

He threw himself at her and cried, "Mama!"

She held him to her breast and whispered, "I'll never let you go again, never. We'll be together always. No matter what."

After she dried his eyes and her own, they sat and talked, slowly, as Rebecca had cautioned her in her letters.

"I remember Pa, but every time I try to put a face to him, it goes out of my mind. Same with Zeb and Becky."

"As soon as you see them you'll remember everything."

"How's my hound Monday?" he asked suddenly.

"There, you see? You remembered without my saying anything," she told him, and he broke out into a smile.

Though everybody in the Brand household tried to be sensible about Suzannah's visit, the next days were a whirlwind of activity. Word spread in Washington that she'd come home, and scores of people trooped to the door to pay their respects. The consensus among the razor-tongued women in Washington was that the frontier had ruined her beauty. "My dear, did you see her hands? Red and raw and the nails all cracked. Appalling; a lady would never appear that way, never."

If Suzannah was aware of what the gossips were saying, she didn't care; beauty wasn't anything she concerned herself with now. But in shunting such frivolities aside, something extraordinary had happened to her, and the discerning people among the Washingtonians spoke reverently about the inner beauty that glowed from the woman. Yes, though she was only thirty, she seemed much older; already gray hairs had begun to appear in her dark-brown mass of hair. But love had illuminated her, and it shone transcendent from her very being.

She spent long hours talking to Bravo about his own plight. She took him more seriously than anybody else; she knew her younger brother wouldn't talk like this unless he felt it in his heart. If it had been Gunning, it would have been something else, for Gunning had been in love with a different person every week. But not Bravo.

For Wingate and Circumstance, she put aside an entire day and the three of them went riding out in the countryside. They guided their horses along the Chesapeake and Ohio Canal, and watched the boats being hauled through the locks on their way to the interior of the country. "I owe the two of you Matty's life," Suzannah said to them simply. "I'll never forget it. If ever there's a time when you need me, or want anything from me or Jonathan, you only have to name it."

Circumstance twined her fingers through her cousin's. "We want your happiness, and the happiness of Jonathan and your children. That's all any of us have ever wanted."

"The boy is destined for something great, Suzannah," Wingate said. "He suffered a great deal; he may still suffer occasional seizures, for who can know how these things will turn out? But surely the good Lord has something very special in mind for him."

Suzannah nodded. "And the Connaughts? What of them?"

Circumstance described what had happened at the inaugural ball, and Suzannah became very distressed. "Oh, Bravo mustn't! He mustn't turn out like them, live by their rules. Theirs is the way to spiritual death."

At last the day came when Suzannah and Matty were to take their leave.

"Remember when I sent you out from this house the last time?" Letitia asked. "Only I knew you were going to meet your Jonathan, hoping you'd run off with him . . . and now you going again, and I'm never going to see you no more."

"But Letitia, I expect you to come to Texas and visit with us. We've got your room all ready. You haven't met Zeb or Becky yet. You'll love Becky; Mother says she looks just like her when she was a little girl."

Letitia shook her head. "This is the last time you'll be seeing your Letitia. You and me, we both knows it; never were much lying between us. I just want you to know how much I loved you, and how much I love this little boy here. So, when I'm gone, think kindly of your Letitia."

"You'll never die for me," Suzannah said. "I owe you my happiness, so every day I live will be in memory of you and all you've meant to me."

The two women held on to each other; then Letitia said, "Best you go now, or you'll see me die of a broken heart."

A final kiss to Rebecca, and then they climbed in the carriage and it rolled down the street and was gone.

Rebecca moped her way around the house for a week. She couldn't bear to go into Matty's room. The youngster had brought new life and energy into the house, and with him gone, Rebecca felt herself slipping into the melancholy moods of old age.

One hot and humid day in early summer, Bravo galloped up to the house, his horse in a lather. He dashed through the front door, shouting, "Mother!"

Up in her sitting room, Rebecca put down her pen. The windows were wide open but the curtains didn't stir. She'd been writing to a novelist in London whose work she greatly admired, a man named Charles Dickens. As she heard the insistence in Bravo's voice, she thought, Oh, he's gotten another letter from Angelica and he's worried himself sick about something or other.

Bravo bounded into the room, his chest heaving, his jacket stained with sweat. "Something terrible's happening in Washington, and in Georgetown too. People are storming the banks!"

"What?"

He nodded, and gulped, trying to catch his breath. "Some banks have already shut their doors—barred them. They're refusing to let people in, refusing to give them their money. Mother, don't you hear me? The banks are failing! There's a rumor that they're failing all over the country."

"Where did you hear this?"

"It's all over the capital, all the legislators are talking about it. Word is that the foreign banks in England and on the Continent have suddenly decided to call in all their loans. Our banks don't have enough gold and silver to cover it. They've all gone broke, and now everybody is saying that the entire country is broke. Bankrupt."

Rebecca got to her feet shakily, mentally figuring their assets, and where she'd placed them for safekeeping. She'd divided them in a number of banks in the District of Columbia, but if all of them were failing...

"Let's get to the Metropolitan Bank immediately," she said, starting toward the door.

Chapter 19

MOBS WERE clamoring at the doors of each bank that Rebecca and Bravo rode to. Shutters were closed, doors were barred. Crowds stood stunned at the doors, women crying, men cursing; occasionally one heard the cry of a baby who'd picked up on the panic of the mob.

In their hapless, helpless state, the crowd responded to the most despotic voice, and one such man urged them, "Let's march on the Capitol! Let those damned legislators tell us what happened!"

All over Washington, people had the same impulse; soon hundreds, then thousands, of people were converging on the avenues toward the Capitol. As they rode along with the mob, Rebecca had a sudden memory of why Major Pierre L'Enfant had designed the city in such a fashion, a series of radial avenues superimposed on a grid of streets: If ever there was a threat of revolution, the cannons of the government could point down the avenues, and rake the advancing revolutionaries. Only today there were no cannons, only distraught, desperate people, many who'd seen their lifetime savings suddenly vanish.

At the sight of the mob converging on them, the Capitol police put up a desultory show of resistance, but since the handful of policemen were also bank depositors, they too joined the throng streaming into the Hall of Representatives.

Unfortunately, the legislators in session had decided that in this instance discretion was indeed the better part of valor, and they'd fled their chambers. The crowd milled about and then, with an air of defeat, slowly disbanded.

The next day only brought more panic, as bank after bank closed their doors to both creditors and depositors. Most businesses ground to a standstill. Those people who'd kept paper money at home suddenly found it was worthless. Shopkeepers wouldn't accept it for anything, be it a loaf of bread or a chicken, and very quickly a barter system sprang up. Eggs for an equal amount of vegetables, or the like.

"Mother—the truth, are we ruined?" Bravo asked.

"I managed to liquidate a good portion of our paper money a few months ago, and converted it to specie," she said. "I've also got some family heirlooms, jewels, silver, and things that might be bartered for food. We own the house in Georgetown, and this house, both free and clear. But as for the Breech-Brand Stone Works, all of our contracts to supply brick and and stone have either been postponed or canceled."

"How did it all come about?" Bravo asked, bewildered.

"I've been trying to figure that one out myself," Rebecca said with a weary shrug. "When Andrew Jackson disbanded the Second Bank of the United States, he did so with the best of intentions, feeling that the bank favored the rich and privileged."

"Well, it did, didn't it?"

"Yes, but it was also a very conservative organization. Nicholas Biddle, being overly cautious, kept a check on runaway monetary practices. I must say I thought Jackson was right to disband it, but now I wonder. Jackson put all the federal monies in 'pet banks'—individual state banks with known preferences for his own fiscal policies. They went a little wild, lending money to the westerners, and in turn borrowing money at exorbitant rates from the foreign banks. An inflationary spiral began, and soon reached such proportions that it had nowhere to go but down. When the foreign banks called in their debts, we in the United States were caught short."

"What's the answer?" he asked.

"We've got to tighten our belts, get ourselves and our economy and our government back on a much sounder financial footing. Jackson balanced the budget; we must keep it balanced. Above all, we mustn't borrow today, hoping that the next generation will pay back debts that we've incurred."

"Mother, whatever money I've got left of the royalties from Uncle Jeremy's invention is yours. Though I confess there's precious little of it, because I invested so much already in Samuel Morse's telegraph."

"I was sorry you chose not to follow my advice, but the money was yours to do with what you would. Perhaps this will make you a little more cautious in the future—if indeed we have a future," she ended with a rueful laugh.

Bravo paced the floor, his hands behind his back. "Maybe I was foolish to invest my money, but Mother, I don't regret it. Nor will I ever regret it if I believe in something. That's the only way we'll ever make progress in this country, when people back their beliefs. Isn't that what our system is all about?"

"To a degree. But it must be coupled with a conscience. Think, Bravo. If it came to feeding somebody, or putting the money into Morse's invention, which would it be?"

He let out a long breath. "Food, without question."

"Well, at least I've taught you something. Sam will just have to wait until a better time. Meanwhile, of course, you won't be likely to get a job in the Patent Office yet—no new positions there. What we must do right this moment is cultivate our own garden. I mean that literally. Letitia's digging up the front lawn right now, and is putting in some vegetables, though I hope we're not too late for the growing season. Tad plans to raise chickens in the stable. Thank God we've never gotten rid of our cow. If this economic depression teaches us anything, it's that to survive, we mustn't get too far away from the earth; we must learn to be self-sufficient again. I'll have to fish in the Potomac."

"I can go duck hunting," Bravo said in a burst of enthusiasm. "I'll take Jeremy with me. Have you seen that lad hunt game? He hunts with a bow and arrow, and whereas my pistol would scare off the entire flock, he can bag three or four birds before they're scared off."

"Extraordinary," Rebecca said. "I shouldn't wonder that it's his Indian blood. He'd be a quarter Indian, wouldn't he? That's right. Well, come on now, if we want to eat, we'll have to work."

With that, she went into the garden to help Letitia and Bittersweet, while Bravo rode off to pick up Jeremy.

The two cousins went duck hunting down the Potomac flats.

Jeremy stood motionless in the rushes, eyes alert, his fingers gently holding his bow and arrow. A duck took wing; in a motion so fast that it blurred before Bravo's eyes, Jeremy raised his bow and shot. The bird plummeted to the marsh.

"I'll never understand how you do that," Bravo said, clapping his young cousin on the shoulder. They collected the bird, then rooted around picking greens for a salad.

"Have you given any thought about what you're going to do with your life?" Bravo asked.

"Why sure," Jeremy said. "I'm going to the university, study medicine, and then join Pa in his practice."

"Are you sure that's what you want to do, that you're not doing it just to please your parents?"

Jeremy frowned, and scratched his head of curly hair. "I never thought of it that way. Every time I see Pa set a broken bone, or deliver a new baby, I think a man couldn't be happier. I mean, being able to help that way. Pa says there's so much to be learned in medicine, so many things yet to be discovered—wouldn't it be something if I could help in that discovery?"

"I love you, Jeremy," Bravo said, "and I consider myself mighty lucky to be your cousin."

Arms around each other's shoulders, they headed back toward the capital.

Within the month, vegetables were growing in every available garden in Washington, Georgetown, and Alexandria. Decorative flowers and shrubs gave way to edibles, and nobody's lawn appeared to be the worse for it. The depression continued, despite the efforts of Van Buren and his cabinet to instill confidence in the economy. It looked like it would get a great deal worse before it got any better.

In the fall, Rebecca received a letter that buoyed her flagging spirits. "Oh, wonderful news!" she cried as she read the perfumed pages. "Dolley Madison is moving back to Washington! She'll be here within a month!"

Dolley Madison's return to the capital engendered great excitement. She'd always been a favorite among the legislators, and though many of her friends had died, there were still many who remembered her, including Henry Clay, John Calhoun, and Daniel Webster.

When Rebecca learned of her arrival, she hurried to the Cutts house on Lafayette Square. The house had been built in 1820 by former Massachusetts Congressman Richard Cutts and his wife, Anne Payne Cutts, Dolley's younger sister. It was a simple building of buff-colored stone, two stories high, with dormer windows on the top floor. It was the first house built on the east side of what was then called President's Square, whose name was changed when Lafayette made his triumphal return to America in 1824.

The Cuttses lived there happily until 1828, when Richard Cutts was thrown into debtor's prison for nonpayment of debts. Dolley and James Madison, ever the saviors of their family, got him released from prison with the proviso that he sell the house to former President Madison so that Cutts could use the money to pay for his debts. The house and grounds were appraised at $5,750, and Madison bought it to please Dolley; otherwise, her sister and family would have no place to live.

Mrs. Madison herself answered the door and threw her arms around Rebecca. "Oh, my Rebecca! I would have recognized you anywhere! You look the same!"

Though Dolley was seventy years old, Rebecca too would have recognized her. There was the same jauntiness in her walk, the same attention to the details of her clothing—though Dolley had been born a Quaker, this didn't prevent her from disporting herself in clothes of her favorite color, any shade of yellow. James Madison's death had had a profound effect on her—she seemed more placid, but not yet resigned to death, and she certainly looked ten years younger than her age.

The two women sat and reminisced, laughing over long-forgotten foibles, crying over their respective loves.

Dolley listened intently to Rebecca's tale about Suzannah and Devroe Connaught. "Well, the Connaughts were always strange ones, weren't they? Tories during the War of 1812, and the whole family just riddled through with spies," Dolley said. "What is Gunning doing these days? That was the handsomest boy in Washington."

"He's the father of two children now, and serving in the army in Kansas—Fort Leavenworth. I haven't seen him in three years."

"And Bravo?" Dolley asked softly.

"I'll bring him round," Rebecca said. "I want very much for you to know him."

"I saw him once, I remember, when I visited here after Mr. Madison and I had moved to Montpelier. He was the very likeness of Jeremy."

"Still is."

"Does he know?" Dolley asked.

"I think he suspects," she said, "though I've never told him in so many words. Incidentally, I'm afraid he's fallen hopelessly in love with your young cousin Angelica Singleton."

"I shouldn't wonder," Dolley said. "She's quite a beautiful young lady."

Rebecca waited for some sign that would reveal Dolley's true feelings about Angelica, but she kept a discreet silence.

"I must go and leave you to your labors," Rebecca said, as she looked at the rooms piled high with furnishings that Dolley had shipped from Montpelier.

As Rebecca turned to leave, a floorboard creaked and sagged ominously beneath her feet.

"My word! What's happening?"

"The house is falling apart," Dolley apologized. "One must walk with care. So much has to be repaired! Though everybody thought Mr. Madison was a rich man, he was so generous with all our relatives during his lifetime that there wasn't much left over."

"I have a little money, put aside . . ."

Dolley shook her head. "Rebecca, I know that everybody is suffering during this depression. I can't let you deprive yourself for me. What I do plan is to sell some of Mr. Madison's papers to the government. I'm hoping that they'll be willing to allot some twenty-five thousand dollars for them."

"You can't be serious!" Rebecca exclaimed. "Why, if you offered them to a publisher, you'd get much more. Those papers are a national treasure. They tell everything about our beginnings, a diary of the entire Constitutional Convention."

"Do you think so?" Dolley asked, a bit befuddled. "That's exactly what my son Payne Todd says. He insists I demand a hundred thousand dollars for them. You see, Payne has this wonderful business venture that he's very anxious to begin, but he needs working capital."

"Dolley, I'm sure that Payne's idea is wonderful, but surely this isn't the time for new business ventures. Certainly he should be able to see that."

Dolley's face set, as it did whenever she felt that her son

was being criticized. Dolley had lost her first husband and an infant son to the fever epidemic that decimated Philadelphia in 1791; consequently, she tended to be fiercely protective about her only living child.

She shook her head slowly and said, "Despite what Payne says, I will settle for twenty-five thousand dollars. I have no desire to bleed the government; I just want to make sure I've enough to live on, so I'm not a burden on anybody."

"You a burden? You mustn't even think such a thing! This country owes you more than it can ever repay. When the British burned the White House, if it hadn't been for your presence of mind, all of our valuable documents would have been destroyed."

"That was a dreadful time for us, wasn't it?" Dolley murmured, her eyes widening as if seeing the flames shooting from the President's house. "I remember tearing the Gilbert Stuart painting of George Washington from its frame, so that it wouldn't fall into the hands of the invaders."

The two women sat quietly for a moment, remembering, and then Dolley shook her head. "If only there was a way that I could get Payne on the right track. I know that's all he needs."

"Children," Rebecca said softly. "We try so hard and sometimes, it's . . ." Her voice trailed off, and her sigh spoke of sleepless nights, and pain and worry. "How many years did I worry about Gunning?"

"Yes, but you tell me he's happy now."

"True, but at the back of my mind there's always the fear that he'll fall back into his old patterns."

Their eyes met and held, with a look of compassion and tenderness. Then Dolley asked tentatively, "Will you bring Bravo to see me?"

"Certainly. But I'm afraid his only free day is Sunday. May he come after church?"

"That would be wonderful. Do you still worship at St. John's?"

"We even have the same pew."

"Well, then, I'll see you there."

Rebecca was somewhat surprised: Dolley was a Quaker, and St. John's was Episcopal.

Dolley smiled. "When a woman gets to be my age, not only does she need to attend church regularly, but the church must be convenient. St. John's is just a stone's throw."

Chapter 20

REBECCA HAD never particularly enjoyed the company of other women; their chatter bored her, and she much preferred to talk to intelligent men. But she was delighted to have Dolley back. Though Dolley had never been known for her keen or discerning mind, her warmth and compassion more than compensated for that.

"Letitia, Dolley Madison looks wonderful," Rebecca said when she got home. "She's hardly aged, and we're going to church together on Sunday."

Letitia told that to the Fairfaxes' maid, who then told the Fairfaxes, who told the Tayloes; soon all Washington knew that the legendary former First Lady planned to live in the capital, and would be going to St. John's Church on Sunday.

The church would normally have been about half full, but this day every seat was taken, and an overflow crowd lined the back wall. Dolley seemed unaware of the stir she'd created. She sat with Rebecca and Bravo; Circumstance and Wingate sat directly behind.

After the warm greeting from Dolley, Circumstance fidgeted in her seat; she was always uncomfortable in church. She felt pinioned here, oppressed by the undercurrent of fear in the religious services, the threats of God's punishment against the transgressor. Circumstance had a different view of life—she saw God's handiwork in everything, in the color and vastness of the sky, the brilliance of the stars, the simple complexity of a leaf. She always found church services something of a travesty, for members spoke of Christian principles on Sunday, then acted like barbarians the rest of the week. She recalled the line of a Coleridge poem she'd recently read: "He prayeth best, who loveth best / all things both great and small." Surely, she thought, the greatest expression of the love of God was the love of one's fellow man. Yet she attended the services for Wingate's sake, and for her children's—though she hoped that one day the children would begin asking questions and make their own decisions as to how they would worship.

Suddenly Bravo grew tense, and Rebecca followed the direction of his fixed stare. The Connaughts entered the church, Véronique looking demure in a plain dark dress and hat, and Devroe impeccably turned out. Bravo half-rose in his seat, but Rebecca grabbed his arm. "Remember where you are!"

"That man doesn't deserve to be here!" he exclaimed under his breath, his eyes flashing to the pulpit. "Why is the Lord silent in all this? Anyone would think that a bolt of lightning—"

Circumstance leaned forward and put her pliant hand on Bravo's shoulder. "Bravo," she said softly, urgently, "God cannot concern himself with such problems. In such matters we're left to our own conscience. Believe me, Devroe's own rage will ultimately destroy him, as it must destroy anyone who surrenders to those base passions."

Bravo let out a deep breath and nodded slightly, but his jaw set and his eyes remained as cold and hard as aquamarines. He turned once to stare at the Connaughts, but instead caught the tentative smile of Anne Fairfax. She sat with her parents; they weren't members of this church but had come to see Dolley out of curiosity. The Fairfaxes sat stiff-backed and prim-lipped. Anne appeared paler than usual. Bravo hated himself for not having visited her in so long, but his heart was off somewhere in South Carolina.

Letitia and Bittersweet stood in the street in front of the church. Though black people never attended St. John's, Letitia had insisted on trying to go. "I been in Washington a whole lot longer than that church, and it's supposed to be free to anybody, and I'm free, and I'm going to see Dolley Madison, and that's all I got to say about that matter!" But she and Bittersweet had been barred.

Bittersweet, afraid to let her infirm grandmother out alone, had accompanied her, but she was very nervous. Ordinarily, she avoided public gatherings; one never knew where a bounty hunter might show up.

Though the Reverend William Hawley was never particularly noted for his oratory, Rebecca listened attentively as he delivered his sermon in a clear voice from the wine-glass pulpit. He wore black kid gloves; one finger of the right hand was split, so he could turn the pages of his sermon.

At the end of the sermon, he urged everybody to contribute to the church fund, to keep the church from going under to the auctioneer's gavel. He explained that the Bank of the Metropolis insisted that its loan be paid back with unstinting regularity; Reverend Hawley modestly announced that he'd taken a voluntary cut in salary to help meet the payments. "We ride in perilous shoals," he said, "and I urge you to look deep into your hearts, and deeper into your pockets, so that we may save St. John's."

While the choir made ready to sing their anthem, the collection plate was passed. Dolley whispered to Rebecca, "I scarcely recognize the church. How it's changed in the past twenty years!"

Rebecca nodded. "From the moment it was completed in 1815, we knew it was too small. They enlarged it in 1820, using a new plan by Bullfinch. But to be perfectly frank, I think Latrobe's original design was much more elegant. I made my opinions known during a meeting of the vestry, but was very quickly voted down. Apparently only my presence was desired, not my voice, it being unseemly for a woman to participate in such matters."

"Oh, men are such fools," Dolley said. "When was the tower built?"

"In 1822, and with great trepidation—since it was three stories high, people feared it would topple in a high wind. A few years ago, we made more room by tearing out the partitions and all those spacious, comfortable old pews." She shook her head. "The only addition I like is the new bell, made from a British cannon captured in the War of 1812, melted down and cast at the Paul Revere works in Massachusetts. It has a wonderfully mellow tone."

When the service was over, the worshippers filed out to shake hands with Reverend Hawley. He made a special point of greeting Dolley. "I hope we shall see you often, Mrs. Madison," he said, then craned his neck over the crowd, motioned to somebody, then turned to Dolley. "I would like you to meet two other members of our congregation who've asked to be presented to you, Mr. and Mrs. Connaught."

Rebecca saw Devroe and Véronique push their way through the crowd, and heard Véronique's high-pitched, *"Enchanté,* Madam Madison. It is indeed a great honor."

"You must visit our plantation," Devroe said to Dolley.

"But of course," Véronique agreed, staring through Rebecca as if she didn't exist. "We would be delighted to make your return to Washington a festive occasion. A grand ball, perhaps; most certainly a dinner—whichever you prefer. I will call on you to make the arrangements."

Only Reverend Hawley's presence kept Dolley from telling Devroe what she thought of him. She finally managed to get away from the Connaughts. Dolley kissed Circumstance goodbye, then she and Rebecca walked slowly back to her house, with Bravo lagging behind.

Rebecca's face flushed with frustration. "When I think of what traitors the Connaughts were during the War of 1812, how they worked to overthrow our government!"

"Now, dear, it's no use getting upset," Dolley said.

Rebecca sighed hugely. "You're right. I guess I'm just one of those old fools who finds it so hard to forgive."

"No matter what you think about that Connaught woman, she is very beautiful."

"Gunning thought so too, and worshipped her, but she betrayed him. She has a brain to match her beauty. Véronique has a hard mind in a soft body, and there's nothing more dangerous than that."

Letitia had seen Dolley Madison, so she and Bittersweet started walking home. As they passed the black-and-gold Connaught carriage, Véronique studied them with a penetrating stare.

"I know the old darkie," she said to Devroe. "She's the Brand maid. But who's the young girl?"

"Begging your pardon, madam," Sisley Urquhart called from the driver's box, "I understand that it's her granddaughter."

"Granddaughter?" Véronique mused. "Why does the girl

have such a frightened look about her? Sisley, find out all you can about this girl—where she comes from, who her parents were, if she's free or a slave. Check the rolls down at the Records Registry office. If she's been freed, then that information will be registered there."

"Why the sudden interest in some no-account nigger?" Devroe asked.

"Nothing, really. But when it comes to the Brands, I like to be apprised of every detail."

"Sometimes I think you hate them more than I do," Devroe said with a laconic gesture. "Or perhaps, you still have a secret place in your heart for your first husband. I understand that Gunning was quite a ladies' man. After all, love and hate aren't so very far apart."

"Idiocy!" Véronique spat, but her furious blush gave the lie to her protests.

Bravo sat on the edge of the sofa in Dolley's house, his leg jerking in agitated rhythm. Since they'd entered the drawing room with its wide, lovely bay window, Dolley had stared at him without a stop.

"Is something wrong?" Bravo asked finally.

She blinked her eyes. "Nothing at all. It's just that you remind me of somebody I was very fond of."

"Who was that, Mrs. Madison?"

"Why, your . . . uncle, Jeremy Brand. Bravo, you must call me Aunt Dolley, since I've known you since the day you were born."

"Thank you, Mrs.—Aunt Dolley. It's an honor." Then, taking his courage in his hands, he said, "May I inquire after the health of your lovely cousin, Angelica Singleton?"

"She's a splendid young lady, isn't she—from a fine family, beautifully brought up. She's been educated at a seminary for young ladies in Philadelphia, so she's very modern in her thinking. She has more in her pretty head than most southern belles, who can be so . . . how can I say it without being unkind?"

"Vapid?" Rebecca offered.

"That's the word exactly," Dolley agreed. "Though it may be unkind after all. Anyway, Angelica has a mind of her own. In fact, Rebecca, she's very much like you in that respect."

"Will she be visiting you?" Bravo asked, and held his breath waiting for the reply.

"Well, I don't see why she shouldn't."

"When?"

"I hadn't given it much thought, since I only recently arrived myself."

"Thanksgiving is a wonderful time in Washington," Bravo said.

"Oh, but I'm afraid that's hard upon us. There isn't enough time to make all the necessary arrangements, and for letters to go back and forth."

"Well, Christmas is even better. It leads right into New Year's. There are all sorts of levees, and the open house at the White House—"

"Dolley, you helped originate that practice, didn't you?" Rebecca interrupted.

Before Dolley could respond, Bravo eagerly went on building his case. "If the Potomac freezes over, there'll be ice skating on the river, and the National Theater will stay open this winter, and I just know that Miss Singleton would have a splendid time."

Dolley smiled at Rebecca. "Do you remember when you and I were young and full of enthusiasm like that? But Bravo, Angelica's visit will have to wait awhile. I must get this house organized, put in a new floor."

"Oh, Aunt Dolley, I'll put in the floor for you! I could come in every morning before I go to Sam's studio, and I could work Saturday afternoons—why, I could have it finished in no time at all, certainly by Christmas."

Dolley, seeing the young man's eyes fairly dance with excitement, allowed herself to be swept along with him. "All right then, I'll write today, and perhaps she'll be able to come. But will you fix the floor even if she can't come?"

Rebecca laughed aloud as Bravo blushed. "Of course I will. I'll go to my workshop right now and get my tools. I'll start this afternoon."

"Bravo, if you do that, you'll get us all arrested," Rebecca admonished. "This is Sunday."

"All right. Aunt Dolley, I'll be here tomorrow with first light. I won't make any noise, so there's no reason for you to disturb yourself. Now I'd better go organize my tools."

He made an attempt at a formal goodbye and left the room. They heard his footsteps in the foyer and then heard the front door close.

"My dear Rebecca," Dolley burst out, "I'm quite shaken. I couldn't take my eyes off him at church, and then again here! He looks exactly like him—I mean *exactly*. With the same ingenuous, sweet disposition. Every moment I thought I was staring at Jeremy!"

Then Rebecca heard footsteps in the foyer and her finger flew to her lips. "Bravo?" she called. "Is that you?"

"Sorry; just forgot my hat!" Bravo answered, trying to keep his voice light. "Here it is! See you tomorrow."

The front door closed again. This time Rebecca went to the window and stared after her son as he kicked his way through the golden autumn leaves on the sidewalks.

Bravo lengthened his stride, trying to get away from what he'd just heard. But the words kept echoing in his ears, making his heart pound until it was so loud he could scarce contain it.

Sooner or later he'd have to confront his mother about this. "I've got to know the truth," he said, accentuating the words as he punched his palm. "I've got to hear it from her own lips!"

PART THREE

Chapter 21

As AUTUMN left its chill mark on the land, the economic depression worsened: trade suffered, ships lay in the harbors collecting barnacles; all government projects ceased, including work on the post office and patent buildings. Among the suppliers who suffered was the Breech-Brand Stone Works.

One bleak, rainy afternoon, a day that reflected Rebecca's mood, she received an invitation from President Van Buren to a small dinner party in honor of Dolley Madison. Rebecca accepted with alacrity, as if reprieved from the depression. The evening of the occasion, she bundled up in her warmest clothes, including a heavy flannel petticoat, before picking up Dolley and driving with her to the White House.

"How well I remember the drafts in this place!" Dolley recalled as she gave her cloak to the White House butler.

President Van Buren greeted them with his usual gracious formality, and said, "Yes, the hall is decidedly cold. I've installed two high screens between the hall and the long corridor hoping to stop the drafts, but to no avail."

Dolley said, "I would love to see what you've done with the East Room."

"Oh, my dear Mrs. Madison, I'd advise against it. I keep it closed during this bad weather; it's impossible to keep warm. I do most of my entertaining in the Oval Room."

As they proceeded along the hall, Dolley crinkled her nose. "What is that I smell?"

"Cheese," Van Buren said with a sad shake of his head. "Just before Andrew Jackson left, some admirers sent a fourteen-hundred-pound wheel of cheese. Jackson put it in the north hall and invited the public to come and eat as much of it as they liked. Well, you can imagine the chaos! Thousands of people flocked here and devoured it. What they didn't eat, they ground into the floor or smeared on the upholstery. We've been scrubbing for months, but we can't get the smell out of the house."

When they entered the crimson Oval Room, they were greeted by Major Abram Van Buren, the President's eldest son. Abram, a graduate of West Point, now served as his father's secretary. He'd just turned thirty, and resembled his father, particularly in his suave, deferential manner.

The President poured sherry for them and toasted Dolley's return to Washington. "Actually, I've an ulterior motive in asking you ladies here this evening," he said.

"You? Ulterior motives? I can't believe that!" Rebecca wanted to say. But since it was Dolley's evening, she kept her peace.

"While my dear friend and benefactor, Andrew Jackson, was in residence," Van Buren was saying, "the White House was as crowded as a stagecoach station. Inundated with thousands of tourists, so that everything has been trampled into the dust. After my inauguration, I had some of the more tattered furniture put up for auction, and I've raised more than six thousand dollars that way. Congress appropriated another twenty-seven thousand dollars to pay for housecleaning, new china, glassware—you've no idea how much of it gets chipped and broken just in ordinary usage. Whatever is left over will be used for new rugs, upholstery, and the like. And that, ladies, in addition to having the pleasure of your company, is one of the reasons I've asked you here tonight."

Abram threw another log on the fire and the sparks popped against the fire screen.

"Mrs. Madison, since you presided here for so many years—sixteen in all, wasn't it?—perhaps you'd be good enough to share your thoughts with a widower on what should be done," Van Buren said.

"Well, my biggest complaint was that there was never an

adequate supply of running water," she began. "When John and Abigail Adams first moved in, their servants had to haul water from a well more than a half-mile away. Then President Jefferson, genius that he was, set up an attic cistern with a system of wooden pipes reaching to all the floors."

"That's right," Rebecca agreed. "I remember Jeremy Brand building it according to Jefferson's design. But Dolley, what you probably don't realize is that President Jackson installed new iron pipes that bring in spring water, and the system even allowed him to take hot and cold showers."

"How perfectly wonderful!" Dolley exclaimed. "Imagine, all the modern conveniences!"

"Then you'll be happy to know that I've gone even further," Van Buren said. "I've built a reservoir in the basement with a double forcing pump that supplies water for the kitchen and the bathrooms and all the water closets."

"Goodness! Are there water closets now?" Dolley asked.

Rebecca nodded. "Yes, John Quincy Adams put them in. Some people say water closets are called johns in his honor."

Dolley laughed gaily. "Do you think if I'd had them put in, they would be called Dolleys?"

Van Buren fingered his side whiskers. "Plumbing aside, I was thinking primarily of how the house should be redecorated."

"Do you think it's wise to spend so much when the country is in the grip of this depression?" Rebecca asked. "Your political enemies might well use it against you."

"That certainly is a consideration," Van Buren admitted, "and I've weighed it very carefully. But I must put my own stamp on this house. I also think it would be a great tonic for the nation if they saw that we had enough confidence in the country to begin restoring the President's House."

Rebecca tilted her head in a noncommittal gesture. She wanted to say that confidence comes from an appreciation of leadership, not from interior decorating, but instead smiled and said, "Well, you're the President, and it's entirely your prerogative."

"Good, good," Van Buren said, rubbing his hands. "Mrs. Brand, do you recall a discussion that you, President Jackson, and I once had in this room?"

"As a matter of fact, I do. I said the Oval Room was entirely too crimson and yellow for my tastes, that I would prefer something more muted—beige or blue, or some soothing color that would allow the beauty of the architecture to shine through, instead of being overwhelmed."

"Oh, Rebecca, I never thought of that, but I believe you're right," Dolley said. "Look at these elegant Bellangé chairs President Monroe bought in Paris. Wouldn't they be divine upholstered in a lovely shade of blue? And instead of that vast expanse of crimson draperies on the windows, a pale sky blue would make this room serene."

"Ladies, I cannot tell you how much you've helped a poor widower," Van Buren said. "Blue it is, then. I'll have the work started tomorrow. Perhaps we may even have it ready in time for my New Year's Day Open House."

Dinner proved to be intimate and elegant. President Van Buren's other three sons, John, Martin, Jr., and Smith, made a brief appearance, but left before the dinner was served. Rebecca thought that Major Abram acted a little snobbish, but that often happened to the children of humble men who'd fought their way to the top.

"Father has imported the very best chef from England," Abram said as he cut the boned chicken with the gold table service, dating from President Monroe's days. "In fact, I'm certain that father will restore this house to its former brilliance."

After dinner, the women departed; Rebecca gave Dolley a lift home in her carriage. The two women huddled under the fur lap rug. "Martin Van Buren may make all the plans he wants," Dolley said, "but what that house needs is a woman's touch. Why with four grown sons living there, the place is beginning to resemble a barracks." She looked significantly at Rebecca. "My dear..."

"Dolley, don't even think it!"

"But I saw the way he looked at you."

"Nonsense!"

"You would be First Lady!"

"Not even for that would I commit such a crime against myself, and against Martin Van Buren."

"Well, then we must find somebody for Abram, that's all there is to it."   *   *   *

At Dolley's house Bravo worked feverishly, convinced that every nail he drove was bringing Angelica that much closer. Not only did he finish the floors long before he'd promised, but he also reputtied all the window frames in the house. The more I do, the more likely it is that she'll come, he told himself. He knew that Dolley had written to Angelica, inviting her, and of course, he'd been writing to South Carolina without interruption. But for two weeks he hadn't heard from her.

"Mother, have you talked to Aunt Dolley? Does she know anything?" Bravo asked one afternoon when he came home from work.

"Not since this morning, which was the last time you asked," she said with exasperation. "Don't you realize that it takes time for the mails to come and go?"

"Now isn't that a perfect reason for Sam Morse's invention? If we had telegraph wires strung between cities, the message would have gotten to Angelica within hours. She could have sent a message back, and we wouldn't have had all this wasteful waiting around."

"Ah, I see," Rebecca said, putting down her pen. "I didn't quite understand until this moment that the whole intention of his invention was to aid and abet true love."

"Oh, Mother, be serious!"

He had such a hangdog look about him that despite her annoyance, she felt sorry for him. "Bravo, you've always been such a young man in a hurry. Now's the time for you to act like an adult, and to be patient."

She bent her head and continued working on her correspondence as Bravo left the room. She'd had a wonderful note from Charles Dickens, responding to her praise of his recently published *Pickwick Papers*. Now she wrote him, inviting him to visit the United States—"so that you may discover for yourself, firsthand, what this new nation is all about"—and to stay with her in Washington.

She'd just sealed the envelope when she heard a rapid knock on the door, and then the breathless voice of Dolley Madison crying out, "Rebecca, Bravo—Where is everybody?"

Rebecca went into the front hall just as Bravo dashed up from the basement. The moment he saw Dolley's sparkling eyes he knew. "She's coming!" he shouted, and picked up a startled Dolley and whirled her around.

"She'll arrive in time for Christmas, stay through the New Year, and perhaps stay even longer if it suits everybody."

At last the day came of Angelica's arrival. Whatever fantasies Bravo had about her, whatever his secret desires, all of them were beggared when he saw her. In the months since their first meeting, she'd become even more beautiful. Thoughts of her filled his every waking moment, and figured his dreams at night. There were times when he became frightened, for the love he bore this creature seemed wild and uncontrollable.

Bravo had thought that he might have her for himself during her visit, but she was the niece of Senator and Mrs. William Preston and the cousin of Dolley Madison, so she was swept into a breathless round of parties. Though the economic situation remained unrelentingly bad, it made many Washingtonians that much more desperate to have a good time.

"It's insanity," Rebecca said to Henry Clay at one such a gathering at the bachelor quarters of fastidious Senator King from Alabama. His intimate bachelor friend, Senator James Buchanan from Pennsylvania, officiated with the eggnog. Rebecca took a sip and continued, "Factory laborers have been thrown out of work, the price of cotton has plummeted, land speculators daily declare bankruptcy, there are bread riots in Philadelphia and Boston—and what do we do here in Washington? We party! Are we nothing but ostriches?"

"It will remain this way as long as Van Buren refuses to act to alleviate the situation," Clay said thoughtfully. "We would all prefer a government laissez-faire policy in business; of *course* it's better to allow the marketplace to determine economic conditions. But there are times when an enlightened government and a strong chief executive can do much to help."

Senator King said in his rarefied nasal voice, "Pawnbrokers and usurers are springing up everywhere—do you know what they're charging? Interest rates as high as seven percent a month!"

James Buchanan agreed that that was dreadful, simply dreadful.

Rebecca studied Buchanan; he was an intelligent man, with strong ambitions, but some female instinct told her that he'd probably remain a bachelor all his life. His relationship with Senator King had raised quite a few eyebrows in the capital, and President Jackson had gone so far as to describe Senator

King as "Miss Nancy." Well, thought Rebecca, it takes all kinds to govern, and the important thing is that a politician be sensitive to the needs of the people.

Then her glance traveled across the room to where Bravo stood with Angelica, the two of them engrossed. They had the capacity only the young had, of being able to shut out the world, and live in their own glass bell of isolation. Dear God, I hope he doesn't get hurt, she prayed. I've never been a doting parent with him, never given him enough of myself, never taught him the things he should know to protect himself. But please, dear God, don't let him get hurt beyond repair.

At the Connaught plantation, Devroe scanned the dispatches he'd just received from England. "Damn!" he swore, and slammed his good hand down on the table.

Véronique, in the sewing room, pricked her finger at Devroe's curse. She put down the strip of needlepoint she was working on. She'd decided to continue the enormous tapestry Devroe's Aunt Elizabeth had worked on for so many years, documenting the events of Washington from its early days, and the feud between the Brands and the Connaughts. She hurried into the drawing room and asked anxiously, "What is it, my dear?"

Devroe's lean face looked haggard. His experience in Texas had aged him, instilled a sense of failure. His refined features look pinched. "I'm afraid our grand scheme to bring America to economic ruin has encountered some pitfalls. When the English banks called in their loans, they never expected that practically every American bank would default. Well, this has created a panic of its own in the mother country."

"But this is not anything you could have anticipated," she said, to assuage his feelings.

"In addition, the United States was one of the principal markets for English cloth—England bought their cotton, and sent manufactured goods back. But with this recession, they've stopped importing English cloth. Hundreds of factories have been forced to close, and the recession has now hit England also!"

"*Mon dieu*," she whispered. "It is as if the whole world is tied together by one banking network, *non?*"

Devroe stood up and threw the secret communiqués into the fire. He watched the papers curl and brown, then burst into flame. Extraordinary that the report had taken only a fortnight to reach him. The new British steamships made the Atlantic crossing in fifteen days now. It filled him with pride that the British navy was supreme at sea, for on that supremacy, the Empire depended.

He turned and faced Véronique. "I must tell you that I'm not in the good graces of the service. They haven't said it in so many words, but I have a feeling that unless my labors here bear better results, I may face a demotion or be recalled."

Véronique clutched her breast. Her sojourn in England, with its rigid society, had convinced her that her chances for success lay in this new nation, not the Old World. "What can we do?" she asked.

"Seize whatever opportunity presents itself to reverse our fortunes. There is one small hope. Great Britain feels strongly that Texas must not join the Union. So far the stupid Americans have played into our hands."

"I am so simple-minded in these affairs," she said. "Please be good enough..."

"If Texas remains an independent nation, then she becomes an excellent market for English cloth and machinery, and it avoids the devastating tariffs the United States has levied against us. Further, an independent Texas stops the expansion of this monster country, which gobbles everything in its path. It is not inconceivable that Texas would then join the commonwealth of English nations, like Canada, which make up the British Empire."

"An exciting dream you describe," Véronique said. "But how is such a thing to be accomplished?"

"By treading very cautiously. I must keep the northern abolitionists in a constant state of agitation, so they'll refuse to allow Texas to join the Union. I may have to return to Mexico, and talk with Santa Anna. That fool! We wouldn't be in this dreadful position if he hadn't tried to be Napoleon! At any rate, he's repudiated the treaty Sam Houston forced him to sign when he was defeated at San Jacinto."

"But how can Santa Anna help?"

"He must be persuaded that he can reconquer Texas—with British help, of course: arms and money. If Texas thinks she's about to be overrun, and the United States is still spurning her bid to join the Union, she'll have no recourse but to turn to Great Britain. I do know that Texas is nearly bankrupt and is very anxious for an alliance with any nation—they've even put out feelers to France."

"This is all so complex for my poor weary head," she said, though her shrewd, calculating mind had immediately grasped the significance of what Devroe had said.

"With Queen Victoria on the throne, with our navy stronger than ever, with our industrialization outpacing the rest of the world, Great Britain is about to enter a golden age. We mustn't allow these upstart colonies to stand in the way of our efforts to bring civilization to the world."

"Oh, the world, the world! It constantly intrudes," Véronique said. "But Devroe, for this moment, now, I'm frightened. Mobs are rioting for food in Baltimore and New York. Plantations have been plundered by angry peasants, who only look for some excuse to resort to violence. It could happen here. Devroe, you must post more guards at the gates, keep out the vagrants and the beggars."

"That's a prudent suggestion," he said. "I think we'll need a new overseer. Urquhart is getting too old."

"That would be wise. And I have another suggestion. Perhaps we should make a greater show of giving to charity. Make gifts of food to the poorhouse, to the hospital. In times of trial like these, he who acts the good Samaritan is less likely to be called a Pharisee."

"My dear, you're sounding positively Machiavellian this evening." Devroe's attempt at a chuckle sounded like a snicker.

"It can only enhance our reputation, and give the lie to the rumors that Madam Rebecca Brand circulates about us."

At the mention of Rebecca's name, Devroe's lips thinned.

Véronique went on, "I learned the other day that Dolley Madison is entertaining Angelica Singleton. Now Queen Dolley is the key to society in Washington. I propose that we give a party for Angelica, invite the British minister, Charles Vaughan, and the French minister, even the President."

"If you think it will help, then do what is necessary."

"Excellent. I'm sure we'll see Dolley and her cousin tomorrow at the President's levee."

"Do we really have to go to that?" Devroe said. "I loathed Andrew Jackson, but at least he was interesting. This little Dutchman—imagine, the son of a tavernkeeper—is a bore."

"We should go, if only for appearances. I understand that he's throwing open the White House so that the public can see how he's redecorated the mansion."

"That pitiful shack—the American Palace!" Devroe sneered. "They should see Buckingham Palace with its six hundred rooms. Now that's a palace!"

"Ah, yes," Véronique said gaily. "But of course, when we speak of palaces, can one think of anything grander than Versailles with its ten thousand rooms?"

Devroe gave an offhand shrug. "Why talk of past glories? Your infernal Revolution finished all that, while Great Britain has become the greatest nation in the world."

Their sparring went on for a bit, then Véronique, as was her wont, allowed him to have the final word. This excited Devroe, and for the first time in many months, he chose to exercise his conjugal rights.

Véronique found their lovemaking patterned and predictable, and as she rose and fell with his motions, clawing his back to excite him further, she remembered her impassioned night with Gunning Brand . . . Gunning, who'd made love like a God. She hungered for that again, hungered for it with her very being.

These thoughts were tormenting her when Devroe reached his climax, leaving her alone, trembling, and unfulfilled.

When he took his leave, she called out plaintively to him, "Devroe?"

He turned, his face remote, his eyes flicking over her in dismissal. "Yes, what is it?"

She fought back what she longed to say, and instead said, "Remember, under no circumstances are you to provoke the Brand boy if we should see him tomorrow. Even if he should strike you, you must turn the other cheek. Remember, dueling is illegal."

Chapter 22

NEW YEAR'S DAY sparkled like an icicle in the sun. Washingtonians, ever curious, came out in force to the White House to see Van Buren's changes.

"How different this is from Andrew Jackson's open houses!" Rebecca said as she and Dolley climbed the steps of the North Portico and made their way into the Grand Entrance Hall. "This is the first time I've ever seen guards at the front door. Van Buren wants to keep out the rowdies and vagrants."

Van Buren's attitude had discouraged most of the riffraff in the District, and only the proper middle and upper classes attended the levee. The fireplaces in all the public rooms had been kept burning for two days beforehand, so that the house was tolerably warm, though not really livable.

"Do you think it's proper that we left Bravo and Angelica alone in my house?" Dolley asked. "A young woman can't be too careful of her reputation, especially in Washington."

"I know," Rebecca agreed. "But Bravo is a decent young man, he adores Angelica, and they both wanted some time alone to straighten things out. If they don't make an appearance within the half-hour, I'll walk back to your house and fetch them myself."

Just then Martin Van Buren bustled toward them. "A most happy and wonderful New Year to the two of you," he said.

Taking Rebecca by the arm, he proudly took the two women into the Oval Room.

Rebecca gasped when she saw it. "Mr. President, it's perfectly marvelous!"

The walls were painted the palest blue, and blue curtains edged with gold ball-fringe hung at the tall windows. The Bellengé chairs and the two couches had been reupholstered in a double-warp blue satin, with a design in gold woven into the seats and backs. The new carpet, a delicate shade of blue, complemented the furniture.

"The Blue Oval Room," Van Buren said softly. "Mrs. Brand—Rebecca, you see how wonderfully well your advice turned out. Now this is surely a room for the ages."

Angelica Singleton stood before the mirror in Dolley Madison's drawing room, arranging her long dark corkscrew curls. "We should go. They're probably wondering what's happened to us."

Bravo came up behind her and put his hands on her shoulders. "Angelica, I must talk to you."

She smiled at him sweetly in the mirror. "That's all we've done since I arrived."

"Angelica, I mean serious talk." He turned her around so that she faced him. "Not the casual chit-chat that's passed for conversation during this party season. Every time I've tried to get close to you, tried to explain what's in my heart, I've felt that you avoided me. Angelica, I'm in love with you—have been from the very first moment I saw you, and I will be until the day I die."

She looked at him with her large, dark, limpid eyes. "You mustn't say such things while we're alone in this house. We must go."

She tried to move out of his grasp, but he gripped her shoulders. "You're going to hear me out. I've got to know whether there's a chance for us."

"Bravo, be reasonable," she said, struggling in his grasp. "You're nineteen years old—"

"I'll be twenty this year."

"—and I'm twenty-two."

"What does that matter when two people love each other?"

"We've known each other such a little time. Love is something that grows, something that must be nurtured."

"I'm prepared to spend the rest of my life doing just that," he said softly. "Angelica, I want to marry you. I want to go to South Carolina with you after the holidays. I want to ask your father for your hand."

Her glance was sharp, and startled. What she had thought was merely a casual flirtation, one that might develop into something more serious, had developed on his side without her consent. Yet she genuinely liked him, felt excited in his presence, wondered what it would be like to kiss him again.

"Bravo, think. There are so many things my father will ask. For instance, what are your prospects?"

"I'll tell him that I'll move mountains for you, make the desert bloom, and lavish on you the most precious gift that God has ever given to man, the gift of love."

"Ah, you don't know my father," she said, a sad look on her face. "After you've said all that, he'll fix you with his gimlet gaze and say, 'Yes, but will that buy bread?'"

"I have a small income of my own—the royalties from my uncle's patented scaffold," he said. "It put me through the university. When times are good, it supplements what I earn. I'm working on a great many inventions with Samuel Morse, and on a few of my own. I know that as soon as our economy recovers, there's money to be made on all of them. And soon I should have a job at the Patent Office."

She snatched at this. "Why then, let's wait until things ease a bit, and until you get a regular job. You'll know your own mind better then, and I—"

"Angelica, you don't understand. I love you for richer or poorer, for better or worse. I love you not because of what I earn, or how much money your father has; I love you because I love you."

His words were so impassioned, his physical presence so overwhelming that suddenly she felt faint and leaned against his chest. He wrapped his arms around her and whispered, "I know you feel the same way about me; a man knows that about the woman he loves. Angelica, forget all the obstacles that people will throw in our path, listen only to yourself."

He lifted her chin and shuddered when he saw that she was crying. He reached down and kissed away her tears, murmuring words of endearment, kissed the bridge of her nose, and then the tip; finally his lips found hers. She trembled in his arms, fighting not to give in to this new sensation, a tremulous feeling in her body that responded to his.

Her lips parted and he felt the warmth of her, sweet and wonderful; he felt himself melting into her being, and he lost all reason. He swung her into his arms; she clung to his neck, their mouths still pressed together. He carried her to the couch, put her down, and then his hands roamed over her, holding, caressing, and she, warmed at first by his ardor, and then inflamed by the sureness of his touch, arched to give herself up to him.

"I love you," he whispered, and with those words, gave her his heart. She answered almost in the same breath, "I love you too."

Then he sat back, gripped her hands between his, and looked deeply into her eyes. "I love you so much that I can do nothing that would in the slightest hurt or dishonor you. But my darling, think of all we'll have the moment we're married."

Startled by this new turn, Angelica quickly recovered herself, then sat upright and burst into tears, sobs wracking her body. "Oh, what kind of creature must you think I am?" she cried. "No better than a wanton, a libertine, oh how you'll hate me."

He pressed his head in her lap. "I could never hate you, never in a lifetime. I could only hate myself for making you shed a single tear. You're everything to me. I'll give up everything, follow you wherever you want to go. I'd defend you against the world, and together, we shall live a life of triumph. Now quickly, dry your eyes. We must get to the White House."

When Bravo and Angelica arrived at the President's House they found a curious lack of excitement among the guests. Van Buren, punctilious, thoughtful, and considerate, didn't have the capacity to let himself go. He rarely did anything without motive, and deemed social engagements, even of this sort, of minor importance. The supply of punch was minimal, nothing was served with it; the cost of the refreshments was coming out of the President's own pocket. But with Angelica at his side, Bravo cared nothing about this.

Dolley saw the happy pair enter the East Room and bustled over to them. "There you are at last. Angelica, my dear, I have explicit orders from the President himself to present you to him." She took Angelica's arm and led her and Bravo to President Van Buren, who was standing beneath the Gilbert Stuart portrait of George Washington. Glancing at the first and present chief executives, Bravo decided that the current President suffered grievously in comparison.

Van Buren and his son Abram were talking, but broke off when Dolley approached. Introductions were made all around.

Abram Van Buren said, "The President and I were just discussing the outbreak of hostilities along the Canadian border."

"I've heard something of it, but know none of the particulars," Angelica said brightly.

Abram plunged into an intense discussion of the problem, his eyes never leaving Angelica's. "A group of Canadian insurgents tried to overthrow their government, and were given aid by some Americans. It was an ill-advised rebellion, quickly quelled, but the Canadian militia retaliated against us. They crossed the river at Niagara Falls, set fire to an American boat, killing an American in the process. Tempers are hot; both sides are arming themselves. Unless we negotiate immediately, war may break out again between the United States and Great Britain."

Standing some distance away from the presidential group, Véronique and Devroe Connaught observed the scene with quickening interest. Devroe's interest was in the Canadian conflict, but Véronique's focus lay elsewhere. "The Brand boy is mad about Angelica Singleton," she said.

"How do you know?" Devroe asked.

"Oh, a woman knows such things." She didn't tell her husband that Gunning Brand had once looked at her that way. Really, the Brand men could be such simpletons when it came to women. The girl was pretty enough, but without any passion or depth.

But now something even more fascinating sparked Véronique's interest: the manner in which Abram Van Buren was reacting to Angelica, and how Angelica was responding. "Ah, there's more than casual interest here," Véronique murmured, as she weighed and measured the glances and smiles that passed between the two. "There is something going on here that can be used to our advantage," she said to Devroe. "I must find a way to see the girl alone."

She waited impatiently for the moment when Bravo would

leave Angelica's side, but he remained glued to her, flaring with jealous annoyance at Abram, who continued to dominate the conversation. Recognizing a trait of her own, Véronique said to her husband, "This little innocent Southern girl is something of a flirt!"

At that point Samuel Morse, who with his full beard looked like a Biblical prophet, entered the East Room. Bravo, unable to take Angelica away from her conversation, excused himself and went to greet his employer and idol.

Véronique went to Abram and Angelica with a flutter of her hands and a gay, piping cry. Véronique was lavish in her praise of Angelica's costume. "The style, the cut, the fabric, it could only have been made in Paris."

"As a matter of fact, it was," Angelica said, pleased that somebody with taste had noticed her gown. With the peculiar delight of people who know that they're excluding the rest of the world from their conversation, the two women began to rattle away in French about the advantages of Parisian dressmakers.

"Washington is fortunate to have you here during these holidays," Véronique said, and her eyes flitted from Angelica's golden gown to the gold upholstery in the huge room. "I must say that these surroundings suit you beautifully."

"I was just thinking the same thing myself," Abram said.

"Oh, this house could use a woman's touch," Véronique said, shaking a naughty finger at him. "For shame, four bachelors living all alone here, and not a woman, a hostess, a *jeune fille* in sight!"

Angelica blushed demurely.

From the corner of her eye, Véronique saw that Bravo was still occupied with Samuel Morse, but she didn't know how much longer that would last. She spoke very rapidly. "My dear, you must allow me to have a small dinner party for you. Shall we say a week from today, January seventh?"

"That would be perfectly lovely," Angelica said.

"I knew it! Seven has always been a lucky number for me. I shall invite your aunt and uncle Preston, and of course, Dolley Madison. Abram, you too must come."

"You may count on it."

"*Charmante,*" she exclaimed. "If your poor overworked father could tear himself away from the affairs of state for an evening, that would make my life complete. I shall have my footman bring you the details. Oh, it will be *intime*, but with you there, Angelica, it will be gala!"

Then with another flutter of her beautifully manicured hands, Véronique bid them adieu and drifted back to her husband. Bravo had seen the end of the interchange, and he strode back to Angelica, his jaw set, his blue eyes glinting. "What did she want?"

"She's perfectly lovely, isn't she?" Angelica said.

"What did she want?" Bravo repeated, his voice a shade more ominous.

"Why, she's going to give a dinner party in my honor at her plantation."

"You didn't accept it, did you?"

"As a matter of fact, I did."

"But you can't!" he exclaimed. "You don't know this woman. I tell you, she's the very incarnation of evil!"

Abram burst out laughing. "Oh, see here, Brand; isn't that a bit melodramatic?"

Bravo turned on him hotly, and Angelica, fearful that something awful was about to happen, drew him out of the East Room and into the Grand Entrance Hall, which was less crowded. They found a corner near the porter's station where they would be undisturbed. "Bravo, what's gotten into you?"

He tried to tell her all that had happened between his family and the Connaughts, tried to explain just how much it meant to him—"She was once my sister-in-law, so I know what she's like"—but he just couldn't seem to transmit his distress to her forcefully enough.

"But I've already accepted," she said.

"Angelica, after all I've told you, isn't that a very minor consideration?"

"But Bravo, you're being unreasonable. You're asking me to take sides in something I know nothing about."

"There are times when you have to trust the person you love, have to side with him."

"The President will be there. I don't see what harm—"

"Angelica, I forbid you to go!" he said suddenly, losing all control.

Then her own temper flared, and she sucked in her cheeks. "How dare you forbid me to do anything?"

"You don't understand!" he cried.

"No, I don't understand! And if you persist in behaving in

this manner, as if you were my jailer, then I don't want to understand."

Before their argument could degenerate into a shouting match, Dolley suddenly appeared, full of good cheer. "My dear, the President and Abram were enthralled with you. But now we must repair back to our own humble dwelling, for people will be arriving there shortly for our own open house."

"I'd be delighted to leave!" Angelica said with a toss of her curls, and marched out with Dolley.

Bravo remained in the White House for another half-hour, trying to think of some way out of this mess. At last, he walked back to Dolley's house. But there, he only became more miserable. Abram Van Buren was very much in evidence, and Angelica danced constant attention on him. A number of times Bravo tried to draw her away for a quiet moment, to apologize, smooth over their first lovers' quarrel. But Angelica would accept none of his overtures.

Unable to tolerate the atmosphere any longer, Bravo left. He walked around Lafayette Square, the icy wind freezing his earlobes and the tip of his nose. He muttered to himself, "They say that the way you spend New Year's Day is the way you'll spend the rest of the year," he said to a stray shivering pup that followed him. "Well, if that's true, this year is going to be miserable!"

But worst thing of all was his feeling of divided loyalties. Could he be a turncoat, dismiss all that had happened between his family and the Connaughts? All for love? Was Suzannah right—was it time to forgive and forget?

Lost in this quandary, he found himself near Circumstance and Wingate's house, and stopped off there. Wingate was off delivering a baby, and Circumstance was doing renderings of Van Buren's redecorated White House rooms.

She made Bravo a cup of tea, and while they drank it, she listened attentively to his woes. "You know, Circumstance, sometimes I think there's something wrong with me, that I'm not like ordinary people."

"Of course you're not like ordinary people," she said quietly, "but that doesn't mean there's anything wrong with you. You live according to an inner vision, but you haven't realized it yet yourself."

"But I love her so much..."

Circumstance tried to soothe his pain, telling him that it

would all work out the way it should, for the best. But she had no idea what way the best was.

Bravo left soon after that, hunching his shoulders against the icy north wind, howling now, bringing snow. The stray dog had followed him to Circumstance's and waited for him outside. He whimpered once when Bravo reached the door of his house. Bravo looked at the forlorn puppy. "I know just how you feel," he said. "All right then, come on in."

Chapter 23

THROUGHOUT THAT WEEK, Bravo suffered unrelentingly as he imagined what might happen at the Connaught dinner: Angelica would be taken in by the pair of murderers; they would turn her against him.

Dolley didn't accompany her young cousin to the affair, pleading an attack of lumbago. The real reason, as Bravo knew, was that Dolley fully understood the Connaughts, and refused to associate with them. "Why can't Angelica see through them?" he demanded to anyone who'd listen.

The night of the dinner, he felt so morbid that he hied himself down to the Indian Queen Hotel to forget his cares in a few tankards of ale. He did forget, but woke the next morning with a pounding head and a dyspeptic stomach.

"But at least this damnable day is past!" he groaned. When he went to call on Angelica that afternoon, he found she'd gone to an impromptu tea dance at the Prestons', escorted by Abram Van Buren. Her week was filled with a multitude of other engagements—a tour of the Capitol with Abram as guide, a ride on the Baltimore and Ohio Railroad, a guest of the Connaughts at a theater party, with Abram making a fourth.

On all these occasions, Véronique never lost an opportunity to extol Abram's virtues to Angelica. "But *ma chérie,* we sophisticated women readily see that he is a man of the world.

Secretary to the President of the United States, a major in the army, and heir to his father's political fortune. I can tell that he needs you, Angelica."

"Why, has he told you anything?"

Véronique lowered her eyes, signifying that she could never reveal such a confidence. "Not only does he need you, but this entire nation needs a woman such as you to bring the genteel, feminine touch to the White House; those four bachelor sons have converted that house into a barracks. I've even heard your cousin Dolley say that."

"But there's somebody else I care for . . . I think. A young man named Bravo Brand."

"Oh yes, I know him," Véronique said. "I know he has some misguided conceptions about me and my husband—ah, I see by your expression that he's already spoken to you. I forgive him; how could one not forgive such an impetuous child? But Angelica, when you compare the two, Abram is a man, and the other? Who can tell how he'll grow up?"

"Well, I suppose you're right," Angelica sighed.

"My dear, I have been raised in Paris and on the Continent. In my travels, I've met many of the crowned heads of Europe. I can assure you that they would clasp you to their bosom. If you had the slightest interest, you could bring that kind of distinction to Washington. Oh, of course we're a democracy, but we sophisticated women know that there is an aristocracy of beauty, of wealth, of intelligence. I beg you, my little one, do not squander yourself on anybody unworthy of your very special gifts."

"Yes, I think you're right," Angelica said, more firmly.

After another week of not seeing Angelica, Bravo couldn't stand it any longer. Early Sunday, he went to see her, without first leaving a calling card. She was still in her morning gown, her hair hanging down to her shoulders, and pouting a bit because he'd caught her without any makeup.

"Angelica, I know we've had a difficult time," he began. "Perhaps I was too demanding. But really, we've got to resolve this. Are you still angry with me?"

She shook her head.

"Wonderful! When do you plan to go back to South Carolina? I want to arrange with Samuel Morse for some time off, so that I can go with you and talk to your father."

"Oh, Bravo, didn't I tell you? I've decided to stay in Washington for another month, perhaps two. There's so much to do here. President Van Buren's asked me to help him redecorate the family quarters on the upper floors of the White House. You know—a widower living there with four bachelor sons. They've made it look like a barracks."

"I see," Bravo said softly. "All right, Angelica, you're impressed, and rightly so. The White House and the presidency are very impressive. But after you've been in Washington for a while, you'll discover that the President is only a man like the rest of us, a man elected by the people. And the White House has its value not as a bastion of privileged society, but as a symbol of our democracy. Angelica, I beg you, don't be misled by false values."

"Oh, Bravo—for a young man, you can be so pompous!"

He flushed under her rebuke, but he cared for her so deeply that he could only persist, hoping that with gentleness and love, he could bring her to the light. "Shall we go riding after church? I know a wonderful place in the hills where we can look down on the capital. You can see how L'Enfant laid out the city, how it will grow into itself."

"It sounds perfectly enchanting, Bravo. But the Bible Society, and the Women's Orphans League..." She rattled off a number of excuses that prevented her from seeing him—not only that afternoon, but all the next week.

"I'm disappointed, but there's every reason for you to be popular. Next week, then?"

"Wonderful!" she said. "Thank you for being so understanding. I'll be in touch with you." She stood on tiptoe and kissed his cheek. Not satisfied with that, he swept her into his arms and kissed her soundly on the mouth, feeling her body resisting, then relaxing and pressing against his, knowing that the precious body he now held in his arms was the real Angelica Singleton. They stood locked in their embrace until, hearing Dolley's footsteps on the stair, Angelica broke free.

He bowed low over her hand, kissed it, running his tongue between her fingers. "Till next week," he said, and strode out the door, feeling as if he'd been given a reprieve from a death sentence.

Angelica stood near the window, watching his tall handsome form striding through Lafayette Park, and she pressed her knuckles to her mouth.

* * *

The week came and went, and then another, with no word from her. He read all about her in the society columns of the *Telegraph* and the *Globe*. And always her name was linked with Major Abram Van Buren's.

Then he read the formal announcement of their engagement in the *National Intelligencer:* "Miss Angelica Singleton and Major Abram Van Buren announced that they plan to be wed sometime this autumn. They will depart on their honeymoon immediately thereafter, spending some time in London and Paris, and then return to the United States, where the major will resume his duties in the government and Angelica will take up residence in the White House. President Van Buren has indicated that she will be his official White House hostess."

"Damn!" Bravo shouted, tearing the pages in half, again and again.

Rebecca came in, startled, and tried to console her son. "I know how you feel about her . . ." Her voice trailed off. Were there any adequate words?

Bravo pulled his gaze up from the floor. "I'm going out, Mother. I may not be back for dinner, so don't wait for me."

He slammed out of the house; the pup bounded after him, tail wagging, but Bravo barely saw him. He saddled up, wheeled his horse's head, and galloped out of the city and into the hills. The wind brought tears to his eyes, tore at his clothes and hair. Still he galloped, riding to escape all the torment that pursued him.

There was an ache in his being more painful than any bullet wound. I'll challenge Abram to a duel! he thought. No, I'll steal to her window tonight and we'll elope; I know she's just trying to test me, see how far I'll go! Then just as abruptly he dismissed his plans as idiotic.

The choice had been hers, clear and simple. No matter what Abram's influence, or the Connaughts', Angelica had chosen a way of life that he could never give her.

"It's me!" he exclaimed suddenly. "There's something wrong with me, there always has been. I grew up feeling that way, different from everybody else, different even from Suzannah and Gunning." He remembered the long-ago fist fight that he'd had with his brother, and heard Gunning's drunken accusation: "You're the cause of my father's death!"

How could he possibly have been the cause of their father's

death? He didn't even remember him. Yet his own brother had accused him. And what of the way his mother treated him? As if he was an orphan, or—

He wheeled his horse, spurred it, and streaked back toward Washington, choosing hazardous shortcuts, topping the stone fences in breathtaking leaps, not caring if he broke his neck in the attempt. I've got to get back, he thought, as his stallion kicked up sprays of water from a stream they forded. He had to find out once and for all about this specter that had haunted him. It had shadowed his existence, brought him to this lonely and desolate place, and now he had to know, couldn't wait another moment, now!

He reached Pennsylvania Avenue, and head low, body thrust over the horse's neck, continued as if his life depended on it. He swung around the grounds of the White House, and for an impossible moment thought of crashing right through the tall windows of the East Room, sweeping Angelica into his arms, and carrying her off. He reined up before his house on New York Avenue.

He stormed into the house, and found his mother in the drawing room, discussing the next day's menu with Letitia. Without a word of greeting he strode to Rebecca, gripped her arms and said, "Tell me!"

"Tell you what?" Rebecca asked, though in that moment she knew very well what he meant.

Letitia lifted her skirts and fled.

"Who's my father?" he demanded.

"Bravo, are you mad? Why now?"

"Because not knowing is ruining my life!"

"I'm afraid that's just the alcohol talking."

"How well you know me! How well you've always known me! I haven't had a drink this entire day. Though I am drunk—on lies and deceit."

"Bravo, you're upset because of Angelica. But one thing has nothing to do with the other."

"It has everything to do with it! You can't put your life into separate compartments; it doesn't work that way. Who is my father? If I don't find out from you, I'll find out from somebody else. But you owe me at least that much."

She swallowed hard, fighting back the fear that assaulted her. All along, she'd known that this day of reckoning would come. One day she would have to lay down this dark burden which she'd been carrying for twenty years. "Bravo, I love you," she whispered.

"That's not enough. God damn you, tell me! I know who it is, but I want to hear it from your own lips. I want to hear the excuses you make about adultery; I want to hear how you justify the fact that you bore a bastard."

She started, and then in a reflexive motion, slapped him.

He neither flinched nor retreated. "A bastard," he repeated, his voice low and dangerous.

Rebecca's face turned ashen and her hands began to tremble. She pressed them together. "I loved your father," she said in a tone somewhere between defiance and a plea.

"I could have told you that was going to be your next sentence," he said. "Just tell me the truth, Mother."

She eased herself down to the settee, her fist clutched against her palpitating heart. She began to roll her handkerchief into a ball with her other hand, trying vainly to control her trembling. "You're right, Bravo, this isn't the time for anything but the truth."

She began in a voice so low that he had to lean forward to hear her. "I married Zebulon Brand in 1806, partly because I thought I loved him, partly because I'd fallen into a fit of pique because of Circumstance."

"Circumstance?" he repeated, dumbfounded. "Why?"

"Jeremy Brand, whom I'd really loved, came back from the Lewis and Clark Expedition with a half-breed daughter. He wanted to marry me, and I accepted, but I asked him to give up the child. He refused."

"But that's not possible! You and Circumstance—you couldn't be closer. Why you're even little Doe's godmother."

Rebecca nodded wearily. "I know. Fate has a way of paying one back in kind. I recognized how stupid and cruel I'd been. I'll spend the rest of my life, if necessary, to make it up to her."

She paused, poured some water from the cut-glass decanter and sipped it. Her throat felt constricted, her heart was pounding unmercifully; she was afraid she was on the verge of having another seizure, but she said nothing. Bravo would have thought she was play-acting, and once started, she needed to unburden herself.

"Zebulon was dashing, handsome, an adventurer, and Chief Justice John Marshall married us. My father was respectably well-off by then, and he built us this house for a wedding present. He also took Zebulon into his business as a full partner."

She paused, remembering those first tumultuous years when Zebulon had expanded the family business, venturing into shipping, and real estate, and how finally his schemes had almost driven them to bankruptcy. But this was nothing akin to the bankruptcy of their love.

"So you married Zebulon. All right, go on."

"Suzannah and Gunning were born in quick succession, and they were the only thing that kept our marriage together. Shortly after the War of 1812, I discovered what I'd always suspected, that Zebulon had plunged into a life of carnal debauchery. I couldn't tolerate it any longer and asked Justice Marshall to arrange for a divorce."

"So that you and Jeremy—?"

Rebecca shook her head vehemently. "No. At that point I had no idea where Jeremy was, or even if he was still alive. You see, the British had captured him when they burned Washington, and took him on one of their prison ships to New Orleans. I found all this out after I'd started divorce proceedings.

"But Zebulon refused, and chose this moment to embark on a shipping venture—I think to transport slaves from the West Indies to New Orleans. The ship was wrecked off the coast of Florida, and all hands were presumed dead. A sailor who'd survived the wreck came to see me here, in this very house. He told me he was sure that Zebulon had drowned."

"In the midst of all this, Jeremy Brand returned," Bravo said.

Rebecca nodded. "He returned to Washington saddened by the death of somebody he'd loved, Marianne Connaught." She smiled wryly. "Yes, a Connaught. Then in our own loneliness we finally found each other."

"You mean to tell me that up until then you hadn't—?"

"No." She saw the look of disbelief on his face and said, "Bravo, you can believe me or not, as you like. There's nothing to hide anymore, and despite your having tried and condemned me before even hearing me out, I am telling the truth."

A long moment passed between them, marked only by ticking of the grandfather clock. "Go on," Bravo said.

"Zebulon was dead. Jeremy was alive. We wanted to marry, but Justice Marshall advised me to wait another year, just to make sure Zebulon was indeed dead. Well, in that year, I discovered what love could really be like, and Jeremy taught it to me. We were older, more mature, both hurt by our own experiences, and grateful that at last we were together. There were problems; Suzannah adored Jeremy, but Gunning resented him bitterly. Still, we thought that with time it would work out."

"And then Zebulon reappeared," Bravo said softly.

"He arrived on the doorstep, half-dead, as if the sea had washed him up. He'd been captured by a band of Seminole Indians, and spent a year in slavery. Finally, he'd escaped, and somehow he made his way back to Washington.

"Jeremy wanted me to leave right then and there, not to spend one night under the same roof with him." She sagged back against the settee. "If only I'd listened to him! But there were the children, and Zebulon was sick unto death. That night, Zebulon forced his way into my room—" She gagged as she relived the horror, being taken by her husband against her will, and experiencing that violation as if she'd been raped by a total stranger.

"I moved out of this house at dawn; I took Suzannah and Gunning and went to Georgetown, to the house that my father left me when he died. Several months later I discovered that I was pregnant with you."

Bravo gazed at her, somehow amazed that this woman, who always acted so proper, so in control, had nevertheless led this tumultuous life. "And of course, you didn't know which of the Brand brothers was my father."

She nodded dully. "The divorce proceedings took forever. A man can get a divorce for almost any reason in this country, but a woman—" She shook her head. "If her husband opposes her, it can drag out for years. By the time you were a year old, anybody with eyes could see who your father was. You favored Jeremy in everything: coloring, disposition, appearance. When Zebulon finally realized that, he turned into a madman. There'd always been a wild streak of competition between the brothers; they were half-brothers, really. Zebulon, because he was older, stronger, more wily, had always won. But now the situation was very different, and he couldn't bear it."

She paused for breath, and Bravo asked impatiently, "What happened?"

"Before anything could be resolved, Jeremy had a dreadful accident. He was repairing the chimneys of the White House, and had positioned his scaffold near the top of the building. A rope slipped, the scaffold toppled, fell three stories. We tried everything to save him, but he died."

Rebecca could control herself no longer and broke down, sobbing. She dabbed at her eyes with her handkerchief and at last gulped back the exhaustion of tears. She thought it best not to tell Bravo about her suspicions concerning the accident. After all, Gunning and Suzannah were still Bravo's brother and sister, and it would do no good if Zebulon were suspected. And what was the point? Nothing could be proven now. Let the dead bury the dead, she thought.

"What happened to Zebulon?"

"He contracted a case of lockjaw and died a little less than a year later."

Bravo paced the room, his temples pounding with all he'd heard. Once he turned to question his mother further, but what really was there to say?

Rebecca saw the torment in his eyes, and in the set of his body, as though he were flinching, expecting to be hit from all sides. "Bravo, if it's any comfort to you at all, your father was a wonderful man. Decent, infinitely talented—all of your own inventiveness comes from him. I'm proud to have loved him. I feel blessed by it, and I hope that one day you'll be proud to be his son."

Bravo stared at her, hearing the words, but without the meaning penetrating, for nothing more could reach him this night.

"Mother, I've got to leave this house."

"But Bravo, it's gotten dark."

"Not as dark as my thoughts."

She gulped for air, and felt the stabbing pain in her chest again. "Where will you go?"

"I don't know."

"Bravo, listen to me. Don't throw away all you've worked for these many years—your education, your work with Sam Morse. I know how painful this must be for you, but in time . . ."

He shook his head violently. "If I stay in this house another minute, I'll go mad! Don't you understand? Everything I've built my life on is in shambles. Gunning and Suzannah—they're only half-brother and half-sister to me. And Circumstance, she's not only my cousin, but my half-sister also! I've got to think this all through, come to some kind of peace with myself." He dashed upstairs to his room.

Rebecca remained on the settee. She thought she had no tears left, but they started again, rolling silently down her face. "This is my punishment," she whispered. My punishment for all my stupidities. In my autumn years, my children should have been by my side, a comfort and a balm, but they're all gone from me. Suzannah in Texas, Gunning in the Kansas Territory, and now Bravo.

Bravo came bounding down the stairs. He'd thrown a few things in his haversack and had it slung over his shoulder. He strode into the kitchen and said goodbye to Bittersweet and Letitia; the old maid was in tears and she hugged the boy fiercely. "Couldn't help overhearing, but everything your mother said about your father, that was the truth. He was wonderful, Bravo. Whatever you do, wherever you go, you remember that."

Then Bravo walked down the long corridor and stopped at the drawing-room door. He glanced in at his mother, still sitting in hopeless dejection on the couch.

"Goodbye," he said. Then he was gone.

Chapter 24

THE OPEN road called to Bravo, and believing that peace might lie just over the horizon, he traveled long and hard. His first impulse was to head west, see Suzannah and then Gunning. But they would have to be told what he had just discovered, and he wasn't ready for that. Will I ever be ready, he wondered? He'd taken nothing from the house that didn't actually belong to him, and he swore that everything he earned from now on, every penny he spent, would come from his own labors.

He decided that he might join the army, fight in the undeclared war on the Canadian frontier, or help quell the Seminole uprisings in Florida. Or I'll homestead a few hundred acres in Oregon, like Suzannah had done in Texas. But after a few days of wandering aimlessly, both in thought and direction, he realized that he was neither his brother or sister. He'd have to find his salvation in his own way.

He worked his way down through Virginia, doing odd jobs for bread and board. The country was still in the grip of the depression, and even in the farmlands things were bad. An infestation of the Hessian fly had decimated the wheat crop and an ordinary loaf of bread was so expensive he couldn't afford it. Acre upon acre of cottonfields lay unplanted; the drastic drop in prices made growing cotton a losing venture. Where cotton had been king, poverty now reigned.

But he did have luck in a few places; at a chandlery in Richmond, the owner was so impressed with Bravo's industry that he offered him steady work. After a week, the wandering urge beset him, and he moved on. The farther south he traveled, the more pro-slavery the populace became. Violence edged the air; scapegoats were needed in these trying times, and he witnessed public floggings of slaves for the slightest infraction of the law. Blacks outnumbered whites in Virginia, and the white citizenry lived in daily fear of a slave revolt.

After a day's work, in a strange place with no friends, Bravo took to the simplest diversion, drink. A streak of belligerence he hadn't known existed surfaced, and one contentious night in a tavern, he roared his feelings about the inequities of slavery. "I know John Quincy Adams," he shouted, "and he'll never give up fighting against the Gag Rule as long as he's alive!" Some plantation overseers jumped him in the alley behind the tavern, and when he woke the next morning, his body was bruised and sore. He pressed on.

Down to the port of Norfolk he traveled, where he considered signing up on a ship that might take him to the exotic lands of the Far East. There he would forget everything, begin a new life, where nobody would know whose son he was, or even care. But few vessels were sailing; the depression had strangled trade worldwide. Somehow he felt relieved that he couldn't find a berth, for he knew he was just trying to run away . . . But how do you run away from your own thoughts? he wondered.

Bravo joined the ranks of the thousands of people who daily went hungry; this made him realize how privileged his life had been. Though never pampered, he had led a sheltered existence, but now that caul was ripped from his eyes.

He crossed the state line into North Carolina and wandered to Raleigh, the heart of the tobacco country. That industry was suffering also, but he managed to find day work baling the dry tobacco leaf and loading it onto wagons that would take it to the auction warehouses.

The weather grew warmer, the daylight hours longer as spring arched toward summer. Stripped to the waist as he labored, his skin turned a golden tan, and his sun-streaked hair looked almost white. His nose burned and peeled and burned again. Always slim, his body now hardened into a weapon as supple and tough as a whip.

He worked and drank, and got a reputation as a dangerous fighter. Though a man might be twice his size and floor Bravo half a dozen times, he just wouldn't stay down. Any number of tavern wenches found him desirable, and there were times when, fortified by ale or rum, he would pound out his torment on a willing body, thinking it might help his wounded pride. But their faces invariably turned to the face of the one he'd lost.

From Raleigh, he moved on again. The deeper south he went, the more rabid the pro-slavery feeling became, often masked under the term "states' rights." Many Southerners believed, with a religious fervor, that the institution of slavery was the only way in which they could avoid economic disaster. One Sunday he wandered into a church service held in a small country town and listened as the preacher cried from the pulpit, "The Negro was meant to work in the fields! Was meant to do the heavy work! Was meant to be subservient to the white man. All this is according to God's will, or it wouldn't be so!"

Bravo called out, "Begging your pardon, preacher, but could you show me just where in the Bible it says that?"

He had to slap leather hard to avoid being tarred and feathered. South, ever south, passing Santee on Lake Marion in South Carolina, where Angelica Singleton had been born, and now lived until her coming wedding. He realized then that he'd been irresistibly drawn here by her siren call.

Hope sprang with the idea that if he announced his presence at the plantation, she'd rush to his arms and they'd ride off together. When he gave his name to the overseer, the man took the information to the main house, then came back, his rifle dangling in the crook of his arm. "Clear off or you'll be charged with trespassing."

"Didn't you tell her—?"

"Miss Angelica's about to be married, and if you bother her again she'll have the law after you."

He continued on then to Charleston, about seventy miles southeast of Santee. An important shipping port for cotton and tobacco, and a port of entry for manufactured goods from the New England states and from Great Britain, the city was one of the richest in the South, and surely the most cosmopolitan.

It was here that James Hoban, the architect of the White House, had first settled when he came from Ireland. Bravo remembered the story from Circumstance's history of the White

House: In Charleston, Hoban had read the advertisement for the competition to design the President's Mansion. He'd entered the contest, won the commission, then moved to Washington to oversee the building.

Charleston had become the most vigorous defender of states' rights. John C. Calhoun, the brilliant senator from South Carolina, had been the principal spokesman for the nullifiers, and only when President Jackson had ordered Fort Sumter, in Charleston's harbor, to be fortified for war had South Carolina backed down from its threat to secede from the Union. But in Charleston, rebellion simmered just below the surface. Carolinians were convinced that the high tarriffs and the abolitionist movement were directly responsible for the great depression.

The humid summer sun burned itself into autumn, while Bravo worked the Charleston docks as a longshoreman. One day he read that Angelica and Abram Van Buren had been married.

"Well, it's done now," he said later that night into his tankard of ale. Bitter as it was to swallow, it did force him to face reality. The following day, he looked around him and said, "What am I doing in Charleston?" He packed his haversack, saddled his horse, and started back to Washington, D.C., arriving at the end of November.

He told no one he'd come back home, and rented a squalid attic room in a grim section of town called Foggy Bottom, originally a marshy area always obscured by the mists that rolled in from the Potomac. Row upon row of wooden shacks huddled against each other. The workers who'd first built the White House and other government buildings had been quartered here. Irish brickmakers, German laborers, Scottish stonecutters, and Italian artisans had lived together and built a city. Foggy Bottom had always been a poor neighborhood, but it had now degenerated into a slum.

In this derelict part of the city, Bravo took on its coloration, and he became a derelict. He drank a lot of rum, consorted with low types. The effects of the dissolute life began to tell on him: his hair grew shaggy and unkempt, his eyes wore a faraway look, his skin became sallow, as if it had never been nourished by the light of day. He worked at the most menial of jobs down at the wharfs; when there was no work, he fished in the Potomac for his food.

One evening, he staggered home from a grog house, clumped

up the outside wooden steps that led to his quarters, and blinked his eyes when he saw the dim outline of a woman waiting for him in his room. He stared at her, the rum making his brain leaden and his tongue thick. But finally he recognized Circumstance. "How did you know I was here?"

"Washington isn't that big a city—how many, thirty thousand or so? We've known for several weeks. Enoch saw you at the wharf one day when he delivered a pallet of bricks, and followed you back here. I wanted to come before, but your mother thought it best if you came back to the family yourself."

"Don't speak to me of my mother!" he shouted. He stumbled over the leg of a chair and fell to the floor.

She helped him up, then took a pitcher of water from the lavabo and threw it in his face. He flung up his arms, sputtering for breath. In all his life, he'd never experienced one moment of ill feeling from Circumstance. But now her face worked with contemptuous anger. He looked at her eyes, the same color blue as his, and said, "How long have you known?"

"I suspected it all along, the same as you."

"Then why didn't you ever tell me?" he demanded.

"Had you asked me, I would have. But I didn't feel that it was my place to volunteer something of that nature."

"But don't you realize that this makes you my half-sister?"

"Is that so terrible?" she snapped back. "Listen to me, Bravo, I'll say this to you only once, and never again. My father, your father, was a wonderful man. You dishonor his memory and you dishonor yourself by acting this way. All right, so you've had a disappointment in love. Well, it isn't the end of the world, unless you make it so. From what I've seen of Angelica Singleton, you're well out of it. You can sink back into your slough of despond, or you can stand up like a man and say, All right, I'll do the best I can, I'll press on.

"I love you. I've loved you from the moment you were born—not only because I suspected you were my brother, not only because you reminded me more and more of my father, but because I saw you growing into a fine and decent man. Then suddenly, this flirtatious self-centered southern belle came along and all your reason disappeared! You've allowed yourself to be unmanned, and by somebody who isn't worth it! You can give yourself a thousand excuses for acting as you do, but in the end it's your own choice, and your own life . . . or death.

Face up to this and call it what it is—a slow, deliberate suicide."

"Is this why you've come here, to preach a sermon?"

"No. I came to tell you that Letitia is dying. She's asked
to see you."

"Dying?" He lurched toward her and then drew back. "What's
wrong?"

"Wingate says everything is just wearing down. She says
she just wants to lay down her burdens and go."

He stood there, stunned.

"I have to go," Circumstance said softly. "If you've a mind
to see her, don't wait too long. She could drift away at any
time."

After Circumstance left, Bravo made his way downstairs
and ducked his head in the rain barrel. He came up gasping
for air. But it wasn't just his head that felt dizzy and dirty; the
months of dissoluteness had made his entire body feel that way.

The night air was chilly but bracing, and suddenly he knew
what he must do. He stumbled down to the banks of the
Potomac, and stripped off all his clothes until he stood naked
in the moonlight. His skin prickled as he waded into the river,
the dark, lapping waters mercurial in the preternatural light of
the moon. Then he dove in.

The shock of the cold water sent shudders through him and
he swam rapidly, wildly, trying to warm himself. The moon
disappeared behind the clouds, but millions of grunnion flashed
by, wheeling, darting, turning, leaving their phosphorescent
trace all about him. The swift current began carrying him downstream, and he felt the sudden urge to abandon himself, to let
the rushing river carry him out to sea.

But then everything that Circumstance said came back to
him, and the blood began to beat through his body, tightening
his muscles, clearing his head, making him feel alive. Yes,
the choices were his, all his. And in the painful exhilaration
of seeing everything made new again, he swam for the shore.

Ten minutes later he'd fought his way to the bank, emerged,
found his clothes, and dressed. Half an hour after that, he
arrived at the house on New York Avenue.

He went directly to Letitia's quarters, and found the entire
family keeping a vigil. Wingate was checking her heart with
his wooden stethoscope; Circumstance had heated up some

bricks, wrapped them in cloths, and placed them in the bed. Bittersweet and Tad stood at the far side of the bed, while Rebecca sat in a chair, holding Letitia's hand.

Bravo nodded to everybody when he entered. Rebecca rose, the shock visible on her face as she reacted to Bravo's condition. A thousand questions were on her lips, but she controlled herself and said, "Thank you for coming. She's been asking for you, but she's drifted off for a little now."

Rebecca gave him her place by the bed, and Bravo reached for Letitia's hand. She lay with her head propped up on the pillows. She'd always been heavyset, but lying here, she looked smaller than Bravo ever remembered. He rubbed her care-worn hands . . . How many tons of clothes had they washed during her lifetime, how many meals cooked, dishes washed? . . . And all to make their lives easier.

He pressed her lips to his fingers. "Letitia, wake up. I've come to say hello."

She stirred at the repeated sound of his voice. Her eyelids flickered, opened, and she stared in his direction through cataract-filmed eyes. "Bravo? Is that my Bravo?"

"Yes, it's me."

"Oh, I'm so glad you came to say goodbye. Got so much to tell you . . . seems I been thinking 'bout it in this shining land I been drifting towards. I came back when I heard you, to tell you, but I clean forgot what it was."

"You can tell me tomorrow."

"No, there'll be no more tomorrows for me," she croaked, her voice thready and weak. "All my tomorrows got clean used up."

"That's nonsense! Why you'll be up and around in the morning, cooking breakfast, and complaining about the new-fangled stove."

She smiled wanly and raised her head. "Bravo, you be a good boy now. Your mother, she may not be right all the time, maybe she's not right most of the time, but that's the way she is; too late to change now. But she tried her best, and I knows that, because I knows her the longest. I tell you for a truth, she be on the side of the angels."

Her speech had exhausted her and she lay back against the pillows, trying to catch her breath. "Rebecca?" she called weakly.

"I'm right here," Rebecca said, and Bravo got up to give

her the chair again. "What is it, dear?" Rebecca asked softly.

"I'm worried half to death," she began, and smiled to herself at that, "worried about my Bittersweet. You know about what—them bounty hunters. Something in this poor old heart tells me I got cause to worry."

"Rest easy," Rebecca murmured. "I won't let anything happen to her."

"You promise?"

"I swear."

"Then I can go," Letitia whispered. She fixed her unseeing eyes on Rebecca. "You were my girl. Long before I had children of my own, I remember holding you, feeding you. You were my very firstest child. The most beautiful girl in all these parts. When your heart hurt, my heart hurt. When you laughed, then I could laugh too. You gave me the most precious things a body could have in this world . . . you gave me my freedom, and you gave me my child."

"And you gave me my life," Rebecca whispered, feeling the tears welling to her eyes, hot and blinding. "Oh my darling Letitia, don't go. Stay with me just a little while longer."

"Too old, too tired, can't hardly see no more, can't hardly lift my hands to do my work. You knows I'd stay if I could, but it's getting so hard . . ."

"What will I do without you?" Rebecca moaned.

"Live," she said simply. "And remember to wear your warm clothes when it gets cold, 'cause you chill so easy."

Rebecca tried to fight back her sobs. Not until this moment had she realized what a gaping void would be left in her life. She hung her head and sobbed uncontrollably, and then felt Letitia patting her head.

"Don't cry," she murmured. "That's just the way it is. Happens to us all, God made it up that way, and there ain't nothing can change it, so no use crying. Thing that makes it easy is knowing that somebody cares. Knowing that there's somebody who's going to remember. Now hold my hand tight, tight, and help me pass over, until He takes my hand on the other side."

Rebecca gripped her hand hard and Letitia whispered, "Going home now, going home, and that's all I got to say about that matter."

Then, still clutching Rebecca's hand, she drifted off. Long after Letitia's fingers slackened, Rebecca held on with all her might, until Wingate took the counterpane and drew it over Letitia's head.

Then Rebecca broke down, great sobs wracked her body as she abandoned herself to her grief. She felt a strong arm on her shoulder, thought it was Wingate, but when she turned she looked into the tear-streaked face of Bravo. She pressed her head against his chest and he held her until she cried herself out.

Chapter 25

REBECCA WALKED down the corridor toward the kitchen, calling, "Letitia, would you get me—" She caught herself in midsentence. So many times during the past six months she'd done the same thing.

Bittersweet had taken over her grandmother's duties long before she'd died, and though Rebecca had grown genuinely fond of the shy, delicate girl, she could never replace Letitia, nobody could. Sometimes when Rebecca voiced her complaints—that prices were exorbitant, that she'd had palpitations during the night—Bittersweet commiserated with her mistress, made whatever helpful comments she could, then went on with her duties. No, Rebecca thought sadly, nobody will ever replace Letitia, and added with a melancholy sigh, "And that's all I've got to say about that matter."

A happy note in Rebecca's life was the improvement in her relationship with Bravo. He'd moved into new lodgings in Washington after Letitia died, and Rebecca believed that was for the best. He was a grown man and needed his own space. He'd moved all his tools and equipment from Rebecca's basement into his new quarters, a two-room suite on I Street, very close to former President James Monroe's old house.

He'd finally gotten his position at the Patent Office, and buried himself in his work. He found it even more fascinating than he had ever dreamed. All over America, people were inventing the wildest and most ingenious devices and sending them to Washington to be patented.

Meanwhile, in his spare time, he continued to help Samuel Morse to refine his telegraph. And he came to dinner at Rebecca's about once a month, usually on a Sunday. Rebecca worried about his self-enforced solitude, but he seemed content to be alone; his only companion was his dog, Shadow.

"Shadow's the only one I can trust," he told Rebecca, ruffling the dog's head.

Whatever pain Bravo felt about Angelica was gradually being blunted by time, and reason. But in the late spring of 1839, when he heard from Dolley Madison that Angelica and Abram were going off to the Continent on a long, belated honeymoon, he experienced a wave of relief. "There must be some truth to the old adage, 'Out of sight, out of mind,'" he said to Shadow, who thumped his tail wildly.

The political climate in Washington grew sullen as the summer of 1839 waxed and waned. The depression increased in depth and ferocity, but still Van Buren refused to take any action to remedy the situation. He retreated from the public eye, entertained rarely, and discouraged the public from visiting the White House, even erecting a wrought-iron fence that served to separate him and the office from the people.

Rebecca was invited a number of times to intimate gatherings, along with Dolley Madison, Henry Clay, and Thomas Hart Benton, and when she mentioned his reclusiveness, Van Buren shrugged. "I've always been a private person," he said. "I prefer it that way."

But the public perceived it differently; denied access to their house and their leader, people began to circulate ugly rumors. "Our dandified President dines off gold plates and uses gold utensils . . . He grows obscenely fat, while his own countrymen starve to death. He even has to wear a corset!"

The presidential elections were a year away, and the Whigs, scenting victory, cast about for a candidate who could beat Van Buren—though at this point, it seemed to Rebecca, almost anybody could defeat him.

Then one brisk October afternoon, Rebecca had a caller whom she always enjoyed seeing, Henry Clay. The upcoming election was very much on his mind. "Rebecca, a number of years ago, we sat in this very room, and I asked for your support in my race against Andrew Jackson. You chose to endorse him, and though I don't fault you, I think that any fair person would agree that many of Jackson's fiscal and economic policies have brought us to this disastrous place."

"Henry, are you here to say 'I told you so'? How ungallant of you," she exclaimed with a gay smile. "But if we were to tally up past mistakes, how would you fare? You were a War Hawk in 1812, and along with John Calhoun, agitated ceaselessly for us to invade Canada and add it to the United States. What was the upshot of that miscalculated adventure? I seem to recall we suffered ignominious defeat, and almost lost the War of 1812!"

Clay flushed. "I was a young, uninformed firebrand then. But your point is well taken."

"Henry, I believed that you and Jackson were both worthy contenders, but I was persuaded that Jackson had a better chance of preserving the Union, and that was my principal concern."

"Granted," Clay said, recovering his poise.

Rebecca reflected on how wonderfully handsome the senator was. Tall, distinguished—exactly how the electorate expected a statesman to look.

"A man votes with his pocketbook," Clay said. "And Van Buren's '*vanburenism*' in the face of our economic disaster has enraged everybody. I truly believe I'm the best man qualified to occupy the White House, and once more I'm asking for your support."

"As Rebecca Breech Brand? or as Rebel Thorne?"

"Why, I should think that they were one and inseparable now."

"Are you convinced then that you'll be the Whig nominee?" she asked, somewhat surprised. Even the Whigs were preparing to send delegates to a national convention to choose their candidate. Clay's sureness about being selected either was premature, or it smacked of a political deal.

"I hope I don't sound immodest," Clay said, before taking a swallow of his bourbon-and-branch. "But who else can the Whigs field?"

"What about Daniel Webster?"

"An excellent senator, without question—but hasn't he ruined his credibility? By accepting monthly retainers from Nicholas Biddle and the now-defunct Bank of the United States, he clearly created a conflict of interest. I've served the nation for thirty years without that kind of taint."

"Henry, you have no argument from me in terms of your qualifications. But you know that I make it a policy never to endorse a candidate before I know all the particulars of the party's platform. A candidate no longer speaks only for himself; he also represents the party's ideology. Perhaps it shouldn't be that way, but that's how our system's evolved. The platform won't be written by your party for several months."

"Let me put forward a hypothetical question. If the election were held tomorrow, who would you support—Van Buren or me?"

"As an esteemed lawyer, surely you realize that your question constitutes cruel and unusual punishment. Our Constitution specifically forbids that. If I were to endorse you, word would immediately get around Washington, and Van Buren would be furious. If I support Van Buren, you'd be angry. At least allow me this additional year of grace, so that I can talk to both you and Van Buren without being a pariah in my own city!"

Clay slapped his long lean thigh and laughed. "Really, Rebecca, you've lost none of your charming ways. If anybody else had spoken so to me, I'd have left here in rage. But, of course, you're right. May I count on you to keep an open mind?"

"Without question." She touched her lips to the glass of sherry, savoring the aroma and taste. She grew serious. "If it's any consolation at all, I do believe that you're one of the greatest statesmen this nation's produced. I never tire of listening to your speeches on the floor of the Senate. You have a way of dramatizing an issue that brings it home with immediacy and force. Sometimes I think you would have excelled as a tragedian."

"I think it's a bit late to change my profession," he said, grinning. "You know, most politicians have a streak of the performer in them."

Rebecca nodded. "Webster, certainly, with his posturing, and his deep golden voice. John Randolph of Virginia kept one mesmerized with his brilliance and his madness, all done in bravura style. But in your case, my intent was to compliment you. It's only when a politician tries to act his way out of a dilemma, without having the necessary substance, that we're plunged into trouble."

She saw Henry Clay to the door, and long after he left she pondered his question. If the election were held tomorrow, she most assuredly would vote for Clay. This despite the fact that she'd received a number of letters from Andrew Jackson at the Hermitage, urging her to endorse Van Buren. She'd never been comfortable with Clay's overweening ambition—how he'd always coveted the presidency. But he was unquestionably a brilliant legislator, knew the workings of government, and enjoyed an excellent relationship with the electorate and his fellow senators. "Henry Clay in the White House?" she mused. In comparison to Van Buren, the idea didn't repel her. "But oh, God, what difficulties this will make with Andrew!"

On a Thursday afternoon in November, Rebecca and Bittersweet went shopping at Market Square, the outdoor market located on Pennsylvania Avenue between Seventh and Ninth Streets. On Tuesdays and Thursdays, farmers and fishermen brought their produce here and set up their wares on pushcarts. Rebecca and Bittersweet made their purchases, and Rebecca noticed a huge, crinkly-haired mulatto, who kept about a hundred paces behind them. Rebecca turned quickly, trying to get a better look at the man, but he disappeared into the crowd.

"I'd swear I knew him," she said to Bittersweet, "but I can't place him."

As they drove home in the carriage, Rebecca had the uncomfortable feeling that they were being followed, this time by a ferret-faced slip of a man, but when he too disappeared after they'd turned onto New York Avenue, she shrugged, and put it from her mind.

While she and Bittersweet were unloading the groceries, Anne Fairfax walked down the street. For once, she wasn't accompanied by either of her parents. Her prim, dark-gray dress and gray hat made her look somewhat like a novitiate in a religious order. The two women greeted each other.

"Mother and Father have gone to Richmond, to a Bible convention, and I'll be alone for the next week."

"Well then, do come in," Rebecca said, "and we'll have a cup of tea, or a glass of sherry."

"Oh, Father would never allow me to drink spirits," Anne said. "But tea sounds delicious."

Over tea and tiny finger sandwiches, Anne and Rebecca chatted agreeably about the weather, the outrageous prices of food, the new styles in clothes, the latest weddings and births.

Rebecca couldn't help feeling the girl's sadness, as if her heart were slowly atrophying as she sat there.

At a lull in the conversation, Anne blurted, "And how is Bravo?"

"I expect he's well. It's been a month since I've seen him, he's so busy with his work." Then Rebecca had a sudden idea. "I know that you and Bravo have had some difficulty, but I want you to join us for dinner on Sunday. Circumstance and her husband will be here also, and they're both so very fond of you."

"They are?" Anne asked, sounding frightened and dubious. "Oh, thank you, but I couldn't, I promised Father and Mother—"

"Anne," Rebecca said with a edge of sharpness, "if you continually allow someone else to dictate to you, including your parents, life will pass you by."

Anne looked down at her hands. "I can't come."

"But why?"

"I can't compete with the belles in Washington, heiresses like Angelica Singleton, and the Tayloe girls. Bravo's made it very clear that he prefers such companions."

Without warning, Anne buried her face in her hands. "Oh, I couldn't! I'm so plain-looking. When I'm with him, I try ever so hard, but I say all the wrong things. Mother and Father said he was leading a dissolute life, and that I wasn't to see him and—"

"One thing at a time," Rebecca interrupted. "Bravo did go through a tormented time, but that madness is burned from him. If I know my son, it won't happen again. The kind of infatuation he had for Angelica is often a kind of trial by fire into manhood. But as for you, why don't you trust yourself? You don't know what to say? I'll tell you a secret that women have known since the Garden of Eden. If you want a man to be interested in you, then ask him about himself. His work, his beliefs, his likes and dislikes. Then listen. It's the surest way to a man's heart."

Anne dried her eyes and managed a forlorn little smile.

Rebecca studied her. "As for being plain, why you're doing that to yourself. Your clothes, for example. They don't suit you, they're drab and unbecoming, and totally wash out your complexion."

Rebecca poured a glass of sherry and pressed it on Anne. "There's nothing like sherry to give you strength after a good cry."

They clinked glasses, and then Rebecca began to get excited about this young creature, enmeshed in an imprisoning cocoon. "I'll tell you what. My daughter Suzannah left some clothes here. Let's pick one out for you; with a little alteration I'm sure it would fit."

"Oh, I mustn't!" Anne exclaimed, her cheeks flushed. But in short order, Rebecca had the girl out of her dreary gray and into an exciting French blue silk gown.

"It's beautiful!" Anne murmured, then took another quick sip of her sherry.

Rebecca was pleasantly surprised to notice that Anne had a wonderful slim figure, full bosomed, and with a lovely curve to her back. "But my dear girl, you've been hiding your best attributes under that obscene gray tent you call a dress!"

After the fitting, Rebecca said, "Now we must try a little experiment. There's nothing like heightening the gifts that nature gave us—after all, that's why makeup was invented. Have a little more sherry, dear. Let me show you how it's done."

Rebecca was having a wonderfully good time transforming the girl. First she applied carmine to the girl's lips, then the faintest blush of rouge to the cheekbones, then added a line of kohl around the eyes. That immediately made her lovely blue eyes more prominent and brought out their sparkle. "Now for the finishing touch," Rebecca said, and before Anne could protest, pulled out the pins that bound Anne's silken blond hair into a tight bun. Rebecca brushed it out, amazed at its length; it fell well below Anne's breasts. Then she handed Anne a mirror.

Anne stared at her reflection, open-mouthed. "But...I look...You see, I've never done this before, not even in play, because Mother and Father would never permit it...Oh yes, I'll do it! I'll come to dinner on Sunday!"

Circumstance and Wingate arrived first Sunday afternoon and Rebecca took them into her confidence about Anne. "I didn't tell Bravo, though," she said. "I was afraid he wouldn't come."

When Anne appeared at the door, Rebecca was immensely pleased with her appearance. She'd learned all the artful little tricks that Rebecca had taught her, and had added a few of her own. The greatest difference was in the eyes. Heretofore, Anne's pale blond eyelashes had always given her face a washed-out expression, but with kohl to darken the lashes, she looked like a totally different person.

Both Wingate and Circumstance were full of praise for the transformation. But Rebecca knew that the real test would be Bravo, and she worried that her meddling might lead to disaster. Yes, Anne's façade was changed, but the wounded creature that she was still lived within her. A short time later Bravo arrived, entered the drawing room, and stopped short.

"Anne? Is it Anne?" he asked. "Why just look at you! I never knew your hair was that long! Or that your eyes—And do you have a pumpkin for a coach, too?" The delight on his face was so evident that Anne experienced a surge of confidence.

"Do I look so different? Well, perhaps. It's just some experiments I've been trying," she said with a glance at Rebecca, who winked at her. "But enough about me," Anne said. "Now, Bravo, tell me everything that you've been doing."

Anne listened with genuine interest as Bravo waxed enthusiastic about the progression on the signal device that he and Samuel Morse were working on, and the difficulty in raising money for the project because of the hard times.

Circumstance, who responded to Anne's gentle spirit, did what she could to support her in the conversation around the dinner table. When Anne grew sad and talked about her parents' intense devotion to God, Circumstance said, "A person can truly be said to be in touch with the Creator if his life reflects the joy of creation. Too much slavish devotion to dogma can be a slow death."

"Oh, many times I felt that way myself," Anne said. "Well, perhaps one day I'll have the courage to stand up for my own beliefs. It's just that Mother faints so easily."

Bravo looked at her questioningly.

"Every time I do something she disapproves of, she faints."

That elicited a huge laugh from everybody. Anne, at first confused, joined in until her laugh was loudest of all.

Baked turbot with a delicate mayonnaise sauce, new potatoes, and a fresh salad made the dinner. The fish had come from the Potomac, the vegetables from the garden. Dessert consisted of hard cheese and fruit. The days of seven-course meals had disappeared. Rebecca was delighted with the way dinner had gone. She liked having her family around her, liked the way Bravo had become animated around Anne. He invited her to Morse's studio—and more's the wonder, Anne accepted.

Twilight was just beginning to fall when Anne rose and said, "I must leave."

"I'll walk you home," Bravo said.

Rebecca saw them to the door, but when she opened it, she started. Two men on horseback were turning the corner; one was the huge mulatto she'd seen at Market Square, and the other was the weasel-faced man who'd followed her and Bittersweet home. Rebecca grasped her son's arm. "Bravo, isn't that man familiar?"

"I couldn't swear for sure—everything happened so fast— but I think he's one of the highwaymen that tried to kill us the night you arrived in Washington."

They called for Wingate and he studied the man, who'd now reached the middle of the block. Wingate wasn't sure either. Circumstance said, "I know the slight man. His name is Ramsey, and he's a bounty hunter."

"Oh dear God, Bittersweet," Rebecca exclaimed.

"What is it, what's happening?" Anne wanted to know.

Rebecca turned to the girl. "Anne, you mustn't get involved in this. Go home, right now. Pretend that you've seen and heard nothing."

"That's impossible. I wouldn't dream of deserting you if there's trouble."

"Delay the men," Circumstance said urgently. "I'll spirit Bittersweet out the back door to the carriage house. Wingate, signal me when it's safe for us to ride out of here. You know where to join me."

Wingate nodded. Circumstance grabbed Bittersweet's hand and hurried her out the back door, just as the two men knocked on the front door. Rebecca answered the door with all the aplomb she could muster. But she found herself looking down the barrel of a pistol.

"We're here looking for a runaway slave," the mulatto, Tortuga, said. "Citizen's arrest."

"Oh, you must have the wrong address," Rebecca said. "There's nobody like that—" Her words were cut short when Tortuga shoved a warrant under her nose.

"All proper and legally executed," he said with his gap-toothed grin. "Her name is Bittersweet, and she's wanted in Mississippi. Where is she? Be quick about it, or you and everybody in this house will be arrested for harboring a fugitive slave. The federal marshal knows all about this," he lied.

"Arrested?" Rebecca cried weakly, and her eyes flicked to the stairway leading to the second floor. "Nothing is worth being arrested. I suppose there's no use pretending."

"Mother, how could you!" Bravo exclaimed, and taking his cue from Rebecca, moved to block the stairway.

Tortuga pushed him aside and bounded up the stairs while Ramsey trained his pistols on Rebecca and the others. Anne moved closer to Ramsey, put the back of her hand to her head and moaned, "Oh, a fugitive slave? I know nothing about that. I'm only a guest here for dinner. I believe I'm going to faint!" With that, she collapsed against Ramsey. He tried to hold her, and she clutched at him and dragged him to the floor.

Using this moment, Wingate ducked his head out the side window and motioned furiously to the stables. Circumstance, with Bittersweet mounted behind her on a stallion Tad had saddled for them, bolted from the carriage house.

By the time Tortuga thundered down the stairs and ran to the front door, the two women had disappeared around the corner of New York Avenue.

"You'll all pay for this!" Tortuga cursed, and started out the door. Bravo tried to delay him again, but Tortuga gave him a blow to the solar plexus that doubled him over. Ramsey and Tortuga mounted up and started after the women.

Circumstance rode as if the devil pursued her. Bittersweet clutched her tightly around the waist as they wheeled and darted through the streets. Circumstance turned a corner every time she could, raced through side streets, avoiding the main thoroughfares. Yet all the time she was working her way west and north through the capital.

"Where are we going?" Bittersweet cried.

"To safety."

"But they'll be watching all the roads," Bittersweet moaned, having been through all this before when she escaped from Mississippi. "I won't go back, I won't! I'll kill myself first!"

"Don't worry, we have a way," Circumstance shouted over her shoulder. "We call it the underground railway!"

Chapter 26

AS THEY approached Georgetown, Circumstance slowed the stallion to a walk. Hearing no sounds of pursuit, she breathed a little easier. But the danger wasn't past. Georgetown, a much older city than Washington, didn't have the enormous open avenues of L'Enfant's plan: Georgetown had taken its configuration from the natural topography.

Threading her way through back streets, Circumstance finally reined in at a three-story house built on a bluff overlooking the Potomac. The house looked substantial, the third story had two dormer windows, and the property behind the house sloped to the river.

"Where are we?" Bittersweet whispered.

"Halcyon House. It belongs to a friend of mine. Come." She stabled the horse, found a key in the drainpipe, unlocked a side door, and entered the house.

Bittersweet began to tremble, an aftereffect of their narrow escape. Circumstance put her arm around the girl's shoulder. "Don't worry, nothing's going to happen to you."

"But suppose they come looking? Suppose they followed us here?"

"They'll never find you."

At that moment, they heard horses galloping up to the house and both women froze. Circumstance darted to the window,

191

pushed aside the curtains, and slumped with relief. "It's Wingate and Bravo." Seconds later, the two men entered. "No one followed you?" Circumstance asked.

Wingate shook his head. "We took the river paths. I didn't want Bravo to come, but he insisted. Said we might need an extra hand."

Bravo patted the revolver he'd stuck in his belt. "Now tell me, what's going on here?"

"Bravo, are you sure you want to pursue this?" Circumstance asked. "Hiding fugitives is against the law. The less you know the better."

"It's too late for that now, wouldn't you say?"

"All right, then. This house is one of a few in Washington and Georgetown that are part of a network to spirit runaway slaves out of the South and to safety in the northern states."

This piece of information came as a thunderbolt to Bravo. Circumstance, the gentlest of creatures, involved in something like this? "How long have you—?"

"Almost a year."

"Who owns this house?"

"A Reverend Terwilliger. I met him when I was researching material about the early days of Federal City. Halcyon House was built by Benjamin Stoddert, one of the commissioners appointed by George Washington to buy up tracts of land when the federal government first decided to move here in the 1790s. Stoddert was very effective, and soon had most of the territory that the government needed, including the acreage owned by Davey Burns, where the White House now stands."

"Benjamin Stoddert," Bravo repeated. "Am I mistaken or was he secretary of the navy under John Adams?"

"That's right," Circumstance said. "His business interests lay in shipping, and he built here overlooking the harbors of Georgetown and Alexandria, so he could see the ships anchoring. Both President Washington and Stoddert had hoped that a great working seaport would develop, to help support the city. But when that didn't happen, Stoddert lost his fortune and died destitute. Now the house is owned by the Reverend Terwilliger."

"Who is he? Why haven't I heard of him?" Bravo asked.

"He's a wonderful man of the cloth from Massachusetts," Circumstance said. "He's gone to Boston on a business trip. Well, since you know this much, you may as well know the rest: He is a dedicated abolitionist. He's gone north to help raise money for our operation. The underground railway costs a great deal of money to maintain."

Bravo shook his head in wonder. "I find this all so hard to believe. I've heard about the underground railway, but to have you involved in it—"

"Somebody's got to do it," she said.

"Have you saved any runaways?"

"Three so far," she said proudly. "We lost two, but at least the others went on to a life of freedom."

She took Bittersweet's hand. "You'll be living here for a bit, until we can make all the arrangements. I must show you where to hide if you see anything suspicious." Taking a lantern, she led Bittersweet and Bravo to a rear door, which led down to the basement.

Because of the proximity of the river, the basement smelled damp, and there were high-water marks on the brick walls, evidence of the river flooding. Circumstance threaded her way around some discarded furniture, and Bravo realized that these pieces had been arranged to provide a kind of maze. They reached a wood bin, and Circumstance opened a hidden door and crept through a false compartment and into a narrow tunnel. Stooping low, Bittersweet and Bravo followed her. Once inside the tunnel, the women were just able to stand up, though Bravo had to keep his head ducked all the time.

"Ingenious!" he said. "Who built it?"

"We did," Circumstance answered, her voice muffled. "Wingate, the reverend, and I."

"Does it lead to the river?" he asked.

"Yes," she said and lifted the lantern high. The walls of the tunnel became damper as they got closer to the river. At last, Circumstance reached another narrow wooden door, and peered out of a peephole. "Clear," she whispered, gingerly opened the tiny door, and stepped out into the starlit night.

Bravo eased his way out and saw that they'd exited about ten feet from the river's edge. The door was well hidden by stands of rushes, and since they were still on the Halcyon property, nobody else would have reason to wander about there. The Potomac flowed by in its dark patterns of waves and rills, and across the river lay the dim outline of the city of Alexandria.

Seized by the excitement of it all, Bravo said, "Explain how the operation works."

"Usually, the slaves come from Virginia, or further south. If they're fortunate enough to get to Alexandria—well, we have friends there who also believe that slavery is immoral. They shelter the runaways until they have a chance to swim the Potomac—"

"But the currents can be treacherous," Bravo interrupted.

"That's how we've lost a number of people. But most are willing to risk it."

"But I can't swim," Bittersweet moaned pathetically.

"You won't have to, child. You're on the right side of the river. I only showed you the tunnel in case you were trapped in the house, so you'd know there was a way to escape. Now that you've seen it, we've got to go back."

When they returned through the tunnel to Halcyon House, Circumstance latched the false compartment in the wood bin and swept the earthen floor to obliterate their tracks. Then they went back upstairs, where Wingate was waiting.

"What will happen now?" Bittersweet asked. "I'm scared."

"You'll have to stay here. A week, a month—I don't know how long, but until we feel it's safe enough to move you. Then we'll come for you."

"All alone?" Bittersweet asked. "Could you . . . tell Enoch?"

Circumstance shook her head. "Bittersweet, the fewer people who know about this the better. Not only for you, but for the entire underground railroad network."

"But Enoch and me, we were planning to get married and go north anyway. Just as soon as my grandmother died and Miss Rebecca was over her grief."

"Ah, well—that puts a different light on it," Wingate said. "I'll tell him, and when you leave, he can join you."

"What about Anne?" Circumstance asked. "How much does she know?"

"I think we can trust her," Bravo said. "You should have seen the way she tripped Ramsey."

"That's right, she did," Wingate agreed. "Without her, you might not have gotten away."

"And Rebecca?" Circumstance asked.

Wingate shook his head. "She wanted to know where we were going, but I wouldn't tell her. Not only for the reasons you mentioned, but because such excitement and danger isn't good for her. She'll be sixty years old shortly; she's not as strong as she used to be. We must keep her out of this for her own good.

"Everything must look normal, so Circumstance, you must spend the night with our children, otherwise there'll be great suspicion. I'll stay here with Bittersweet tonight. If anybody asks, I can say I was called out to the country to minister to a patient."

The plan agreed upon, Bravo and Circumstance left. They rode north from Halcyon House, and when they'd gotten about a mile into the countryside, swung wide and entered Washington from the northeast. It took a good deal longer to reach the capital this way, but caution was imperative.

Circumstance sagged in the saddle; the tension of the escape had exhausted her. Bravo pulled his mount closer to her. "I think you and Wingate are wonderful for doing this. So many people talk out against slavery, but you're willing to risk everything to change the system."

"I'm glad you feel that way. Anybody who diminishes any human being, diminishes us all. Slavery is just as much a form of bondage to the master as it is to the slave. Our father taught me that. When I was very young, we had a wonderful slave named Tanzy, whom father freed. I loved her as if she'd been my own mother. She even risked her life to save me when the British invaded Washington. Ultimately, it was father who convinced Rebecca to free Letitia."

"Really? I didn't know that. The more I hear about him, the more impressed I am. I wish I'd known him."

"Then look deep inside yourself," she said softly.

"I feel like such a fool for putting everybody through that hell," he muttered.

"The important thing is that it's over. Mark me well, Bravo, there'll come a day when you'll thank the Lord that Angelica Singleton married Abram Van Buren."

Just before leaving Circumstance at her door, Bravo said, "Tell me the truth. Will we really be able to spirit Bittersweet out of Washington?"

"I don't know. The authorities are in such a difficult position here. Though many of them abhor slavery, the law is the law and they must observe it. And Washington is a southern city. We'll have to be ingenious, that's for certain."

"We'll get her out," Bravo said, determination strong in his voice. "We made a promise to Letitia, and we have to keep it. We'll get her out. I'll think of a way."

"I have a feeling that there's more to this episode than the accident of a bounty hunter discovering Bittersweet," Circumstance mused. "Bittersweet told me this man they call Tortuga had been tracking her and Rebecca. Now you think he's one of the highwaymen who tried to kill you. What does that all suggest?"

Bravo turned it over in his mind. "Of course! The Connaughts."

"Precisely. Now that the Connaughts know we're involved, they'll increase their surveillance. We daren't make a false move. Not only for Bittersweet's sake, but for the sake of the family."

Bravo ground his fist into his palm. "I know mother preaches peace, but I know that one day Devroe Connaught and I must face each other, and only one of us will live."

Chapter 27

AT THE Connaught estate, Véronique paced the Italian tiles of the solarium floor, annoyed beyond measure. She had an important engagement elsewhere, but her father Audubert had appeared suddenly and she was doing her best to be civil to him.

"I do not wish to be a complaining father," Audubert said, "but I never see you or my grandchildren anymore."

"I know, but what can I do?" Véronique said. "Devroe has taken it into his head that you're a bad influence on them."

"I confess to loving them overmuch," Audubert said. "Is that such a bad influence?" He suddenly looked quite old and very lost. The thing that he'd wanted most for his daughter— security, a good marriage—all this had taken her from him. He almost yearned for the old days when they'd lived by their wits, dancing their way across Europe, and then coming to America to make their fortune. Audubert looked around at the grandeur of the Connaught house. Not as grand as his chateau had been, to be sure, but grand enough for this country.

"May I see the little ones before I go?" he asked, and the request was so plaintive that she didn't have the heart to refuse him. At her orders, the nurse brought the children down. They appeared in their stiff starched clothes, and Audubert threw out his arms to them. "My angels!" At first none of them moved;

then little Carleton ran to his grandfather. Audubert swept him up into his arms. Then Sean ambled over, followed by Romance.

Romance was Audubert's favorite; she knew this, and often made the old man suffer all kinds of indignities before she would give him a kiss. "What did you bring me?" she asked.

"A picture book, all about the National Theater in Washington. You know that the theater couldn't operate without your grandfather. I make sure that the curtain goes up on time, and that everybody is in his place."

Audubert was the stage manager for the theater. He was a man who needed fantasy in his life, and only the theater could supply these dreams of the glory he'd never gained. "Do you know what else?" he asked Romance. "Angelica Van Buren, a very important person in Washington, has asked me to come to the White House and help her plan the levee she's giving on New Year's Day."

"Is this true?" Véronique asked sharply.

Audubert nodded proudly.

"What does she have in mind?"

"I don't know. I haven't seen her yet."

"You must tell me the instant you know," Véronique said. "It could be very important."

When Audubert made ready to depart, Véronique pressed some money into his hands. He shook his head vehemently. "I have not come for that. I came out of affection for you and the little ones." He thrust her hand away.

She reached up and kissed him, "Oh *mon père*, don't make it any more difficult for me than it is!"

"Ah? Is it so terrible then?" he asked, his concern for his daughter overriding his own unhappiness.

She recovered and said, "Not so terrible, really, save that Devroe changes his mind from one minute to the next—sometimes so complimentary to me, and the next moment . . . Well, there are days when I truly think he loathes me."

"I'm so sorry," he murmured. "I did not think it would turn out this way. Take heart. If it becomes impossible, then leave him. You and I, we've been in difficulties before, and always survived." He kissed her goodbye, and this time didn't resist when she pressed the money on him.

After her father left, Véronique told the children that she

had to go out. "But if you're all very good, then Mama will take you ice skating when she gets back."

She rode to a little-used horse shed on the fringe of the Connaught estate, where Tortuga and Ramsey were waiting for her. When they told her what had happened with Bittersweet, she slammed her riding crop against the wall.

"*Stupide!* I've hired myself a pair of fools!"

Tortuga said nothing, his eyes on this delicate-looking nymph who nevertheless had the soul of a killer. That combination excited him, and he wondered what it would be like to love such a woman.

Véronique caught him staring at her and flushed; she'd seen that leer too often from the stage not to know its meaning. Curiously, though, instead of angering her, it unnerved her. Devroe was away in Baltimore, talking with the Whig leaders about selecting a candidate for the election. But even if her husband were at home, it wouldn't have mattered much, for he often went months without expressing any interest in her. *Tiens,* there were times when she wondered if she'd made the right choice in throwing over Gunning Brand for her limp asparagus of a husband.

She paced the stalls, then stopped in front of Tortuga and rapped her crop against his burly chest. "I suppose you've no idea of what to do next?"

"Every road out of Washington is being watched. We know what the girl looks like, the authorities have been alerted, as far away even as Baltimore and Philadelphia. She won't get away."

"Fool! There are a hundred small roads out of the city. She can go through the fields, she can go upriver. There's only one way to track her down, through the Brands. Increase your surveillance on all of them, including their servants. If we're lucky, they may lead you to her."

"Such a thing requires money," Ramsey said, "more than you've given us."

Cursing softly under her breath, Véronique reached into her reticule and handed them some silver dollars. "You will get double that if you find her. Now get out of my sight. Don't return until you bring me good news."

Ramsey and Tortuga left, but when they'd gotten about a

half a mile down the road, Tortuga wheeled his horse around. "I'll meet you later," he said. "There are some things that I've forgotten to ask that hellion."

Ramsey shrugged and rode on; Tortuga doubled back toward the plantation house. There was a large barn about a quarter of a mile from the main house, and Tortuga approached it from the rear, so he wouldn't be seen. He slipped inside, then climbed up into the hay loft. He cracked open the hayloft door; it gave him an excellent view of the house. Nightfall—he would have to wait till then. His designs could get him killed, he knew; all she would have to do was denounce him to that strange husband of hers and he would be shot. But he'd seen the gleam in her eyes. He decided to risk it.

In the late afternoon, Véronique, the children, and their nurse went down to the little pond near the barn to ice-skate. Carleton was too young to do anything but slide around in his shoes, but Romance and Sean had skates of their own and were quite accomplished for their age. Then Véronique put on her skates and thrilled the children with some dazzling turns and spins. She grew quite flushed with her exertions, the blood rushing everywhere in her body. Then nurse took the children back to the house.

Véronique lingered near the pond, gazing across the gentle slope to the stately house with its wide veranda and tall columns. The house that she coveted so eagerly had become a prison. I must come to peace with this, she commanded herself. Yet her body yearned for a different kind of fulfillment, one that had nothing to do with riches—an insatiable hunger that had been slaked only by one man.

Thinking of Gunning, she grew dizzy, could almost smell his distinctive, wonderfully male odor. She imagined his chiseled body, always so firm to the touch. He'd been a golden satyr of the woods, and she his dark bacchante. Then something hit the ice off to one side of her. She saw a pebble skittering across the frozen surface. Then a second one! She turned to see where they'd come from, saw the barn—and the dim form in the hayloft, beckoning to her.

He was too far away to see clearly, but she had a suspicion, and her heart began to race as she walked toward the barn. With each step a voice within her warned, *This is madness,* while a stronger voice screamed, *It doesn't matter; nothing matters except this torment in my body.*

She looked around cautiously . . . nobody was in sight. The field slaves had been locked away for the night; the house slaves were busy with their chores. She wouldn't be missed until the evening meal.

She reached the barn door, and she stepped into the dim interior. The deathly quiet made her skin crawl; she fought off an impulse to run and run. Then she lifted her eyes and saw Tortuga in the hayloft, looming larger than life.

"Oh, it's you!" she cried, feigning surprise. "You gave me a fright. Why have you come back? What do you want?"

He didn't answer, but started to descend the ladder. She saw the powerful haunches come closer. I must find out what he wants, she rationalized, otherwise he could jeopardize everything. Such were the lies she told herself until he was upon her.

When he reached for her, she realized what an error she'd made and opened her mouth to scream, but he clamped his hand over her mouth. His grip was so powerful that she couldn't move. If I resist him, he'll kill me! she thought in a panic. All the while his hands violated her body, disgusting and thrilling her at the same time.

"I know what you want," he muttered. "You and I are made from the same clay."

She bit his forearm, almost breaking the skin. With an oath he grabbed her shoulders and shook her so hard that she thought her head would snap. *Mon dieu,* the man is as strong as Hercules! He swung her into his arms, carried her to a back stall, and tossed her onto a stack of hay. The stall smelled richly of hay and manure, and of his sweat. She tried to scramble away, but he threw himself on top of her.

He had her out of her clothes in a moment, then shucked off his own. From the corner of her eye she saw his monstrous body, frightening in its elemental power. The prickly sensation of the hay against her skin sent shudders through her. For six long years she'd led a corseted life with Devroe, laboring in vain to arouse him to the fever pitch of carnality so necessary for her survival. The kind of sensuality that she'd known with Gunning. In her mind, in her spirit, that's who she coupled with now, Gunning of the magnificent body, Gunning, who'd taken her to other, rarely seen worlds, Gunning, who'd taught her the deep satisfactions of being a woman.

He pounded out his rhythms on her, until she felt she was

no more than a piece of flesh, mauled by this beast, until she gave herself up to it, stretching, reaching for the promise, and was cast down and down to a place beyond sensation.

She lost all sense of time . . . she thought she must have fainted, for when she regained awareness, she found that the brute was teasing her, running a straw over her nipples. Then the straw tickled its way down her stomach . . . to her thighs. "Can you do no better?" she groaned, placing an insistent hand on the back of his neck.

He read her intent correctly and did as she wanted. After some moments, he entered her again. He moved more slowly, with more calculation, but it was she who took command now, moving in such a way that enabled her to extract the last drop of pleasure from him. When they climaxed again, he groaned and rolled off her, heaving for breath.

Raw, yet desiring more, she gauged the time. She would be missed shortly, and they might come looking for her, but this made her sin all the more dangerous—and desirable. "More," she commanded, reaching for him.

He shrugged helplessly, and she slapped at him with disdain when he couldn't respond. "Tomorrow," he said.

"Fool, there can be no more tomorrows for us."

But he'd exhausted himself; seeing that it was a lost cause, Véronique dressed hurriedly. Suddenly she felt she must get away from this stall. If he were out of sight, if she could get this smell out of her nostrils, she could make believe it had never happened. She understood why Cleopatra, after a night of carnal debauchery, would often have her unlucky favorite imprisoned or put to death. If she could have killed Tortuga right now, she would have.

"Tomorrow," he hissed after her as she hurried out of the stable. "At the shed, this time. Twilight."

Véronique returned to the house, and when her maid asked where she'd been, she slapped her. That night, she had her first good night's sleep in years, dreaming contentedly of Gunning. Toward dawn, she woke and reveled about in bed, stretching and yawning. As she pressed herself against the pillows, remembering, she almost came to her own climax. If only Gunning were lying here beside her! She knew he'd married some tavernkeeper's daughter and was living thousands of miles away in the wilderness. Should I have gone with him? she wondered. But she was a city girl, born and bred in Paris; even this silly excuse for a city called Washington was almost too countrified to tolerate. Yet to experience again what she and Gunning had known would have made living in hell worth it.

"Of course I will not meet Tortuga again," Véronique told herself over her morning hot chocolate. Yet the mellow color of the brew reminded her of the texture and color of his skin. Their first encounter she could rationalize as rape—she had feared for her life, and she clung to that as an excuse for her wanton behavior. But if she went this time, it would be of her own volition. Another such meeting with him was so dangerous!

She fretted about it all day, was snappish with the children, then said to herself, "I'll go riding instead." When she told the nurse and her maid, "I must get away from this noise and commotion," they were bewildered: the day had been unusually quiet, with everybody walking on eggshells because of her mood.

Véronique planned only to ride over to the shed, to convince herself that he hadn't come. But she saw him at the open door, stripped to the waist. She galloped over to him to order him off the property. She hurried inside the shed, and he grabbed her. Without a word, without a kiss in preparation, they fell to, she taking everything he had and demanding more.

"Tomorrow," he called after her as she rode off.

During the weeks that Devroe was away, Véronique met Tortuga every afternoon. She always made certain that she took precautions, but even with precautions one could never be sure, and so she lived with that Sword of Damocles hanging over her head. Unable to control her passions, unable to break off meeting with him, she could only breathe with relief when her time of the month came, and she knew at least that for another month she was safe.

Chapter 28

CARRYING A FRUITCAKE, Dolley Madison called on Rebecca.

"You might as well have your present now, too," Rebecca told her. "It's only two days early." She took a large box out from under the Christmas tree.

Dolley opened the box, and her eyes lit with joy. She took out a beige turban with a tall ostrich plume that waved gracefully when she tried it on. "It's beautiful!" She gazed at her reflection in the mirror. "Exactly what I need."

Knowing Dolley's preference for turbans, Rebecca had ordered this one from the best milliner in Georgetown. "I hope you'll wear it to the President's levee."

"Oh, I will." Then her face began to twitch. "Rebecca, I'm afraid I have some very sad news. I must leave Washington."

Rebecca reacted with shock. "But why?"

"The depression is so serious that if I'm to keep my house on Lafayette Square, I must rent it out. Senator Preston, Angelica's uncle, has offered me a price I daren't refuse."

"But what will you do?"

"Return to Montpelier."

"I won't have it! After waiting so many years for you to come back to Washington, I can't bear the thought of your leaving. Dolley, listen to me. I have this large house, I'm living in it all alone. You must move in."

Dolley's eyes filled with tears. "Oh, Rebecca, I'll never forget your offer. But there's so much more involved. Montpelier is going to rack and ruin. I left Payne Todd in charge, and he's done such a remarkable job, but this depression is ruining everybody. So I must return and oversee things myself, or I'll lose Montpelier too."

They argued alternatives until the tea grew cold in the china pot, but at last Rebecca gave in. "You must promise me that anytime you want to come to Washington, you'll stay with me," she said, patting Dolley's hand. "After all, as we grow older, our circle of friends diminishes, and we must cling to each other."

Dolley nodded and sighed. "Why do such sad things always happen around the holiday season? I suppose I have the option of either sinking into a foul mood, or in joining in the holiday spirit. I do owe it to Angelica to be present at the New Year's levee."

Angelica and Abram Van Buren had recently returned to Washington after their honeymoon on the Continent. Angelica had taken up her duties as White House hostess, and this was to be her first official function since her return.

"Angelica made a great sensation in London," Dolley began, and then paused. "Rebecca, does it pain you if I speak of her? I know that she and Bravo . . ."

Rebecca waved her hand slightly. "It's perfectly all right. We can all see now that it would have been a dreadful mistake. Angelica requires a different sort of life than the one Bravo could have given her."

"Oh, I agree absolutely," Dolley said. "Well, as you know, her cousin Andrew Stevenson is our minister to Great Britain, and he made sure that Angelica was presented to Queen Victoria. The queen was enchanted with her, and Angelica became the rage of London. Then she and Abram went off to Paris—for what's a honeymoon if it doesn't include Paris?"

"As I recall, Dolley, you never honeymooned in Paris, and neither did I."

"Well, yes; but women today are accustomed to so much more," Dolley said. "In Paris our minister, General Case, presented Angelica to the French king and queen, and do you know what? Louis Philippe invited them to dine at St. Cloud and personally gave them a guided tour of the palace!"

"It all sounds very heady," Rebecca said.

"I can't recall when an American has so completely captured the hearts of the Continent. All of Washington is buzzing about it. Angelica is just full of ideas about how the White House should be run. I understand that she has great surprises in store for us all at the New Year's levee."

"I wouldn't miss it for the world!" Rebecca said.

Bravo was so impressed with Anne's behavior during the Bittersweet crisis that he wrote her a note expressing his admiration, and asked if he might call on her.

Unfortunately, Anne's parents intercepted the letter and read it.

Mr. Fairfax shouted, "I forbid you see this reprobate, this drunkard, this Godless lost soul!" Mrs. Fairfax looked as if she was about to faint.

Anne suffered for a number of days, and then for the first time in her life, willfully disobeyed her parents. She answered Bravo's note, mailing it at the post office herself. In the letter, she explained the difficulties with her parents, and said she was going to be in the bookstore on Pennsylvania Avenue Wednesday next at six o'clock, and would consider it fortuitous if he happened to be browsing there also. She hated the deception, cringed at being so forward with him, but didn't know how else to handle her dilemma.

Bravo jumped at her suggestion and they spent a pleasant half-hour wandering through the dusty stacks at the bookshop. They arranged to meet again at the Hall of Representatives at the Capitol.

With each meeting, their affection grew. Though this pleased Anne enormously, she could never be sure that Bravo's feelings for her were real; was it only because he'd lost Angelica? She fretted more about this than about being discovered by her parents. One afternoon, at a small tea shop near the Treasury Building which was under construction, she asked him, "Do you plan to attend the President's New Year's levee?"

Bravo shook his head. "I have very little interest in such things."

"Is it because of Angelica?"

He sat back hard in his chair, looking defensive and angry. "Can't we let the past be?"

Not to be put off, she took her courage in her hands. "I plan to go, and I do so wish that you'd escort me." Her cheeks burned with the brazenness of her having asked, yet she also felt relieved.

"Anne, ask me anything but that."

"But Bravo, don't you see? That's the most important thing standing between us. Not so much to go to the levee, but for you to find out once and for all if . . ." Her voice faded as she found herself unable to go on.

"If I've gotten over Angelica, isn't that it?" he finished.

She nodded, miserable that she'd brought herself so low by exposing her heart to a man who hadn't declared himself first . . . Yet the room hadn't swallowed her up, nor had he run away.

"If that's what it takes to convince you, then of course we'll go," he said. "I'll call for you at noon on New Year's Day."

"Perhaps it would be better if we met someplace other than my house."

He was about to agree, but then said quietly, "If I'm willing to take a stand about Angelica, then you must be brave enough to do the same with your parents. I don't plan to spend the rest of our lives hiding."

She started to protest, asked for more time, but he remained firm. He reached across the table for her hand. "I know you've spent a lifetime catering to their wishes, but you're an adult woman, one that I'm growing to love . . ."

She thrilled when he said the words, almost not hearing the rest of his sentence: "But you've got to make your own life, and you've got to do it soon, or you won't find the courage to do it."

His words lingered in her head like a threat, and she knew that he was pushing her to make a choice. "I don't know," she whispered, her eyes averted. "I want to; you know that. But when Father begins to shout, all my strength ebbs from me."

"Why won't you let me speak to them? Declare my intentions to call on you?"

"Oh, no, no!" she said hurriedly. "You're dear and generous to offer that, but we both know that this is my battle."

"I'll make this one concession," he said. "I'll come to your house on New Year's Day. But I'll wait for you outside. I'll wait until the bell of St. John's tolls the noon hour. If you don't join me by then, I'll know that they've won, and I'll never trouble you again."

She protested, maintained that such ultimatums were silly;

but he remained adamant. She gathered her belongings and walked home, pondering everything he'd said. She needed to talk this over with somebody; a parent would have been the best, but hers were out of the question. She told herself all the reasons why this would never work—it was only because Angelica had married somebody else that he was at all interested in her. Could she spend the rest of her life being second-best? Besides, he had very little prospects in the way of earning a living; his dream was to be an inventor, and so many of them starved. The Patent Office was full of the dreams of men that would never be realized.

"But those are all excuses," she whispered to her reflection in her dresser mirror as she brushed her hair. How she loved the feel of it as it lay on her shoulders; how she loved all the freedom it exemplified. She'd even come to think that its color and sheen were pretty. "He's right. Unless I seize this moment, I'm doomed to become a spinster."

Since President Van Buren had entertained very little at the White House, Washington society eagerly awaited this levee. Rumors had reached the capital from Europe that Angelica had indeed conquered the Continent. Anxious to make their own judgments, the ladies of Washington prettied themselves up for the occasion; even the men took extra pains.

Up until the day of the event, Anne hadn't found the courage to tell her parents that she planned to go to the levee with Bravo. But she did spend the better part of the morning locked in her room, dressing. Angelica would look ravishing—of that one could be certain—and though Anne could never compete with her, she thought it imperative that she look her best.

She applied her cosmetics the way Rebecca had taught her, arranged her hair in soft, becoming waves, then put on the French-blue dress which she'd hidden in her closet. With her cloak over her arm, she descended the stairs and found her mother and father in the sitting room. Her father was intent on deciphering a passage in the Bible, thumbing through concordances, the better to determine precise meanings, and her mother was sewing initials onto a handkerchief. Anne waited.

Her mother shrieked when she finally noticed her, and her father raised his head from the pages, his eyes looking as if they might turn her into a pillar of salt. "Have you gone mad?" he sputtered.

Anne opened her mouth to answer him, but the words choked in her constricted throat. She swallowed and said, "Not mad at all, Father. In fact, this is one of the few sane things I've done in my life."

"But you look like one of those painted women of the streets!" Mrs. Fairfax moaned, and began to gasp for breath.

"Oh, Mother, surely that isn't true. I'm going to the White House, and I'm appropriately dressed."

"What's happening to children these days?" her father demanded, as he slammed the Bible shut. "To think that I should hear my own flesh and blood speak so disrespectfully to her parents! If you wipe that filthy stuff off your face, and put on a decent dress—one more suited to a daughter of mine—your mother and I may forgive you and take you to the White House ourselves."

"Father, I've already accepted Bravo Brand's invitation to go with him. He's picking me up at noon."

Mr. Fairfax jumped to his feet. "You've done such a thing behind our backs? Have you been meeting him? Has he touched you?"

"Of course I've met him; of course I did it behind your backs—would you have permitted it if I'd told you? And yes, he has touched me, he's held my hand when we've crossed the street, he's opened doors for me, he's done the hundred and one things that people do in simple daily contact, and you see, Father, none of us have been contaminated."

"I don't see that at all!" he boomed. "I'd say that you were very much contaminated. If not already *fallen*." A blue vein bulged in his temple with such rapidity that Anne was frightened for him, and for herself. "You're not going anywhere with Bravo Brand! Don't you know the rumors about him?"

"I know them, and they make not the slightest difference to me."

Mr. Fairfax advanced on her. Anne felt her heart skip but stood her ground. "I've recently turned twenty-one. I'm considered an adult legally. In short, Father, I'm no longer a minor, and not answerable to anybody but myself. I'm going to a public function with somebody whom I admire, and furthermore, I'm proud to be going with him."

"Anne, remember your affliction, remember—" Mrs. Fairfax began.

In the distance, Anne heard the mellow bell of St. John's

begin to toll the noon hour. "I'm leaving now, and you can like it or not, as you choose," she said, whereupon Mrs. Fairfax fainted.

"Have you no decency?" Mr. Fairfax shouted. "Look what you've done to your mother. See to her this instant!"

Anne took a small vial out of her bag; she'd brought it along just for this emergency. She handed her father the vial. "Smelling salts will revive Mother just fine."

Mr. Fairfax bellowed, "If you leave this house now, you'll find the door locked on your return."

Anne hesitated a moment, a look of infinite sadness on her face, then she stepped over the fallen body of her mother and swept out the door.

The moment he saw her, Bravo threw his hat in the air, and arm in arm, Anne's heart fluttering, they walked and ran and skipped off to the White House.

A line of people had queued up outside the North Portico, waiting to get into the mansion. Each person was inspected and passed on by the guards, so that none of the disreputable characters in Washington could get in. Often, all too often, that meant the poor and the indigent. "One gets the feeling that only the privileged are welcome," Bravo said. "President Van Buren ought to know better. After all, he was the son of a tavernkeeper."

"Sometimes, when the humble have risen, the first thing they want to do is forget their background," Anne said.

Bravo saw Rebecca and Dolley coming their way, and the four of them walked through the Grand Entrance Hall, toward the East Room, where Angelica was receiving. The entryway was crowded so that they couldn't see what was going on, but there was a commotion about something.

Then they caught sight of Angelica, and Rebecca gasped, "Oh, my God, I don't believe this! What has she done?" Even Dolley appeared to pale.

"How dare she?" Rebecca kept repeating, unable to find the words to express her shock. A dais had been constructed in the East Room, about a foot and a half higher than the floor. On the dais stood a chair that looked suspiciously like a throne. Angelica sat in the throne-chair, looking quite regal. She wore a purple velvet gown—the color was too exact to be anything but royal purple—and its long train curled around her feet.

Three long ostrich plumes rose imperially from her brown hair, the plumes the sign that she had been presented to the monarch of England. A pendant held by a rope of pearls hung on her forehead, and that and the ostrich plumes completed the impression that she was wearing some sort of crown.

The guests stared at Angelica with a mixture of curiosity and annoyance. Just then President Van Buren came into the East Room, looking more jowled and portly than ever. He approached Rebecca and Dolley.

"What do you think, eh?" he asked, beaming at his daughter-in-law. "Isn't she enchanting? Come, let me personally present you to my official hostess." He took Rebecca's elbow, but she pulled free.

"Martin, do you understand what you're doing? What she's done?"

"Why, what do you mean?" His sprightly blue eyes blinked with genuine confusion.

"I find Angelica's performance shocking," Rebecca exclaimed. "There she sits under the portrait of George Washington, he who was offered the crown of this new nation, and refused it! Yet Angelica willfully creates the impression that she's royalty. Our forefathers would be rolling in their graves if they saw this."

"I should have warned Angelica," Dolley moaned. "Rebecca, do you remember what happened when Elizabeth Monroe did a similar thing?"

"Indeed I do. The public accused her of having an acute attack of Queen Fever, and shunned her throughout James Monroe's first term."

"Oh, Rebecca, you're making too much of this," Van Buren said deprecatingly. "Angelica's a high-spirited young girl, she's come back from Europe after observing all the protocol there, and thought she'd introduce it as a way of refining our conduct and sensibilities. Is that so terrible?"

"Outrageous and scandalous," Rebecca insisted. "I have no desire to be presented to anyone who's that insensitive to our heritage. A generation of Americans fought and died to rid our land of the yoke of royalty. We hammered out one of the finest political documents that man has ever achieved. Now you're prepared to throw it all aside, and all its meaning, philosophically and ideologically, because of the whim of an insensitive young woman? Martin!"

"Tut, tut, tut," Van Buren clucked, treating Rebecca's outburst as if it were a piece of dismissable gossip.

Rebecca straightened. "President Van Buren," she said, addressing him formally, "you inherited a great deal of difficulty in your administration, some of it of your own making, much of it not. People are miserable about the depression, and the government's inactivity in solving the problems. The slightest incident could affect your chances to be reelected. Unless I seriously misjudge the character of the American people, your precious high-spirited daughter-in-law has just cost you the election."

President Van Buren glowered at Rebecca, then turned and walked away with a petulant waddle. Rebecca said to whoever was listening, "I cannot stay in this royalist den another moment!" and she swept out of the East Room.

"Goodness, your mother is certainly vehement about this, isn't she?" Anne said to Bravo.

"It's always been one of her 'causes.' But come on, we can't get involved in that, we've other things to do." Then he took Anne's hand and joined the receiving line that wound around Angelica's dais.

When Angelica saw Bravo, her lips thinned slightly, but nothing else betrayed an iota of feeling. He bowed politely to her. "Happy New Year, Mrs. Van Buren."

She nodded graciously, her questions the appropriate ones, asking after his health, his work, but the words were bloodless, delivered by rote. He was glad when the people behind made them move on.

"Well, that's over with," Bravo said with a sigh. "I could use a glass of punch."

But there were no refreshments anywhere, and the crowd grumbled about that. Here Angelica Singleton Van Buren was made up like a queen, but the President didn't have a glass of punch or even a cookie to serve his guests.

"Angelica's very beautiful, isn't she?" Anne said. "I can well understand why men admire her so."

"Beauty has never been Angelica's problem," Bravo answered. "But I look at her now and I see something very different. I suppose it was there all the time, but I was too young and too witless to see it."

"What?"

"A self-involved woman enjoying her power, without understanding any of the responsibilities that go with it. You know, I don't often agree with my mother—she can be a little boring about 'democracy'—but in this instance, she's right."

Then Bravo gripped Anne's hands. "A long time ago Letitia told me that beauty shone from the heart. I didn't really know what she meant until I met you."

She lowered her eyes, shocked, thrilled, delighted.

"You know about me, don't you?"

"What—?" and then she understood his meaning. "I've heard the rumors, but it doesn't matter to me at all. You're Bravo Brand. I don't care who your father was; you're making your own life, and that's good enough for me."

His face broke into a broad smile. "What will happen when you get home?"

Her eyes opened wide, and she hunched her shoulders. "This has never happened to me before. I imagine that Father will have locked the door."

"You're not serious!"

"Oh, it will only be to punish me. After he's left me banging on the door for a bit, he'll let me in, and then glower at me for a year or so."

"Anne, don't go back. Come with me!"

"Bravo!"

"Oh no, I don't mean that way!" he added hastily. "Anne, I know I'm not the best husband material, and the East Room isn't the most appropriate place to propose marriage. But it's a New Year, and a new start. Let's make it a new life, together."

His proposal left her sputtering, but he hurried on, gathering energy with each word. "We should be able to find a Justice of the Peace somewhere in Washington. Oh, I know—let's go to Georgetown! Reverend Terwilliger's just gotten back from Boston, and he can marry us. I don't want to wait another day."

She thought she must surely faint from the shock. All the reasons why she shouldn't sprang to her mind. There was nobody more surprised than she was when she heard herself exclaim, "Yes!"

Chapter 29

BRAVO AND Anne rode first to her house, where Anne found
the door barred. For some strange reason, this sent her and
Bravo into gales of laughter, but she called out anyway, "Mother?
Father? I'm getting married. I'd like you to attend the wedding."

Mrs. Fairfax hurried to the window, saw Bravo with her
daughter, and this time really did faint. Mr. Fairfax rushed for
the old musket that hung over the mantelpiece, and while he
fumbled to load it, Anne and Bravo fled.

They ran across the street to Rebecca's, and before she could
protest, they swept her along. Then the three of them were
riding hard, leaving Mr. Fairfax standing in the middle of New
York Avenue, waving his musket.

A quick stop at Circumstance and Wingate's, where Bravo
shouted, "If you're at Halcyon House within the hour, you can
stand as our best man and matron of honor!" Wheeling their
horses, they were off again.

In their breathless excitement, they did not notice the hulking shadow of a man mounting a horse and following after
them.

When Rebecca entered Halcyon House, she saw Bittersweet, and was overcome with surprise. She'd been told that
Bittersweet had gotten out of Washington safely. "But isn't it

dangerous for you to still be here?" she wanted to know.

Reverend Terwilliger, whom Rebecca knew from having served on various charity functions, including the Children's Orphanage, nodded. "It's dangerous, but we had little choice. Roadblocks have been set up, and a place has to be found for the child someplace north. It all takes time."

It didn't take Rebecca long to realize that Halcyon House was being used as a way station for the underground railway she'd heard so much about. She began pressing everybody for details when Circumstance and Wingate arrived.

Circumstance took Rebecca's hands. "You must understand that the less you know of this, the better for everybody. The entire network could be endangered."

Rebecca looked at her intently. "You're the one behind this whole thing, aren't you?" she asked.

"I'm active in it, yes," Circumstance said. "Do you find that so shocking?"

"I don't know what to think anymore," she said. "Our whole world is turned upside down these days. You know I'm an abolitionist, so I have no problem there. But you and Wingate, if you were to be caught... our entire family..."

"We tried very hard to keep you out of this," Wingate began.

Bravo interrupted. "It's my fault for making you come here today. I just wasn't thinking."

Rebecca saw the forlorn looks on everybody's face and said quickly, "Well, if you've set your minds to this, against all good common sense, then I can only tell you—that you're children after my own heart. Anything I can do to help, just tell me."

Huge smiles of relief flashed between everybody in the drawing room. Then, warming to the subject, Rebecca said, "As a matter of fact, there's no reason why I shouldn't write about this, alert the people in America to this horrid injustice."

"That's a noble sentiment, Rebecca," Wingate said. "And perhaps one day the country will be ready for it. But this isn't the time. Even in our own capital, John Quincy Adams faces daily villification because he's trying to lift the Gag Rule that prohibits any discussion of slavery on the floor of the House. So you can imagine the further furor you'd create. It might seriously harm our cause."

"Of course you're right," Rebecca agreed. "It's just my usual manner of plunging into something without thinking."

"I do believe that we've come here for a wedding!" Bravo interrupted, and everybody laughed.

As Reverend Terwilliger prepared for the ceremony, Rebecca said rather forlornly to Wingate and Circumstance, "You know, I've never had the pleasure of seeing any of my children married in a traditional and proper ceremony. Suzannah eloped; Gunning married in Kansas; and now here's Bravo, my last hope." She put her hand on Circumstance's arm and said, "Now as your daughter's godmother, I insist that when Doe marries, you allow me to take care of all the details. I want a church wedding with all the trimmings, and a reception for all of Washington."

"But Doe is only ten years old," Wingate said.

"Are you implying that I may not last until she's ready to get married?" she demanded. "All the more reason for you, as my doctor, to keep me alive until then."

Rebecca's attitude about a traditional wedding surprised Circumstance; she'd never thought of her as being particularly sentimental. Yet beneath the strong façade she showed the world, there obviously beat the heart of a romantic. She leaned over and kissed Rebecca. "The kind of wedding that Doe will have will naturally be her decision. But if it's all right with her, Wingate and I would be honored by your generosity."

Reverend Terwilliger returned carrying a gold-embossed Bible. Bravo beamed as he stood before the minister, and Anne, usually so reserved, was radiant.

The young couple heard the reverend's words, and listened to his advice about the sanctity of marriage, and their shining eyes bore witness to their belief in what he was saying. Then he said, "Will you love, honor, and obey, forsaking all others, until death do you part?" To Anne, those words formed a bond for eternity, one which she embraced with all her heart.

Amid the hugs and the tears, Rebecca asked, "Have you made any arrangements for a honeymoon?"

Bravo shook his head. "We haven't even thought of it, but I don't think I can leave Morse's workshop right now. We're just on the verge of a major breakthrough."

"You can't leave him now; you've both worked on this for so long," Anne added quickly. "There's so much that I must do anyway, to get settled."

"I'll help you with that," Rebecca said, slipping her arm around the girl's waist. "Where will you live?"

"At my studio," Bravo told her. "It's only two rooms, but they'll do for the moment."

"We have the house in Georgetown," Rebecca said. "Why not take that? You'd be so much more comfortable there."

"Thanks, Mother, but we'll start out small, and move as soon as we're able." He said it with such quiet conviction that Rebecca knew better than to argue. He was no longer her youngest boy, but a man with a wife and responsibilities of his own . . . and though she felt happy for him, how to explain the twinge of sweet sadness?

The young couple were eager to be on their own, and leaving the others behind at Halcyon House, they rode off.

In the shadows near the top of Prospect Hill, a giant mulatto lurked, his spyglass trained on the house.

"Mrs. Bravo Fairfax Brand, I can't believe it," Anne said when she and Bravo arrived at his apartment on I Street. "A few hours ago I was in danger of becoming a spinster, and now I'm a happily married woman. Can anybody doubt that there is a God?"

He swung her into his arms, carried her up the stairs to the top floor, then carried her over the threshold. "I know it's really not much," he began, but she put her finger on his lips. "As long as you're here, it's wonderful."

He put her down and cupped her face in his hands. "I'll be here for you forever."

They kissed slowly, and he felt her trembling against him. "Don't be frightened," he murmured. "Surely you know that I'd never do anything to hurt you."

She gazed up at him, her face open and vulnerable, and she whispered, "It's just that there are so many things that I don't know. I mean the ordinary things that a mother should tell a daughter—well, those things my mother never told me."

"All in good time. I've just as much to learn; after all, this is my first attempt at being a husband. And my last," he added hastily.

He laid a fire in the hearth and lit it, and soon a cheery blaze crackled, taking the chill from the skylighted main room. With twilight, dark clouds furled across the sky, bringing a heavy snow. As they sat before the fireplace, leaning against each other, they watched the flakes fall on the skylight panes, then dissolve.

Suddenly, neither of them could stop asking questions. They both realized that they hardly knew each other: She wanted to know all the foods he liked to eat. He wanted to know if any of his habits annoyed her, and if so, she must tell him at once.

"I think when two people get married, it's like being born anew," she said quietly. "Two people are made one in the eyes of the Lord, and their destinies entwine, for better or for worse, as the minister said . . . until death do us part."

"But we have a whole lifetime ahead of us. A lifetime beginning with tonight."

With that, she gave a little nod, then went to the other room to prepare for bed. Bravo threw another log on the fire, took off all his clothes, feeling the warmth of the fire on his bare skin. He had a moment of panic and thought, Oh, my God, will I be able to?

Circumstance had had the presence of mind to pack a few things for Anne, including a new nightgown, pale blue ribbons for her hair, and fragrant soap. When she came back into the main room, her face scrubbed, her hair tied back, Bravo said huskily, "You look like an angel."

He took her in his arms and kissed her very gently, feeling the sweet warmth of her lips, lips that no other man had ever kissed. She allowed the shift to fall from her shoulders, and she stood naked in the firelight.

He drew her down until they reclined on the large sheepskin rug before the fire. He held and caressed her for a long time, not rushing, knowing that what happened this night could establish the course of their marriage. In wanting it to be good for her, in wanting it to be right for both of them, he found that he'd forgotten his own fears.

While they were locked in each other's embrace, their lips pressed tightly, there came a moment when he felt the blood rise to her body, a pulse of passion never before wakened in her. He moved ever so gently to become one with her.

She cried out once when she lost the last vestige of being a maiden, and he held her until she stopped shuddering and she whispered, "I'm all right, all right." He moved deep within her, loving her in a way so wondrous that she knew nothing could ever describe it save the experience itself. She was fiercely glad now that her mother had told her nothing, proud that she'd discovered this joy on her own, and could love this man as he deserved to be loved, completely, without holding anything back because of guilt or fear or shame. No, she thought, thrilling to the rising and falling motion of her husband and lover, only love would live in this house, now and forever.

All through the night they reveled in each other's touch, dozing, waking, making love. The snow piled high in the streets and on the skylight, a dazzling blue-white in the midnight light, wind-carved into fantastic shapes. When dawn finally did come, the roseate gray light filtering through the snow-covered panes wakened Bravo.

He crept from her embrace, dressed noiselessly, and left the house. He galloped over to the Patent Office, slogging through the drifts, and informed his superior that he'd just gotten married, and to ask for the day off.

Then he rode back home, and crept back onto the pallet without Anne ever realizing he'd gone. She woke at nine, appalled that she'd slept so late. She was about to scramble up and make breakfast, but he said, "There's nothing in the house anyway, and that's really not what I want now," and so their lovemaking began anew.

She pressed her face against his smooth, rock-hard chest. "I feel like such a wanton," she whispered. "Instead of being exhausted, the way I've heard some women complain, somehow I feel replenished."

"That's the miracle of love. I mean, when two people are *truly* in love, then they never tire of it, because it's made new and wondrous each time."

"Do you know something else, my husband? The one thing I want more than anything else is to bear our child, to hold in my arms the visible proof of how much I adore you. If God is listening, and has in his mind to grant us a wedding present— well, that's the one that would please me."

"Then you shall have it," Bravo said, "and as Benjamin Franklin wrote in *Poor Richard's Almanac,* God helps them that helps themselves!"

Anne found the first month of marriage idyllic. She loved Bravo—there'd never been any question of that in her mind— but she discovered to her amazement that she also liked him, liked his constant good humor, his forgetfulness, his absorption in his work. But when he did turn his attention to her, he returned her love with a passion that left her breathless.

The difference in her life was so drastic that there were

times she actually felt that she was growing younger. Her laughter sounded through the rooms; she sang while she did her chores, delighted in fixing dinner, savored the Sundays when she would have him for the entire day.

One afternoon in February, she heard a heavy tread on the stairway and recognized her father's lumbering gait, and her mother's step that seemed to sandwich itself between the steps of her husband's. Bravo wouldn't be home for another two hours, and she flew into a panic, her first thought being to bar and lock the door.

"That's ridiculous!" she told herself. "They're your parents." A wonderful idea occurred to her: they'd come to apologize, to make it up to her!

She hurried to the door and opened it; her heart fell when she saw the unforgiving look on her father's face. He pushed his way into the room, his grim visage speaking eloquently of what he thought of her.

"We've come to take you home," Mr. Fairfax said. "Your mother and I talked it over and realized that you've had a momentary aberration, that you've been duped by this spawn of the Devil, but that we owe it to you to—"

"Just a minute!" Anne interrupted. "That's my husband you're talking about."

"He won't be for long, dear," Mrs. Fairfax said with a self-satisfied nod. "Mr. Fairfax has arranged to have this entire travesty annulled. Coercion, undue influence, and the like. He's already consulted several lawyers."

Anne paled. "If you say one more thing against my husband, I'll ask you to leave my house."

"You call this hovel a house?" Mr. Fairfax blustered. "It's no more than a slum. You were raised better than this."

Anne opened the door. "When the two of you can act in a decent, civilized manner to me and to my husband, then you'll be welcomed in my home. Not before then."

"I will not ask you again," Mr. Fairfax said, his voice heavy with threat. "You'll be cut out of our wills, and you'll forfeit the right to be called our daughter."

"As you like," Anne said softly. "I've chosen a way for my life, one that gives me a true feeling of being blessed, without the need for a lot of cant and hypocrasy. I wish you and Mother nothing but the best. But I'm Mrs. Bravo Brand now, and I intend to remain that until my dying day."

"Then God's punishment be on your head!" Mr. .Fairfax thundered. "You and your husband will pay for your sins. Honor thy father and thy mother! The Lord will surely smite you for not obeying the Commandments!"

With that, they left, leaving Anne standing in the center of the room, the echo of her father's curse resounding in her ears. Tears welled to her eyes as she murmured, "I never got a chance to tell them that they're going to be grandparents."

Chapter 30

REBECCA RODE over to the Senate chamber one day in May to listen to Henry Clay debate Thomas Hart Benton on the economy. After the session was recessed she went down to the floor of the chamber to congratulate Clay on his speech. But Clay looked quite glum.

"You've heard the news about the Whig convention, I take it?" he asked her.

"Yes. I *am* sorry they refused to give you the nomination. You're the strongest candidate they could have."

"Of course," Clay agreed sourly. "The fools opted for the candidate who was the least controversial, as though that were the prime requisite for a President, rather than intelligence or honesty!"

Rebecca's sorrow was genuine. As the titular head of the Whigs, Clay deserved better from his party. But the Whigs, seeking a success such as the Democrats had had with Andrew Jackson, cast about for a popular folk hero of their own, and seized on General William Henry Harrison.

In 1811, at the Battle of Tippecanoe, Harrison had scored a solid victory over the Shawnee Indians, who were led by the Prophet Tenskwatawa, brother of the great Chief Tecumseh. That victory had given Harrison the nickname "Tippecanoe" or "Old Tip."

Rebecca tapped her temple lightly and said to Clay, "Henry, in my aging, addled brain, I seem to recall some dire curse that Tenskwatawa leveled against Harrison and the presidency. Do you remember what it was?"

Clay shrugged. "I recall that the newspapers were full of it, because Tenskwatawa had a reputation for being able to foretell the future. But damned if I can remember the details. At any rate, we have a great deal more to worry about now than some silly Indian prophecy." He looked around the Senate chamber and exclaimed, "I've served here most of my adult life. I'm almost sixty years old and I won't have many more opportunities to run for President. But by God, one day I shall have it!"

Several nights later, in the midst of a fierce storm, Bravo put his revolver in his belt and prepared to leave his dwelling.

"Why do you have to go out tonight?" Anne asked. "The weather is so dreadful." As if in confirmation, a gust of rain-driven wind rattled the panes of the skylight.

"There's no other way," Bravo answered gently. "Don't wait up for me. I doubt I'll be back before morning."

"It's about Bittersweet, isn't it?"

Bravo nodded. "Reverend Terwilliger's decided that she must be moved, the sooner the better. He's seen some suspicious people nosing about. Wingate's away, so Circumstance asked me to help."

"I wish the weather weren't so miserable. I won't sleep until you get back."

"The bad weather works for us. People are less likely to be about." He kissed her goodbye, then strode toward the door.

"Bravo!" she called. He turned expectantly, and she flushed and murmured, "I love you." He waved at her and bounded down the stairs.

The wind moaned through the capital, sending lines of rain marching along the deserted avenues. Bravo drew his cloak tightly about him as he set off for Georgetown. The rain had turned much of the still-unpaved avenues into a quagmire, and he had to proceed very carefully lest his horse step in a pothole and break a leg. By the time he reached Halcyon House, he was soaked through. He stabled his mount, then hurried into the house, where Reverend Terwilliger, Circumstance, Bitter-sweet, and Enoch were already waiting.

"I'll run through the plan once more," Reverend Terwilliger said to them. "Bravo, you and Circumstance will escort Bittersweet and Enoch as far north as Gaithersburg, Maryland. If for any reason you're stopped along the way, you have these falsified papers to prove that Bittersweet and Enoch are your slaves."

"What happens at Gaithersburg?" Bravo asked.

"You'll be met by another courier, who'll take Bittersweet and Enoch to our next way station; this will be repeated until they cross the border into Pennsylvania. Once they get into the northern states, the risk of capture will be much diminished."

"Wish it weren't storming so," Bittersweet said in a small voice. "This kind of weather always scares me."

Enoch put his arm around her. "Don't worry. In a few hours we'll be out of Washington. You'll be free, and we'll be able to do whatever we want. Get married, raise a family of our own, without worry about slave traders and bounty hunters."

She nodded absently, but her eyes still looked haunted.

Circumstance gathered their belongings. "We must be on our way," she said, and opened the door. They ran toward the stables to get the horses, and were quickly soaked through.

Bravo cocked his ears when he heard the clatter of hooves bearing down on them. "Get back in the house!" he shouted to Circumstance and Bittersweet, and the two women fled just as Ramsey, Tortuga, and two other hirelings charged into the driveway.

Bravo drew his revolver, but Tortuga's horse threw him against the wall, stunning him. His revolver skittered away into the mud. Enoch fired off a shot that brought down one of the marauders. But Ramsey slashed down with his saber, cleaving Enoch's collar bone in two. Enoch pitched forward to his knees, bright red blood gouting from his wound.

The other raider, a heavy-set man named Lemuel, made for Bravo to finish him off, but Tortuga called out, "Don't harm him. Madam wants to see him hanged!"

Bravo regained his senses, only to find Tortuga's pistol pressed against his head. "Move, why don't you?" Tortuga chuckled. "I'd enjoy putting a bullet through your brain."

Lemuel and Ramsey lifted Enoch under the arms and dragged him onto the porch while Tortuga shoved Bravo forward. Reverend Terwilliger had barred the door, but Tortuga kicked it into splinters with a couple of blows of his booted foot, and went crashing through. "Where are they?" Tortuga shouted, his wild eyes sweeping around the empty drawing room. "Ramsey, get upstairs, search the basement. Find them!"

Ramsey scurried off. Bravo tried to stem the flow of blood from Enoch's wound, but Tortuga hit him a stunning blow on the side of the head that sent him sprawling. Then Tortuga spat at Terwilliger, "Tell me where the girl is or I'll let this man bleed to death."

Enoch shook his head wildly. "Don't tell them anything—"

Tortuga pistol-whipped Enoch until the blood oozed between his lips. Reverend Terwilliger cradled Enoch's head in his arms and looked at Tortuga. "Are you some kind of beast?"

"Touch him and I'll run you through," Tortuga said. "The law's on my side. I've got warrants to arrest all of you."

Ramsey came back then, puffing. "I've looked everywhere, the attic, the basement, there's nobody anywhere."

Tortuga drew his sword and pressed it against Terwilliger's breast. "Where are they? I speak in the name of the law."

"There's a greater law than yours," Terwilliger said softly, and pressed a cloth against Enoch's wound.

Bravo, still reeling from Tortuga's blow, saw the big mulatto draw back his arm, then plunge his saber through Terwilliger's chest. Terwilliger collapsed over the blade, fell to the floor, and lay still.

"Fool, what have you done?" Ramsey cried. "It's one thing to kill a nigger, but this is a man of the cloth!"

"He's a criminal nonetheless!" Tortuga insisted, but he himself was shaken by his own rashness. He pointed to Bravo and said to Ramsey, "Keep your eye on that one. If he tries anything, anything at all, shoot him. I'm going after the girl. When I get my hands on her, she'll pay for this night."

"But I've looked everywhere," Ramsey said.

Tortuga's eyes narrowed craftily. "Follow their wet tracks," he said with a grunt of satisfaction, and began to trace the footprints that Circumstance and Bittersweet had made. The trail led him to the basement door, and then down the steps.

Bravo heard Tortuga and Lemuel's footsteps clumping down into the basement. He had to do something, and fast—Tortuga was an animal, and Lemuel obviously no better. Terwilliger was dead, nothing he could do about him, and Enoch's wound looked like a mortal one . . . but Circumstance and Bittersweet—God, he couldn't let anything happen to them!

"Money," he said desperately to Ramsey. "I'll give you whatever you want, just let me free. You saw how he killed the minister. He'll kill you too, whenever it suits him."

Ramsey shifted uncomfortably. "I don't think you got as much money as we're being paid. The Connaughts, they must hate you something fierce to go through all this trouble, eh?"

Bravo felt the rage well up deep within him. The Connaughts. Whenever disaster loomed for his family, they were always behind it! He kept talking to Ramsey, trying to convince him.

Tortuga, meanwhile, had followed the trail of footprints to the far wall of the basement.

"Where have they gone?" Lemuel demanded. "They disappear into a blank wall?"

Tortuga tossed aside the furniture that blocked his path, and after rooting around, found the secret compartment in the woodbox. "Here it is!" he exclaimed. "You go back," he said to Lemuel. "That Brand boy is a tricky one. Help Ramsey keep an eye on him. I'm going after the women."

Tortuga entered the tunnel, feeling his way in the darkness. In a few minutes he would have the young little slave, as fair as a white woman, and anticipating what he would do when he got his hands on her, he began to get aroused.

Upstairs, Bravo had fully recovered his strength, but kept up a pretense of being dizzy. He struggled to his feet but fell back, all the while seeing Ramsey's pistol trained on him. The next time Bravo tried to stand, he used a small table for support, and then grasping it under the drawer, hurled it at Ramsey. Ramsey fired at the same time, but the bullet plowed into the tabletop, and before he could make another move, Bravo was on him, fists smashing into his face. Ramsey's knees buckled and he fell close to where Enoch lay. With the last of his ebbing strength, Enoch pressed his forearm down on the man's windpipe.

"Go after the women," he whispered hoarsely to Bravo. "I'll take care of him." When Bravo hesitated, Enoch rasped, "Go man, before he kills them!"

Bravo raced toward the basement steps just as Lemuel came up, and they collided. Lemuel fell backwards, his flailing arms trying to catch the bannister, but he tumbled, his head hitting a step at an awkward angle. Bravo heard the distinct snap of a neck being broken. He vaulted over the body, ran to the

tunnel and chivvied his way in, scraping himself against the
sides in his haste.

"A weapon," he cursed, "I should have taken a weapon!"
Too late to go back now, he'd have to think of something to
use against that giant.

Tortuga bulled his way through the tunnel, stooping low
because of his size. He caught the two women just as they
reached the exit of the tunnel and he grabbed for Bittersweet's
skirts. As he did, his bulky shoulder crashed against the supporting beam, sending a fall of earth down on them. Bittersweet
screamed and Circumstance turned and came back, pulling on
Bittersweet's arm to free her from Tortuga's grasp.

He bellowed with laughter and cried out, "Two of you, eh?
Then I'll have double the fun this night. First this pretty little
thing, before the whip scars her body and she's used by a lot
of men."

Circumstance reached past Bittersweet and clawed at
Tortuga's face, but he hit her such a blow in the chest that she
fell against a hillock and sat there, unable to catch her breath.
Tortuga tore at Bittersweet's clothes, while his raucous laughter
echoed in the tunnel. He threw her down in the soft earth at
the tunnel's mouth, and then, hands fumbling with his pants,
he started to mount her.

Bittersweet tried to roll out from under him, but his weight
was unsparing. Circumstance, still gasping for breath, looked
around for anything that could be used as a weapon, but she
could find nothing in the darkness, and so she threw herself
on his back, biting and tearing at him. He bounded to his feet
and shook himself, dislodging her. He raised his leg, aimed
for her skull, and brought it down, but she saw it and scrambled
away in time. At that moment, Bravo came around the bend
in the tunnel.

Tortuga whirled, whipping a long, double-edged knife from
his belt. "You've got more lives than a cat, but I'll finish you
off once and for all." With a sideways swipe he slashed at
Bravo, tearing his chest. Bravo jumped back, drawing Tortuga
after him.

Seeing Bravo about to be killed, Circumstance sprang at
the man and sank her teeth into his calf. He bellowed and
straightened suddenly, his head hitting the supporting timber.
The beam, weakened by the heavy rains, began to give way;

Bravo grabbed it and yanked down with all his strength.

"Circumstance, get away!" Bravo shouted, and she rolled from the mouth of the tunnel as the beam fell on top of Tortuga, crushing his chest.

The tunnel had collapsed only at the opening, and Bravo quickly dug his way free. He, Circumstance, and Bittersweet stood there, holding onto each other in the driving rain. The shapeless mass of Tortuga's body lay under the fall of earth. "What are we going to do?" Bittersweet whispered.

"Drag his body into the river," Bravo said. "Let the currents wash him out to sea. The less the authorities know about this, the better."

They dragged Tortuga down to the riverbank, then rolled his body into the Potomac. The swift currents bore him downstream. The three of them went back through the garden to the house.

Once inside, Circumstance and Bittersweet gasped at the carnage. Enoch was dead, his forearm pressed down heavily on Ramsey's windpipe. Ramsey's lifeless eyes were popping out of his head. Bittersweet knelt by Enoch, trying to rouse him, until Circumstance led her away from the body.

"Reverend Terwilliger is dead also," Bravo said.

"All because of me," Bittersweet whispered.

"Yes," Circumstance said suddenly. "All because of you! That's why we can't have any more tears. That's why we have to get you away from here right now. So that all these people will not have died in a vain and empty cause. Bravo will take you to Gaithersburg right now. I'll have to stay here and explain all this to the authorities. Bittersweet, when you get to Gaithersburg, from there you'll have to go on alone. Can you do it?"

"I don't know," she whispered.

"Remember, this is what Enoch would have wanted."

"That's right," Bravo said. "He made me go after you rather than try to save him. You've got to do it for his sake, and for the sake of your grandmother. For all of us. Bittersweet, you mustn't fail us!"

She hung her head, but nodded.

"Good girl!" Circumstance said. "Bravo, we're far behind schedule. You must start right now or you may miss your contact."

"What about you?"

"I'll tell the authorities that these men broke into the house with their accomplices, and tried to rob us under the pretext of searching for slaves. That we tried to fight them off, and this was the result."

"Do you think you can convince them?"

"I have no choice," she said. "Otherwise, the entire underground railway will be threatened. Bravo, this mustn't stop us. There are many more lives to save. But none more important right now than Bittersweet's. Go, and God be with you."

PART FOUR

Chapter 31

BRAVO AND Bittersweet rode hard through the darkness and made their connection in Gaithersburg. From there, she moved on north toward Frederick, and Bravo returned to Washington. He wished he could help Circumstance explain to the law officials what had happened at Halcyon House, but that would have put them on Bittersweet's trail, so he had to leave Circumstance to fend for herself.

The supposed robbery and the real slaying of Reverend Terwilliger caused great consternation in the District of Columbia. Though Ramsey and Lemuel were rogues with bad reputations, many people believed that there was more to the tale than was being told. But since Circumstance was the only known witness, her story finally prevailed.

Eventually word reached Circumstance through the underground railway that Bittersweet had gotten to Lancaster, Pennsylvania, and had headed farther north. So she would be safe, at least; that made all the danger worthwhile, and it helped to compensate for the deaths of Reverend Terwilliger and Enoch.

The Connaughts knew the truth about the Halcyon slayings, but couldn't reveal it without incriminating themselves. "If that runaway slave had been captured," Devroe said to Véronique, "it would be different. But without her as proof, we have no case."

Devroe had just recently returned to the estate and was seriously disturbed that the Brands hadn't been caught red-handed. "How annoying," he complained to Véronique.

"It will happen," she responded. "They are so foolhardy they'll never give up this slave adventurism. Sooner or later they'll make a fatal mistake. Then you shall have them, all legally, and with no jeopardy to yourself."

"Any word of Tortuga?" he asked.

"No word," she said. "He's disappeared completely. A body was found floating in the Chesapeake; from the description, I'd venture to say it was him. No matter. He was just another hired hand, and not very effective."

"I'd assumed that you'd miss him a great deal more than that," he said mildly. "I'd heard you were spending an inordinate amount of time with him, my dear. You know the way slaves gossip."

Véronique hunched her shoulders haughtily, but her heart was pounding. Had she been found out? If he suspected, he would kill her without a second thought. "Slaves gossip about everything," she said. "They'd do whatever they can to keep from performing an honest day's labor. You know better than to pay attention to them."

"If you say so, my dear."

All during that night, Véronique tossed and turned, beset with chilling concerns. Thank God Tortuga was no more. She had learned her lesson; she would never put herself in jeopardy again. When she woke that next morning, she felt nauseated and convinced herself that it was the creamed mussels she'd eaten the night before. But when her morning sickness persisted through the week, she could no longer hide the truth from herself.

She gazed into her mirror, seeing the dark circles around her eyes. "Oh my God," she whispered, her lips trembling, "I'm pregnant!" She began to calculate how much time had elapsed since she and Devroe last slept together. Then another horrifying thought pressed in on her. What if the baby was born with noticeably dark skin? She knew of several cases on the plantation where a light-skinned Negro had fathered a child as black as coal.

She paced her sitting room, waiting for the day when Devroe would absent himself from the estate. Finally one afternoon he rode into Washington with the children, to have new saddles made for them. The moment he was away, Véronique rode to the cabin of an old Haitian woman who lived several miles away. The woman, named Mizras, rumored to be in her eighties, looked remarkably young, with hardly a line on her face. The more superstitious people in the area whispered that her youth was a consequence of her dining on . . . well, the less said abut that, the better. Mizras had been a slave in her youth, but had earned her freedom by casting spells for her mistress, now dead.

The walls of her shack were hung with items that Véronique didn't recognize but which she took to be charms used in casting voodoo spells. Mizras sat with her head bent, smoking a pipe filled with a pungent, aromatic leaf that Véronique had never smelled before. She crinkled her nose, but the old woman puffed more deeply and said, "It brings me visions on the smoke."

Mizras never looked at Véronique, yet her concentration was so intense that Véronique grew uncomfortable. "You came here because you're with child," she said at last. "You fear the child is not your husband's, and so it must be destroyed."

Véronique gasped, about to deny everything; but that would be stupid, since the reason she'd come here was indeed to rid herself of Tortuga's bastard. "What will it cost to be rid of it?"

"More than you can pay," Mizras said.

Véronique started, sorry that she'd come here in the first place. She should have journeyed to Baltimore or Philadelphia and found a reputable doctor there, rather than exposing herself to this madwoman. She rose to go.

"I'm an old woman, and I've lived a long time," Mizras said, breathing out a stream of smoke. "I want nothing, need nothing, except for some more years. There will come a time when I will ask you for something."

Véronique waited.

"If you don't bring what I ask then, your husband will find out you've deceived him, he'll drive you from your home like a whore, and you'll spend the rest of your days in the gutter. But if you do as I say, you'll live out your days as mistress of the Connaught plantation."

"How do you know my name?" she gasped, but Mizras made no reply, acting as if the question were a piece of stupidity. "What is it you want?" Véronique demanded, near hysteria now.

Mizras's words came through a pall of smoke. "I will want the heart of a child."

Véronique thought she was surely going to faint, and she leaned against the wall. "The heart of a child?" she repeated. "But that's madness! Why do you need such a thing?"

"That is my concern, not yours. Now stare into the flames, deeply, and see if I haven't told you the truth."

Véronique tried not to look into the fire, but her eyes felt heavy, and as she stared at the embers, she thought she saw all that the crone had predicted. "She's mesmerized me!" she cried inwardly, but that made the vision no less horrible. She felt her mouth move of its own volition as she whispered, "All right, you shall have the heart of a child."

"Good, good," Mizras said, rubbing her hands together. She began to grind some ergotic grain in a mortar, mixed it with a foul-smelling liquid, and handed it to Véronique. "Drink this, to the dregs."

Véronique held her nose and drank it, convinced she would retch on the spot. In moments, she felt her stomach begin to roll and churn. Then Mizras told her to lie on her back. She mixed another potion, put a large swab of cotton on the end of a stick, and after dipping it into the new mixture, inserted it as deeply as she could into Véronique's body.

She cried out once with the discomfort, but Mizras snapped, "Be quiet. You pleasured yourself; now you must pay in pain. Leave the packing inside for twenty-four hours. Tomorrow, when you remove it, the child will come with it."

Véronique rode away from there, so filled with terror that when she got home she began to bleed, and two hours after that, she miscarried. She didn't call her maid; she had to do this alone. It was with the greatest relief that she accomplished her task, and got rid of every vestige of her guilt before Devroe returned from Washington that evening.

By week's end, Véronique was back to her old self, and managed to push the incident from her mind. She even forgot her promise to Mizras. Except there were times in her sleep, the hours between three and four, the hours of the wolf, when the old crone's voice came to haunt her.

Rebecca had taken a passionate interest in all that John Quincy Adams was suffering in the House of Representatives.

Each morning as the session began, he raised one motion or another in an attempt to lift the Gag Rule, which prevented any discussion of slavery on the floor, and each morning his motion was beaten down. Fellow congressmen threatened to censure him, threatened him with bodily harm, swore they would have him killed, but still Adams fought singlehanded for the right to debate any issue as guaranteed the American people in their Constitution.

One Sabbath after church, Rebecca paid a social call on John Adams in his house on F Street. The Federal-style house was furnished sparingly, but with great good taste, Louisa Adams being a woman of exquisite sensibilities. "How is your dear wife?" Rebecca asked John Quincy.

"Ailing, I fear. She has little stomach for all this political infighting. Her constitution was ever frail."

"As ours," Rebecca said with a slight laugh, and John Quincy smiled appreciatively. Rebecca sipped her sherry and said, "I thought I'd stop by and offer you whatever support I could in your battle."

"Thank you, Rebecca. Frankly, I need all the help I can get. I despair of winning, but I'll never stop as long as there's a breath in me. We must have the right to discuss our problems, else how shall we ever solve them?"

"That seems axiomatic to me," she said. "You'd think the supposed brains of the House would see that also."

"Are you going to be involved in this election?" he asked.

"I have little heart for it. Whom do we have running—Van Buren and Harrison? When I think that these are supposed to be the best that the country has to offer, I'm filled with despair. How I wish that you'd consider . . ."

"Truthfully, I'd like nothing better than to be President again. In fact, when my constituents in Quincy elected me, I had in mind using it as a springboard to regain that office."

"The country could do worse," she said.

"I'm afraid that I'm a political anomaly," he said. "Now it's all party politics—what's best for the party, not what's best for the country. Anybody would think that the two parties were at war. I find it disgustingly tribal and I won't have anything to do with it. I'm my own man, and I'd rather be my own man in the House than a party hack in the President's Mansion."

"Have you heard the latest nonsense about Harrison?" she asked. "The Whigs are trying to turn their candidate into a frontiersman—spreading tales that he lives in a log cabin and drinks only hard cider!"

John Quincy reacted angrily, his face becoming even more dour. "You know as well as I that Harrison is an erudite man, a classical scholar, though a bit dull and pedantic. He's graduated from college, and served in both the House and the Senate. Wouldn't you think that was good enough for the people? But no, they have to debase him to their lowest common denominator."

"I know," Rebecca sighed. "Now Henry Clay tells me that Nicholas Biddle has taken a hand in Harrison's campaign. His advice is 'Let Harrison say not one single word about his principles, or his creed—let him say nothing—promise nothing. Let no committee or convention—no town meeting ever extract from him a single word about what he thinks now, or what he will do hereafter. Let the use of pen and ink be wholly forbidden, as if he were a mad poet in Bedlam!'"

"Extraordinary!" Adams exclaimed. "So once again we're faced with an election not of issues, but of personalities. Sometimes I think that Alexander Hamilton was right when he said, 'The public, sir, is a great beast.'"

"Oh, John, you don't believe that at all."

"I suppose not. But it does make one wonder sometimes about the intelligence of the electorate. Do you know who most frightens me? Not Harrison; he's a mild enough man. But I fear Henry Clay. Because I believe that Harrison will become Clay's puppet."

"Well, at least Clay is open about his desire for the power of that office. Every political move he's ever made has been to that end."

Adams stroked his chin. "It's the greatest prize that this country has to offer," he said softly. "To serve for the public good, with little thought of personal aggrandizement, or party affiliation, but to govern solely so that the democracy can evolve into the most perfect and perfectable form of government...can any man ask for greater glory than that?"

Rebecca leaned over and kissed Adams's whiskered cheek. "This country is made greater because of such sentiments. It's a pity that more of our legislators don't hold similar beliefs."

Adams drummed his fingers on the table, embarrassed but also obviously pleased. "Well, give us time, Rebecca, and one day the country will grow into itself. Whatever the outcome, I have a feeling that this will turn out to be a most unusual election."

Chapter 32

"HAVE YOU ever seen such a glorious day?" Anne asked as she and Bravo strolled along the Mall. He had to ship a package to Baltimore for Samuel Morse, a small electrical armature for their magnetic telegraph; Bravo, though now an inspector of patents, still devoted his spare time to working with Morse. The afternoon being so lovely, Anne and Bravo had decided to walk to the Baltimore and Ohio railroad depot at Pennsylvania Avenue and Second Street, N.W.

The fresh breeze carried off the odors from the open canal which ran near the Mall. A brown-and-white cow grazed contentedly on the greensward, oblivious to the passing pedestrians and carriages, while birds flew hither and yon, gathering food for their young.

"Are you getting tired?" Bravo asked. "It's a long walk."

"It's good for me, it will help me keep my girlish figure. Though I fear that in a few more months, nothing will help."

He slipped his arm around her waist and pressed her close to his side, and they walked along in matching stride.

"I look around, see everything budding, and feel in rhythm myself," she said. "I never knew that I could be this happy. Life before you was like some long, gray corridor, with my mother blocking one end and my father guarding the other. Now there's life in my body and joy in my heart, and sometimes

I love you so much that I hurt with the sharpness of it."

Bravo brushed back his long white-blond hair. "Were there ever two people as lucky as we? In a way, we were both limping along in life, but now look at our stride!"

"I want a large family," she said resolutely. "I've had none of the ordinary complaints that other pregnant women tell of. I think I was just designed to bear children."

"I see I have my work cut out for me," he laughed.

She felt a tiny stab of pain in her shoulder and arm, but said nothing about it. Nor had she ever mentioned the weariness she sometimes felt in her limbs, or her shortness of breath. She saw no point in worrying Bravo needlessly. He was working so hard with Samuel Morse, had experienced so many disappointments, that she felt she couldn't add to his burden.

They soon reached the small, narrow, three-story train depot and Bravo dropped off the package. Rudimentary train service had first been established between Baltimore and Washington in 1835. The first excursions were comic, and sometimes near-disasters, with trains derailed after hitting grazing cows, engines running out of fuel, and passengers having to walk for miles. Once an engine even blew up; fortunately, no one was hurt. But in the course of the past five years, service had become quite reliable.

"Can you believe it only takes two and a half hours to travel the thirty-seven miles to Baltimore?" Bravo said. "It's incredible. Why, I can foresee the day when we'll have railroads spanning the entire continent."

She looked at him rather dubiously.

"It will happen, and sooner than we think. I'd say within twenty-five years. They say that necessity is the mother of invention, and with our continent so vast we must have the fastest transportation possible."

"To begin with, we don't own the entire continent."

"We will," he said. "It's our destiny. Andrew Jackson told me himself."

"Even if we did, there'd still be rivers to ford and mountains to climb."

"Anything a man dreams of, he can do. Otherwise, why would the good Lord have given us the capacity to dream?"

"You believe all this, don't you?" she said, feeling a vague uneasiness that in his genius, he would grow tired of her and leave her far behind.

"I do. I also believe that America is the chosen land, the new Jerusalem. I believe that Americans are the chosen people—chosen to lead all mankind to new heights of freedom and dignity."

"That sounds a little hypocritical, especially here in Washington where the slave trade still flourishes," she said.

"But we'll change all that—slowly perhaps, but change it we will."

They started the slow walk back home, nodding to several acquaintances who drove by along the Mall, delighting at the sight of children flying kites, of adults on velocipedes, and savoring the serene beauty of spring greening the landscape.

"I feel so full of love, so full of life, that sometimes I think my heart will burst."

He twined his fingers through hers. "Anne, I'm not given to flowery speeches, and though I don't say it often enough, I do love you. It's been such a long journey for me to find the right person, one I could trust and cherish. I've taken a number of wrong turns. But the Fates, or God, or whoever guides our destinies, heard me, pitied me, and sent you to me."

With summer, the trees grew heavy with leaf. Rebecca suggested that Anne move into her house on New York Avenue to wait out her time there, but Anne preferred her own quarters. She and Rebecca spent every Wednesday and Saturday afternoon sewing the baby's layette; Anne didn't sew in the colored ribbons, thinking to save that until she knew for certain the sex of the child. But Rebecca blithely sewed blue ribbons on everything.

"My dear, you're carrying just the way I did when I had Bravo, high and up front. So it will be a boy, take my word for it. And that's all I've got to say about that matter!"

She stopped suddenly and tears welled to her eyes. "Every so often I'll think of Letitia, say something to her as if she were still alive. She was the most exasperating human being I ever met, and the kindest, and oh, Lord, how I miss her."

The sun burned through August, stultifyingly hot. With all her added weight, Anne found herself sometimes gasping for breath. But she kept her own counsel about that. Only a few more weeks now, she told herself, and she could certainly bear that. One afternoon, Circumstance came to help her with the chores, and she noticed Anne breathing heavily. When she questioned her about it, Anne said that she thought it was normal for her condition.

"Maybe," Circumstance said, "but I'm going to ask Wingate to come and see you. He'll be able to tell us."

The following day, Wingate and Circumstance walked over to the house on I Street; Bravo was still at Morse's studio. Wingate gave her a thorough examination—pregnancy wasn't usually considered the proper concern for a physician, and this was the first time that he'd seen her professionally. During his examination Wingate questioned Anne intently. Had she experienced shortness of breath, difficulty climbing stairs, pains in the chest and arms, dizziness, hot-and-cold sweats?

Anne said she'd experienced some of that, but wasn't it all just part of the pregnancy?

"It can be, but there's something more. Do you have palpitations, times when your heart seems to beat irregularly?"

She looked at him craftily. "No."

"Anne, there's no point in your lying to me. I can hear it with my stethoscope."

"What does it all mean?" she asked, trying very hard not to give in to her fears.

"I believe there's a strain on your heart, one that I don't much like."

"But I've always had an erratic heart, as long as I can recall. Doctors have told me that I mustn't exert myself. But please—you mustn't tell Bravo."

"Of course he must be told," Wingate said sternly. "It's his right and duty to know. Now I don't anticipate anything untoward happening. But I want to be cautious about it. From what I can determine, you should give birth in a matter of days."

A sudden thought crossed her mind. "What about other children?"

"For the moment, let's just concern ourselves with this one."

She looked at him earnestly. "Now there's no point in your lying to *me*. Will I be able to have other children?"

"All right then, I'll give you my considered opinion. You shouldn't have any more children. It's far too great a risk."

She considered that for a long moment. "Will you let me tell that to Bravo myself? In my own time?"

"Of course."

"One other thing. No matter what happens, this child must live. It must. Do you promise?"

"I'll do everything I can," Wingate said.

"No, promise!"

"Anne, I'm only a physician, not the Lord."

She sank back in the chair and said dully, "I knew it was all too wonderful to last. I knew that when mother and father came here and said—" She broke off as her face contorted with a wrenching pain. "My God, I think it's begun."

By the time Bravo got home, Anne's labor had commenced. His joy was quickly tempered when Wingate gave him the particulars of her condition. "What's to be done?" he demanded.

"Nothing now, except let nature take its course, and hope for the best."

Bravo thought that he'd go mad as he listened to Anne's low moan that would grow into a piercing cry. The most terrible thing was that he could do nothing to relieve her of the pain, pain that he'd helped cause.

The hours dragged by, and all this while, Circumstance and Wingate stayed with Anne, ministering, helping her as best they could with encouraging word and prayer. By midnight, Bravo convinced himself that Anne's pains were coming faster, she'd barely time to recover from one bout before the next onslaught hit her. It went on all through the night until Bravo worked himself into a dull rage about this child that was tearing Anne apart.

At dawn, Anne slipped into a merciful coma, exhausted beyond endurance. But the pains started soon again, and this time Wingate knew that they were threatening her life. "Unless she gives birth quickly, I'm going to lose her," he said, his stethoscope on her heart. "She can't stand much more of this."

"Perhaps if we have her squatting," Circumstance said. "Sometimes that makes the child come more easily."

Wingate nodded. "If that doesn't work, then I'll have to do something I hate doing. Cut the baby from her. Or else both child and mother may die."

Bracing Anne between them, they positioned her so that she was squatting, but by now she was so weak that she couldn't retain her equilibrium and kept falling over. At one point, he had difficulty locating her pulse; when he finally did it was so erratic that he said, "I'll have to operate."

Circumstance asked, "Can she withstand an operation?" But before Wingate could answer, Anne went into the final labor.

After another hour of excruciating pain, the child was born. With its appearance, Anne collapsed. Circumstance washed the baby, put it in a swaddling blanket, and when Anne opened her eyes, Circumstance placed the child in her arms.

"It's a beautiful boy," Circumstance murmured. "Weighs at least eight pounds."

"Which is part of the reason it was such a difficult birth," Wingate said.

Bravo hurried to Anne's side. "How are you, darling?" He was appalled at her appearance. She had an unearthly pallor about her. Her lips were bloodless, deep dark circles lined her glazed eyes. Her breathing was rapid and very shallow.

"Bravo," she whispered. "It's a boy . . . Promise that if anything should happen to me—"

"Nothing's going to happen," he said, stroking her forehead. "You were just wonderful. Nothing's going to happen. It's all over."

"Promise me you'll raise the boy yourself. Oh please, don't put him into an orphanage. You mustn't let my parents have him!" she exclaimed on a wave of fear. "Never. They'll ruin him as they ruined me."

"Anne, what are you talking about? You're going to be all right." He turned to Wingate. "Tell her that she's going to be . . ."

She shook her head wearily. "It's taken the last of my strength, and there's none left over for living. Now it's you and the child who must do my living for me. Remember me sometimes. Know that I did the best I could."

Her eyelids flickered and he clutched her hand. "Anne— don't close your eyes, don't!"

She smiled at him, and he could barely hear her as she mouthed the words, "Don't grieve for me. There are some people who can only tolerate so much happiness. I've crowded a lifetime of loving into these past few months. Enough to last me for an eternity."

Then she closed her eyes for a final time and was gone.

"Oh no, God, no!" Bravo cried out, clutching at her.

Circumstance put her arm around him and held him while he wept for this gentle creature, wept for himself, wept for the cruelty of life itself that had torn her from him.

Wingate took the baby from Anne's arms, and gently drew the blanket over her face. Bravo looked at the child, his tears turning as brilliant as ice.

"I hate him," he whispered. "He killed her, and I hate him."

Chapter 33

ANNE FAIRFAX BRAND was buried in the Brand family plot in Rock Creek Cemetery. According to Bravo's wishes, the funeral services were kept short, but they were still heartbreaking; Anne had been just twenty-two. As the first spadeful of earth hit the coffin, Bravo believed that it was the end of everything.

Rebecca grieved not only for Anne's untimely death, but also for the other members of her family who were buried here. In this plot her father, Mathias Breech, rested. Alongside each other lay Zebulon and Jeremy Brand. A lifetime flashed before her eyes as Rebecca gazed at the headstones . . . Jeremy Brand, born 1782, died 1820. He'd been only thirty-eight years old, and in the prime of his life when he'd fallen from the top of the White House. It didn't seem possible that twenty years had passed, yet here was her son, Bravo, standing beside her, witness to the passage of the years.

Rebecca was chilled by Mr. and Mrs. Fairfax's reaction to their daughter's death. "It's God's will," Mr. Fairfax murmured, "and we must all bow before God's will. I can only pray that the Lord will forgive her sins."

Mrs. Fairfax, weeping in her handkerchief, nodded in agreement. "It will be a burden for us, but it's our bound duty to raise our grandson in the ways of the Lord."

Bravo hardly heard what they were saying, hardly realized that he'd agreed to give the child to them. Nothing seemed important anymore—not his work, his life, his son—and he walked away from the cemetery and through the days as if he too had died. Is this my destiny? he wondered. My father died because of me, and now Anne . . . Is my love then such an evil thing?

Bravo named the baby Forrest, his paternal grandmother's maiden name. About a week later he brought the child over to Rebecca's, before handing him over to the Fairfaxes. They'd already had papers drawn up and he'd agreed to sign them.

Rebecca was beside herself. "Bravo, how can you?" she asked. "This is your own flesh and blood. Do you know what kind of hell you're consigning the child to? They'll twist Forrest into something unrecognizable. You told me that Anne didn't want her parents to have the child."

"Mother, what can I do? I can't take care of him."

"But I can!"

He glanced at her in surprise. She said, "Why not? I've raised three children of my own." She kept up a persuasive argument as Bravo leaned over the small cradle, gazing at his son.

The boy's hair was so blond that he looked almost bald, and his blue eyes were the startling Brand color. Then the baby's tiny hand closed around Bravo's finger, and held on for dear life. For the first time since Anne's death, Bravo smiled.

About an hour later, Mr. and Mrs. Fairfax appeared at Rebecca's door. "We know that this is for the best," Mr. Fairfax said, proffering the adoption papers.

Bravo shook his head slowly. "I've decided not to part with my son. My mother's offered to care for the boy, and that suits me just fine."

Mr. Fairfax grew red in the face. "The child needs the care and guidance of a man and a woman to raise him properly," Mr. Fairfax insisted, "and your mother is a woman alone."

"I'll be coming here every day after work," Bravo said. "Now if you'll excuse me, it's time for Forrest to be fed." With that, he led the outraged Fairfaxes to the door.

"It won't end here," Mr. Fairfax threatened. "I'll institute proceedings to gain custody!"

Bravo gripped his father-in-law's lapels. "On what grounds?"

Mr. Fairfax ripped free. "On the grounds that you're an unfit parent. There's more than enough in your past to damn you! And that includes your mother also! I won't have my grandchild subjected to such immoral people!"

Bravo slammed the door in their faces.

"They're poisonous," Rebecca said. "Little Forrest is well rid of them, and so are we. Don't worry about what they said, Bravo. Their threats are all idle." She said it with a conviction she was far from feeling.

By fall, the election campaign had turned into a complete fiasco, leaving Rebecca disgusted. "That something as vital, as sacred as an election should be turned into a carnival. It's unconscionable!"

William Henry Harrison's managers, disdaining any degree of political responsibility, refused to debate the issues. The "Log Cabin and Hard Cider" appellation had stuck to Harrison. Log cabin headquarters were set up in all the major cities, where giant rallies were held, fueled by hard cider passed out to the boisterous crowds. The public, debilitated after years of the depression, wanted something, anything to take their minds off their own misery, and they seized avidly on this diversion.

The Whigs flooded the country with rollicking pamphlets called *The Hard Cider Press, Old Tip's Broom,* and the *Log Cabin.* Rebecca crumpled the paper she was reading into a ball and threw it in the fireplace. "Idiotic scandal sheets, all of them, without a single redeeming feature. There isn't one issue of substance discussed," she complained to Circumstance, who was playing with Forrest.

"Whenever I go to Center Market or to Georgetown I'm inundated with log-cabin nonsense—log-cabin handkerchiefs, log-cabin sunbonnets, buttons, teacups, plates—until I just want to scream. Has the entire country gone log-cabin crazy?"

The country had. A host of products sprang up around the campaign, including Tippecanoe tobacco, Tippecanoe shaving soap, Old Cabin whiskey, and suddenly everybody across the country was dancing the Harrison Hoe-Down and the Tippecanoe Quick-Step.

Such mindless inanities were enough to make Rebecca sick, and as Rebel Thorne, she said so repeatedly in pamphlet after pamphlet. "General Harrison has probably never even seen the inside of a log cabin." Thorne protested. "Surely a man's qualifications for the highest office in the land should rest on something more substantial than a campaign slogan—'Tippecanoe and Tyler too!' I'm neither for nor against Harrison—but then, how could I be? I don't know what he thinks about any of the substantive issues. What I am for is an open forum—better yet, a debate between the candidates to discuss the course of this country."

But nothing Rebel Thorne said or wrote could stop the mad surge.

A week before the election, Circumstance, Wingate, and Rebecca were discussing the phenomenon. Wingate said, "I've never seen an election like this one. What does all this mean? Is there some underlying reason for it?"

Rebecca considered that long and hard. Finally she said, "People have always responded to catchy slogans, and I'm afraid that the politicians have finally realized that. Unless I miss my guess, from now on all elections will have this kind of circus atmosphere. Candidates will become like hucksters, selling their patent slogans to gullible voters."

Circumstance dandled Forrest on her knee and the baby cooed at her. "If this election proves anything, it's that the West has become an important part of the nation. First we had Andrew Jackson, and now Harrison."

Rebecca nodded in agreement. "The days when the eastern seaboard alone can control the destiny of the nation are over."

They heard a hubbub in the street and Rebecca went to the window. "My Lord, what's happening now?" They stood at the door and watched a crowd of people rolling a huge leather ball along the avenue. The ball stood more than ten feet high, and slogans were written all over it. It took more than a dozen men to roll it along.

"What's going on?" Wingate called to one of the men in the crowd.

"A Whig delegation from the Alleghenies rolled this ball all the way to Baltimore, and now we're rolling it through Washington. It symbolizes the irresistible momentum of Harrison's campaign, and that's why we must keep the ball rolling!"

The crowd shoved the ball along while they sang:

What has caused this great commotion, motion, motion,
    Our country through?

It is the ball rolling on,
For Tippecanoe and Tyler too—Tippecanoe and Tyler too.
   And with them we'll beat little Van, Van,
       Van is a used-up man,
   And with them we'll beat little Van...

"This would be laughable if it weren't so idiotic!" Rebecca called to the revelers, but her admonition was drowned out by the second verse of the song.

In the days that followed, the Whig attacks against President Van Buren increased in intensity. Congressman Charles Ogle of Pennsylvania stood up in the House of Representatives and cried, "I am here to talk to you today about the royal splendor of the President's Palace!"

Immediately, the dozing, drinking congressmen bestirred themselves. They'd always been jealous of the accommodations given to the chief executive, and they egged Ogle on as he lambasted Van Buren.

"This palace is as splendid as that of the Caesars, and as richly adorned as the proudest Asiatic mansion. The garden has rare plants, shrubs, and parterres in the style of the Royal Gardens in England, and the men who look after these things are paid with the people's money to spend their time, plucking up by the roots, burdock and sheep sorrel. The Blue Elliptical Salon of the presidential mansion is hung with gilt mirrors as big as a barn door, and in this nefarious room are chairs that cost six hundred dollars a set!"

"Ogle's mouthing a pack of lies," Rebecca said, when she heard of his speech, "but his task has been made easier by Angelica Singleton's high-handed ways. After she tried to fob herself off as royalty, the people will believe anything."

The Whig papers picked up the charges of royal pretentions and wrote, "Is it a democracy where the President sleeps on French bedsteads, walks on Royal Wilton carpets, sits on French taborets, eats his *paté de foie gras,* and *dinde dosse* from silver plate with forks of gold, sips his *soupe à la reine* with gold spoons from a gold tureen, and rides in a gilded maroon coach? No, it's time for Old Tip's broom to sweep the President's mansion clean and return it once more to the common people!"

The next day the Whigs held a torchlight parade along Pennsylvania Avenue. The rally brought out most of the populace, bellowing a new ditty at the top of their lungs:

> Old Tip he wears a homespun coat,
> He has no ruffled shirt-wirt-wirt.
> But Mat, he has the golden plate,
> And he's a little squirt-wirt-wirt!

The *wirt* sound was made by spitting through the front teeth, which the crowd did as they passed the White House.

The Democrats tried vainly to stem the tide; they nicknamed Harrison "Granny," a reference both to his cautiousness on the battlefield and to his age—sixty-seven; he was the oldest candidate ever to run for the presidency. As a signpost of how good a chief executive Harrison would be, the Democrats suggested that the voters spell his name backwards: "Nosirrah!"

Andrew Jackson threw his formidable support to Van Buren. The Democrats took heart in the fact that the voting franchise had been broadened, giving the vote to many more people of the lower classes, traditionally sources of Democratic strength. The census of 1840, recently completed, showed that the population of the United States had soared to seventeen million. Perhaps Van Buren could squeak through if all those who were eligible voted.

On election day, the turnout proved to be phenomenal; more than seventy-eight percent of the electorate voted. When the results were tallied, Harrison garnered 1,275,011 votes to Van Buren's 1,129,102, a difference of only 140,000. But in the electoral college, Van Buren fared much worse. He'd lost the large states of New York, Pennsylvania, and Ohio by very slim margins, and he could only claim 60 electoral votes to Harrison's 234.

"Well, we've seen the con men and the hucksters and the politicians triumph," Rebecca said. "But does anybody know what William Henry Harrison really stands for?"

"Harrison arrived in Washington by train on February 9, 1841, the first President-elect to arrive in the capital by this new form of transportation," Rebecca wrote in her article for the *National Intelligencer*. "His wife, Anna Tuthill Symes Harrison, is ailing, so she didn't accompany him. She's expected to join the President when the weather gets better, sometime in May. Snow was falling when Harrison arrived, but a goodly crowd was gathered at the depot."

Rebecca thought that Harrison looked older than his years,

and very tired, but she didn't mention that in her article, lest she be accused of being pro-Democrat.

"After a warm greeting from the crowd, Harrison repaired to Gadsby's Hotel, where he refreshed himself, and afterwards went to call on President Van Buren." Rebecca also didn't mention that Van Buren told her, "Harrison's as pleased with the presidency as a lady with a new hat! But little does he know that it's Henry Clay who plans to call the tune in his administration!"

Harrison went off to Berkeley, his ancestral home in Virginia, where he stayed until a few days before the inauguration, scheduled for March 4, 1841. Sixty thousand people from all over the United States began to stream into the capital to witness Harrison's swearing-in. In Center Market Square, elated Whigs erected a log cabin headquarters, and hard cider flowed night and day, while drunks caroused through the streets.

The mob has taken over, Rebecca thought, as she watched the people dancing around the huge victory bonfires, their shadows thrown onto the night. What a far cry from the passion and idealism that was the benchmark of our Founding Fathers. Well, she thought wearily, perhaps I'm growing old, and have lived too long for these times. Am I out of step with this new wave of the future? Or is our country heading for ruin?

Chapter 34

AT SUNRISE on March 4, Rebecca was wakened from a sound sleep by a twenty-six-gun salute fired from the Mall, one round for each state. Little Forrest expressed his displeasure in a continuous howl throughout the salute.

Shortly after ten o'clock, Harrison mounted a white charger and slowly rode to the Capitol. The day was bitter cold, but he'd purposely not worn a hat, nor a greatcoat, nor gloves, but had on only a plain black frock coat.

"But he'll catch his death of cold!" Rebecca exclaimed to Wingate as she watched the President-elect pass by. Harrison was on the short side, only five foot eight, but because of his military bearing, he appeared taller, particularly in the saddle. He was surrounded by seven citizen marshals wearing yellow scarves, and was attended by the marshal of the District of Columbia and his aides. Ladies leaned from the windows of the surrounding houses, waving handkerchiefs at Harrison.

"He does look weary," Wingate said to Rebecca. "Well, he is sixty-eight, and that's a venerable age for anybody. But in the office of the President, it can be a killer."

A gust of wind from the northeast whirled down on them and they turned their backs to it, but Harrison bent his head into the wind and continued on his course.

A deafening shout went up when Harrison appeared on the

inaugural platform, erected on the east front of the Capitol. The crowd huddled against the wind that howled around the building.

Harrison began his inaugural address. Being a student of Roman history, he liberally laced his speech with a plenitude of classical allusions, most of which the listeners didn't understand.

"This is the man who lives in a log cabin and only drinks cider?" Rebecca asked derisively. "I wish he'd finish with his classical references; I'm freezing!"

Fifteen minutes ticked by, then half an hour, and still Harrison droned on. His knuckles turned white with the cold, and his breath froze, but he continued. An hour . . . an hour and a half. Finally, after almost two hours had elapsed, Harrison turned to Chief Justice Taney, who stood shivering in his black robes. Taney manged to administer the oath of office through chattering teeth.

Harrison repeated the oath in firm, solemn tones, and the men in the crowd, reacting to the gravity of the situation, removed their hats. At last Harrison was President. But the first thing he did in the official capacity was to continue with his inaugural address!

Rebecca groaned, "Why in heaven's name is he subjecting us to this? We're all going to come down with pneumonia. I wouldn't mind if his speech had any significance, if it addressed our problems. But his lecture is designed to show us how erudite he is about ancient Roman history."

Wingate beat his arms against his shoulders to keep the blood flowing. "The Democrats claimed that Harrison was too old for the job, so naturally the old soldier had to prove that he could outlast us all."

"If he doesn't finish in the next five minutes, I'm going home to soak my feet in a pail of hot water," Rebecca grumbled.

But then she and the others were absolutely startled when Harrison said, "I promise all of you standing here today that I will serve only one term." When the gasp of surprise subsided, he added, "And I will be obedient to the will of the people as expressed through the Congress of the United States."

"Now that will have Henry Clay licking his chops," Rebecca said. "It's the first time I've ever heard a President *willingly* give up any of the powers in the executive office."

With that last sentiment, Harrison concluded his address.

Still bare-headed, he mounted his horse and led the boisterous crowd back toward the White House, as the bells of the city's churches pealed. Former President Van Buren was in the crowd lining Pennsylvania Avenue, and former President John Quincy Adams watched from a window in his F Street home; later, he would write in his diary that not since George Washington had a President received such an ovation.

Tippecanoe clubs marched in random cadence; the students of George Washington University had been released from classes for the day and were there in their colorful uniforms. Circumstance spotted her son Jeremy in the parade of students and waved to him. He'd just turned fifteen, and had enrolled in the university to study medicine. That decision had pleased Wingate enormously, and he looked forward to his son going into practice with him as soon as he graduated.

Many floats rolled down the avenue, but one in particular dazzled the crowd. The largest in the procession, it was drawn by six splendidly matched white horses. On the float stood a complex weaving machine; operators worked the machine as fast as they could, and the moment a piece of cloth was woven, it was taken from the machine and thrown to the applauding crowd.

"From the looks of that, we'll soon be giving England and the rest of Europe competition in the manufacture of cloth," Rebecca said.

"Bravo says that's going to be true in all forms of manufacture," Circumstance said. "England now has the upper hand in an industrial revolution, but we'll soon be catching up, he says, because we have so many of the raw resources right on hand. Frankly, I find those concepts hard to understand, but when Bravo explains it, it seems possible."

President Harrison, fully aware of the enmity that Van Buren had created because of his refusal to make the White House accessible to the public, had invited everybody to the open house he was hosting at the mansion. His daughter-in-law, Jane Irwin Harrison, was acting as his official hostess.

When Wingate, Rebecca, and Circumstance reached the White House, they had to wait for almost an hour before they could get in, the crowds were so huge. The Whig party regulars worked hard to keep the milling mob under control; nobody wanted a repeat of the near-riot that had accompanied Andrew Jackson's first term.

They finally made their way into the jammed East Room. As Rebecca surveyed the gathering, she saw Daniel Webster, Harrison's new secretary of state, and the President, laughing and chatting. But nobody appeared to be having a better time than Henry Clay. Though Clay hadn't realized his dream of being President, Harrison had publicly promised to be obedient to the will of Congress—and Clay controlled Congress. A new era in government is about to begin, Rebcca thought, an era in which Henry Clay could easily become the most powerful man in the nation.

A month later, in early April, Wingate received a hurried summons from a medical colleague. "President Harrison has taken desperately ill. You must come immediately to the White House."

Wingate galloped over there and found a number of other doctors in Harrison's bedroom. The President lay in bed, propped high on pillows, barely able to breathe. Wingate examined him.

"Pneumonia," he said tersely to the other doctors. They all nodded sagely. "How have you treated him so far?" Wingate asked.

The doctors rattled off a litany of cures—heavy doses of castor oil, snakeweed root, opium, crude petroleum, brandy, and a dozen others.

It's a wonder he's survived this long with all those poisons, Wingate thought, but said nothing. One doctor now advised bloodletting, another advocated mustard plasters all over the chest and back, another insisted that the man would die unless the debilitating diarrhea was stopped. But all the physicians were in agreement that the President was literally drowning from the fluid in his lungs. Wingate felt that short of a miracle, the President was too old and too tired to fight off the ravages of the pneumonia.

On April 4, thirty-one days after he'd taken office, William Henry Harrison, the ninth President of the United States, died in his bed in the White House.

He lay in state in the East Room. Afterwards, the funeral cortege proceeded along Pennsylvania Avenue to the train depot, where his body was to be shipped back to North Bend, Ohio. His horse walked in the procession riderless, his stirrups turned backwards.

The death shocked the nation. Rebecca saw the ramifications

which reached far beyond the personal tragedy. She said to Bravo, who was trying to help Forrest stand up by himself, "Do you understand what this means? This is the first time in our history that a President has died in office. Who controls the executive branch of the government now? What happens now?"

That question was asked all over Washington in the House of Representatives, in the Senate, and among the members of the Supreme Court. At one of the many memorial services, Henry Clay, John Quincy Adams, and Rebecca chatted quietly about the predicament.

"We're faced with a grave constitutional crisis," Clay said somberly. Adams added, "I'm of the opinion that John Tyler, the Vice-President, is only the *acting* President, until a new election can be held."

"Henry, how do you feel about that?" Rebecca asked.

"The people will demand a new election. After all, they didn't vote for John Tyler to be President."

Of course he wants a new election, Rebecca thought, this would be the perfect opportunity for him to slip into the White House.

Adams bounced up and down on the balls of his feet. "Chief Justice Taney tells me that the learned members of the Supreme Court are burning the midnight oil, searching the Constitution for a clear definition. Naturally, there's no precedent; and this is one contingency that our Founding Fathers hadn't thought of."

Rebecca pursed her lips. "Do you remember that old legend we once talked about? Concerning the curse of the Shawnee prophet Tenskwatawa?"

"My God, I'd forgotten all about that. But surely this is only a coincidence," Clay said.

"Of course," Rebecca agreed, and they went on to talk of other things. But when Rebecca got home, she searched out some old newspaper clippings she'd filed away. She finally found them, articles printed in the *National Intelligencer* in 1811, right after the Battle of Tippecanoe.

She read the curse aloud slowly: "Every President elected in a year ending in zero will die in office." There was another condition also—that the planets Jupiter and Saturn would be conjoined in an earth sign—Capricorn, Taurus, or Virgo. Long ago she'd asked Bravo to work out the specifics for her, but she couldn't find the notes for it, and when next she saw him she asked him to do it again.

"But mother, it's only a superstition," he said. "Why not do it yourself?"

"Come, Bravo—do it for me, if only out of curiosity."

He returned the next day and said, "It looks like those conditions will be satisfied every twenty years—in 1840, 1860, 1880, 1900, 1920, 1940, 1960, 1980, and in the year 2000."

"Does that mean that every President elected in those years will die in office? What a horrifying thought!" Rebecca exclaimed.

"Well, you can see that it makes no sense," Bravo said.

Nevertheless, the mere possibility called for a bracing tumbler of bourbon. As she sipped it, Rebecca tried to rationalize away the curse. "The Shawnee medicine man had been half-crazed because he'd suffered a disastrous defeat at Tippecanoe; he'd say anything to get even. But Bravo, you're right, his prediction couldn't possibly be true, because that would mean that everything was preordained. Then what would become of free will?" she asked. "No, I can't believe in the ravings of a mad medicine man. I'll never give up my belief in free will."

Yet when she finally went to sleep that night, she tossed with horrifying nightmares. A President dying in office every twenty years—could the nation survive such repeated traumas?

When she wakened the next morning, the fear associated with the curse diminished, for the problems facing the country were far more immediate. Who *was* President? Would a new election be called? Most important, could a constitutional crisis be avoided over the accession to the highest office in the land?

Chapter 35

"HOLD ON. I'll be right down," Rebecca called to the insistent rap of the doorknocker. She'd been reading in her bedroom when she was aroused by the commotion at her front door. She glanced out the window and saw the foreshortened form of a woman with three children clutching onto her skirts. For the life of her, she couldn't figure out who it was.

She couldn't have been more astounded when she opened the door. Facing her was Kate Geary Brand, Gunning's wife. "My God!" Rebecca exclaimed. "Kate, what's happened? Gunning—?"

"Gunning is fine," Kate said.

"Is he with you?"

She shook her head. "I left him back in Kansas."

Something was terribly wrong, that much Rebecca could tell from the strained look on Kate's face. She herded the brood inside. The children were adorable, well-dressed, neat; the two boys looked very much like Gunning as a child, with bright thatches of unruly red hair and huge hazel eyes.

"So you're our grandmother?" the older boy said. "Well I knew I wouldn't like you, and I don't."

"I'm not sure yet," the other boy said.

Kate rolled her eyes in mortification. "Don't speak to your grandmother that way or I'll tan your hides." The older boy stuck out his tongue at Rebecca and dodged away when Kate went to swat him. She shrugged eloquently at Rebecca. "Takes after his father, that one does. The Devil himself lives in those golden eyes."

"What's your name?" Rebecca asked, trying to act stern but all the while absolutely enchanted with him.

"That's for me to know and you to find out," he answered belligerently and punched her in the thigh.

Rebecca promptly boxed his ears. "In my house, you'll answer when you're spoken to, and civilly." The boy rubbed his ears, surprised that this old lady had been able to move so fast. "What's your name?" Rebecca repeated, and when he didn't answer quickly enough she reached for him again. He said hurriedly, "Peter. This here's my brother Geary. He's only five, but I'm seven. This is my sister Sharon, she's almost four. Box their ears, too."

"I will if it's called for," she said. "Now from the look of you, you're all mean and frazzled as wet cats because you've been traveling for so long. So I'm going to get you something to eat, and then you're all going off to bed, and tomorrow morning when you wake up, you'll have your good manners back."

Rebecca went to the kitchen and set out some cold meats, a loaf of whole-wheat bread that she'd baked the night before, and a large platter heaped with fruit that she'd just bought at Center Market.

Forrest woke up from his nap just then, yowling, and Kate went upstairs to get him. "What a beautiful child!" she exclaimed, as she brought him down. "This must be Bravo's son. Oh, you're as wet as a little tadpole." She was in the midst of changing the boy's undergarment when Bravo arrived from work; quickly she covered the boy's nakedness.

Bravo came to her in a rush and embraced her, kissing her soundly, and Kate, seeing this-boy-turned-man, looked like she would faint from embarrassment. "How you've changed!" she exclaimed. "When I left Washington you were no more than a teenager, barely shaving, and now you're a father on your own."

"Who are you?" Peter demanded. "You leave my Ma alone!" He charged at Bravo, pummeling his leg with ferocity.

Bravo scooped him into his arms and crushed him in a bear hug. "I'm your Uncle Bravo, your father's brother, and I love you all." Soon he had all three children clambering all over him as if he was some sort of Gulliver.

After they'd eaten, the children talking at once about all the things they'd seen on their trip east, Rebecca took them upstairs to the guest room and tucked them safely into bed.

"I cannot believe that I've got seven grandchildren," Rebecca said to Kate and Bravo. The three new ones commanded her attention. Already, Peter's wide shoulders and hipless body mirrored the heroic physique of his father. Geary's gap-toothed smile and happy disposition made him seem a bit clownish, but he had a quick, eager mind. Sharon had Kate's raven hair, blue eyes, and sweeping black lashes, and she was as much a fairy-tale princess as the boys were roughnecks.

As twilight stole into the drawing room, Rebecca lit the whale-oil lamps, and Kate heaved herself into the large Chippendale armchair, looking forlorn and lost in it.

"Tell me," Rebecca said softly.

Kate's tiny shrug hinted at a weariness in her spirit. She started to speak, then her glance flicked to Bravo. He said, "Kate, it's all right. We're all family, here to help."

She bit her lip and it was a few moments before she could manage, "I think you've probably guessed. You warned me about it before I went out to join Gunning in Kansas."

"Another woman?" Rebecca asked.

Kate nodded and tears started to her eyes. Bravo leaned forward in his chair. "Tell it, Kate. Get the poisons out of you."

"Our first year at Fort Leavenworth, we were so very happy with each other. Of course they were still building the fort then, and we all had to help, and there wasn't much time for anything but work. I was always in love with Gunning, from the day that I saw him shot and dying out in Bladensburg, but I fell even more in love with him that first year. When Peter was born, you never saw a man so happy. Why, he spent a month's wages buying everybody at the fort a drink. About a year later, I found out he was sparking a lieutenant's wife. Oh, it wasn't anything serious, I thought—only a flirtation."

Bravo shook his head slowly. He'd never understand Gunning. Why would he even look at another woman if he had Kate? Since his youth, Bravo had always idolized this devoted woman who'd helped save his brother's life. The passage of the years had made her an even more attractive female.

"Now maybe it's just because we were that far away from civilization," Kate continued. "The closest town was a hundred miles away. Naturally, people confined in the small space of a fort get on each other's nerves, and Gunning and I were no different. We had a tiff just about the time that the lieutenant went out on a scouting expedition. Gunning wanted to go, but was ordered to remain at the fort. Well, one night, he just couldn't resist. I didn't know anything about it until the lieutenant's woman came to me and said she and Gunning planned to go off together, and if I was a decent person I would give him his freedom. I was pregnant with Geary then, and when I confronted Gunning he said the woman was addled, suffering from a case of fort fever, being cooped up too long with a lot of hostiles around.

"We fought and argued, Gunning swore that it would never happen again, and when Geary was born, he did mend his ways for a bit. That's what's so awful about it all. He doesn't *mean* to be unkind, the children adore him, and in everything but this, I couldn't ask for a better husband. But once he's had a drink in him, then it's the Devil goading him. Sooner or later a woman's got to decide if she's going to live like that. I took sick after Sharon was born, and we couldn't live together for a bit, and that's when he began casting his eyes on the daughter of the Indian agent. I saw my future then—one infidelity after another, until I would end up a beaten and miserable woman. I waited until Gunning was sent out on a long expedition to Santa Fe."

"Santa Fe?" Bravo interrupted.

"Oh, yes, we have scouting parties that probe deep into that part of the Spanish southwest. The moment he was gone, I left for Washington."

Rebecca sat quietly for a bit. "What do you plan to do?"

"I don't know. I need time to think, to decide."

"You're not thinking of divorce, are you?" Bravo asked anxiously.

Kate shook her head with vehemence. "I was born and raised a Catholic, and hope to die one. I believe with all my heart in the sacred vows of marriage. God heard me when I swore to love, honor, and obey, and if I go back on my word, I deserve to spend an eternity in purgatory."

"Kate, just a moment," Rebecca interrupted gently. "Surely you know that I was divorced?"

Though she realized the awkward situation she'd just created, Kate could only answer truthfully. "Aye, I know that you were divorced, but then you don't believe the way I do. Maybe the punishment is meant only for those of us who believe."

Rebecca thought that was an odd way of looking at it. She started to take Kate to task about it, but then paused. Hadn't she experienced some part of purgatory every single day since Jeremy's death? What difference did it make if one experienced the fires of hell during one's lifetime, or after death?

"I'll stay married to him, I will," Kate continued. "But I'll not be shamed this way. If it's other women he wants, then he can't share my bed."

Rebecca pondered this dilemma. Where did her loyalties lie? With the son she favored more than her other children? He'd had a notorious history with the tavern wenches in the District, he'd been duped by Véronique. One would think he'd have learned by now. Kate had agreed to marry him only after his solemn promises to reform. In many ways he had—he was slowly building a distinguished career in the army. But when it came to things of the flesh, he had the weaknesses of his father.

"What do the children want to do?" Rebecca asked.

"Oh, they want to go back, and why wouldn't they? Spoils them rotten, Gunning does, and since I'm the one who has to be heavy with the rod, they think of me as some kind of ogre."

"I know it will sort itself out," Bravo said encouragingly. "Gunning loves you, he loves his children, I can tell that much just from the few letters he's written. When he gets back to Fort Leavenworth and finds you've left, he'll come to his senses and be after you like a shot. How much longer does his enlistment run?"

"It's up in a few months. Matter of fact, Gunning was undecided about reenlisting, or for us to move to Oregon or California."

"Well, perhaps that would be an answer," Rebecca said. "Once he's in a new land, away from all the army restrictions, he could change."

"Would to God it were so," Kate said. "Though knowing Gunning as I do now, I wouldn't hold my breath. Now, Mrs. Brand, the children and I will just stay the night, and come tomorrow morning, I'll be off to find work. Perhaps my father will have me back in his tavern. Though everybody in my family will shake their heads and say, 'I told you so.'"

"You'll do nothing of the kind," Rebecca said. "First of all, you're to call me mother, or Rebecca, whichever suits you. Secondly, I've a perfectly good house in Georgetown, and it's empty at the moment. You and the children are welcome to stay there as long as you like. As for money, Gunning has some on deposit at the bank—money due him from a family invention. Fortunately, I still control the disposition of those funds, and I'd much rather see you use them to take care of the children, than to try to work at something you hated, which would only make you and the children more miserable."

"Mother's right, Kate," Bravo said. "However bad your troubles are, you're not alone. You're part of the family, and we'll solve this all together."

Kate started to cry softly then. Rebecca went to her and put her arm around her shoulder. The feel of the girl was solid, salt-of-the-earth, and Rebecca felt sure that this fine young woman had imparted that strength to her children.

"The worst thing of all is that I still love him—love him enough so that I don't know if I can live without him. Help me," she whispered to Rebecca, the misery shining in her eyes. "I ask not so much for myself, but for the children. Else they'll grow up in a family full of hate, and their lives will be twisted beyond repair. Help me to do the right thing."

The thought crossed Bravo's mind that Gunning didn't deserve this gentle, generous woman, and anger long buried in him flared up against his brother.

The following day, Rebecca got Kate and the children settled in the Georgetown house. Kate busied herself cleaning up and wouldn't consider hiring or buying anybody to help her. "Now what in heaven's name would I do with a slave underfoot?" she asked. "I'm no stranger to work; it strengthens the spirit, and it will help keep my mind off things."

Rebecca wrote immediately to Gunning and told him that his family was safe and with her. She urged him to come to Washington and salvage his marriage. She went to see Kate about twice a week, but only when invited. She would have gone every day, because she found her grandchildren as endearing and amusing as a passel of wildkittens.

Peter was clearly the leader of the pack. Geary used his ingenuity to best his brother, though that happened infrequently. Sharon had Kate's practicality, and constantly made peace between her sparring brothers. Early one evening, Rebecca was reading the children a bedtime story—Washington Irving's tale of the headless horseman. She finished and closed the book. Then Peter asked, "When's Pa coming?" and the other two joined in.

"I don't know," she said, caught unawares. "Soon, we all hope." She sat with them until they fell asleep. Oh, Gunning, she sighed, trying to think of one day when he'd given her a moment's peace. He was flawed—that much she realized—and though she'd always attributed those flaws to his father, she was too old now, and too wise, not to realize that some of the fault lay with her. Whatever weaknesses she had had been magnified in her son.

He would follow Kate to Washington, of that much she was certain. But what would happen then?

Chapter 36

"REBECCA, I tell you I've never seen anything like it," Daniel Webster declared as he downed another shot of bourbon, followed promptly by a third of the tea sandwiches that Rebecca had prepared.

Webster had always had a bullish sort of build, and in the past decade, his inordinate love of food and drink had given him a generous paunch. He still wore his dark-blue coat, beige waistcoat, and white cravat, but a great deal more fabric was used in the making of the garments. The fires that had burned in his coal-black eyes seemed to be damped somewhat by the folds of flesh.

Webster had visited Rebecca at her invitation, for she was fascinated by what was happening in the government. Vice-President Tyler had refused to consider that he was anything less than President of the United States, and had been sworn in by a justice of the Supreme Court at Brown's Hotel. Webster, who'd been appointed secretary of state by Harrison, believed that Harrison's death would allow him to control the office of the presidency. So many secretaries of state had gone on to become chief executive that the position was considered a springboard to the presidency. Webster was regaling Rebecca with the details of the first cabinet meeting Tyler had attended after being sworn in as President. "The cabinet was naturally made up of tried-and-true Whigs, whom President Harrison had appointed. So I said to Tyler, 'It was our custom, in the cabinet of the deceased President, that Harrison should preside over us. But all measures whatever, however relating to the administration, were brought before the cabinet, and their settlement was decided by a majority—each member, including the President, having one vote.'"

"How did Tyler respond to that?" Rebecca asked.

"The room was deathly quiet while we waited for his response. Then Tyler stood up, and looking like a great predatory bird, he said, 'I beg your pardon, gentlemen. I am sure I'm very glad to have in my cabinet such able statesmen as you've proved yourselves to be, and I shall be pleased to avail myself of your counsel and advice. But I shall never consent to being dictated to as to what I shall or shall not do. I, as President, will be responsible for my administration. I hope to have your cooperation in carrying out its measures; so long as you see fit to do this, I shall be glad to have you with me. When you think otherwise, your resignations will be accepted.'"

"Mercy!" Rebecca exclaimed. "Well, you certainly can't accuse Tyler of taking a weak stand. Imagine, throwing down the gauntlet that way to the entire cabinet!"

"I always suspected that he was really a Democrat in disguise," Webster sneered.

"What do you think will happen?"

"A great deal depends on how Tyler handles the issue of the new United States Bank," Webster said. "You know that Henry Clay is pushing hard for its passage. If Tyler signs it into law, we may have some peace in the government. Otherwise, it will be war between the executive and legislative branches. Since the Whigs control both houses of Congress, I doubt Tyler has a chance. Henry Clay plans to do nothing less than grind Tyler into the dust unless he goes along with Congress."

The bill for the new bank was passed by Congress, but some of its provisions weren't to Tyler's liking. Clay took this as a personal affront, and a bitter battle of words erupted. Tyler vetoed the bill. Enraged, Clay moved to chastise the President.

On September 11, 1841, every member of Tyler's cabinet resigned. Tyler, nonplussed, accepted the resignations and appointed conservative southerners to his cabinet. Only Daniel

Webster stayed on, with the excuse that he was conducting intense negotiations with Great Britain over the undeclared war on the Canadian border. That was the excuse he gave Rebecca, but she was far too astute to believe that selfless altruism lay at the heart of Webster's actions. Clearly, the secretary of state believed that his political star had a far better chance of rising if he stayed close to the source of power. What if Tyler should die? There was now no Vice-President, so the secretary of state would succeed to the presidency.

At a Thanksgiving dinner held at John Quincy Adams's house, Clay—looking thinner than ever, and slightly in his cups—held forth about the turncoat in the White House. "Tyler is a doomed man," Clay insisted. "He's a President without a party, and how long can such an anomaly last in this country? Everywhere, legislators are calling him 'His Accidency.'"

"They tell me that Tyler is trying to form a new party," Rebecca said, "one that will incorporate some middle-of-the-road policies from both Whigs and Democrats, with an emphasis on states' rights."

"It will never happen," Clay insisted. "The people aren't behind him, and that's the lesson he hasn't yet learned. Do you know that the influenza epidemic that hit the country is being called 'Tyler Grippe'?"

Everybody around the table laughed with the exception of gentle Louisa Adams. "I can't say that I like Mr. Tyler very much," she said softly, "for he wasn't elected President, and chooses not to implement the programs that won Harrison the presidency. But somehow I think that the *office* deserves more respect from the people."

"Hear, hear," Rebecca seconded her, clinking her spoon against her port glass.

"We must be rid of this man, or this country is ruined," Clay said. "The people voted for the policies of the Whig party, but this ingrate is doing everything he can to thwart us. He wants to bring Texas into the Union so that we may have more slave states." He turned to the head of the table. "Adams, you must investigate ways to bring impeachment proceedings against him."

"On what grounds?" Rebecca interjected, her pulse quickening.

"On the grounds that he's usurped the office of the presidency," Clay shot back.

Adams pulled at his sideburn whiskers. "I doubt that it will work, but it may put a scare into him, so he'll be less cavalier about using the veto. The country is grinding to a standstill. Every time we pass an important piece of legislation, Tyler digs in his heels like an obstinate southern mule and vetoes it."

"John," Rebecca asked, "how does it go with the Gag Rule? Have you made any headway in having that rescinded?"

"The wheels grind slowly, but we are making progress. At one point, mine was the only vote calling for the Gag Rule to be lifted, but now we're polling as many as fifty votes."

"How many years has it been now?" Rebecca asked.

"Almost six," Louisa Adams said in her high, sweet English-accented voice. "Every single day that the House is in session, John introduces a motion to have the slavery issue debated, and every single day he endures the villification of his fellow congressmen. Sometimes I wonder where he finds the strength to continue."

"I continue because it is our inalienable right to debate all issues, anywhere in this nation. It is guaranteed to us as free people by our Constitution, and not even the Congress has the right, morally, or legally, to prevent such an open debate. You all know me to be a moderate on the issue of abolition, but I shall never be a moderate on the right of freedom of speech. I shall continue this battle until we win, or I am dead!"

The dinner party broke up shortly thereafter, and Henry Clay and his wife Lucretia offered to take Rebecca home, but she had her own carriage with her. As Tad drove her home, she drew the fur lap rug closer around her feet. The late November air was so clear and piercing that it was all she could do to keep from sneezing. Despite the rutted roads, and the trees denuded of their leaves, Washington looked lovely this night.

"This is my city," she mused aloud. "I've seen forests cleared, swamps drained, streets paved, new gas lamps installed. I've seen it grow into the capital of this nation. Though there's still much to do, it's becoming a city worthy of its people."

Where else but in America could the problem of presidential succession have been settled so peacefully? Had it happened in one of the monarchies on the Continent, blood would have flowed. Even Mexico had one dictator after another, and now she'd heard that Santa Anna had been deposed.

As she approached her house, she saw a lamp burning in the window. She hadn't left any on when she'd gone out . . . It must be Bravo or Kate, she thought, both of them had keys to her house.

She hurried inside, and found Kate in the drawing room, pacing the floor in a state of extreme distress. Rebecca looked at her face and realized what had happened even before Kate blurted, "Gunning's come to Washington!"

"Is he all right?" Rebecca asked, as she went to the sideboard and poured two glasses of sherry. She handed one to Kate. "I know you don't drink, but this will do you good."

Kate hesitated, then downed it in one gulp, making a wry face as she did. "Aye, Gunning's fine and healthy, he is. Though angry enough to wrestle a grizzly to earth and win. Said he'd come to take me back, and when I refused, he slapped me. Can you imagine? He struck me. He'll never lay a hand on me again!"

Rebecca allowed her daughter-in-law to vent her anger. "Can I stay here tonight?" Kate beseeched her. "The children will be all right, Gunning's with them."

"Of course you can stay. But you know that you're only putting off the day of judgment."

Kate nodded, her eyes looking a trifle vacant. Then she said, "I know this is a very unfair thing to ask, you being his mother and all, but I think you're a fair woman. What would you do in my place?"

"That's impossible for me to answer. You've got to search your own heart for that."

Their conversation was interrupted by the sound of hoof-beats approaching along the avenue. Kate shuddered and gripped the arms of her chair. Then the front door burst open and Gunning charged into the house shouting, "Kate, Kate, where in blazes are you?"

She sprang to her feet when he came into the drawing room. "What have you done with the children?"

"They're all right, though crying for you. I left them with a neighbor. Kate, you've got to come back home. This is ridiculous. I haven't traveled fifteen hundred miles for you to spend the night in a separate bed."

Rebecca studied her son as he argued with Kate. The seven years he'd been away from Washington had been good. Though the flush of youth was off his face, he'd grown even more handsome. He wore his red-blond hair in a thick leonine mane, with sideburns that almost reached his jawline. The harsh winds of the prairie had weathered his features, giving him character. How old is he? she thought, and did a fast reckoning. Thirty-two . . . full grown, with the rugged physique of a frontiersman. This wasn't a schoolboy she could dominate anymore, and suddenly Rebecca felt uneasy. The elemental quality that had always existed in him—something akin to a natural disaster, like a tornado, or a waterspout—seemed emphasized, dangerously closer to the surface.

"Hello, mother," Gunning said, and gave her a quick, matter-of-fact kiss, along with a dazzling smile that showed his genuine affection for her. Then he turned his attention to Kate. "Get your cloak. Whatever problems we're having, we can straighten them out when we're alone."

"I'll not go with you," she said, stamping her foot. "For too long we've solved all our problems in bed, or at least you thought you were solving them. But then in a month, sometimes less, we'd have the same fights again. You're a philandering man, and I'll have no more of it."

He moved toward her, his face darkening. "Hold your tongue, woman," he demanded. "I'll not be spoken to that way."

"And I'll not be treated that way either," she retorted, her Irish temper flaring. "You've fooled me for the last time, Gunning Brand. I'll not spend another night with you, I don't care how many miles you've traveled."

He raised his hand and Rebecca called out sharply, "Gunning, don't you dare!"

He whirled at the sound of his mother's voice, then spat, "Mother, this is none of your business, and I'll thank you to stay out of it."

Rebecca marched to her son and poked her finger in his chest. "You are in *my* house, and anything that happens here is my business. You're not going to solve anything by beating your wife. Now you either act like a rational human being, or you get out."

"Mother, I have a great deal of affection for you, but don't push it too far. This is my wife, my family, and my problem, and you've no place here."

"Kate asked me if she could spend the night. I told her she could."

"You had no right to do that," he shouted. "No right to come between us."

"I have a right to do whatever I want in my own home," she answered, feeling the erratic pounding starting in her chest. You've got to keep your temper or all this will be for naught, she warned herself. Nevertheless, she heard herself saying, "Judging from what Kate tells me, you're behavior has been abominable."

"A fine one you are to judge," Gunning shot back. "Why don't we just say it runs in the blood? You who deceived my own father and had a bastard son by another man?"

Kate's mouth fell open and her hand moved out toward Rebecca in a gesture of shock and support.

Rebecca steeled herself, trying hard to keep her voice from breaking. "Gunning, any transgressions I've committed, I've paid for every single day. But that shouldn't concern us here. We're dealing with your life right now. You raise your hand against your wife as though she were some dumb beast you can kick or whip whenever it suits you. But she's a human being, mother of your children, and somebody you promised to cherish and protect until death do you part."

"Ah ha, Kate, you hear that?" Gunning demanded. "Till death do us part. Is this how you honor your vows? The minute I'm off on a scouting expedition for our government, you sneak away, stealing my children from me."

"You *dare* talk to me about vows?" she cried. "You who warmed the beds of all your fancy women, and God knows how many Indian squaws?"

Their vitriolic argument raged back and forth. Rebecca listened, trying with all her sense and compassion to be an arbiter for these two fiery people.

After an hour of exhausting recriminations, Gunning shook his head wearily. "Kate, when I found out that you'd left, I didn't know what to do. I was lost. I realized just how much I loved and needed you. But if it's not the same for you, then what's the use? What is it you want, Kate? Do you want a divorce?" When she shook her head he asked, "Then what?"

"I'll not have you sleeping with anybody else while you're married to me. I'll not have our children exposed to such shame. If that's what you want, then you can have it, but you can't have me. And that's my last word on it."

"Then what do you suggest?"

"I don't know. I don't know anything anymore."

Gunning moved to her in one bound and wrapped his arms around her, crushing her in his embrace. She tried to fight him off but he was so strong that resistance was useless. "You love me, you know you do," he said. "There's too much between us for you to deny it. We have three wonderful children to prove it, if nothing else. Please come home to Georgetown with me. We don't have to sleep together. We'll just talk. We've so much to talk about. Besides, I don't want to leave the children alone any longer."

At the mention of the children, Kate weakened.

"I didn't follow you all the way across the country because I didn't love you. I've always loved you, from the day you nursed me back to health, right until this very moment. All right, I've made some mistakes—" He broke off and smiled wryly, that delightful off-center grin that was so much like Zebulon's. "But men are weaker than women, and that's why we need women around—to keep us walking on the straight and narrow. I've got you for that, Kate, so come on home."

"Only if you promise that you'll never..."

"You have my word on it," he said, and kissed her forehead. Then he took her hand and led her out of the house.

Rebecca stood in the doorway, watching them as they rode off into the darkness. She wrapped her shawl tighter around her shoulders, shivering not only from the cold, but from the disaster that they'd just avoided. Thank God Kate had had enough strength and courage to give their marriage another try. Because Rebecca feared that without Kate, Gunning could easily slip into the same kind of excess that had ruined Zebulon. "Stay with him, Kate," she breathed her prayer into the night, "stay with him."

An uneasy truce existed in the house in Georgetown, and as is so often the case, the embattled sides were particularly courteous to each other. The children didn't know quite what to make of this, and more often than not, Peter's devilment was rewarded with the back of his father's hand. The boy learned to walk softly, as did Geary and Sharon.

Gunning's hitch in the army was up, and he decided not to reenlist. "Not for the moment, anyway," he told Kate.

"Do you have something else in mind?"

"The next six months or so we ought to remain right here in Georgetown. Winter's coming on, any kind of traveling we plan will be damned near impossible. Here, we can take our time and decide what we want to do with the rest of our lives."

"We talked once about moving west permanently," she said.

He nodded. "But we really can't settle in the Plains territories because the Indian reservations are all there, and I don't think it would be healthy. Sure, they're quiet now, but who can ever tell with these unpredictable hostiles? I'd rather go where we don't have to worry about the terrible winters, where we won't be looking over our shoulder for an arrow or a tomahawk everytime we step outside our front door."

"We did talk about the Oregon country. Maybe even California. They say that it's a land with trees and mountains so tall giants must have lived there."

Gunning tossed a large envelope full of leaflets on the table and said with a great laugh, "That's right, giants—and that's what we'll become when we move there."

Kate picked up the leaflets and scanned them eagerly while Gunning went on. "I like the frontier life. It's not easy—and in some ways even harder for you, because you're often stuck at home with the children. But the country is young, and we're young, and we can grow with it. There's no reason why we couldn't wind up with a ranch some thousands of acres. Look, if my sister Suzannah could do it, then I can too! We're Brands. What do you say, Kate?"

"It sounds so wonderful! Let's do it. California, or Oregon, or wherever you like." She looked at him and tears sprang to her eyes. "Gunning, let's forget everything that happened and start anew."

He reached out and gripped her hand hard.

That night, as the children lay asleep in their rooms, Kate and Gunning sat up in bed, reading through all of the leaflets about western lands. The yellow light flickered across the pages that promised cheap, plentiful acreage to anybody with the strength and will to work it.

"It will be such a wonderful life for the children," Gunning said, caught up in the adventure. "They can grow up with room to breathe, instead of being stuck in a dirty little city—for that's what Washington's become, a little city."

He reached for her hand and gently caressed her fingers. She made the slightest motion to pull back, but he put her hand on his chest and she felt his rhythmic heartbeat tingling her fingers. "That's my heart, Kate, and it beats only for you."

When he moved toward her, she didn't resist, and they made love then, a love that was as much a delight as it had been on their wedding night. She gave herself to him, renewed in her love for this man who could still reach her, still make her thrill to the call of love. She had never known another man in her life, and she knew that she never would. And for what reason? He was all that she'd ever wanted.

Throughout the night, Gunning made love to her, each time moving to an exhausting climax, yet always ready to begin anew after a brief respite. He had to imprint his mark on her, make her his, for he sensed that in this woman lay his only hope for a life of reason and peace.

Yet there was another part of him that wanted so much, wanted everything he saw . . . but she, only she was his true love. How could he ever explain that to her? That his other transgressions meant nothing to him, and only served to make him appreciate her all the more. Knowing that she could never understand this, he could only continue making love as proof of his devotion, and love yet again, until there came a time when love submerged all her doubts in her ecstasy.

Chapter 37

IN EARLY January of 1842, Dolley Madison, who'd recently returned to the capital, paid a social call on Rebecca. "I had to come back to Washington," she said over a cup of tea. "Things became far worse at Montpelier than they were here. Payne Todd tried ever so hard to manage the estate, but..." Dolley shrugged defeatedly and dabbed at her eyes.

Rebecca didn't press for details; rumor had it that Dolley's son Payne Todd had run Montpelier into the ground with his drinking and gambling debts, and had squandered all of her reserves—even the funds she'd gotten from Congress for James Madison's papers. Montpelier had been sold for debts. All Dolley had left was the house on Lafayette Square, and she had moved back in.

"At any rate, my dear Rebecca," Dolley said, "I'm not here to complain, but to extend an invitation to the wedding of President Tyler's daughter Elizabeth."

Rebecca raised her eyebrows. "But Dolley, I hardly know the Tylers. Oh, I've met John during the time he served as senator, but I've never laid eyes on Mrs. Tyler."

"That's the point," Dolley said. "Letitia Tyler, a perfectly wonderful and gentle creature, is an invalid. She and John have a wonderful marriage, and she's borne him eight children.

When she lost her youngest, the shock was so great that she
had a stroke. She's been invalided for the past four years. Since
she's moved into the White House, she hasn't officiated at any
of the functions. Her daughter-in-law Priscilla Cooper Tyler
acts as hostess. But for the wedding, Letitia's asked me to help
with the arrangements."

"I'm sure you'll do a perfectly wonderful job."

"Nonsense, my dear. I'm getting old and forgetful. You
and I both know that nobody can handle that kind of detail as
well as you. Will you help? I've already talked to Letitia about
it, and she's sending you a formal invitation in the mail."

"Dolley, if you need my help, of course I'll do it."

"It will make it so much easier for me," Dolley said, clasping
Rebecca's hands. "You and I are two of the maturest matrons
in Washington. Now, now dear, don't fret, I know you're years
younger than I, but after a certain age, there's little difference.
I don't think it would be too untoward if we escorted each
other to the wedding, do you?"

They laughed at that, then set about making plans for the
wedding day. For the ceremony, only immediate members of
the family had been invited, but the following day, the Tylers
were hosting a grand reception at the White House.

On Monday, January 31, 1842, Elizabeth Tyler was married
to William Waller in the East Room. Reverend William Hawley
of St. John's Church officiated. The simple ceremony was done
with style and taste, and the bride, a vivacious twenty-year-
old wearing white satin and lace, looked radiant.

President Tyler, tall and slender, carried himself with distinction. At fifty-two, he had thinning light brown hair, piercing
blue eyes, and a sharp aquiline nose that gave him a rapacious
expression, but his manner was that of a southern gentleman.

Mrs. Tyler, confined to her wheelchair, had been a great
beauty, but now she looked worn. She wore an unostentatious
dress and a becoming lace cap. Rebecca liked her immediately.
Like so many selfless, devoted wives of American politicians,
she'd carried all the burdens of being a wife and mother, had
raised eight children, and had depleted her own health to give
life to others.

Rebecca and Mrs. Tyler chatted briefly, and Letitia, as she
asked to be called, said, "You see, Rebecca, I don't really
know Washington very well, and I was so afraid of committing

some terrible social blunder. Thank you for your help in that regard."

"I can't imagine a woman of your refinements committing any kind of social blunder. Besides, if we women don't stick together, then whom can we count on?"

"When I married John, I never dreamed I'd wind up living in the White House," Letitia said softly. "He's had such an extraordinary career...Perhaps he'll come and chat with us." She looked across the East Room to where her husband stood, talking with the beauteous Julia Gardiner—the Rose of Long Island, as the fabulously rich debutante was called—and her current beau, Richard B. Waldron, a navy purser. President Tyler was paying Julia such lavish compliments that everybody within earshot couldn't help but remark about it.

"She's very beautiful, isn't she," Letitia said softly. "Such clear olive skin, and that hour-glass figure."

"That's not too difficult when you're that young," Rebecca said. "The girl can't be more than nineteen."

"I understand that she's twenty. Sometimes I think John would be far better off with a younger woman than with an invalid."

"Now you mustn't even think such things," Rebecca admonished. "After all, you've been his helpmate in everything he's done. Doesn't that count for anything?"

She nodded absently. "We met when he graduated from William and Mary College—four generations of Tylers had gone there. He was just seventeen then, and already intent on a life in politics. My parents disliked John, and they forbade us to marry. We continued to meet secretly, and I was so proud when he was admitted to the bar at nineteen. He wanted me to run off and marry him then, but I wouldn't dream of defying my parents. I had to win them over. Finally, when they saw me turning down all my other suitors, and I'd reached the ripe old age of twenty-three, they realized I'd never have another for a husband, and they relented.

"I was delirious with joy, and we spent two wonderful years on John's plantation. But my husband wasn't somebody to be confined, and when he was twenty-six, he ran for Congress and was elected. He traveled to Washington, but I disliked the city. It seemed like some kind of battleground to me, and not at all conducive to the rearing of children."

"It may seem that way to you," Rebecca told the First Lady,

"but I've lived here all my life, and though the District does have its drawbacks, it also creates a certain excitement in a person's life."

"Oh, I didn't mean to imply—" Letitia began, trying to apologize. "I'm sure it's a lack in my own character that prevented me from being comfortable here. At any rate, by the time John reached the tender age of thirty-five, he was governor of Virginia, and at thirty-six, he became senator. He'd been a strong supporter of Andrew Jackson's, but broke with him over the Nullification crisis."

"Yes, I remember that. His was the lone voice against giving Jackson extraordinary powers to put down a rebellion as spelled out in the Force Bill."

Letitia nodded. "It caused John to become a Whig, and so here we are."

Rebecca looked bemused. Extraordinary, that this chain of events, and the death of Harrison, should have brought Tyler to the White House. She wondered what effects Tyler's avowed states'-rights policies would have on the government.

Letitia Tyler craned her head at the laughter coming from the quarter where Julia Gardiner and her beau were standing with the President, only now the beau seemed totally eclipsed by Tyler.

There's something unfair in all this, Rebecca thought. Yes, Mr. Tyler was healthy, and though in his early fifties, still very much in his prime. But there was something uncomfortable in all the attention he was paying Julia Gardiner in the presence of his incapacitated wife.

The grand ball in celebration of the wedding was held the following day, and the mansion was thrown open to the public. The slaves that President Tyler owned saw that the guests were well supplied with food and champagne.

"Everybody in Washington of any importance is here," Dolley said to Rebecca. "Even those arch-Whigs Clay and Adams have put aside their battle in the face of love."

"The East Room is fairly ablaze with jewels," Rebecca said. "It certainly looks like Washington is going to give Philadelphia and New York competition in the social arena."

Rebecca looked around for Mrs. Tyler but was told that she'd decided to remain in her room.

Gunning had persuaded Kate to attend the ball, and though

Kate seemed a trifle ill at ease in the midst of all the splendor, Rebecca thought that her son and daughter-in-law were the handsomest couple in the room. Kate had never been one to trouble herself too much with clothes, and she'd had nothing appropriate to wear, so Rebecca had altered one of her old ballgowns, a maroon velvet dress with off-the-shoulder puffed sleeves. Kate's flawless Irish complexion was shown to advantage by the wine-colored gown, and if it clung a tifle too snugly to her buxom frame, it served to emphasize her statuesque figure. After she had danced a gavotte, a reel, and a waltz with Gunning, her blue eyes began to sparkle.

President Tyler's eyes lit up when Julia Gardiner made a gossip-provoking entrance, for this time she was escorted by *two* men. Representative Francis W. Pickens, a thirty-seven-year-old South Carolina widower with four children had asked Julia to marry him; so had Supreme Court Justice John McLean, who held her other arm. Julia hadn't yet committed herself to either man, or to anybody else for that matter.

"Oh, Dolley, I know I'm getting old when I find such flirtatious behavior just a little too silly to bear."

"I guess we forget all too easily that there was a time when we did the same thing."

"Why does it seem so cruel to me now?"

Dolley shrugged. "Perhaps it's because we now know the pain it can cause. But Julia is young, and if men have the opportunity to sow their wild oats, then why shouldn't women?"

President Tyler made his way to Julia, who was now surrounded by every unattached man in the room. They parted to make way for the President and he bowed formally and asked her to dance.

"That would be wonderful," Julia said in her lilting, musical voice. Her clear gray eyes looked searchingly at the President. "Will you have the band play a waltz?"

It was common knowledge that Tyler had expressedly forbidden his daughters ever to dance the waltz, for he considered it immoral the way couples' bodies touched during the high-spirited step. But when Julia commanded, the President couldn't say no, and at his signal, the Marine Band struck up a waltz.

At that point, Gunning and Kate joined Rebecca and Dolley. "I say, that's a splendid-looking female," Gunning said, as he watched Julia do all the intricate steps she'd learned during her grand tour on the Continent.

"She's flamboyant, I'll say that for her," Rebecca said. "But for my tastes, there's not a woman in this room who can hold a candle to our Kate."

Kate blushed furiously as Gunning slipped his arm around her waist and squeezed her. Everybody was laughing and chattering, having a splendid time, when suddenly Gunning's arm stiffened, and his eyes looked on the woman who'd just swept into the East Room.

Never did a more fragile apparition float across the Versailles parquet floor, taking steps so rapidly beneath her trailing gown that she seemed suspended. Her dress was black peau de soie, with an overlay of black lace, the waist incredibly nipped, the skirts flaring. A heavy diamond bracelet flashed on her left wrist, a river of diamonds cascaded down her throat and bosom, and long thin strands of diamonds coiled in the loose knot of her raven hair. Had the gown been any other color, the display of diamonds would have been ostentatious, if not crass. But she wore them with an artless air, and sparkling with white fire, she drew every eye to her, including those of Julia Gardiner, who was unaccustomed to being upstaged.

"My God, it's Véronique," Gunning croaked, and tried to clear his throat.

Kate tensed, suddenly feeling very coarse and lumpy alongside this airy creature who had the quality of a firefly.

Rebecca looked around quickly, to see if Devroe had accompanied his wife. But he was nowhere in sight; then she remembered hearing that he'd gone off to England on a business trip. "We can be thankful for that," she whispered under her breath. With a sick, sinking feeling in her stomach, she recalled the last time that her son and Devroe had met, on the dueling fields of Bladensburg. There, through Devroe's deceit, Gunning had almost lost his life. At that time, Gunning had been married to Véronique, and the duel had occurred because Gunning discovered his wife in bed with Devroe, the whole nefarious episode prearranged by Devroe. Gunning had been more than willing to let Devroe have Véronique, but Devroe insisted that his honor had been compromised, and demanded satisfaction. Though Gunning had discharged his dueling pistol harmlessly in the air, thinking that Devroe couldn't shoot because of his crippled arm, Devroe had then shifted his pistol to his other hand—he was ambidextrous—aimed for Gunning's heart, and fired. The bullet had lodged in Gunning's chest, and only

Wingate's skill as a surgeon, Kate's attentive nursing, and a great deal of luck had saved Gunning's life. While Gunning was recuperating, his marriage to Véronique was annulled, and he had later married Kate.

Véronique glided to the British minister plenipotentiary; when the waltz was over, he made a point of introducing Véronique to President Tyler and Julia Gardiner.

The two women immediately recognized that they were cut from the same bolt, and probed and tested each other, trying to find the weak spot. But when Julia learned that Véronique was married to the wealthiest man in the District, was fifteen years her senior, and had no designs on anybody, particularly not the President, she relaxed.

Véronique gushed, "My dear Julia, if I may be so forward as to call you by your lovely first name—but then I feel that I have known you forever; sisters, *non?*—I saw you in the advertisement in the newspapers, and you looked wonderful. What a courageous thing to do."

Julia pursed her lips, trying to determine if Véronique was castigating her, but she could detect no hint of dissembling on the Frenchwoman's part. Julia had always been a daring female. Darling daughter of David Gardiner, who owned Gardiner's Island just off Long Island, Julia had been instructed that a lady's name appeared in the newspapers only three times: at her birth, at the announcement of her wedding, and at her funeral. But Julia, a free spirit, thumbed her nose at such silly social restrictions and appeared in a newspaper advertisement for a department store in New York City. The caption on the ad read, "The Rose of Long Island," and showed Julia, sumptuously gowned, wearing a lace cap and veil, in addition to carrying a parasol to shield her face from the sun, and holding a placard that read, "I'll purchase at Bogert and Mecamly's, 86 Ninth Avenue. Their goods are beautiful and astonishingly cheap."

Her endorsement was the beginning of testimonial advertising in the United States, and she came to be considered the first fashion model.

Véronique discovered that Julia spoke French, and soon they were chattering away, becoming as thick as conspirators as they discussed the men in the room. Julia liked Véronique's hard cutting edge, and strangely enough, Véronique felt that she'd found a kindred spirit in this sophisticated, witty youngster. She was a bit too fleshy to be really beautiful, but then American men preferred their women with meat on their bones.

Véronique kept chatting away, for she knew that if she stopped she might scream. She'd come to this reception because she'd heard a rumor that Gunning had returned from Kansas. When she'd first seen him, standing a head taller than most of the other men in the room, she thought she'd faint from the shock. Then she realized that shock wasn't the reason for her distress; her trembling was desire. As she gazed at him, remembering the rippling muscles of his wonderfully endowed body, remembering the days and nights when they'd made endless love, she swore to herself, "I will have him again."

Chapter 38

SEEING VÉRONIQUE stealing glances at Gunning, Kate said, "That's your first, isn't it? I don't think I've ever seen a more elegant woman. She's very beautiful."

"I once thought so," Gunning said. "But her beauty is only a façade. Beneath that taut skin and makeup lies a soul all worm-eaten. Anyway, Kate, our marriage was annulled, so in the eyes of man and God, it never happened, more's the blessing."

Kate took heart from that, took heart that Gunning avoided any contact with Véronique. When they returned to Georgetown later that night, she and Gunning made love with tenderness and compassion drawn from a new wellspring.

Two months later Kate discovered that she was pregnant again, and there was much rejoicing in both Brand households. Rebecca insisted that they delay their trip west, at least until the baby was born. "Gunning, it's unfair to ask Kate to travel and work as hard as she'll have to when she's carrying a child. Wait another year. Stay in Washington, save your money. Find out exactly where you want to settle, and by that time the baby will be old enough to travel."

"What do you say, Kate?" Gunning asked.

Kate would have preferred to be gone, but this pregnancy

wasn't an easy one, and finally she gave into Rebecca's arguments. Gunning took over the running of the Breech-Brand Stone Works, and with the recession easing, and his own gregariousness, business began to pick up. Gunning was a man that most men liked, and women adored, and within six months, he'd doubled the business.

By the beginning of summer it became evident that President Tyler and Congress were never going to have a peaceful moment between them. Then something happened that had never happened to a President before; the Whigs, infuriated with his endless vetoes, drummed him out of their party. The Democrats, considering him little more than a turncoat, turned away from him also, and Tyler found himself with little if any power. His plans to have Texas admitted to the Union were constantly thwarted by the Whig Congress, who saw in it nothing but a plot by southerners to increase slave-holding territory. Tyler set about trying to build a power base for a new political party in the country, a mélange of southern conservatives, middle-of-the-roaders, and advocates of states' rights.

In early autumn, personal tragedy struck the Tylers when Letitia died. "She just drifted away," Dolley told Rebecca, "almost as if she'd lost the will to live. Her daughters placed a damask rose in her hand, she closed her eyes, and in her own gentle way, she was gone."

President Tyler went into deep mourning, which was eased somewhat by the appearance of Julia Gardiner, who returned to Washington to express her condolences personally to the President.

In October of 1842, when Kate was in her seventh month, she began to stain, and Wingate became quite concerned. "You're not to have any relations with Gunning at all," he warned her. "Not until after you've given birth."

"And how am I going to tell Gunning something like that? It's hard enough as it is with this great lump I've become. But none at all? That won't sit easy with him, I can tell you that."

"We're talking about your life, and the life of the child," Wingate insisted. "He's a mature man and he'll just have to learn how to control himself."

To make sure that Gunning fully understood the dangers,

Wingate warned him himself. Gunning was upset, but understood completely.

One evening, fretting under the strain of two weeks of enforced abstinence, Gunning rode over to Bravo's house, just to get away from the temptation of Kate. The brothers were getting along a bit better than usual, though Gunning still acted with the overbearing quality of an older brother. Gunning found Bravo working in his studio, finishing some last-minute adjustments on a model of the magnetic telegraph he'd helped Samuel Morse develop.

"Congress finally voted us enough funds to run a line from here to Baltimore to see whether we can really transmit messages by wire. In a year or so, as soon as the lines are up, we should know once and for all."

"It sounds like a toy to me," Gunning said. His frustrations were beginning to wear him down and he said, "Bravo, what do you say we go over to the Indian Queen and hoist a few? I'll give you a chance to drink me under the table, see what kind of man you've become."

"I'd like nothing better, Gunning, but I promised Morse I'd have this new armature wired by tomorrow. What about tomorrow night, then I'll have a real reason to celebrate."

"All right then, tomorrow," Gunning agreed. He hung around the studio for a while longer, but Bravo was so preoccupied that he finally left.

"I don't feel like waiting for tomorrow," Gunning said to himself and rode over to the Indian Queen. In the inn, he met some old friends and bought a round of drinks for them, they returned the favor, and in a short while, Gunning was feeling immeasurably better.

That day, Véronique Connaught had come to Washington to do some shopping. When it grew too late to return to the plantation, she decided to stay in the suite at the Indian Queen that Devroe kept. Her presence in the capital wasn't totally by chance, for since she'd discovered that Gunning was back in Washington, she'd made frequent trips into the city, hoping they'd eventually run into each other. Devroe had returned from his mission to London, but within the week had left for Norfolk, Virginia.

"But why in heaven's name Norfolk?" Véronique had asked.

"Because, my dear, a new steam-powered American frigate,

the *Princeton*, is being outfitted there," Devroe said. He massaged his crippled arm endlessly, a sure sign that he was upset.

"I cannot for the life of me imagine why you are so distressed about a ship."

"This is no ordinary vessel," he snapped. "Our informants tell us that when it's completed and armed, it will be one of the most powerful ships afloat. One of its guns is capable of hurling a two-hundred-pound shell more than three miles!"

"*Formidable!*" Véronique exclaimed. Suddenly, she understood the cause of Devroe's distress. "Ah, a fleet of such American ships could conceivably challenge England's supremacy of the high seas."

"Precisely. So I must go to Norfolk and learn all I can."

Véronique wasn't displeased at Devroe's leaving, for it gave her freedom to pursue Gunning.

About ten o'clock that night, when the tavern at the Indian Queen closed, Véronique happened to be standing at the hotel window, out of sorts. She saw the half-drunken patrons stumble out of the front door, and then she spied Gunning. Throwing aside every vestige of caution, she flung on her cloak, ran downstairs, and followed him through the dark streets.

He was weaving his way down the streets, singing at the top of his lungs and not quite hitting the notes. He stopped to pet a stray cat, hunkering down to talk to it. This allowed Véronique to catch up to him. He stared up at her, the alcohol fuddling his brain, and as he tried to stand, he stumbled against her. She caught him and steadied him.

"We must get you off the streets," she said urgently, "or the constable will arrest you for being drunk, and you will have to spend time in jail."

"The constable?" he slurred. The odor of her exotic, expensive perfume overwhelmed him. She allowed her cloak to fall open and his eyes fastened on the delicate curve of her bosom. "Véronique," he mumbled.

"Yes, it's Véronique," she whispered, as she placed his arm over her shoulder. Staggering under his weight, she led him to a vacant building on a side street. She knew about this warehouse, because Devroe was buying it as an investment. They made their way into the bleak, empty-smelling space. She thought she heard some small night creature scurrying across the floor, and she stamped her foot to frighten it off.

Moonlight filtered through the dusty panes, painting a moon-window on the floor.

To Gunning, drunk and disoriented, the world seemed up-side down. "Where am I?" he muttered.

"You're with me," she answered firmly, and in the breathing darkness, reached up to brush his lips with hers.

He stared at her full heavy lips, lips that had once taught him so much, and then she kissed him again, this time using her full and formidable knowledge. For a moment, some decent part of him said no, and he fought back. Kate was home, waiting; this woman had deceived him once, and would deceive him again. But the alcohol in his blood and her scent met and mingled in his brain, and that potent alchemy fogged his reason. Her passion became so insistent that it ignited his own. Her lips, warm and yielding, began sucking his resistance from him until he could no longer think, but just moved to a primitive lust of the blood.

They were out of their clothes in moments. She employed all the tricks she'd ever learned. There came a time when Gunning was brutal with her, pounding away at her betrayal, taking violent pleasure in the fact that she was now cuckolding Devroe, as she'd once done to him.

But if he thought his brutality would be a punishment he was mistaken, for this only roused the dormant beast in Véronique, and she matched him in passion. They rolled around on the floor, tearing at each other with their teeth, leaving marks on each other's bodies, and sometimes even drawing blood.

At last they lay limp from exhaustion, and she sprawled alongside him, her hair disheveled, her chest heaving, her body sated. *"Mon dieu,"* she whispered huskily, "I had forgotten how wonderful we were together." Some dim corner of her brain warned her how dangerous this was—not the prospect of being discovered, though that was a consideration. This fear struck deeper, the fear that she might be falling in love with this extraordinary creature again.

With that on her mind, she dozed off briefly. When she wakened, she found herself alone in the empty warehouse. She hissed, "Gunning! Gunning, where are you?"

She heard nothing but another scurry of clawed feet and it made her flesh crawl this time. She dressed quickly, alternately frightened and angry that he'd deserted her. But she knew that she must pursue him until she had him again. What would happen when Devroe returned from Norfolk? She would have to choose then...the choices were so devastating that she couldn't bear to think of them.

She remained at the Indian Queen the following day, desperate to see Gunning. All night long she'd struggled with herself, relived the kind of life she'd led with Devroe, and found it lacking. Hourly, her desire for Gunning grew into an obsession which she couldn't control. She would leave Devroe and all the comforts he offered—yes, she would even leave her children.

Late that afternoon, she set up a watch at Gunning's house in Georgetown, and when he left, followed him. Before he could reach Bravo's studio on I Street, she intercepted him. She dismounted and caught the bridle of his horse. "I must talk to you, my darling."

Gunning, perfectly sober now, looked at her and spat. She blanched and reached out for him, but he snarled, "Whore! That's all you've ever been, a whore. Get out of my sight. I detest myself for what I did. I'll never have anything to do with you again."

Tears started to her eyes, and her cheeks flamed with the shame of it all, for she'd come to tell him she would run off with him that very day. "Oh, Gunning, no, please, you don't understand—"

He shoved her away roughly and she fell in the mud. She watched him gallop off.

Véronique went back to the hotel. That night, in her rage, she wrote an anonymous note to Kate Brand. "Your husband is a monster," she wrote. "How could I know that he was going to deceive me? I'm a poor girl, not yet fifteen, and he's gotten me with child. He refuses to help, and so I implore you to see that justice is done. If you don't believe me, look at his body tonight when he gets home. You'll find my teeth marks all over him, from when I tried to fight him . . . teeth marks everywhere. How can he deny the truth of those marks? From a fallen friend who would not see you deceived as I've been deceived."

When Kate got the note, she began to retch violently. This pregnancy had distressed her terribly; she didn't know why, but the months of carrying new life hadn't been as wonderful as her other pregnancies. This note only intensified her fears. When Gunning came home that evening, after carousing with Bravo, she helped him to undress before he fell into bed; she saw the telltale black-and-blue marks all over his body... everywhere.

Who can gauge what betrayal can do to the human heart? Who can measure and weigh its consequences?

She went into labor then, but Gunning had passed out. Kate suffered until first light, then sent Peter riding to get Wingate. He came as quickly as he could. For hours Kate labored to bring the child into the world, and when she finally did, the little girl was born dead.

Kate acted as if she wanted to die too. When Gunning came into the room to console her, she turned her face to the wall and wouldn't speak to him. Wingate tried to break through to her, but she just repeated, "Just leave me alone. Oh, my poor, sweet little girl."

At wit's end, Wingate left Rebecca and Circumstance alone with Kate. Finally she broke down and sobbed out the story. She showed them the note.

Rebecca, in a bloodless rage, took the letter into the dining room where Gunning sat and slammed it down on the table in front of him. "Is there any truth in this? Think carefully before you answer, for your future with Kate may depend on it."

Gunning stared at the note, and said incredulously, "It's that damned bitch, Véronique."

"Véronique?" Rebecca cried, aghast. "Did you sleep with her?"

"No, I didn't *sleep* with her. One night I got drunk and she waylaid me. I didn't know what I was doing. When she approached me again, I fought her off. Told her to go to hell. That's why she sent Kate the letter, to make everybody as miserable as she is."

Gunning's explanation didn't help Kate, not after the death of her child. In her exhausted and tormented mind, she viewed this as the death of her marriage also. She whispered to Gunning, "I'll never let you touch me. When we decided to salvage our marriage, we made a vow to God. You've broken that vow, and I'll never trust you again."

Gunning groaned, and then his temper flared. "Kate, I was drunk! I didn't know what I was doing. But the moment I realized what had happened, I corrected myself. Why, even the Prodigal Son was accepted back."

"Prodigal Son, is it? You know how to quote the Good Book, but only when it suits you. How many times will you sin, come crawling back, only to go off and sin again? Gunning, I don't have the strength for you anymore. I loved you, but you've killed that love, the way our child was killed . . ."

For days, Gunning tried to reason with Kate, but she remained inconsolable. Wingate told Gunning that many women who'd lost children went through such a period, and that it would just take time.

It reached a point where every time Kate saw Gunning, she dissolved into silent tears. He couldn't take that constant condemnation; he fretted, then grew hardened to what he believed was her willful unreasonableness. One day he told her that he'd heard of an expedition being formed by Zebulon Pike to explore the interior of the country, and thought that he might go on such a journey. Or he'd just met John Frémont, who'd married Thomas Hart Benton's daughter. Frémont was leaving to map the territory west of the Rocky Mountains. "I'm thinking maybe of joining up with Frémont," Gunning said.

"Do what you like," she said dully, "for that's what you'll do anyway."

Pushed to his limits, Gunning investigated both the Pike and Frémont expeditions. They were only in the planning stages, and Gunning felt so choked by Washington that he had to do something immediately.

That week, Gunning reenlisted for two more years in the army. He asked for, and received, duty with his old outfit in Fort Leavenworth, serving under Major Kearny. Shortly thereafter, he made ready to leave for the Kansas territory.

"Time, that's the only thing that will cure Kate," Gunning said to Bravo. "Time to forget the death of our little girl, time for forgiveness to soften her heart."

"You do understand that in part you're responsible for her state of mind, don't you?" Bravo asked.

"Ay, but it's not a lecture I need now. I love the girl, but I'm not so stupid that I don't know there's something uncontrollable in me. I've brought misery to her, to myself, and if I stay around Washington any longer, I'll bring misery to our children."

Gunning went to Rebecca and told her to give Kate and the

children every cent of his share in the Brand inheritance. Then
he rode west.

When Kate discovered what Gunning had done, it pried her
from one somber mood into another. Now she felt abandoned.
"It's true that I asked him to get out of my life," she told Bravo,
"but I suppose I never expected him to listen to me."

"If you truly feel that way, then you must go after him,"
Bravo told her.

She shook her head slowly. "I'm not yet well enough to go
traipsing after him."

Bravo knew that pride had a great deal to do with her
decision.

"I'll stay here in Washington with the children, and make
some kind of life for myself. Bravo, I would ask you something.
Your little Forrest—don't you think he'd be better off growing
up with other children? Rebecca isn't so young that she can
handle a rambunctious child. Let Forrest come and live with
me. I'll love him as if he were my own. You can come see
him whenever you want, and somehow . . ."

Bravo knew that in Kate's mind, Forrest might take the
place of the little girl she'd lost. When he told Rebecca about
it, she hesitantly agreed that Kate might have a point. So Forrest
moved to Georgetown to be with his aunt and his cousins, and
was soon absorbed into that family.

The days followed one after the other for Kate, and soon
the demands of the children, their growing pains, their scrapes
and illnesses, blunted what had happened and brought her back
once more into life. She knew that she'd never give her heart
again, and there was some small consolation in that . . . At least
she'd never again be hurt.

Chapter 39

SIX MONTHS after the death of his wife, President Tyler found himself so bereft that he did the only thing he could to bring himself heart's ease: he asked Julia Gardiner to marry him. A number of his children were older than the Rose of Long Island, and they were distressed. Several government officials and friends of Tyler's suggested that such a May-December marriage might be unseemly for a man in his position, and might damage his career. But Tyler had never taken orders from anybody, and he was not about to change now, particularly when the cause was true love. He pressed his suit with Julia.

The Rose of Long Island wouldn't say yes, she wouldn't say no, but rather enjoyed her position—being courted by the most important man in the nation, yet also available to the younger swains who still panted after her.

"And why *not* have the best of all possible worlds?" Véronique assured Julia. With Gunning gone and Devroe back, Véronique had slipped back into her role of devoted wife, mother, and mistress of the Connaught estates. She entertained the Gardiners lavishly and so ingratiated herself that she became Julia's confidante. The Gardiners were weekending at the Connaught estate, and the two women had spent most of their time planning strategy.

"The most important question is, Do you love him?"

"How can I tell something like that?" Julia asked. "Can one love a man thirty years older with the same passion as a contemporary? Still, when I'm with him, I feel comfortable, safe, the way I do with my father."

"Whatever you decide, you mustn't say yes too quickly, otherwise it would look insensitive, so soon after Mrs. Tyler's death. Nor must you say no so vehemently that you permanently discourage the President."

"Oh, there's no fear of that, I can assure you. Why the President hangs on my every word, applauds everything I do. Véronique, I've come to cherish you as a sister, and sisters have no false modesty between them. I tell you that the President believes that I am the most beautiful woman of the age, and the most accomplished. I'm quoting him exactly."

"To be sure," Véronique agreed. The silly snit did have a certain *joie de vivre*, but as to being *the* most accomplished or the most beautiful woman of her age—*tiens!*—how blind and stupid youth could be.

"Tell me, my dear Véronique, do *you* think he's too old for me?"

"My dear sister, when it comes to true love, has age ever really meant anything? Look at Caesar and Cleopatra. She was younger than you when Caesar paid her court, and Caesar was far older than Tyler. Did they not go down in history as one of the most passionate couples of all time? Why, empires rose and fell all about them. Nor did having Caesar ultimately prevent Cleopatra from also having her Mark Antony."

"You know, I never really thought of that! Oh, Véronique, you're so clever; that's why I feel I can talk to you rather than to those gossipy old biddies in the capital. President Tyler does have a lovely voice. I could listen to him declaim all day long."

"Of course, you would also become First Lady of the land. That alone should be an inducement. Knowing what I do of you, I can safely predict that you'll bring style and tone to that mansion, something this country sorely needs. Who is the supposed social arbiter in Washington? Dolley Madison, that mummified relic. You, who have traveled on the Continent, could be responsible for a golden age at the White House, and history would record you as a heroine!"

"Do you really think so?" Julia asked. "I do have a certain flair for entertaining."

"Think so? I *know* it with all my heart. Now here is what
you should do . . ."

Three months later, President Tyler again asked Julia to
marry him, and one evening chased her all around the East
Room as the Rose shrieked her delight. When he caught her,
she still wouldn't commit herself, pleading that she needed the
summer in East Hampton to plumb the depths of her true feelings.

She departed, but she and President Tyler corresponded
almost every day. Somehow, the President's declarations of
love became known all over East Hampton, pretty soon it had
spread to include all of Long Island, and then the entire eastern
seaboard. Julia insisted that she'd no idea how the information
ever leaked out, but she did revel in all the attention being paid
her by eager reporters, and by local politicians anxious to have
a speaking acquaintance with her should she ever marry the
President.

In December of 1843, Kate Brand received her first letter
from Gunning. The children crowded around her as she read.

"My darling Kate, I arrived in Fort Leavenworth amid all
sorts of rumors about Indian uprisings, and so I've been out
on patrol until now and haven't had a chance to write. The
Indians are miserable here; many of them come from warmer
climates like Georgia and Florida, and can't adjust to the brutal
winters on the plains. As a matter of fact, neither can I!

"How are the children? Tell them that they'd better behave
themselves, or I'll take down their britches and tan their hides."

Kate put the letter down for a moment and thought, Gunning
could have used some of that discipline in his youth. Perhaps
things would have turned out differently. She began to read
again.

"Kate, I've thought so much of what's gone on between us,
thought of how wrong I've been, and I do humbly beg your
forgiveness." At this point Kate broke off, unable to see through
her tears.

"We've come such a long way in our marriage, Kate. We've
given life to three wonderful children, and that should be more
important than the one we've failed with. I know how painful
it must be to you; many nights I lie awake and wonder what
our little girl would have looked like, as I wonder now . . . But

we must all opt for life, Kate, we must do the things that keep
us going, and help the next generation on its way.

"I love you. I want you here by my side. If you come, I
swear on my eyes that you'll never be deceived again. I know
I can't force you to make any decisions in haste; the pain must
still be too fresh. But think on it, Kate, let time heal the wounds,
and know that I'm here and waiting whenever you decide that
we've punished each other enough. Your loving husband, Gunning."

"Let's go back to Pa!" Peter cried out, and Geary chimed
in, "I want to go back too. I like it better out there, not so
much school and things." Sharon, who was holding Forrest,
said, "When we go, I want to take Forrest with us."

Kate quieted her children. "Maybe one day we'll go back,
but not just yet."

That night, when she prepared for bed, Kate lit a candle for
the repose of the child she'd lost. She also prayed to God that
she would be able to live with her husband again someday, lie
with him, love him as she had once loved him. Right now, the
thought of such a thing was so abhorrent that it turned her flesh
to stone.

Julia Gardiner returned to Washington in February of 1844
after a dazzling autumn social season in New York. Her sister
Margaret and her father David Gardiner accompanied her as
chaperones; it was well that they did, for rumors spread through
Washington like brushfires. The Gardiners were constant visitors at the White House, where intimate soirees were held,
which often included the Connaughts. For an evening's entertainment, President Tyler, an accomplished violinist, would
accompany Julia while she strummed her guitar. The President
was hopelessly smitten; his children hardened their position
against Julia, some of them even leaving the White House to
return to Virginia. Daniel Webster, who'd finally resigned from
Tyler's cabinet and returned to the Senate, poked fun at the
"aging paramour," and John Quincy Adams wrote in his diary,
"The President is a subject of ridicule to most people in the
capital."

Ladies gossiped behind their fans, legislators nudged each
other in the ribs in the corridors of Congress. What could
possibly be the outcome of this bizarre match? Even the President's valet, who'd been with him for years, walked around

shaking his nappy white head. "No good's going to come of this, I tell you, no good's going to come of this."

"But why?" Tyler asked, somewhat amused by his slave's concern. "I'm in my prime. I can fulfill my marital functions. I'm in my prime."

"That may be, Mr. President, but when she's in *her* prime, where's *your* prime going to be?"

Early in February, Bravo received an invitation from the new secretary of state, Upshur, to cruise down the Potomac on the navy's new steam frigate, the *Princeton*. The navy was inordinately proud of this first screw-propelled vessel, because it carried two of the largest cannon then afloat, dubbed the Peacemakers.

Bravo was one of three hundred prominent Washingtonians invited on the cruise. He'd been included, not only because of his work with Samuel Morse, but because he'd recently submitted a number of ideas to the ship's designer, a Swedish inventor named John Ericsson, on how to increase the efficiency of the *Princeton*'s steam engines. Ericsson had incorporated some of Bravo's ideas.

Rebecca, Circumstance, and Wingate had also been invited, Wingate had wangled an invitation for his son Jeremy, and the Granges and the Brands decided to make a special outing of the occasion. A gay crowd boarded the vessel, docked at the Navy Yard, on a beautiful sunny morning in late February. As Rebecca walked up the gangplank she remarked to Circumstance, "Why, everybody who's the least important in Washington has turned out for the event. Even the Whigs."

President Tyler was piped aboard and greeted with a smart salute from Commodore Robert F. Stockton, captain of the *Princeton*. Tyler escorted Julia Gardiner, swathed in sables, and attended by her sister and father. Jaunty plumes announced the arrival of Dolley Madison, with several cabinet members in tow, including the secretaries of the navy and state. Véronique and Devroe arrived in the black-and-gold Connaught carriage. Devroe appeared quite nervous, and at the last minute hesitated about boarding, but finally did. The gangplank was pulled up, and the *Princeton* slipped from its berth and eased out into the Potomac.

The sun sparkled off the waters of the river, and the capital slowly receded. Soon swamp and forest lined both shores of the river, waterfowl abounded, and the haunting cry of gulls followed the boat. Belowdecks, cooks and stewards busily prepared lunch for the horde. The *Princeton* continued to steam down the Potomac, its power evident in the mighty surge that the passengers felt beneath their feet.

Then came the moment that everybody had been waiting for: Commodore Stockton prepared to demonstrate the Peacemaker. Devroe Connaught took Véronique's arm and led her away from the gun. "There's no telling what can happen with an untried weapon." Though she wanted to see it close hand, something in the tone of his voice made her follow him.

The perfectly drilled gun crew took the two-hundred-and-twenty-five pound shell on a dolley from the main munitions magazine to the monstrous twelve-inch gun. They loaded the shell, and at a signal from the commander, fired it.

The gun thundered and recoiled, striking silence into the awe-stricken crowd. The shell whistled through the air, to explode three miles downstream, sending a plume of water high into the air. A riotous cheer rose from the onlookers.

"If we'd had one ship like that patrolling the Great Lakes, there never would have been a threat of war with Canada, and Webster could have negotiated a much better treaty for us," said the secretary of war, and the secretary of the navy agreed wholeheartedly.

The gun was fired several more times; each time prearranged targets were demolished by the gunners' accuracy. "With a few frigates like these, it's not England who'll rule the waves!" a slightly inebriated senator shouted and the cry was picked up by other patriots. Véronique felt Devroe stiffen; he began to massage his crippled arm.

As the bombardment continued, Bravo said to Circumstance and Wingate, "I don't like this. They're firing too often. John Ericsson perfected one of the guns, but the other was built by Commodore Stockton to Ericsson's specifications. The navy should have tested Stockton's gun for several months before allowing the public to participate in something like this."

"If you're that worried, shouldn't you tell Commodore Stockton, or perhaps Secretary of the Navy Gilmer?" Circumstance asked.

"I've talked to both of them," Bravo confided, "but both men waved aside my objections."

"Why wouldn't they?" Wingate observed. "This has been

a dreary administration for Tyler and his cabinet, with very little in the way of constructive legislation. Now this demonstration of our power is making them look good."

Julia Gardiner was chatting with Dolley Madison, Rebecca, and her father when a steward came up to her. "Miss Cardiner, the President wishes to escort you to the collation which is just being served."

"Oh, I suppose I will have to obey orders," Julia laughed. "Father, will you come? I must have my chaperone with me at all times, or God knows what the gossips will say."

David Gardiner accompanied his daughter belowdecks. Dolley took Rebecca's arm and hastened to follow. Dolley ate whenever she could at these functions, there being precious little food in her own house. Though Rebecca didn't feel much like eating, she was curious to see what the rest of the frigate looked like.

When Rebecca and Dolley reached the officer's mess, they found that President Tyler had already seated Julia at the head of the table with him, and both were sipping glasses of champagne. Julia's father stood directly behind her chair. The food being quite agreeable, Dolley finished her portion quickly, and Rebecca quietly passed her friend her own plate.

Then Devroe and Véronique appeared, and Julia insisted that they have champagne with her and the President.

"It makes my gorge rise to see the Connaughts so intimate with the President," Rebecca muttered, and Dolley clucked, "It just shows you that money can gain you entree almost anywhere."

Several minutes later, a navy lieutenant ducked his way into the officer's mess and said, "Mr. President, we're preparing to fire another round, and would be most honored if you'd light the fuse."

President Tyler half-rose, but Julia hadn't yet finished with her dessert of strawberries and champagne, and so he said, "I'm afraid that I'll have to forgo that honor; I'm otherwise engaged."

"Oh, Mr. President, perhaps you should do it," Devroe began. "It is, after all, such a splendid accomplishment."

Having eyes and ears only for Julia, Tyler declined. But Mr. Gardiner, the secretary of the navy, and the secretary of state went topside to witness the new round of firings.

On deck, the gunners were going through their ritual; the

cannon barrel was swabbed and loaded. Then the gun commander touched the lighted taper to the gunhole, and as Bravo
watched, a mighty explosion rent the air, throwing him off his
feet. The cannon exploded into thousands of fragments, and
amid the geyser of fire and the black pall of smoke, shrapnel
raked the decks, flames of fire fountained everywhere, one
tongue searing toward the main ammunition magazine.

Screams of horror blended with cries of pain as men were
cut down by the deadly shrapnel or were engulfed in the fire.
Those who'd been belowdecks hurried topdeck. Rebecca fought
her way up the ladder and searched frantically for members of
her family. She saw Wingate crouched over Circumstance who'd
been lacerated in the arm and neck by the shrapnel. But Rebecca
couldn't see Bravo anywhere. She clutched her handkerchief
to her mouth and nose against the acrid smoke as she picked
her way among the fallen bodies. The ship's whistle sent up
an unending scream, which only added to the confusion.

Then Rebecca found Bravo lying stunned against the bulk-
head. "Are you all right?" she cried, shaking his shoulder.

He nodded groggily. "I think so." He hiked himself to his
feet, then caught sight of the blaze headed toward the ammunition magazine. "Mother, the fire—"

She turned and saw what he meant. He staggered toward a
group of sailors who were helping the wounded and cried,
"Never mind them, if the fire reaches the magazine, we'll all
be dead!"

They began beating at the flames with their coats, calling
for the fire brigade on the double. Other sailors joined in and
gradually the flames were beaten back.

Julia Gardiner arrived on the deck amidst all the turmoil.
When she was told that her father had been killed, she went
berserk. She screamed in agony, her eyes rolled back in her
head, and she fainted dead away in the arms of President Tyler.

The ship limped for the nearest dock. The President started
to carry the unconscious Julia off the *Princeton;* they got halfway across the gangplank when she revived, remembered what
had happened, and struggled so hard that she almost pitched
them both into the river. Tyler finally managed to get the
hysterical woman to shore.

When a final body count was taken, five people had been
killed, including David Gardiner, the secretary of state, the
secretary of war, and the captain of the ship. Many more were

wounded, and Wingate and his son Jeremy labored long and valiantly to save the lives of those they could.

"I cannot believe this," Véronique cried to Devroe. She was shaking uncontrollably. "Just a few minutes ago we were standing here and—"

He didn't say anything, but his gaze drilled straight through her. And the truth swept over Véronique and she clasped her hand to her mouth to stifle a whimper. He'd wanted that gun to blow up! He'd wanted the *ship* to blow up! Even if it meant that the two of them would have been sacrificed! For if the *Princeton* had sunk with all hands aboard—the President and his cabinet all dead, God knows how many senators and congressmen and other highly placed officials—it was conceivable that the entire American government would have collapsed. Or at least been thrown into such a state of turmoil that the country would have been incapacitated. At that moment Véronique realized that nothing was as important to Devroe as his duty to his monarch. Nothing, not even his own life.

Chapter 40

WHAT HAD begun as a pleasant cruise down the Potomac had turned into a tragedy. The five dead men were taken to the White House, there to lie in state before being buried in the congressional cemetery.

Julia Gardiner remained in seclusion in the White House, attended by President Tyler. When she was well enough, she left for her home in New York City.

An inquiry was held to determine the cause of the explosion. Though there were several unresolved questions, nothing could be proven, since most of the evidence had blown up when the cannon exploded. The official determination was that an unfortunate accident had occurred—an act of God. Devroe, who'd testified along with many other witnesses about his recollection of what had happened, breathed a sigh of relief when the inquiry panel's judgment was announced. The accident set the navy back several years.

Though never quite satisfied with the board's findings, Bravo could not get any official support to continue further investigations, and so once more he focused on the project on which he'd been working for almost seven years. In 1843, Congress had grudgingly appropriated thirty thousand dollars for an experimental electromagnetic telegraph line to run from Wash-

ington to Baltimore. Bravo had overseen the running of the
lines, often having to contend with lumbermen who wanted
the poles for their own businesses, and with farmers who cut
the wires down and used them for fencing in their pastures.
But at last, the final wires had been run, and on May 24, 1844,
all was in readiness.

Samuel Morse, gray-haired now and bearded, but just as
vigorous as in the days when he'd painted his glorious scenes
of Congress, stood at the telegraph sender's station which had
been set up in the Supreme Court chambers in Washington,
D.C. Bravo made some last-minute adjustments on the telegraph key, then gave the place to Morse, who prepared to send
the word.

Chief Justice Taney was in the chamber, along with several
important legislators and cabinet members. Morse began to tap
out his message: "What hath God wrought!"

Moments later, the message was received in Baltimore, and
then to the amazement of the observers in the room, was sent
back to Washington.

"By God, we did it!" Morse said, and embraced Bravo. The
two men had tears glinting in their eyes.

When Bravo was able to break away from the celebration,
he galloped to his mother's house to tell the news to her and
Forrest, who was visiting for the day. He burst through the
door, picked up Forrest, and threw him in the air as Rebecca
shrieked, "Careful, you'll drop him!"

But Forrest knew better and laughed. "Again!"

Bravo told Rebecca what had happened. "You've no idea
what this means. For the moment, only Baltimore and Washington are linked, but there's no reason why this couldn't be
done to every major city in America. All it takes are the telegraph lines."

He stopped for a moment, his intense blue eyes gleaming
with a vision that only he could see. "We'll be able to tie this
entire nation together; events that happen in one section will
be only minutes away from the rest of the country. Some day,
we may even be able to do that with the entire world!"

"Oh, Bravo, really!"

"I remember telling Anne once that anything that a man
dreams, is possible. We're only limited by our own shortsight-
edness and our own fears."

"I must confess, when you first brought me the news about

this telegraph some years ago, I told you not to get involved. That should teach us both something," Rebecca said. "—teach you to follow wherever your dreams lead you, and me to keep my mouth shut!"

Bravo laughed at her good humor, but grew serious again. "We don't see it yet, because it's happening a bit every day, but things are about to change drastically in this country. The telegraph, the steam engine, the railroad are all contributing to it. With something like the telegraph, we can now have real time schedules for the railroad, and even for steamships, and that should make them more attractive to passengers."

"Where do you think the future of commerce lies, on the rivers or with the railroads?" she asked.

"The railroads," he said. "Sure, for the past half-century, rivers have afforded the easiest means of transport and travel, but much of this nation doesn't have navigable rivers. Look around you at how railroad lines have grown. In a decade, I bet, you'll be able to take a train as far as the frontier."

"I suppose, but what I find so awkward about railroads is that you have to keep changing trains all the time. An engine and cars of one line can't operate on the tracks of another line."

He stopped suddenly and stared at her. "Of course, it's that simple! Forrest, your grandmother is a genius!"

"Well, I have always been of that opinion myself—" she began, but Bravo cut her short.

"You don't know it, but you've just given me an idea. Standard-gauge tracks for every railroad in America! Uniform throughout, so that trains can be interchangeable, able to move from one locale to another depending on the traffic."

"Oh, Bravo, it will never work, because every railroad line will want *its* track size to be the one used."

"Think of what an advantage that would be in times of war," he said, as he developed his idea. "The side that had the efficient transportation system would have such an advantage. Troops and ammunition could be moved quickly to any battlefront. Mother, this is important, really important. I'm going to submit such a proposal to the President first thing tomorrow."

"Bravo, you know a great deal about inventions, but you're politically very naïve. Tyler is now a lame-duck President, and you'd surely injure your chances by confiding in him. Wait until there's a new man in the White House. If you let the new President think the idea is originating in his administration, you're bound to get much more action."

"That's a very small-minded view, isn't it? But I suppose you're right."

After Bravo left, Rebecca considered what her son had told her. She felt proud of his accomplishments, and yet also a bit unnerved, for they were further proof that he lived in some rarefied atmosphere she would never be able to reach. Suzannah was cozy, and Gunning charming and demanding; but Rebecca could talk, cope, argue with them. But Bravo . . . he was totally beyond any such family commonplaces, and that saddened her profoundly.

Nevertheless, the following week, she very quietly invested some more of her savings in several railroad stocks. There were nine Brand grandchildren to take care of now, and she wanted to make sure that before she died, all of their financial futures would be secure.

Julia Gardiner had been very close to her father; in fact, only because he was a pillar of the community, and her loyal protector, had she been able so flagrantly to flaunt society's conventions. With her father gone, President Tyler became a much more attractive suitor. He petitioned her mother for her hand, and consent was finally granted. On June 26, 1844, the couple were secretly married at the Church of the Ascension on Fifth Avenue in New York City.

When Washington learned the news, it reacted at first with jeering condemnation. John Quincy Adams told Rebecca, "They're the scandal of the capital, if not of the nation. The President is a perfect example of the adage, 'There's no fool like an old fool!' She's thirty years his junior! Has the man no shame?"

"The age difference doesn't upset me as much as the thought of that woman becoming First Lady. Is she the example to be held up to American womanhood? I'm afraid our flamboyant heiress has no more idea of what a democracy is about than the Sultan of Turkey!"

Rebecca's fears were soon justified.

President Tyler had tried to form a third political party; a shrewd politician, he'd offered Martin Van Buren a seat on the Supreme Court, hoping to keep Van Buren out of the race for the presidency. But Van Buren declined the appointment, positive that he would be selected as the Democratic candidate for the election of 1844. The Whigs had already chosen Henry Clay. Tyler's third-party plans came to naught, so it was just a question of whom the Democrats would choose to run against Clay.

But at the Democratic convention, Van Buren committed the blunder of crossing Andrew Jackson on the issue of Texas. Van Buren was against annexing it, certain that it must lead to war with Mexico.

Andrew Jackson, still the most potent force in the Democratic organization, began to manipulate the party from his home in Tennessee. He insisted that Texas must be annexed now, or it would be forever lost either to Mexico or to Great Britain. As the Democratic convention ground on, ballot after ballot was taken; Van Buren's strength slowly eroded, and nobody could get the necessary two-thirds majority to secure the nomination. Then Jackson let it be known that he would prefer to see a compromise candidate selected, a dark horse like James Polk of Tennessee. Polk was a staunch supporter of all of Jackson's policies, and not a turncoat like Van Buren. Finally, the convention acceded to Jackson's wishes, and Polk was nominated. Nobody could have been more disappointed than Van Buren, or more surprised than Polk.

Up until the last, Julia Gardiner Tyler had hoped that the Democrats would come to their senses and nominate her husband; after all, he was her husband. "Polk? I've never even heard of the man." she exclaimed. Nevertheless, she had to resign herself to having only eight months left to reign in the White House.

"They say that my husband doesn't have a party?" she confided to Véronique. "Well, then, *I* shall give him a party!"

True to her word, she instituted a round of levees and balls that left Washington gasping.

"The woman has no shame," Rebecca said to Dolley Madison. "Here her father died in February, she married four months later, and now her life is one continuous party."

"Well, she does observe the code of mourning," Dolley said weakly. "She wears only black lace, or white satin."

"Dolley, really!" Rebecca exclaimed. "Not even you, with your forgiving manner, can find any justification in what Julia Gardiner Tyler is doing to the White House."

Rebecca turned her condemnatory gaze to the center of the East Room, where Julia sat on a large gilt chair upholstered in

red velvet. Twelve ladies-in-waiting, including Véronique Connaught, surrounded her; the ladies were all dressed in cream-
colored satin, though their gowns were forbidden to be more
elaborate than Julia's. Julia wore a diadem in her hair which
looked very much like a crown, and absolutely gorged herself
on the compliments lavished on her by the sycophantic guests
who'd come to drink the President's champagne and eat his
food.

When John Calhoun addressed Jula as "Mrs. Presidentress,"
she positively cooed, though actually she delighted in being
called "Her Serene Loveliness." At her insistence, the Marine
Band learned to play all the new Viennese waltzes, and Julia
went so far as to introduce the daring new dance craze from
Europe, the polka. Though she was supposed to be in deep
mourning, no one danced it more often or with more zest. Then
Julia got a new notion, and demanded that the Marine Band
play "Hail to the Chief" every time her husband made an
appearance, and the music resounded at every major and minor
function, until Rebecca thought she would scream. She forced
herself to go to these functions, intending to document an era
in the White House she felt was so reprehensible that it must
never happen again; the only way to prevent that was to bring
it to the attention of the public.

"Oh God, anything," Rebel Thorne wrote in a tirade. "I'll
suffer the social policies of James Polk, a teetotaler, or the
ambitions of Henry Clay, only get that woman, that debased
royalist out of the people's house!"

The election campaign of 1844 wasn't quite as colorful as
the "Tippecanoe and Tyler too" carnival, but then what could
have matched it? The Whigs chose the raccoon as the symbol
of their party, Clay supposedly being as smart as a coon. But
at least the candidates had some issues of substance to debate.

Clay was against the annexation of Texas, and its inclusion
into the Union as a slave state. He also was not very positive
on the issue of the Oregon Territory. But Polk, following the
lead of Andrew Jackson to such a degree that he was called
"Young Hickory," insisted that Texas be admitted into the
Union, and that the Oregon Territory was owned by America,
since the Lewis and Clark expedition had already established
the country's right to it. "Fifty-Four Forty or Fight!" became
the energizing Democratic slogan—a claim to all the western

territory on the Pacific, right up to 54°40', the latitude of Russian-owned Alaska.

Henry Clay was confident of victory, and told Rebecca as much. "This time I shall have it!" he crowed. "Who in this country ever heard of James Polk? Oh, we here in Washington know the little man as a toadying follower of Andrew Jackson's. He was Speaker of the House, and served as governor of Tennessee, but if I may be immodest, his record in no way compares to mine."

"Henry, I believe you're right," Rebecca said. "You've waited a long time for this, you've fought hard for it, you've been a good loser, and now I'll be the first to admit that you deserve this chance at the highest office in the land."

A disturbing factor did develop in New York. A group of people, disenchanted by both the Whigs and Democrats, formed a new third party of their own, and since it condemned slavery in every form, they called it the Liberty Party. They nominated James Birney as their candidate for President.

Up until election day Clay remained supremely confident of victory. But when the votes began to trickle in, it gradually became clear that he'd seriously misjudged the attitude of the American people. They wanted to push their borders as far as they could; they wanted Oregon, they wanted Texas, and they would vote for the man who promised it to them.

In spite of that, Clay would have won, but the Liberty Party siphoned off sixty-five thousand votes from the Whigs in New York State. Clay lost that vital state by a scant four thousand votes; losing its electoral votes cost him the election. When the final results were in, Henry Clay broke down and cried.

Chapter 41

LOUISA ADAMS passed the tray of watercress sandwiches. "My dear Rebecca, one reason I asked you here today is that I'm terribly worried about John." Louisa shivered slightly and placed another log on the fire; the late November air was wet and raw, and she had never had a robust constitution. Both women continued to do their embroidery as they talked.

"You know, John is seventy-six years old," Louisa went on, "but the way he comports himself in Congress, one would think that he believes himself still in his salad days. I've remonstrated with him endlessly, but he won't heed. Rebecca, you're one of our oldest and dearest friends in Washington. John respects you, and I was wondering if you might persuade him to ease up."

"I'd be delighted to do anything to help," Rebecca answered as she finished a rosette on the cuff of a dress for her granddaughter Sharon. "But Louisa, I don't have to tell you of all people that John is one of the most obstinate of men."

Louisa sighed. "I suppose that's an accurate description of him. Imagine, every single day for the past eight years, he's fought to have the Gag Rule repealed. Reviled by his fellow congressmen, threatened with bodily harm—it's a wonder that it didn't kill him."

Rebecca patted Louisa's fine-drawn hand. "But he is making

such wonderful headway. When he first started this crusade, his was the only voice opposed to that heinous rule. Now the solid front in Congress is beginning to crack, and he almost has the necessary votes to rescind it."

"Your articles about the rule were a great help, and John's indebted to you."

"Thank you, dear Louisa, but in this battle, he deserves all the credit."

At the first session of the Twenty-eighth Congress, in January of 1844, eleven months earlier, a group of northern Democrats had split with their southern brethren, and backed Adams's petition to repeal the Gag Rule. That attempt had lost by just one vote. The handwriting was clearly on the wall.

"The second session of Congress is hard upon us, isn't it?" Rebecca asked.

Louisa nodded. "It commences on the second of December, though John doesn't believe any real business will be conducted until the third."

"I tell you what we must do that day," Rebecca said conspiratorially. "We'll put on our best clothes, hats, and all, go sit in the gallery, and when John gets up to propose his motion, applaud like *mad!* Who knows, this time he may have enough votes to win."

"I pray for that so fervently. Another defeat is liable to crush him."

On December 3, shortly after the presidential election results were formally announced, Rebecca and Louisa Adams bestirred themselves and went to the opening session of the House of Representatives. The gallery was packed; win or lose, this promised to be a momentous day. Rebecca gazed down at Adams, who sat at the same worn oaken desk he'd occupied for the past fourteen years. He looked his age; his hair, what little fringed his pate, had turned totally white, and his shoulders were stooped.

When Adams rose to speak, the chamber grew hushed.

"I demand that the Gag Rule be abolished, and I call upon the House to vote on the matter!"

Once more the voting commenced. Rebecca kept track of the tally. Midway through, she nudged Louisa and whispered "Do you realize what's happening? A great many of the northern Democrats are voting with the Whigs."

The northern Democrats were angry with the southern Democrats for refusing to nominate Martin Van Buren and instead choosing James Polk. Now these disenchanted Democrats saw their chance for revenge.

When the final ballot was cast, the Speaker of the House read the results. "Eighty votes for retaining the Gag Rule, one hundred-and-five votes for repeal!"

Pandemonium erupted in the chamber. Many of the congressmen, including some who'd previously villified Adams, rushed to congratulate him. It grew to a groundswell until finally everybody, legislators and spectators alike, leaped to their feet, to give Adams a standing ovation. After a long eight-year battle, against odds that had seemed insurmountable, Old Man Eloquent, and justice, had prevailed.

When the commotion finally subsided, Louisa and Rebecca joined John Quincy Adams on the floor of the House. Adams's eyes looked red and watery; so did Louisa's. Rebecca was sure that her own looked very much the same.

Louisa kissed her husband. "At long last the fight is over."

"At long last," he repeated. Then he shook his head. "Madam, this is just one battle, for the war against injustice is never-ending. But blessed, ever blessed be the name of God who gave me the strength to continue."

When Rebecca offered her congratulations, he squeezed her hand. "Thank you for all your support in your pamphlets and articles. You understand, I'm sure, that this is a significant turning point in our history. Once more we have freedom of petition and debate in Congress. Without it, there was no way to regress any wrongs. The people of this great nation, through their representatives, have turned away from slavery, and are moving toward freedom for all. The repeal of the Gag Rule means nothing less than that. Oh, it may take many more years, and may require many more battles, but we are witnessing the beginning of the end of slavery."

After the drama of the repeal of the Gag Rule, the inauguration of President Polk on March 4, 1845, proved to be something of an anticlimax. Winter's last gasp turned the weather foul, and a hard-driving rain forced Polk to deliver his inaugural address to a sea of black umbrellas.

Bravo Brand had set up a telegraphic sending station on the platform on the East Front of the Capitol, and Samuel Morse tapped out Polk's entire speech to newsmen waiting in Baltimore. Bravo was standing with his twenty-year-old nephew Jeremy Grange, who said with awe, "This is the first time that a presidential address has been relayed by wire. And you helped make it possible."

Bravo smiled proudly, then listened with growing interest to the speech: "The Republic of Texas has made known its desire to come into our Union . . . to enjoy with us the blessings of liberty secured and guaranteed by our Constitution. Texas was once part of our country . . ."

Bravo took this to mean that Polk considered Texas part of the original Louisiana Purchase, a point of view Jackson had always espoused. Bravo felt a sudden burst of pride that his own father should have journeyed across the vast, unchartered continent on the Lewis and Clark Expedition.

Polk went on, "I congratulate my country that by an act of the late Congress of the United States, the assent of this government has been given to this reunion, and it only remains for the two countries to agree upon terms to consummate an object so important to both."

"Did you hear that?" Bravo asked Jeremy. "The President's just put Mexico on notice that he absolutely intends to annex Texas."

"But Mexico's repeatedly warned us that annexation means war," Jeremy said. "It could put Suzannah and her entire family in danger again."

Bravo bit his lip. "I know, and there doesn't seem to be anything we can do to stop it. Gunning's at Fort Leavenworth, so he'll probably get involved. He's somebody who likes to get into the thick of things anyway."

Polk sipped some water, then went on about the Pacific Northwest. "Our title to the country of Oregon is clear and unquestionable, and already our people are preparing to perfect that title by occupying it with their wives and children. Eighty years ago, our population was confined on the East Coast by the ridge of the Alleghenies. Within that period—within the lifetime I might say of some of my hearers—our people, increasing to many millions, have filled the eastern valley of the Mississippi, adventurously ascended the Missouri to its headwaters, and are already engaged in establishing the blessings of self-government in valleys of which the rivers flow to the Pacific."

"Do you realize what Polk just said?" Bravo asked incredulously.

"It's just hit me," Jeremy answered. "Polk's put the British on notice that we mean to have Oregon! He's prepared to fight a war on two fronts, with England *and* Mexico!"

Bravo studied the President-elect with new interest, trying to get the man's measure. Was this speech all bluster, another ploy of a politician, or was Polk prepared to exercise real strength to get what he wanted?

The President-elect was a slight man, so spare of frame that his clothes hung on him. But he had a solid and an interesting face—determined, it seemed to Bravo. His cool gray eyes looked penetrating and intelligent. He had a high forehead, dark eyebrows, and a strong nose and chin. Strands of silver shot through his dark-brown hair, which he wore long, brushed back behind his ears.

"During the time I worked as a page, Polk became Speaker of the House," Bravo said. "He had a reputation as a stickler for details. 'Polk the Plodder' the other congressmen called him. But after what I've heard just now about Texas and Oregon, I think this little man may surprise us all."

Another thought came to Bravo. "Jeremy, can you imagine if the entire country had learned all at once of Polk's intentions? Why, the news would've been electrifying."

"But how could such a thing happen?" Jeremy asked.

"We ought to have a telegraph line running to every city in the United States. Somehow, I'll have to talk to President Polk about it. Maybe I'll get a chance tonight."

"Tonight? Are you going to the inaugural ball tonight?" Jeremy asked.

"I'm taking Kate. We thought we'd give the children a treat and allow them to see the festivities for a bit, then send them home. What about you, are you going?"

"You bet. This will be the first time I've gone to one—I was only sixteen for the last one—and I'm really looking forward to it."

"Taking anybody special?" Bravo asked.

Jeremy shook his head. "Haven't found her yet, but I'm searching real hard."

Several days before the ball, Rebecca had discovered that Bravo planned to escort Kate, and it made her very uneasy.

When Forrest first moved in with Kate, she'd reluctantly approved; she thought the boy would be better off growing up with other children rather than with a grandmother growing more crotchety each day. But the move had thrown Kate and Bravo together in an alarming way. They were both young, both healthy, and both very lonely. Whatever rivalry had existed between Bravo and Gunning mustn't erupt again, Rebecca thought, and especially not over Kate. Such a turn would be disastrous for everybody.

This past week, what with the miserable weather, Rebecca's lumbago had been plaguing her, and she hadn't planned to attend the ball. But at the last minute she changed her mind.

She sent Tad over to Georgetown to pick up Kate and all the children, and then he came back for her. When Rebecca swept out of the house, in an ecru satin mink-lined cape, the children jumped up and down in the carriage. Rebecca climbed in amidst cries of "Sit next to me, Grandma!" "No, next to me!"

"Hush!" she commanded, and they fell silent for the moment. Sharon slipped her small hand into Rebecca's, saying "You smell so pretty." Geary leaned against Rebecca's legs. "Do all those jewels belong to you?"

"Yes, but most of them are really fakes—but don't tell anybody."

Eleven-year-old Peter's eyes darted one way then another, trying to think of some piece of mischief he could commit without getting his ears boxed. "Grandma, I have to tell you, you look beautiful tonight, and if you let me come to the ball, I'll ask you for the first dance."

"Well, Peter Brand, I'm highly honored that you think so, but you can't come to the ball," she said and tweaked his nose.

"Aw Grandma. I never get to do anything."

"Where's Bravo?" Rebecca asked.

"The carriage was full, so he said he'd meet us at the hall," Kate told her.

"My Pa helped invent the telegraph," Forrest said to Peter. "Didn't he, Grandma?"

"Aw, anyway, so what and who cares?" Peter snapped belligerently. "My Pa's the best Indian fighter out in the Kansas Territory, and that's much more important than a silly old telegraph."

"It is not!"

Rebecca clapped her hands over both their mouths. "There's more than enough room in this world for both Indian fighters and inventors. You should be proud of them both." She leaned around the cluster of children and said to Kate, "Have you heard anything from Gunning?"

"Not since the last letter I showed you."

All during the ride, Rebecca guided the conversation to Gunning . . . his good qualities, how much he really adored Kate and the children, then posed tentative questions about when and if she planned to join him on the frontier.

Kate was sensitive enough to understand what Rebecca was doing, for she too had qualms about how close she and Bravo were drifting.

The Democrats were throwing two galas: one at Carusi's, costing the astronomical sum of ten dollars per ticket, open to people of all parties; the other, for "pure Democrats," held at the National Theater, at two dollars per ticket.

When Rebecca's carriage rolled up to Carusi's, they saw Dolley Madison coming out, her ostrich plumes gaily jouncing. "Don't even bother going in there," Dolley called. "It's the dullest party imaginable. Everybody's looking at everybody else, afraid to make a move, so nobody is having a good time. Follow me to the National Theater!" she cried, as she climbed into her carriage.

Just then Bravo appeared on horseback, so they all followed Dolley's carriage at a rapid clip to 1321 E Street, N.W. Crowds were queued up at the theater entrance. Rebecca and Kate got out of their carriage. "Now Tad will take you children right home and you are to go straight to bed," Kate told them. But Peter jumped out of the carriage. "Now where do you think you're going?" Kate demanded.

"Grandma said I could have the first dance."

"Grandma says that another word out of you, and you're going to hear ringing in your head," Rebecca said, making a menacing gesture toward him. Peter scrambled back into the carriage.

It was the first inaugural function held at the National, and a theatrical festivity prevailed. Rebecca saw Audubert Ville-franche in the lobby, and she wanted to compliment him on the decorations he'd designed. But because of the continuous difficulties between their two families, she thought it best not to engage the old dreamer in conversation.

The two-dollar jamboree had attracted everybody in Washington. Shortly after they got inside the packed theater, the band broke into "Hail to the Chief" to announce the arrival of President and Mrs. Polk.

Polk waved to the gathering, saw the feathers of Dolley's turban above the crowd, and made straight for her. Mrs. Polk, a striking woman in her mid-forties, greeted Dolley warmly. When she was introduced to Rebecca, the First Lady took her hand.

"Mrs. Brand, I understand that you and I both serve on the board of the orphan asylums in Washington. Well, I have some wonderful news. For the first time in the history of inaugurations, this affair is showing a profit. I believe we'll have over a thousand dollars to divide between the two orphanages."

"How splendid!" Rebecca exclaimed. She was deeply impressed with the sensitivity of this woman, who even at the height of her husband's success would talk about the orphanages first. What a refreshing change from the self-centered little snob who'd just been First Lady, with all her attention getting soirees—twelve ladies-in-waiting indeed!

Not that Mrs. Polk wasn't very elegant herself. Her gown was of blue-ribbed silk and satin, trimmed with blonde lace, and figured with blue ribbons in a poinsettia design. She wore it off the shoulder, which showed her lovely neck and high firm bosom to advantage. She had dark hair, refined features, and superb posture. As an inaugural gift, President Polk had given her an ivory-handled fan with the portraits of all the Presidents of the United States painted on one side, and on the other, a painting depicting the signing of the Declaration of Independence.

"Your gown is breathtaking," Rebecca said.

"Thank you," Mrs. Polk answered. "Worth of Paris designed it for me. I had serious trepidations about using a foreign dressmaker; I really would have preferred an American—but, oh well, our relations with France are good at the moment."

"This may make them better," Rebecca rejoined with a laugh.

The band struck up a quadrille, expecting the President and his lady to lead the dance, but Mrs. Polk shook her head firmly. "We're Calvinists. We don't dance, nor do we drink."

The Polks were spirited off to greet English Minister Plenipotentiary Richard Pakenham, and Rebecca commented to

Dolley, "No drinking or dancing in the White House? These should be four very unusual years."

"Or four very dull years," Dolley sighed. "Nevertheless, I'm devoted to Sarah. As you can see from her gown, she isn't exactly poverty-stricken—she comes from quite a wealthy Tennessee family. One of her greatest disappointments was not being able to have any children. That might have twisted a lesser person, but she just turned her energies to her husband's career. James Polk has a great asset in her."

"What a pity that a woman like that can't have a career of her own," Rebecca snapped. "Must we always bury our own desires in the careers of our husbands?"

"Now Rebecca, this is a night for laughter and *joie de vivre,* and we mustn't get into things like that."

In another part of the theater, Jeremy Grange, Bravo, and Kate were standing together, laughing and chatting. When Bravo saw the President enter he said to Jeremy, "I charge you with a sacred duty. You're to keep an eye on Kate, lest some roving bachelor snatch her away from us."

"Where are you going?" Kate asked.

"I've got to talk to President Polk. Jeremy, remember what we were talking about earlier this afternoon?"

"Bravo, this is supposed to be a celebration. Do you really think this is the right time?"

"If you want anything done, the right time is always now."

With that, Bravo pushed his way through the crowd to where President and Mrs. Polk were holding court. Sarah Polk was busily discussing the Oregon situation with Richard Pakenham, and Bravo was able to draw President Polk away from the Mexican minister, Juan Almonte, whose face flushed with anger.

"Mr. President, my name is Bravo Brand, and this afternoon I worked with Samuel Morse to telegraph your inaugural address to Baltimore."

"Ah yes," Polk said, looking up at Bravo. "I asked Morse who you were, and he was highly complimentary about you and your work. I suppppose you're about to petition me for some position in the government?"

"Not exactly, Mr. President."

"You're the only person in Washington who isn't, then. Ever since I was elected, I've been hounded to death."

"I've something to discuss that I believe is vital to our

country," Bravo said. Seeing President Polk's eyes glimmer with interest, he went on, "Suppose this nation had a network of telegraph lines connecting all our major cities—do you realize what that would do for us in the way of communications? Particularly in the event of any major calamities."

President Polk stared at the Mexican minister, who was gesticulating wildly to one of his aides. "Such as war?" Polk said softly.

"Exactly, sir. Now is the time that we should be preparing for any such eventualities. The country that has the best communication system is surely the one that has the advantage in time of crisis."

Polk's gray eyes grew even keener. "What do you suggest?"

At that moment, Juan Almonte threw up his hands, and with an oath, started back toward President Polk. The President put his hand on Bravo's arm. "Have you talked to anybody else about this?"

"Only to Samuel Morse. He and I have been dreaming of this possibility since the day we started working on the telegraph."

"Not a word of this to anybody else. I think there's something in what you're saying, but here comes a Mexican with mayhem on his mind. Come and see me tomorrow at the White House. We'll talk about it then."

Chapter 42

WHEN BRAVO reached the White House the next day, he was surprised to be directed to Mrs. Polk. President Polk had appointed his wife his secretary; she made and oversaw all his appointments, both social and political, which gave her a position of extreme importance. Anything that the President did, anybody he saw, had to be cleared first by Mrs. Polk.

The President received Bravo in the Cabinet Room. Once again Bravo was amazed at how tiny the President appeared, his size made even more diminutive by the grand proportions of the White House. Polk unrolled a map of North America; all twenty-seven states were indicated in bold lines. He tapped his finger on the Republic of Texas. "When Texas is admitted, there'll be twenty-eight states in the Union."

"Perhaps more," Bravo said.

Polk looked at him quizzically, so Bravo said, "I understood that Texas was to be divided into four separate states."

"That's a rumor put forth by the abolitionists. They believe I want to annex Texas to balance the power in Congress between slave and nonslave states. But that's a lot of nonsense. To the best of my knowledge, Texas will remain one state. Now, you said you had a proposal."

Bravo cleared his throat, suddenly feeling a bit nervous. "Sir, the country is growing tremendously—"

"Seventeen million in 1840, and I'd wager we had at least two million more now. Waves of immigrants from Europe view this as the Promised Land, and they're not far wrong."

"At this moment, we're erecting telegraph lines along the eastern seaboard—"

"Approximately fifteen hundred miles of line," Polk interrupted again. "But as you say, it's all confined to the East, with nothing going beyond the Appalachian mountains."

"Sir, I must tell you I'm impressed with the knowledge you've brought to this meeting."

"I believe in studying all facets of a problem before I make my decisions. Mrs. Polk is very helpful in this area; she amassed this information for me."

"Well, I visualize a day when every major city in the United States will be connected by telegraph lines, and news that would have taken weeks or months to reach a distant town, will only be minutes away."

"It's an exciting notion," Polk mused. "How would you propose to do such a thing?"

"The easiest way would be for Congress to send out a team of surveyors, and then appropriate the necessary funds. Then you'd appoint a commission, probably working through the Army Corps of Engineers, and they'd run the lines."

Polk frowned. "You're talking of millions in expenditures even before the first new line was run, and at a time when we're just recovering from the worst depression in our history. I can tell you unequivocally that even though it may be in the country's best interests, Congress will never vote for such an appropriation."

Bravo let out a long sigh. He was disappointed, but felt in his gut that the President was right. "Then there must be another way. I truly believe that such a communications network would generate more business and more money than we ever thought possible. This continent is a sleeping giant, abundant in raw materials, ready to be tapped."

"My sentiments are with you, but that still leaves a recalcitrant Congress."

Bravo studied the map, trying to come up with a solution. "Suppose the telegraph lines could be laid by private industry, along already existing rights of way, like along canals, or even the new railroad lines." He grew excited as he developed his thoughts. "That land's already been cleared for the passage of trains; with any new railroad lines, there could be some sort of contractual agreement so that the railroads would have to provide for telegraph lines also. Lord knows the railroad companies are being given enough free federal land to build on; they can afford to do something like this, particularly because it will benefit them in the end."

"It sounds like a capital idea," Polk said. "It bears further investigation. Frankly, young man, when you said you wanted to see me, I thought it would be another crackpot interview. I cannot tell you what the President has to go through in resisting the inane ideas of inane people."

Then he turned his attention to the map. "You heard my inaugural speech, so you know that I intend to expand the borders of this country to their natural limits. That means all of Texas, right to the Rio Grande River."

"But Mexico claims that the legitimate border is the Nueces River."

"Well, it's not," Polk barked. "If they had their way, they'd make the border the Sabine River, which divides Louisiana from Texas. But I'm a peaceful man, and I'd prefer to settle things amicably. I'm prepared to offer Mexico fifty million dollars for the disputed Texas Territory, and the New Mexico Territory, and the California Territory."

"That's an awful lot of land," Bravo said, shaking his head. "Do you think Mexico will agree?"

"I'm hopeful. In the autumn of this year, I'm sending Henry Slidell to Mexico City to negotiate just such a purchase. Mexico hasn't colonized any of that land. But our people have, and settlement is surely the principal claim to the rights of ownership."

"I agree. I have a sister and brother-in-law who homesteaded in Texas, Suzannah and Johnathan Albright. Jonathan originally came from Nashville, by the way. Did you know him?"

"Of course! He was Andrew Jackson's ward, one of the general's favorites."

"Mr. President, I believe that a survey of the country is necessary now, one that will determine where the best lines of communication should be located."

The President regarded Bravo thoughtfully. "In the light of what we've said, who'd conduct this survey?"

"Somebody who's familiar with the requirements of running telegraph line."

"How long do you think such an enterprise might take you?"

"Me?" Bravo almost choked, then considered. "Six months to a year, depending on how far west I went. I would have to take leave from my job at the Patent Office."

"I think that can be arranged." Polk turned to the map again, focusing on the territory west of the Mississippi. "If I were to say yes to such a survey, I'd want you to concentrate initially on the South—New Orleans, the Texas frontier. That's the virgin territory we know the least. We don't have to worry too much about the North—it's industrializing rapidly along the Ohio and the Great Lakes—but the South still lives its agricultural backwater life. That must change if the South is ever to break its dependence on the North."

Bravo nodded, getting a whole new insight into the problems of sectionalism.

"Because of the delicate nature of the coming negotiations with Mexico, your mission would have to remain unpublicized; the Mexicans tend to see any exploration of that region as a military threat." He paced the floor for a moment and then asked rhetorically, "How would we finance such a mission? I suppose we could find enough money in the White House's special reserve fund."

Bravo felt himself growing excited. Could his dream be coming to pass?

"It's conceivable that if you were captured by an enemy, you might be charged with spying. Knowing that, would you still be willing to undertake this?"

"Absolutely, Mr. President. I'd consider it an honor."

"Excellent. I do anticipate instances where you'd need to talk to members of our own Army Corps of Engineers, get their best thinking on certain problems. Suppose I were to get the secretary of war to give you a temporary commission—second lieutenant in the Washington militia, perhaps—for the duration of your explorations?"

"That would be fine, sir."

He looked at Bravo. "I want you to draw up a prospectus for me. Indicate what you'll need in the way of equipment, provisions, money, and men."

"Mr. President, under the conditions you've outlined, one man working alone might be the best way to handle this."

"The thought occurred to me, but I leave that choice to you. Can I expect your proposal within the month?"

"Without question."

"Remember, the fewer people who know about this, the better."

Several weeks later Bravo returned to the White House. During this time he'd burned the midnight oil, checked all of the army's records and maps about the territory he planned to visit, and had drawn up a detailed proposal. But when he was greeted by Mrs. Polk she said, "I'm afraid the President is indisposed."

"Nothing serious, I hope."

"We're not quite sure," she said, the strain evident on her face.

"Forgive me for being forward, Mrs. Polk, but a member of my family is a doctor in Washington, and he acted as Andrew Jackson's physician. His name is Wingate Grange."

"I've heard the name. Andrew told us to keep him in mind should anything go wrong."

"May I fetch him?"

"I'd be obliged. We had another doctor here the other day, but I wasn't at all reassured by his examination."

Bravo rode off and brought Wingate back. Wingate asked his son Jeremy to accompany him.

While Wingate examined the President, he explained Jeremy's presence. "It's always best to have a back-up doctor, one who knows the details and who can fill in should I be away for any reason."

"But he looks no more than a lad," Polk grumbled.

"I'm twenty," Jeremy said. "I hold a degree in medicine from Georgetown University, and I've assisted my father for years."

Half an hour later, the two doctors concluded their exhaustive examination of Polk.

"Could you describe what happened?" Wingate asked.

"I was working late, and suddenly I felt so tired that I just collapsed. Mrs. Polk found me an hour later."

"Any dizzy spells?" Jeremy asked.

The President shook his head.

"How late was it?"

"About two in the morning."

"How many hours a day do you work?" Wingate asked.

"Oh, twelve or fourteen."

Wingate raised his eyebrows. "Well, you're suffering from a severe case of fatigue. You need rest and a tonic; nothing less will do. A vacation at the seashore; some bracing air, sleep, and good food will soon set you to rights."

"I'm afraid that's impossible," Polk sighed. "You've no idea of the demands of this office. Everything must pass through the President, everything. No President who performs his duties faithfully and conscientiously can have any leisure. If he entrusts the details to subordinates, constant errors occur."

"Begging your pardon, Mr. President, but no one man can oversee all the demands of this office."

"I'm beginning to find that out, but I intend to do as much as I can—and then a little more. When I took this office, I set four goals for myself. I plan to reduce the tarriff, re-establish the independent Treasury, settle the boundaries of the Oregon Territory, and acquire the territories of New Mexico and California. Nothing less will suit me."

"Well then, Mr. President, you've set yourself a Herculean task, and you may well kill yourself attempting it."

"That's why I intend to serve only one term. Four years. Not too long a time for a man to give to the service of his country. I'm forty-nine years old now; when I retire I'll be fifty-three. Then Mrs. Polk and I can look forward to our quiet years."

Jeremy often wondered at the ease with which patients talked to his father. Something so intimate existed in the relationship between patient and doctor that a man would tell his physician things he'd never utter to anybody else.

Later, when Wingate and Jeremy met Bravo, Wingate said to him, "Polk seems like such a slight man, but I tell you there's a will of iron there."

"Or obstinacy," Jeremy said.

"Whatever you call it, this is a man who'll be President in his own right, and will badger Congress until he gets what he wants."

"Is he really ill?" Bravo asked anxiously.

"A man can make himself ill by too much carousing, too much drinking, or too much work. The more I see of patients the more I'm convinced of the biblical admonition, 'To every thing there is a season'—there's a time to work, and a time to rest, and if President Polk doesn't learn that, then I'm afraid he's going to wear himself to death."

* * *

Wingate had prescribed a week of rest, but the following day Bravo received a summons from the White House and went there with his proposals.

After studying the plans carefully, Polk made some suggestions that surprised Bravo with their intelligence, then gave him leave to begin his investigations. "You've had no trouble with the Patent Office, I trust. When do you plan to start?"

"As soon as possible. There are a few personal matters I must tend to here in Washington; as soon as I've taken care of them, I'll be off."

"In your travels, I'd be obliged if you'd stop in Nashville and talk to Andrew Jackson. I think that the general might provide you with some useful information."

"That would be a pleasure, Mr. President. From there I'll head to New Orleans and then on to San Antonio. Jonathan Albright knows Texas and its requirements; he can save me a great deal of time."

"Let me hear from you whenever you have something to report. Address the letters to me personally, and Mrs. Polk will see that I get them. Good luck. Give my best to General Jackson."

Chapter 43

"I JUST received the most upsetting letter from Andrew Jackson," Rebecca told Circumstance and Wingate. She'd arrived at their modest, rough-hewn house with a new yellow shawl she'd knitted for her godchild Doe. The fourteen-year-old girl wrapped it around her shoulders and whirled in a little dance around the pine-paneled room with its oversized fireplace.

Circumstance's house held such memories for Rebecca. When she'd first seen it, half a century ago, it was little more than a worker's shed belonging to James Hoban, the architect of the White House. Ten-year-old Jeremy Brand then worked for Hoban, who allowed the boy to live there. But when Jeremy turned eighteen, Hoban gave the shack and the land to him. With his own hands, Jeremy built it into a livable, then comfortable dwelling, adding on a studio, a substantial living room, and a kitchen.

Through the peculiarities and inequities of the law, Zebulon Brand inherited the house when Jeremy died rather than his daughter Circumstance; but at Zebulon's death, the deed passed to Rebecca, and she gave the property to Circumstance and Wingate when they married. In a city fast becoming all brick and white marble, the Granges preserved the house's rustic nature.

"How's General Jackson feeling?" Wingate asked.

"Judging by his handwriting, not very well. It looked like the tracks of a wounded bird and took me forever to decipher. At first reading I thought it much like the other letters he'd written me, complaining that he was ailing and not long for this world. But on rereading it, a certain unwritten despair seeped through the pages."

"Let's see, Jackson must be seventy-eight by now," Wingate said. "That's eight years more than the Bible allots to us mere mortals."

"Andrew Jackson is no mere mortal!"

Wingate and Circumstance laughed. "Frankly, Rebecca, I never thought he'd last this long," Wingate said. "He's lived by an effort of will, but even that must eventually weaken."

Circumstance handed Rebecca a glass of lemonade sweetened with wild honey. "You're thinking of visiting Jackson, aren't you?"

"Oh, but that's impossible! Even if I had the strength for such a journey, it would be far too forward of me; he hasn't extended an invitation."

"I'd say that his writing to you in the first place is as good as an invitation," Wingate said.

Circumstance added, "Suppose he were to die before you had a chance to see him again, you know you'd always regret it."

"A trip to Nashville at my advanced years would probably kill me," Rebecca countered.

"Nonsense. As your personal physician, I give you leave to go. I'll do even better; I prescribe it."

"Why don't you start packing right now and save us all a lot of grief?" Circumstance asked. "We'll keep an eye on everything in Washington while you're gone, Kate and the children, and the stoneworks."

"Somehow I get the uncomfortable feeling that I'm being railroaded out of Washington," Rebecca joked to Doe.

With the ends of her shawl flying, Doe whirled over to her godmother. "Aunt Rebecca, I'll go with you. We could have ever so much fun together."

At fourteen, Doe had her mother's erect, proud carriage. Though she wore the conventional clothes of a young lady of Washington, her dark hair plaited into braids, her thin, high-bridged, slightly aquiline nose and prominent cheekbones were incontestable evidence of her Indian blood. Because of that, she'd already encountered a number of unpleasant experiences in the capital, where prejudice formed the daily fabric of life.

"Doe, that's a lovely idea," Circumstance said to her daughter, "but it's just not possible." The idea of two women traveling alone to the frontier was just too unsettling for Circumstance.

"Just a minute," Wingate interrupted. "Some weeks ago Bravo told me he was heading west, and that he was going to stop off at the Hermitage."

"He mentioned it to me also," Rebecca said. "But I doubt that a grown man would be interested in traveling to the frontier—with his mother. No, if I do go, I'll go alone."

Later that week, the question did arise when Rebecca was having dinner with Bravo and Forrest. "I think your going is a wonderful idea," Bravo told his mother. "I can take you as far as Nashville, then leave you there when I go on to Texas."

"Pa, can I go too?" Forrest asked eagerly.

"I'd like nothing better, son, but I'm going to be traveling hard and fast, and it's best that I do this alone."

"Aw, I never get to go anywhere."

After dinner, Forrest went down to the basement to putter around in his father's old workshop, leaving Rebecca and Bravo alone.

"I wish you'd tell me why and where you're going, Bravo, instead of letting me worry. All I know is that it's some sort of mission for the White House, but about what?"

"Now, Mother, you had your secrets and kept them from us for years, so why can't I have mine?"

On an overcast day in May, Rebecca and Bravo said their goodbyes to Kate and the children. Rebecca shook her finger at the brood lined up before her. "Now all of you remember, if I find out you were any trouble while I was gone, I'm not going to bring back any presents."

"I want an Indian scalp," Peter cried.

"Me too," sang Geary, Sharon, and Forrest.

"That's the last thing any of you want, or that you're going to get," Rebecca scolded. Then she scooped up each child in turn and hugged him. When she got to Peter she grimaced. "My back! You're getting a little too old and heavy for this sort of thing."

To her surprise, Peter didn't fight her off as he usually did, but hugged her fiercely. "Grandma, take me with you," he whispered. "We won't tell the others. I don't take up much room, I don't eat a lot, and I'll carry your bags. I want to see my Pa."

She smothered the red-haired, freckle-faced boy with kisses. "I have a feeling you'll be seeing him before very long," she whispered back to him.

With a final goodbye, she and Bravo set off. They took the Chesapeake and Ohio Canal inland to Cumberland. They had quite a pleasant journey, the canal boats rising and falling in the locks to cross the mountains. From Cumberland, they caught a luxurious stagecoach to Pittsburgh. It had heavily padded red velvet seats and was drawn by six spirited horses.

"Fifteen years ago I came this way," Rebecca said, her voice laden with memories.

"When Suzannah eloped with Jonathan."

She nodded ever so slightly. "How determined I was to get her back! Extraordinary, the lessons that only time can teach. I was so convinced that unless Suzannah married Devroe Connaught her life would be miserable, and all the while that fiend was planning to kill her. How could I have ever been such a fool?"

Boarding a riverboat at Pittsburgh brought forth another burst of recollections, and Rebecca spoke with some agitation about what had happened on the Ohio River.

"Devroe Connaught and his henchmen tracked Suzannah and Jonathan to Pittsburgh, but discovered that they'd eluded us and were heading downriver on an old paddleboat. We gave chase on another steamboat, the *American Flyer,* I think it was. Two days later, we finally caught them, and the most fearful fight broke out. That's when I realized that Devroe meant to kill Suzannah, to revenge himself against our family for all that had happened to his."

"Wasn't that when Devroe's arm was mangled?"

Rebecca nodded, reliving that horror. "Devroe went to stab Jonathan, and as he drew back his arm, his sleeve got tangled in the boat's paddlewheel. Before we could pull him free..."

Bravo leaned forward. "Mother, it's time to forget all that and press on to a new life. Why in heaven's name don't you get married again?"

"Are you mad? I'm past sixty."

"Nobody would know it. You're still attractive, you still have a wonderful figure—and all your teeth!"

"But I've also got lumbago, and palpitations, and dizzy spells. No, Bravo, after you reach a certain age, it's easier to be left alone. I need my solitude, my peace of mind, and those things are decidedly contrary to the conditions of marriage."

"What about just ordinary companionship?"

"I have my children and my grandchildren. I get my nourishment from watching them grow."

"That's not the real reason you won't even entertain another man in your life, is it?" he asked softly.

She looked to the darkened sky, watching the sparks from the tall smokestacks leave a trail of glowing embers behind them. When she spoke, it seemed in cadence to the muffled whoosh of the paddlewheel that sounded almost like a heartbeat.

"Some people love only once in their lives. I suppose I fall into that category. I loved your father so deeply, and with such joy, that it's sustained me through the years. The idea of another man . . ." She gave a tiny shrug.

"Yet there was Andrew Jackson. Would you have married him?"

She thanked heaven for the darkness, so that he couldn't see her embarrassment. Then she became angry that he'd even brought the subject up. Finally she let out a long sigh and thought, why the deceit? He's a grown man, he deserves to be treated as one.

"Andrew Jackson and I were drawn together out of mutual loneliness: he could talk about Rachel, I could talk about Jeremy. What we had was very special, I hope for both of us. But it was more abstract in nature than the passion I bore for your father. I'm grateful for having known Andrew, but as I said, I've had only one love in my life."

Long after Rebecca retired to her stateroom, Bravo sat up and watched the rushing waters of the river. He thought a great deal about Anne, the gentle creature who'd been his wife, he thought about his motherless boy, and wondered if he would ever remarry. Something had happened to him when Anne died, something akin to a malady, and he wondered if that malady would ever be cured. There on the dark mercurial river, he felt his loneliness, as keen as an instrument of torture . . . Then another thought came to him that shocked him. Lord, what a lonely, tormented woman his mother was. That could be his destiny too, unless he reached out for life.

* * *

Throughout the journey, Rebecca couldn't help but notice that Bravo was constantly taking notes, drawing diagrams, making entries in a thick notebook. Everytime she questioned him, he'd only flash his infuriatingly ingenuous smile. One day he did say, almost as an afterthought, "I'll bet in ten more years we'll have train service going directly from Washington out to the frontier."

His rather laconic statement only mystified her all the more.

When they reached the Cumberland River, they transferred to another steamboat, a smaller one this time, and several days later arrived in Nashville. It was now the end of May, and the Cumberland Valley burgeoned with growth.

Rebecca gazed at the rolling hills. "It's lovely, placid country, but I'm afraid it's a little too landlocked for me." As they approached the Hermitage, her eyes widened in surprise. "I had no idea Andrew's property was this large."

They passed wheatfields, orchards, cottonfields, stables, smokehouses. The driveway leading to the main house was designed in the shape of a guitar, and was bordered with a riot of spring flowers; Rachel had loved both flowers and music.

From the outside, the two-story house looked rather awkward, the consequence of eight oversized white columns. "I remember Andrew writing me about a fire that destroyed the front of his house; I guess this was his way of repairing the damage as best as possible," she mentioned to Bravo.

When they entered the spacious entrance hallway, they were both agreeably surprised. The walls were covered with a quite famous French wallpaper, depicting Telemachus awaiting the return of his father, Ulysses. "I suppose I'll have to revamp my opinion of the vulgar frontier," she murmured. She recognized certain pieces of furniture that had been in the White House, including a couch covered in horsehair. At the far end of the hallway, a lovely curving staircase led to the second floor.

Rebecca and Bravo were greeted by old Uncle Alfred. "The General, he's expecting you," he told them. "Wants to see you right away after you've refreshed yourselves."

Jackson had assigned Rebecca one of the guest rooms on the second floor of the main house. Bravo was to be quartered at the Tulip Grove, the house just across the road where Jackson's adopted son lived with his wife.

Rebecca tidied up, then went downstairs. At the doorway to the library, she straightened her dress, brushed back a few loose strands of hair, and knocked on the door.

"Get in here, you old bitch!" came a raucous squawk. "Get in here and lift those skirts!"

Chapter 44

"OH MY NERVES, I may faint," Rebecca muttered under her breath as she entered the library.

"Hello, dearie," a magnificently plumed parrot called to her from its perch.

Rebecca made a face at the bird. "Andrew, that creature will never cease to shock me."

"Quiet, Old Poll," Andrew Jackson ordered. The parrot shifted from leg to leg, rumbled deep in its chest, pulled its neck in, and settled down.

Jackson was sitting, or rather reclining, in a very unusual chair. When Rebecca finally caught sight of his face she drew in her breath sharply. He'd lost so much weight that his bone structure showed . . . The mark of death was on his face.

"Andrew, how wonderful to see you," she said, struggling to remain composed.

He looked at her with his sunken eyes, the only part of his being that still seemed alive, and smiled wanly. "Forgive me, my dear, but I can't get up."

She held out a restraining hand. "That's a wonderful chair."

"It was made especially for me," he said proudly. "It's called a recliner chair." He paused to catch his breath. "Dr. Holmes of South Carolina invented it. He built the first one for me, then made another for Queen Victoria, and one for a damnable

334

southern senator who shall remain nameless."

"Damnable could only mean John Calhoun," she laughed.

"I should have hung that traitor!" he exclaimed, harking back to his old, persistent theme. "Fomenting rebellion, preaching secession. I warned Jim Polk that if he even considered giving Calhoun a position in the cabinet, I wouldn't support his candidacy. So Calhoun is out of government, and a public citizen once more—though not for long, if I know that wily scoundrel."

Jackson, despite his infirmities, was obviously still an unforgiving man.

"I hunger for news of Washington. Tell me everything. Has Polk really appointed James Buchanan secretary of state?"

"Oh yes, and he's been confirmed."

"Damn! I asked Polk not to."

"But Andrew, you yourself named Buchanan minister to Russia during your first term."

"That I did. It was as far as I could send that popinjay out of my sight. I'd have sent him to the North Pole if we kept a minister there. What news of Oregon?"

"The British are making threatening noises, but Polk is insisting on the fifty-four-forty boundary line."

"Excellent. I told him that was the course he must take. He must stand firm, look John Bull square in the eye, and stare him down. Their bold claim to all of Oregon must be met as boldly by our denial, and confidence in our own right. It will take courage; I vouched for Polk's courage during the election campaign, and now he mustn't fail me. But between you and me, Rebecca, when it finally comes down to it, Polk will settle for a boundary drawn along the forty-ninth parallel."

"He will?" she asked, startled. "But that was one of the strongest planks in his platform."

"To get what you want, you always start out asking for more."

"I see you still keep your finger on the political pulse," she said with a wry smile.

"I have the Washington papers sent to me every day. I'm concerned about Texas. The dream we had so long ago is about to be realized, if only Congress remains firm and isn't intimidated by the Mexican threat of war. What do they really think of it in Washington?"

"Most of the legislators are pleased. The Whigs, understandably, believe it's a southern plot to add slave states to the Union."

"Oh, God, it's not—on that you must trust me. But my fears are in other directions. I believe that John C. Calhoun has far more nefarious plans. He wants Texas and all of the New Mexico Territory, and California, to join the southern states, and then break away from the Union and form a new nation."

"That's not possible!"

"It is, it is, Rebecca; that's what's in the back of his mind. When history judges me, the one thing I'll be condemned for is that I didn't hang John C. Calhoun."

"Andrew, you mustn't upset yourself so. There's nothing you can do about it right now."

"That's the trouble—I die leaving so much undone. Rebecca, attend me on this. It has been my contention, and the contention of the elder statesmen of this nation, that Texas was always part of the United States. That land was included in the original Louisiana Purchase made by President Jefferson in 1803, and only the deviousness of Napoleon prevented us from getting that put down on paper."

"I know Jefferson felt that way; it was common knowledge when Jeremy went out on the Expedition of Northwest Discovery."

"Agreed, then," Jackson said. "President Madison continued his efforts to get a satisfactory boundary line drawn, and this continued well into President Monroe's term of office. When he bought Florida from Spain for five million dollars, Spain gave up any territorial claims it had to the north and west extending all the way to the Pacific Ocean. However, when Mexico rebelled against Spain, she insisted that the territory belonged to her."

"But when John Quincy Adams became President, he did try to buy all that land from Mexico," Rebecca put in.

"So did I when I took office. Each President tried, because we felt that we'd already paid for the territory. We didn't go to war over it; we tried to settle it peacefully. But Mexico would have none of it. Did Spain ever colonize that land? She did not! Neither have the Mexicans, but they brought in our fellow Americans to do that, like your Suzannah and my Jonathan."

MAP OF AMERICAN AND MEXICAN BOUNDARIES.

"And they've been living on a tinderbox ever since."

"When Texas won her independence, Santa Anna agreed to Sam Houston's terms—until he was safely back in Mexico City. Then the harassment began, and the border raids. You know that the Mexican army attacked San Antonio as recently as 1842. Is that the act of a peaceable neighbor? Mexico will never give up its claim to Texas; they want it back in their empire. Even now they're enlisting foreign support for their aggressions."

He began to cough so badly that Rebecca thought this might be the end. He grew ashen, then red-faced, then broke out in a cold sweat.

"Shall I send for the doctor?" she asked anxiously.

He shook his head and pointed to a decanter of brandy on the table. She gave him a spoonful and this eased the cough. He lay heaving, his fingers shaking with a palsy. "It's this damnable tuberculosis," he wheezed.

"Andrew, Wingate's told you a hundred times that you don't have tuberculosis. The bullet from your old dueling wound punctured your lung, and that's what's causing the bleeding."

"Whose lungs are they, anyway?" he demanded. "I say it's tuberculosis."

The afghan she'd once knitted for him fell from his legs, and she could see that his legs and feet were incredibly swollen. No wonder he couldn't stand!

"Dropsy," he told her wearily. "Rebecca, it isn't any fun getting old. As long as you can keep your faculties, and a modicum of strength, living is worthwhile. But not this way, not this unending pain. Rebecca, I promise you, I'm dying as fast as I can!"

She didn't know whether to laugh or cry at that. She stood up. "Andrew, I fear that I'm tiring you."

He nodded. "I am tired, and must lie quietly for a bit. In an hour or so, I want you to send your son in to see me. Then later this evening, when all these visitors have cleared out, you and I must finish what we have to say to each other—matters of vital importance to this nation."

Rebecca was amazed at the stream of callers at the Hermitage, for word had spread that Jackson was near death. In addition to the morbidly curious, people came to ask for special favors, office seekers wanting his blessings, autograph hunters—some who even wanted locks of the General's hair. Rebecca remembered that when George Washington died and was lying in state, the mourners had pulled almost every hair out of his head. Whenever Jackson had his hair cut, he had the barber save the clippings, so he could pass the snippets out to those who asked for them.

Later Bravo went to see Jackson in the library. The General's nap had somewhat refreshed him; he sat listening to the song of the field hands as they came in with twilight. When the music faded he turned to Bravo. "It may surprise you to learn that I'm privy to the details of your mission."

Bravo blinked, taken by surprise.

"President Polk wrote and asked me my opinion of you. I told him that I had little direct knowledge of you, but that I knew both your mother and father." He hesitated for a moment and then said, "I'm a dying man, so I've little time for dissembling; Rebecca's told me that you know the truth."

Bravo's jaw tightened.

Jackson went on. "Your father served with me at the battle for New Orleans. In fact, he built the redoubts across the bayous that stopped General Pakenham. I couldn't have asked for a better soldier. You've a great deal to measure up to in that man; I only hope you're capable.

"When your father fell in love with your mother, he asked me for my advice. I told him to seize all the happiness he could, as I'd done with my Rachel. I'm thankful to say that he listened to me, and you're the legacy of the love he bore for that wonderful woman."

Bravo didn't know what to say; hearing about his parents from this new vantage point totally confused him.

"I know you've had difficulties with your mother—but then, I don't know anybody in Washington who hasn't. I did, and I was President of the United States!"

The buzz of cicadas began with twilight and Jackson turned his head to the window, imprinting on his mind all the delights of sight and sound that the earth could offer. "Sometimes I think that your mother was born in the wrong time; her ideas are so strange—Like giving the vote to women. But a person must be judged by the totality of his deeds throughout his life, and your mother has performed a great service for this country. Though I've disagreed with her many times, she's used her pen, to be a gadfly, a watchdog, and an avenging angel all in

one. Someday you must look at her as a human being separate
and apart from yourself. You'll find an extraordinary person."

"Thank you, sir. I have had difficulties, and for reasons you
know. Doubtless I'll have difficulties with her in the future.
It's taken me a long time to reach this point, but I know you're
speaking the truth, and I'll always remember what you've said
about her, and about my father."

"Good. Then we've no need to worry that further. At any
rate, I told Polk to keep an open mind about you. When you
submitted your plan, he was favorably impressed, and he decided to proceed."

Bravo was struck with the power Jackson still wielded in
Washington; but after all, Polk was his hand-picked man.

"I don't pretend to understand a good deal of what you're
after," Jackson continued. "But certain things in your proposal,
I know will benefit this country. You see, I fear war will come.
An old soldier knows this; he can almost feel it in the air, sense
it in the mood of the people. We've tried for so long to avoid
it, to get the territory that rightfully belongs to this nation, but
the Mexicans won't sell it, and they won't or can't colonize
it, so the land sits there like a great prize for any nation that
covets it, like France or England. We mustn't allow that to
happen.

"I've been studying the situation from a military viewpoint—God, if only I were twenty years younger!" Jackson
exclaimed, hitting his blanket weakly. "In all likelihood, Polk
will appoint General Zachary Taylor to command the army if
hostilities break out."

"Why Taylor? He isn't the ranking officer in the army."

"Why indeed?" Jackson asked, his frown eloquently indi-
cating what he thought of the general. "Simply because Zachary
Taylor is commander at Fort Jessup in Louisiana—the United
States post closest to the Mexican border. You are going to
New Orleans, aren't you?"

Bravo nodded.

"It's a key city, the major supply point for our army in the
South and Southwest. Unless I miss my guess, the Mexicans
will attack us first, and in force. They have a standing army
of more than thirty thousand. We have less than five thousand."

Jackson leaned back in the recliner and extended his frail
hand. "Now you must leave me, for I fear I don't have much
strength left."

Bravo shook Jackson's hand. He felt honored to have been taken into the general's confidence, honored that this giant of a man should have thought so highly of the father he'd never known. As he was about to leave he heard Jackson clear his throat and he turned.

"Don't forget what I told you about your mother."

"I won't. Thank you again, Mr. President."

"May God walk with you on your journey."

After the evening meal was eaten and the house had settled down for the night, Jackson sent for Rebecca. She found him this time in his bedroom, lying in the high four-poster bed. Uncle Alfred was rubbing his feet with liniment to help increase the circulation. Jackson was humming "Auld Lang Syne" in a high-pitched voice. He dismissed Uncle Alfred when Rebecca entered.

"How are you tonight, Andrew?"

He made a sound somewhere between a sigh and a groan. "I'm dying as fast as I can, as fast as I can. I don't mean to complain; it's something that all men must face. My lamp of life is nearly out, and I'm ready to depart when called. I feel that I'm in God's hands, and I have full confidence in his goodness and mercy."

He said it in a prayerful litany, and she was awed by his courage in the face of impending death. He put his hand on the Bible that he kept on the bedside table. "I remember once, during a dark night of my soul, you read to me, and it brought me great comfort. Read to me again, wherever the book falls open."

With her eyesight blurring with tears, she reached for the worn Bible and let the pages fall open. "The Sixty-First Psalm. 'Hear my cry, O God, attend unto my prayer . . . From the end of the earth I will cry unto thee, when my heart is overwhelmed; lead me to the rock that is higher than I . . . For thou has been a shelter for me, and a tower strong from the enemy . . . I will abide in thy tabernacle forever; I will trust in the covert of thy wings . . .'"

Her voice caught and she couldn't go on, tears streaking her cheeks. Jackson wiped his eyes. "Rebecca, my dear Rebecca, thank you. Ah, you've a mote in your eye. Don't cry, there's no good to be done crying, not when we've so little time left, and so much to discuss."

She dabbed at her eyes with her handkerchief and managed a smile.

"You and I have had our disagreements, but both of us have always had the country's best interests at heart. Now you must attend me on this. It's absolutely imperative that the United States have the territories of Texas, New Mexico, California, and Oregon. We must expand to both oceans, so that our nation can grow into itself without interference from foreign powers. I've always felt that we had a destiny . . . you described it once as a shining destiny, to bring the message of freedom to all men. But if we allow Great Britain, or France, or anybody else to establish a foothold directly in the path of our westward expansion, then we'll never be able to achieve that destiny."

She wasn't sure she agreed, but she didn't have the heart to argue with him, not in his condition. Perhaps he was reacting to something deep in his being, something more profound than anything she felt. Did he have a vision of the mystical course of the nation, as George Washington once had?

"I pray that we can do without war," he whispered. "But if not, then let war come. There'll be patriots enough to repel foreign aggression." He pulled himself higher on the bed, growing excited. "Rebecca, you must write a letter for me to President Polk, outlining what I've just said, so that he can use these arguments with Congress."

"Andrew, don't you think it would be better to wait until morning?"

"I may not be here come morning."

She penned the letter, and though his arguments were eloquent, she got the uncomfortable feeling that in trying to persuade her he was also trying to persuade himself.

During that week, Jackson's condition deteriorated, and by Sunday, June 8, death was near. The servants did their chores while singing old hymns and weeping. As he heard the grief sighing through the house, Jackson murmured, "My dear children, don't grieve for me. I'm going to leave you . . . I've suffered so much pain."

The doctor administered another spoonful of brandy, which revived him enough to say goodbye to the servants and kiss each member of his family. "My dear children and friends and servants, I hope and trust to meet you all in heaven, both black and white, both black and white."

Jackson lingered for a few more hours, and even as life slipped away from him, he sent messages to Senator Thomas Hart Benton, to Francis Blair, and then a last and final note to President Polk, insisting that he remain firm with Great Britain and Mexico.

"Has Sam Houston come?" he whispered.

"No, he hasn't arrived yet," his adopted son told him.

"I'll wait then, but I don't know how much longer."

At six o'clock in the evening, General Andrew Jackson's head fell to the side and life left him.

At nightfall, a dusty carriage rolled onto the plantation; in it were Sam Houston and his young son. Sam rushed into the house. Rebecca met him at the door and shook her head.

"Oh God, no," Houston lamented. "I whipped the horses until I thought they'd drop under us, and still too late."

He took his son into the room where Jackson lay, and the towering bear of a man knelt sobbing before the general's bedside. Houston turned to his boy and whispered, "My son, you must remember all your life that you looked on the face of Andrew Jackson, one of the greatest men that this country has produced."

The funeral was held two days later before a crowd of three thousand people who'd pressed onto the Hermitage grounds. Everybody within a hundred miles who could travel came to pay his final respects. There was an awkward moment when somebody began to curse like blue thunder—but then Uncle Alfred threw a cover over the cage of Old Poll.

Jackson was buried beside his beloved wife, Rachel, of whom he'd often said, "Heaven will be no heaven for me if she's not there."

Rebecca and Bravo stood side by side listening to the eulogy and found it wanting. Andrew Jackson had been as elemental as a force of nature; mere words could never do him justice.

Rebecca and Bravo left the Hermitage right after the services, he on his way to New Orleans, she returning to Washington, D.C. As Rebecca boarded the steamboat on the Cumberland River, she felt old, and tired, and very much alone.

PART FIVE

Chapter 45

"DEVROE, DARLING, I cannot believe you're planning another trip," Véronique said to her husband. "The children complain that they hardly see you anymore. Where are you off to this time?"

"Cuba."

She did a mental calculation of how long it would take him to get there, how long to return. At least two months in all—two months of something like freedom for her. Of late, Devroe had become almost unbearably irascible. "Why Cuba?"

"Because that's where the illustrious General Antonio López de Santa Anna is living at the moment, very honorably engaged in the statesmanlike pursuits of wenching, drinking, and cockfighting. He was exiled to Havana when those silly Mexicans had their last coup. Their government is about as stable as gelatine pudding, and I believe it's time for Santa Anna to make a triumphant return."

"But must you go?" she asked, running her hand along the sleeve of his good arm. "Can't you delegate this to an underling?"

"It's far too important. I've put the idea in President Polk's head that if there were a strong man ruling in Mexico, it would be easier for the United States to purchase the territories it wants."

"That's precisely what you *don't* want," she exclaimed, confused.

"Ah, my dear, will you never understand the Machiavellian requirements of politics? Santa Anna will never sell any Mexican land. His dream is to reconquer Texas, to set up an independent empire stretching from Louisiana to the Pacific Ocean. But I didn't tell Polk that, of course."

"But returning Santa Anna to his native country, why would the President even consider such a dangerous course?"

"He's desperate; he wants the territory without war. He knows Congress won't support him if it comes to hostilities. Santa Anna will take the money, and when he's back in power, use it to finance his battle against the United States."

"Devroe, your machinations leave me dizzy."

"If war does break out, Mexico mustn't lose. The moment Mexico declares war, it will be time for Great Britain to attack on the Oregon frontier."

"And is Great Britain willing to do that?" Véronique asked.

In answer, he showed her a clipping from the London *Times:* "We too have rights respecting this territory of Oregon. We are resolved—and we are prepared—to maintain them. If necessary, we will call on the All Powerful God of Battles, and the thundering broadsides of Her Majesty's ships!"

"Tiens," Véronique breathed, "this really could mean war."

"Let us hope so. The United States has no standing army to speak of—a paltry five thousand men. How can they possibly hope to fight on two fronts? Véronique, I've worked for this opportunity for more than twenty years, I mustn't let anything stand in my way."

"How long will you be gone?"

"I don't know. After my sojourn in Cuba, I may go to San Antonio."

Her hand flew to her mouth. "After what happened there, that's madness!"

"Perhaps, but it was more than ten years ago, and as far as Jonathan and Suzannah Brand Albright are concerned, I'm back here in Washington." He massaged his crippled arm. "The scales of justice must be balanced once and for all."

"Devroe, in God's name, be careful. If you should be recognized. . . ."

"Albright would kill me on sight," he finished. "I have no intention of taking chances. With money, anything can be

achieved. I'll hire renegade Mexicans and Comanche Indians
to carry out my plans."

Véronique regarded her husband, feeling that peculiar chill
that overcame her whenever his passionate hatreds surfaced.
He was how old now, thirty-four, thirty-five? His thin brown
hair was turning gray at the temples, and his face had settled
into a permanent grimace, as though his thoughts were always
vaguely distasteful. She knew him to be brilliant, obsessed,
and willing to wait as long as necessary, even decades, to
implement his schemes. Perhaps he'll die on one of these ventures, she thought suddenly and wondered what it would be
like to be absolute mistress of the vast Connaught estate. Of
course, he hadn't left her anything in his will—all that had
been settled with their prenuptial agreement. Harking back to
the ancient English laws of primogeniture, everything went to
the eldest son, Sean. That way the estate wouldn't be broken
up, and the fortune could perpetuate itself. But Sean was only
eleven, and as the boy's mother, surely she would have a great
deal to say about the disposition of the Connaught wealth. I
must visit that old Haitian witch again, she thought. Perhaps
she can reveal something of the future.

"Have the children brought," Devroe ordered, interrupting
her thoughts. "I wish to say goodbye to them."

Minutes later, Romance, Sean, and Carleton entered the
drawing room, each child immaculately dressed and groomed.
Romance curtsied to her father, a low deep bow executed with
such elegance that he almost applauded.

"Bravo, my girl. I've rarely seen a curtsy better executed,
even at the royal court."

Romance smiled demurely. At thirteen, she was a dazzling
beauty, with hair so black it shone blue. Her complexion was
paler than her mother's, and her eyes were a clear sea-green.
In this one year she'd become a woman, and she carried herself
as if she planned to use that new status as a terrible weapon.

Sean, at eleven, looked like a miniature of his father, thin,
wiry build, an inordinately high forehead, pale blue eyes, and
lank brown hair that fell to one side of his face. Being the heir
apparent of the plantation, he was deferred to by everybody,
including brother, sister, and servants. So far his mother had
eluded his power, but she wouldn't for long, that much he'd
promised himself. Devroe had personally overseen the boy's
education, and had found him an apt pupil. He could discourse

on *Plutarch's Lives* as intelligently as Napoleon's battles. From birth on, Devroe had implanted in Sean's mind the conviction that he was better than most people, and certainly better than any American. Sean had absolutely no difficulty in accepting that idea.

Carleton was a disappointment; if he didn't look so much like a Connaught, Devroe would have insisted that the child wasn't his. To begin with, nature had erred; he looked entirely too gentle for a male, and his sensitivity was apt to be excruciating. Whenever a slave had to be whipped, Carleton would run and hide, whereas Sean and Romance would applaud. Once when Devroe asked his youngest son what he would like to do for his birthday, expecting the lad would say riding, or hunting, or shooting, Carleton shook his mop of blond curls and cried, "Could we go to see grandfather at the theater in Washington?" When Devroe refused, great tears squeezed from Carleton's large blue eyes. The priesthood, Devroe thought as he studied his youngest son. In a monastery, the boy would never be an embarrassment . . . he might even be happier.

"I must go away again for a bit," Devroe said to his children. "I expect you to be on your best behavior, for you're all Connaughts. Learn your lessons well; I shall test you on them when I return."

He kissed Romance on the cheek, then shook hands with the two boys. The entire family escorted him out to the colonnaded veranda and watched as the servants loaded his trunks onto the carriage. "Carleton," Devroe said suddenly, "from what you've learned in your geography lessons, how will I get to Cuba?"

A look of terror crossed Carleton's face and he began to stammer. Devroe snapped his fingers impatiently, and then Sean interrupted with a smirk. "You'll go to Baltimore, father, and take a ship from that port, then set sail south, for the Caribbean."

"Excellent," Devroe said, placing his good hand on Sean's shoulder. Tears started to Carleton's eyes; he turned away, for if his father saw him crying, he really became angry.

Véronique waved as the carriage rolled away. The Caribbean, she mused. Hurricanes were spawned there at this time of the year . . . Oh, if only one had the gods' ears . . . Barring that, she would have to do something very soon, for she felt her unhappiness stretching to a point of desperation. Even madness.

* * *

A week later, the butler announced, "Madam Connaught, there is a rather old woman, disreputably dressed, asking to see you. Naturally, I told her that you were unavailable, but she insisted. Shall I have the caretaker escort her off the property?"

Véronique tapped her pen sharply on the pages of her household accounts. "Has this woman no name?"

"I believe she said it was Mizras."

Véronique stiffened but kept her expression implacable. "Where is she now?"

"Outside the front door. I refused to let her in."

"Quite right. She's a poor, demented old soul to whom I occasionally give charity. I'll see to her myself."

With that, Véronique dismissed the butler, and heart beating rapidly, she flung on her cloak and hurried downstairs. She swept out the front door, hooked Mizra's matchstick arm through hers, and propelled the startled old crone along the gravel path away from the house and the prying eyes and ears of the servants.

Mizras, who looked even more ancient and infirm than when Véronique had first seen her—and yet somehow ageless— pulled back, but she was no match for the younger woman. When they were safely out of earshot, Véronique hissed, "Are you mad to come here? What do you want?"

"I want—"

"I have some money for you. Take it, but you must promise never to come here again." She thrust some coins into her hand, but Mizras allowed them to slip through her fingers.

"I have no use for money, not now. I'm old; my time is fast coming on me. There is only one thing that I need. And so I've come for the payment you promised. I've come for the heart of a child."

"You are mad, totally mad!" Véronique exclaimed. "To think of such a thing, to demand such a thing!"

"I want—"

"If you say one more word, I'll have you arrested and thrown into prison."

"When you were pregnant, when you needed me, you swore—"

Véronique slapped the old woman hard across the face. She reeled back and fell. "There! That's what you need to bring you to your senses. Now take the money and get out. If I ever see you on this land again, I'll have the caretaker set the dogs on you."

Mizras slowly picked herself off the ground, rubbing her bruises. She stumbled off, muttering, "She promised. She broke her promise. She'll regret this."

Long after Mizras had disappeared into the dusk, Véronique remained rooted to the spot, clenching and unclenching her fists. All sorts of fears wormed their way into her mind, but at last she managed to dispel them. After all, the woman really was at death's door. Devroe would be away for months, and by the time he returned, the old witch would be safely dead and buried.

Chapter 46

BRAVO'S JOURNEY took him through Tennessee, down into Alabama, west into Mississippi, and finally to New Orleans. He'd bought a horse when he left the Hermitage, and both he and the beast suffered woefully from the swarms of mosquitoes, ticks, and chiggers everywhere. He drew extensive maps as he proceeded, making routes he thought might best accommodate rail and telegraph lines between the cities that lay along his route.

In late summer he reached New Orleans to find that city in the grip of a heat wave that stultified its citizens: women fainted in the streets, men shot each other, old people died under the relentless sun. The levees couldn't contain the Mississippi and much of the riverfront lay underwater. He stayed in the Queen City for almost a month, trying to determine the easiest access to the port through the labyrinth of bayous that surrounded it.

He made a pilgrimage to Chalmette, where Andrew Jackson had fought the battle for New Orleans. Bravo sat on the battlefield for a long time, trying to visualize what had happened; he could almost hear the crackle of musket fire and the roar of the cannon. He wished that he'd known his father, however briefly, and then recalled what Circumstance once told him, "If you want to know what your father was like, then look into yourself."

When he rose to leave, he felt curiously at peace.

New Orleans wasn't all work for him; a man would have to be a fool not to enjoy himself in the City That Care Forgot. The food was the best he'd eaten, a mixture of French, American, and Creole. He visited a fancy house once, and left it ten dollars poorer and just as frustrated. He'd never been like his brother Gunning; love was the only thing that made him capable, so he would have to wait for that.

From New Orleans, Bravo headed north and west toward San Antonio. He rode for days, which stretched to weeks, and still he rode, living off the land, shooting game when necessary, and always mapping the terrain. Texas was endless. He reached the San Antonio area in mid-November, and his excitement rose as he approached Suzannah's ranch.

He'd written her that he was coming, but hadn't been able to give her a definite date. As his horse ambled toward a ranch house set in rolling hills, he saw a lanky youth cutting a stallion out of some wheeling horses in a corral, while another lad sat on the split-rail fence, shouting encouragement.

Bravo reined his mount and watched. He noticed then that the slim-hipped youth whirling the lariat was really a girl; the boy sitting high on the fence looked enough like her to be her twin. Bravo's heart filled to overflowing as he watched them: Suzannah's twins, Becky and Zeb.

"Do like I taught you, Becky," Zeb shouted. She shot him an annoyed look as she shouted back, "I taught you."

Becky threw her lasso and caught the stallion neatly, at which point Zeb slid down from his perch and lassoed the horse from another quarter. They worked together in an unconscious harmony until they'd quieted the stallion, a beautiful roan. Then Becky slipped a halter over the horse's head. As they led him around the corral, they noticed the tall stranger watching them.

Bravo dismounted and walked over to them. His face was begrimed with dust and a broad-brimmed hat hid his hair and shadowed his face; he knew he must look like a saddle-tramp.

"Hi! My name's Zeb, and this here's my sister, Becky. You-all looking for work? Lots of horses to be broken."

"Well, not exactly."

"If you're just passing through, Pa's not much on drifters. If you expect a meal and a bed for the night, it's only fair that you work for it."

"Is that any way to treat an uncle?"

Recognition lit their eyes at the same moment, and the twins threw themselves at him, making such a racket that Suzannah came running out from the house, while Jonathan came from the barn where he'd been working with the Mexican hired hand. Even their old hound Monday dragged herself out from under the house to join the excitement.

"It's Bravo!" Suzannah cried, and rushed to embrace him. Then Jonathan was pumping his hand and exclaiming, "My God, you've grown yourself into a man. Haven't seen you in fifteen years, yet it seems like yesterday."

Lupo, a grizzled Mexican, limped out of the barn and took Bravo's horse to feed and water him, while the Albrights went into the house.

"It's got two stories," Suzannah said proudly. "Most of the houses in these parts only have one, but Jonathan wanted ours to be a little different."

It looked comfortable, sparsely furnished with utilitarian wooden furniture, and lots of bear and puma skins on the floor. Bravo felt that the house exuded happiness—it sang from the bunch of wildflowers on the hewn table, from the yellow chintz curtains at the windows, from the miniatures of the family that stood on the shelves of a corner cupboard, but most of all it shone in the eager faces of the twins. Bravo had fallen under their spell from the moment he'd laid eyes on them.

"Where's Matty?" Bravo asked.

"Out on the range," Jonathan said.

"How is he?"

"Doing pretty well," Jonathan answered, but Bravo could tell from the look on Suzannah's face that something wasn't quite right.

Suzannah ran her fingers through her dark hair that was streaked with gray. "Matty's fine most of the time. You won't recognize him; he's sixteen and almost as tall as Jonathan. But there are times when he gets dizzy spells, and he can't remember anything that's happened."

"Getting better or worse? The dizzy spells, I mean."

Suzannah bit her lip. "Better I'd say, wouldn't you, Jonathan?"

He nodded. "Hasn't had a spell in six months, and I reckon it was four months before that." Jonathan chose his words with care. Bravo thought that he hadn't changed much since the last time he'd seen him, sparer of frame, maybe, and his cheeks

scored from the sun and wind. But he still looked like a
scarecrow with shoulders so wide they poked through his shirt.
Bravo had always admired his brother-in-law—thought him
taciturn and at times abrupt; but he was honest and decent.
And he loved Suzannah, which was the most important thing
of all.

"Wingate said to tell you that he thought the spells would
diminish as Matty got older," Bravo told them. "He's almost
certain that he'll outgrow them."

"That would be a blessing," Suzannah sighed.

During this part of the conversation Zeb shifted uncomfortably from leg to leg; he'd always carried a burden of guilt
over Matty's condition. Zeb's hijinks had set off a series of
events that ended in Rebecca and Matty confronting Devroe
Connaught, and it was then that Devroe had fractured Matty's
skull with his saber.

Sensing Zeb's distress, Becky slipped her arm around his
shoulder and murmured, "It was long ago, everybody's forgotten, and nobody blames you."

For dinner, Jonathan had Lupo slaughter a steer and cut
fresh steaks from it. Becky and Suzannah picked vegetables
from the garden on the south side of the house. Bravo studied
Suzannah as she prepared dinner. His sister had once been a
great beauty, gifted, gentle in her demeanor. Now at thirty-
eight, she looked her age . . . and a little more. The toll of living
on the frontier showed. But there was a quality about her that
defied description. Everything she did was done with joy . . . and
her happiness lit those around her.

By twilight Matty still hadn't returned and though Suzannah
tried to appear calm, Bravo knew his sister well enough to
realize that she was worried.

"Maybe Zeb and I should ride out and look for him?" Bravo
asked.

Jonathan tamped the tobacco in his corncob pipe. "That'd
be a mistake. The worst thing we can do is let Matty see our
fears for him; that way he'll never get over his ailments."

An hour later they heard hoofbeats approaching; then Matty
came through the door. "Uncle Bravo!" he shouted. He gripped
him in a hug. Suzannah was right; Bravo wouldn't have recognized the tall gangly youth. Bravo picked him up and tried
to whirl him around, and just barely got Matty's legs off the

floor. Whereupon Matty did the same to Bravo, to everybody's laughter.

"You missed supper," Jonathan said.

"That's okay. The cattle's all fine, Pa—gaining weight; wolves haven't got any of them."

"What took you so long?"

"My horse threw a shoe, so I thought I'd better stop off at the Kelleys' and get it fixed. Had a bite of dinner there."

"The Kelleys', huh?" Zeb hooted. "I'll bet Maureen Kelley helped you fix it!" He had to dodge around the room as Matty came after him.

A couple of good-natured punches were thrown and Suzannah explained, "The Kelleys are our nearest neighbors, and our closest friends. Matty and Maureen Kelley—well, they're looking at each other kind of seriously."

"Things start early out here on the frontier, don't they?" Bravo said.

"Why let life pass you by?" Jonathan grinned, and Suzannah blushed becomingly.

"Well I don't plan to get married, not for a long time," Becky said. "I'm going to Washington and study law, like Grandma said I should."

Zeb rolled his eyes and made circles with his finger around his forehead.

"Pa, Mr. Kelley said to tell you that there are reports of some more Mexican and Comanche raids north of San Antonio," Matty said. "They hit the Steinhoff ranch hard, killed off half their herd and shot two of their hired hands before they were driven off."

Jonathan slammed down his pipe. "Damnation, we ought to wipe out those mauraders once and for all. This has been going on ever since we beat Santa Anna at San Jacinto," he told Bravo. "That's why we formed the Texas Rangers, to protect the families living out here."

When everybody else had gone to bed, Suzannah and Bravo sat up and talked far into the night. Memories, laughter, sadnesses . . . Bravo realized that brothers and sisters had a bond between them that was unspoken, yet very strong; after all, they'd known each other long before husbands and wives entered the picture.

He told Suzannah what had happened to Kate and Gunning,

and she was heartbroken. "Mother wrote me about it, and so did Gunning. I honestly think he's repentant, and is just waiting for Kate's hurt to be over before they get back together."

A dying ember in the fire popped onto the hearth and Suzannah brushed it back into the fireplace. "Odd, I've never had a problem like that. In all the years of our marriage, Jonathan's never looked at another woman... of course, there aren't any other women out here to look at." This threw them into a fit of the giggles which they hopelessly tried to muffle.

Thinking it was best gotten out of the way, Bravo raised the question of his parentage. Suzannah looked at him with her dark-brown eyes. "I know that it must have caused you great pain... We all suspected, because you looked so much like Uncle Jeremy. It never made any difference to me, because I adored Uncle Jeremy, I knew he made mother happy, and of course, I loved you."

"What about Becky and her plan to go to Washington?" Bravo asked, amused. "She serious?"

"Oh yes, she's quite insistent about it. She wanted to go this year, but Jonathan said no. If she hasn't changed her mind in another year, then he'll consider it. Jonathan's not much on cities. He thinks they can pervert a person."

"Would Becky stay with Mother?"

"I hope so! She was the one who put the idea in her head in the first place."

"Of course Mother would love that; it would give her another life to meddle in!"

At last they went to bed, and as Bravo climbed the stairs to the guest room on the second floor, he felt so warmed by the life that Suzannah was leading that he thought her blessed.

Bravo intended to stay with the Albrights for a week, perhaps two, but Jonathan was such a fount of information about the terrain throughout Texas that his visit stretched out for three weeks. Bravo would join Jonathan, Lupo, and the boys doing the necessary work around the ranch, and then they'd spend the remainder of the afternoon and evening going over maps and plans.

Lupo, the old Mexican hand, had lost his family to the cholera plague back in 1834, and never remarried. After Enoch left with Rebecca in 1836, the Albrights hired him and he'd been with them ever since. Though he was now quite old,

Suzannah wouldn't have dreamed of putting him off the ranch, and everybody tended to pitch in and take up the slack of his chores.

There was a stir of excitement when word reached the ranch that President Polk had ordered General Zachary Taylor to move from Fort Jessup and set up camp at Corpus Christi on the Gulf Coast, Taylor to take up a better position to press United States claims for the contested Texas land to the Rio Grande.

"Soon as I'm finished here I'll be joining General Taylor at Corpus Christi," Bravo told the Albrights. "See what's happening there."

"Can we go too, Uncle Bravo?" Zeb wanted to know, itching with the excitement of it all.

"Seems to me you've got enough to do around here," Jonathan said mildly.

Then Christmas was upon them and Suzannah insisted that Bravo stay. As a present for the family, he built a tall windmill that drew water from the well and delivered it into Suzannah's kitchen.

"I hope you don't think this is spoiling me too much," Suzannah said to Jonathan. He blushed furiously, until she threw herself in his arms and kissed him. "I'd rather be with you than anywhere else on earth," she whispered.

The Kelleys came for Christmas dinner—six boys and three girls, every one of the boys capable of handling a rifle. After dinner they sang Christmas carols. Lupo strummed a few on his guitar and sang in Spanish, and in the foreign tongue the songs sounded haunting. Matty and Maureen just sat and stared glassy-eyed at each other; Zeb snuck behind them and imitated them, though with crossed eyes.

Three days after Christmas, Mr. Kelley galloped into the Albright ranch, his face grim. "There's been another raid on the Steinhoff ranch; burned them out. This time they killed Mr. Steinhoff. We're going after them."

Jonathan strode into the house and buckled on his holster. "We've been living this way for more than ten years," he said to Bravo. "A plow in one hand, and a rifle in the other. If only the Mexicans and the Indians would let us live in peace."

Jonathan, Matty, and Zeb saddled their horses. When Lupo saddled his, Jonathan shook his head. "I want you to stay here and watch out for Miss Suzannah and Becky. If anything happens, make sure to let the livestock out of the barn, especially Mean Red. That bull is our ticket to a decent life."

Bravo joined them and Jonathan said, "This isn't your fight."

"The hell it isn't," he swore gently, rolled the chamber of his revolver, then mounted up.

"Stay close to home," Jonathan said to Suzannah and Becky. "You've both got your rifles; keep them loaded and ready. We'll be back as soon as we can."

"Be careful," Suzannah called after them.

As they rode out Bravo said, "Do you think one of the boys should stay behind?"

"I'd feel better myself, but we need every rifle we can get. Lupo's a little old, but he's reliable and good with a gun. Besides, Becky's a better shot than I am—take the eye out of a puma at a hundred yards—and I left her one of those new repeating rifles."

Suzannah and Becky watched the posse ride off until their forms were tiny on the horizon. Suzannah put her arm around her daughter's shoulder. "We've got a lot of work to do, so it's best we keep busy, keep our minds off things until the men get back."

The day dragged by interminably, gave way to night and another tensely silent day. Their old hound Monday was fifteen years old now, arthritic, blind in one eye, and did little except lie in the sun, waiting for her time to come. But her nose was still sharp, and late the second afternoon she set up a fearful baying.

Suzannah and Becky ran to the window, thinking that the men might be back, but they saw a lone rider coming in.

"Who is it?" Suzannah asked.

"I can only make out that he's wearing a sombrero."

"Bolt the shutters and get the rifles," Suzannah ordered, and Becky sprang to do her mother's bidding. "You cover me. I'll go out and see what he wants."

"Be careful, Ma," Becky said, as she slid the rifle through the gun hole in the shutter.

Chapter 47

SUZANNAH STEPPED out onto the porch; when the rider came within a hundred feet, she held up her hand. "Don't come any closer. Who are you and what do you want?"

"Only some water, *por favor*," the swarthy man said in a Spanish accent, as he slowly continued toward her. "I've been riding for days, my horse needs water."

"He's lying, Mama," Becky whispered from her position behind the shutters. "There's plenty of water around."

"I told you to stop," Suzannah said to the man who had now closed the gap between them to fifty feet. "I want you off this property and right now."

The man half-rose in his saddle and looked around. His eyes swept the barn and the house. His tongue flicked to his sweeping black moustache. "Ah, *muchacha*, are you going to stop me? A lone woman?"

Suzannah turned toward the barn and shouted, "Lupo!"

The Mexican laughed. "Don't worry about the old man. I tied him up." Then he suddenly dug his spurs into his horse's flanks and bolted toward Suzannah, at the same time drawing his pistol. Before he could get off a shot, Becky fired. Her bullet caught the man in the chest and lifted him right out of his saddle. He hit the ground and lay still.

"Get back in the house, Mama!" Becky called as she saw

361

a half-naked Comanche spring up from the tall grass and race
toward them.

Suzannah dashed inside and slammed down the cross bar
just as an arrow sank into the wood outside. She reached for
her rifle and cocked it. "How many of them are there?"

"I think I saw two, but there may be more," Becky said,
drawing a bead on the Comanche now creeping forward in the
grass. She fired and there was a yelp of pain as the Indian
clutched his biceps and then zigzagged off.

"Becky, they have Lupo tied up in the barn."

"I know, Mama, I heard."

"How much ammunition do we have?"

"Papa left us a hundred rounds."

"When they see that they can't get to us, the first thing
they'll do is try to burn down the barn. I've got to save Lupo;
I've got to let the livestock out. Do you think you can cover
me?"

"Mama, don't go!"

"Becky, Lupo's been with us for more than ten years. When
Zeb broke his arm out on the range, Lupo carried him for five
miles. If this situation were reversed, I know he'd try to save
us. Both of our horses are in the barn, and Mean Red. You
heard what your father said, I've got to set them free. Now
cover me, and don't come out of the house, no matter what."

With that, she lifted the crossbar on the door, waited and
when she didn't see anything stirring, started running toward
the barn, about two hundred feet away.

Jonathan, Bravo, Matty, Zeb, and the rest of the posse had
ridden through the night to reach the Steinhoff ranch. Among
the smoldering ruins of the ranch house they found the body
of a slain Mexican, and discovered an English gold sovereign
on him.

Jonathan held it up. "Somebody's paying these men to stir
up trouble. Where would a poor Mexican get this kind of
money? Wouldn't put it past the English, the way they supplied
arms to Santa Anna when we were fighting for our independence."

All day long they rode hard on the trail of the renegades.
At one point Jonathan called a halt. "Looks like they're dou-
bling back on themselves."

Suddenly Zeb stiffened in his saddle. His horse spooked at

the sudden move and reared, and Zeb fought to keep from
being thrown.

"What's the matter, Zeb?" Jonathan called.

"I don't know, Pa." Zeb's face turned bloodless, his head
lolled forward on his shoulders, and then he jerked it back,
breathing hard. "Something's not right. Becky . . . Becky's in
trouble."

"How?" Jonathan demanded.

Bravo looked with fascination at Zeb. His mother had described how Becky had once had a premonition about her twin
brother when they were attacked by a puma. Now Bravo was
witnessing a similar experience and it raised the gooseflesh all
over his body.

"At the ranch," Zeb whispered. "There's trouble at the ranch,
Pa. We gotta get back there right away."

Without waiting for an answer, Zeb wheeled his horse and
galloped for the Albright ranch, with Jonathan and the others
following.

Suzannah ran as fast as she could, past her vegetable garden,
past the corral, where the horses churned, their noses alert to
the danger. Suddenly an arrow whistled through the air and hit
the ground just in front of her. She dodged, and another ripped
through the hem of her skirt. She didn't break her stride but
kept running for the barn.

She got within fifty feet of it when she saw the crouched
figure of a Mexican come around the side of the barn. Her
heart sank when she realized that he'd reach the barn door
before she did.

She raised her rifle and fired, but the recoil made the bullet
go wide of its mark. She saw a thread of smoke rising from
the back of the barn and whimpered; they'd set fire to it already!

"Lupo!" she cried out.

The grinning face of the Mexican loomed closer as she ran,
clutching the barrel of her rifle to use it as a club. But then
another shot rang out and the Mexican clawed at his face and
crumpled to the ground.

"Oh, Becky, thank God!" Suzannah breathed as she ran
inside the dim interior of the barn. In a corner stall, bales of
hay had been set afire and rivulets of flame were crawling
everywhere at once. She'd never be able to put it out.

"Lupo!" she shouted. Then she saw him lying on his back.

She knelt beside him and gasped when she saw that his throat had been slashed. "Oh the murderers, the damned murderers!"

A horse whinnied and crashed its hooves against the stall. Suzannah sprang to her feet and opened the stalls, slapping the horses on the flanks, shouting at them. Thick smoke began to fill the barn and she knew that she only had a few moments left.

She raced to the pen where Mean Red was chained, the ring through his nose. The great hulking beast pawed the earth and bellowed his rage while the fire inched closer. "The key! I forgot to bring the key to the chain!" she cried.

Fumbling, Suzannah reloaded her rifle, then fired a shot at the chain that smashed it. From the corner of her eye she caught a glimpse of two men at the barn door; she searched wildly for another way out, but behind her, the back wall was engulfed in flames.

She opened Mean Red's pen; the bull whirled around a few times, lowered his horns and galloped out through the open door. The two Mexicans saw him come charging and fled. Suzannah ran after Mean Red, streaking out of the barn, her dress on fire. Mean Red and the other livestock dashed into the open fields to safety.

"Only a few more yards and I'll be back in the house, only—" She heard the crack of the musket at the same instant that the numbing blow of the bullet caught her in the shoulder and pitched her forward. She fell, tried to drag herself to her knees, to crawl to the door, get to Becky, save her . . .

She heard a coarse laugh and felt her head snapped back as an Indian yanked her hair, exposing her throat to his knife. As he brought it down another shot rang out and he reeled away from her, his hands clutching his stomach. But the second man, a Mexican, grabbed Suzannah, and lifting her to her feet, used her body as a shield.

"Open the door or I'll kill her!" he shouted to the house.

"Becky, don't!" Suzannah started to scream, then gasped as the blade of the Mexican's knife slipped between her ribs and entered her back. She couldn't move, for the man still held her in front of him. She saw an Indian in a loincloth and breeches steal onto the porch and flatten himself beside the door. If Becky came out, the open door would hide him from her view.

"Oh, God, Becky, don't," she tried to scream but only blood bubbled to her lips.

As the door opened a crack, Suzannah whirled on her captor with the last of her strength and raked for his eyes. He raised his knife and slashed at her, tearing off the sleeve of her dress and leaving a long gash on her arm. Becky fired just as the Comanche behind the door swung it hard at her, throwing her off balance. Before she could take aim again, the Indian leaped on her, pulling her to the ground.

The two men, all that were left of the force of seven who'd originally attacked the ranch, dragged Suzannah and Becky into the house. Becky saw the blood staining her mother's dress and screamed. She tried to go to her and the renegade Comanche, the one she'd first wounded in the arm, knocked her across the room. She recovered and dove for the pitcher on the table and hurled it at him, but he laughed as it hit him, then bounced off without breaking.

Suzannah reached out for her daughter. "Don't, please, she's only a child, she's..." She gasped as rough hands tore her dress from her, and dimly she heard Becky screaming, "Mama!"

Suzannah passed out briefly; when she regained some semblance of reason, she felt the unsparing weight of the Mexican taking his vengeance on her. Through the pain, and the approaching specter of death, her one thought was for Becky... Dear God, protect her, she cried out with all the passion of her soul. She flinched with agony under the unrelenting assault of her attacker.

Her hands scrabbled across the puncheon floor, searching for something, anything she might use as a weapon. Her fingers closed around the shaft of the arrow that was still caught in the fabric of her skirt. She clutched it, and as the Mexican rose and fell on her with his abandoned motion, she waited for the right moment, then held the arrow up and plunged it into his stomach. His full weight came down on it. The arrow pierced home, and his strangled cry came out as a death rattle.

The Comanche saw what was happening and rolled off Becky. He sprang to Suzannah and plunged his knife into her breast. Becky saw her mother's head fall back and knew that the wound was fatal. With a piercing scream of anguish and rage, she scooped up the pitcher again and hit the Comanche with all her strength. The pitcher shattered, stunning him, and Becky, naked, fled from the house.

Outside, the burning barn lit the sky, sending a pall of smoke into the dusk. It seemed to Becky that her entire world was in flames—her mother dying, she herself violated in a way that made her want to die. Yet life still beat its relentless message of survival through her body and she ran for the corral.

A horse, she had to get a horse and ride away from here! Anywhere. She and Zeb had broken a few wild ones and she thought she might be able to ride one now. She caught up a rope harness as she ran, then screamed when she saw the naked Comanche start after her, a knife in one hand, a pistol in the other, his entire body a weapon.

A half-dozen wild horses milled in the small corral, panicked by the fire, racing around the split-rail fence, trying to get out. She slipped between the rail and into the corral, hearing the tread of the Comanche gaining on her.

Running, dodging, sobbing all the while, she fought to avoid the careening bodies of the horses that plunged and swelled around her. The Indian followed her, drunk on blood, and eager to finish what he'd begun. The girl is young, he thought, with a wonderful tight body. He would toy with her in the corral, let her exhaust herself. Then he would drag her back in the house and make her watch while he scalped the other woman. He would use the young one then, tie her up, take her with him, keep her as long as she continued to please him. A woman could be trained to do many things if she feared for her life. The Englishman with the crippled arm had paid them well for this raid. Six men had died at these two women's hands, and the girl would have to pay for it. When he was finished with her—in a week, or a month, or whenever she ceased to please him—he would slit her throat.

Becky managed to elude the Comanche, keeping the horses between them. But she was growing exhausted, and her feet were bleeding. Twice the horses knocked her down, and it was all she could do to keep from being trampled beneath their flailing hooves. The smell of the sweaty animals, the recollection of the sweaty man on top of her, pinioning her to the ground, causing her a pain so piercing that she thought she must die . . . and now she knew what awaited her if he caught her again. At that moment she slipped into a madness in which nothing mattered save survival.

In the darkness she could see the white teeth of the whinnying horses, like death's heads, and then came the resounding crash of the barn as the burning structure collapsed in on itself, sending a shower of sparks leaping into the night sky.

"Oh please, somebody come and help, please," she sobbed.

She could run no more and stumbled to the ground. She lay there, panting. The Comanche grabbed her by the hair and started to drag her out of the corral and toward the house, his high-pitched laughter seeming to resonate in her own madness.

They'd gotten halfway to the house when the Comanche stopped in his tracks and peered into the darkness. He reached for his pistol, but before he could make another move Jonathan sprang at him and almost cut off his head with the Bowie knife.

Jonathan ripped off his buckskin jacket and put it around Becky. "Where's your mother?" he demanded.

When she recognized his voice she burst into tears. "Oh, Papa, what they did. Oh, Papa, Papa."

He held her, trying to comfort her, but she was beyond such things, the horror seared forever into her brain.

Bravo, Matty, and Zeb rode up. They hurried into the house. Suzannah lay dying in a pool of blood. Jonathan knelt beside her and tenderly cradled her head.

"Becky," she whispered, tiny bubbles of blood forming on her lips.

"She's all right," Jonathan said, pressing her head to his chest, as if by holding on to her he would cheat death.

A tiny smile lit Suzannah's face. She looked at Jonathan for a long moment, the expression in her warm dark eyes encompassing the endless love she had for this man, her husband, father of her children . . .

"I love you," she whispered. "Build again."

Then her lids flickered, and the brown eyes that had warmed everyone they'd ever looked upon went blank and unseeing.

"Suzannah!" Jonathan screamed, his anguish tearing across the night. "Suzannah!" But she was gone.

Chapter 48

THEY BURIED Suzannah two days later on a knoll overlooking the winding stream and the line of trees heavy with
honeybees. As the first spadeful of earth hit the coffin, both
the Albright boys broke into heartrending sobs, but Becky still
appeared too dazed to know what was happening. Shock was
still imprinted on her pallid face, in her listless movements, in
her inability to say more than a few words at a time.

In his own bereavement Bravo saw something that frightened him: he saw Jonathan virtually die before his eyes. Oh,
his body was still functioning—he continued to breathe, he
continued to see—but as Suzannah's coffin was covered over,
so was his spirit buried.

The neighbors came from miles around to pay their respects;
Suzannah had been much loved in the community. After the
funeral, they stayed on and helped to rebuild the barn. When
it was all done but the finishing work, they left, and then
Jonathan called Matty, Zeb, and Becky to him.

"You all heard your mother before she died. We're to build
again. Well, that job's got to be yours now. You're not children
anymore, not after what happened. I've got other duties to tend
to. This pillaging and murder can't go on. It's got to be stopped
once and for all."

"What do you aim to do, Pa?" Matty asked.

"The Texas Rangers are joining General Taylor's forces at Corpus Christi. So I'm going there with Bravo to offer Taylor our services. I don't know what the people in Washington think, but as far as I'm concerned, there's a war going on here right now."

"Pa, Zeb and I figured you had that in mind. We talked it over and we'd like to go with you," Matty said.

Jonathan shook his head. "Matty, you're the oldest, so you're in charge. You know what to do to keep the ranch running. We've got responsibilities to the livestock, and to the land. You boys have been doing your work all of your lives, so it won't be anything new. One thing though, Matty: there's no time for you to be sick, or to get any of your spells. There's—just—no—time—for it! Do you understand?"

"I'll try my best, Pa."

"I know you will." Then Jonathan turned to his daughter, trying to penetrate the veil of shock and pain clouding her face. "Becky, Mrs. Kelley wants you to stay with her for a bit. She thinks maybe a woman's touch will bring you around a little faster. Do you want to go?"

Becky, unable to face anybody outside the family, shook her head violently. "No, Pa, please," she whispered, "don't make me."

He put his arm around her shoulder and held her to him. "Becky, my dear Becky... you've been through something terrible, but it's like your ma said, you got to build again. You need to rebuild yourself, come out of the shell you're in, walk in the sunlight again. You must do it, so that your mother's soul can rest in peace. Every day of your life, ask yourself, what would she have done? If you listen close, I know you'll hear the right answer. The last thing on her lips was concern for you. So go on living, or else you'll make her death the worst waste of all. Do you promise?"

Tears filled Becky's eyes, and she clutched her sides to keep from trembling. Finally, she nodded.

"Pa, when will you be back?" Zeb asked.

"When the job's finished once and for all. Not before."

With that, he mounted up. Bravo kissed his niece goodbye, hugged his nephews, then rode after Jonathan. Bravo knew that Jonathan was right about the kids no longer being children, yet he felt uneasy leaving them alone, without either parent.

When he mentioned this to Jonathan, he didn't hear him. Jonathan couldn't hear anything.

The two solemn men traveled south at a steady pace. A number of times Bravo tried to draw Jonathan into conversation: about rebuilding the ranch, what they might find in Corpus Christi, whether or not there'd soon be a formal declaration of war. But Jonathan wouldn't be drawn into talk. He found it an effort to breathe, let alone think and give an opinion.

The second day out a norther struck, a Gulf storm peculiar to the area; the dark-gray howling winds and the cold rain penetrating right to the marrow of the bone reflected Bravo's mood. How he wept for Suzannah, alive and vital one moment, dead the next. And why Suzannah, of all people, she who'd never harmed anyone? Where was justice and God's compassion in such a thing? It left him feeling numbed, and bereft, and angry.

He and Jonathan camped in the lee of a grove of trees and huddled in their ponchos, eating beef jerky and cold soggy biscuits. They bedded down early. In the middle of the night Bravo was wakened by soft moans, and saw his brother-in-law leaning against a tree, his body convulsed with sobs.

The rain had lessened to a fine drizzle, and Bravo got up, made a small fire, then led Jonathan to the warmth of the blaze.

"There's nothing I can say that will make it any easier for you," he said softly. "The only thing you can do is live through it."

"Why?" Jonathan asked dully.

Bravo searched for an answer to the enigma that had once plagued him. "Because you've got three fine children who need you. Because Suzannah's last words were to build again."

Jonathan stared at the fire, his long arms around his knees. "I remember when we were running before Santa Anna's army in 1836 and she said to me, 'Come back to me. Because if you die, I don't want to go on living. Not even for the children.' That's the way I feel right now."

"I know." He told Jonathan a little of what he'd gone through when Anne died. "The first thing you want is to die yourself. But somehow you go on. You build a hard shell around yourself, because if you didn't, the memories would tear you to pieces. You never forget, but somehow you do go on."

They talked until first light made the tragedy a little more bearable, and then they rode on.

They reached Corpus Christi the first of February and found a bustling army camp. The town had been little more than a trading post on the west bank of the Nueces River. A half-dozen sheds with thatched roofs had comprised the permanent settlement, but now more than a thousand white army tents were pitched around the curve of the bay. On the extreme left of the tented camp, shanties were springing up like poisonous mushrooms, housing lawyers, gamblers, whores, and all the other hangers-on that trail every army and feed off it.

Jonathan and Bravo went directly to General Taylor. They found the old soldier sitting outside his tent, mending a tattered coat while he conversed with his field officers. Bravo thought him a significantly homely man, short, squat, thick-featured. Yet there was something homespun and very friendly about him.

"Captain Jonathan Albright of the Texas Rangers presents his compliments and awaits your orders, sir. I'm here representing Colonel Sam Walker of the Texas Rangers, who'll join you as soon as he's organized the Ranger forces."

Zachary Taylor, affectionately named "Old Rough and Ready" by his men, put little stock in formalities and readily agreed that Jonathan would act as liaison between Taylor's regular army and Colonel Walker's Rangers.

Bravo's status proved a little more complex. Feeling that the situation warranted it, he told General Taylor, in private, of the special project he was doing for the White House. "But if hostilities should break out, then I'd like to stay on here with your forces." He showed Taylor his credentials as a second lieutenant in the militia.

Taylor scratched his head, scratched his chin, waggled his eyebrows, then said he'd decide what to do about Bravo later.

Corpus Christi had little to offer in the way of diversion. When the weather was decent the men went hunting and fishing; some braved the cold waters of the Gulf. But for the most part, the three thousand men in camp roamed around with little to do except drink and get into mischief. In the short time the army had been bivouacked there, more than thirty saloons had sprung up.

Early one afternoon, while Bravo was reconnoitering the campsite, he came across a lieutenant struggling to get a mule out of a mudhole.

"Need a hand?" Bravo called, as he slogged through the mud to the officer. He was thin and almost boyish-looking, for all the braid on his uniform.

"I could sure use one," the lieutenant said with a midwestern accent.

"You're a regular, aren't you?"

"West Point," he said proudly.

Bravo and he began yanking and pulling at the mule, but she had other ideas and bucked, throwing the lieutenant ass-over-teakettle into the mud. Bravo tried not to laugh, but then gave up. Remembering an old trick, he called to the officer, still sitting in the mud, "Here's something they don't teach you at West Point."

He bit the mule's ear, fully expecting it would make her move. Instead, she let out a fearful bray and butted him in the stomach, sending him flying into the mud alongside the lieutenant.

Then the mule shook herself gingerly, and trotted off. The two men looked at each other and broke up with laughter.

"You don't find too many lieutenants who can laugh at themselves," Bravo said and extended his hand. "Name's Bravo Brand."

"Mine's Ulysses, but most everybody calls me Sam—Sam Grant."

Slipping, sliding, holding on to each other, they finally managed to ease themselves out of the sucking mud and trudged down to the Gulf.

"Only one way to take care of this mess," Bravo called. With a whoop, he dove into the water. As he broke surface he sputtered, "It's cold!"

Sam Grant then dove in; in short order both men had chivvied out of their clothes and swirled the garments around to rinse out the mud. They hung them on a couple of bushes to dry and then dove back into the water.

"What do you think of Old Rough and Ready?" Grant asked.

"Quite a character; refreshing after the pompous fools who pass themselves off as generals in Washington. Old Zach didn't seem to have too high an opinion of me though, and I can't think why."

"You're from Washington, you say?" Sam asked. "Maybe Taylor thinks you're one of Polk's spies."

"How's that?" Bravo asked, confused.

"The general claims that the War Department and Polk are asking him to do the impossible. Send out an army of four thousand men, most of them untrained volunteers, to confront a Mexican army that at last report numbered over thirty thousand. We don't have the proper supplies, or wagons, or ammunition. And I know, because I'm General Taylor's chief supply officer."

"Why would Washington do something like that?"

"Because we're here and they're there, and it's always easier to fight a war from behind a desk. Besides, Polk and Taylor don't get along; Polk's a Democrat and Taylor's a Whig."

"Politics even in the army? I can't believe it!"

"It's worse in the army than anywhere else. Did you see the way Taylor dresses?" Grant asked.

"Yes—like the town tramp."

"I think he does it to make fun of us West Pointers. All spit and polish, he calls us. Doesn't think that kind of discipline helps a man to fight. But this is our big chance to prove that a man can be *trained* to be a soldier."

"How come you picked the army as a career?"

"My father's a tanner in Ohio. Soldiering sure beats that, so I applied to West Point and got accepted. Nobody was more surprised than me. Especially when I graduated. Now I've got to get out of this water before I freeze."

They scrambled out and put on their still-damp clothes. "Thank God the sun's warm today," Sam said, his teeth chattering.

"Where are you off to now?"

"Requisitioning some food for the general. Ever seen prices as high as they are here? Potatoes five dollars a pound, butter thirty-seven cents a pound, and milk at twenty-five cents a quart? If I had my way, I'd throw these price-gougers in jail. I don't know why it is, but every time a man puts on a uniform, folks think he's ripe for a plucking. Seems like it's their only entertainment."

Bravo looked around at the vast empty plain. "Not too much to do here of a night, is there?"

"Well, there's a new bowling alley, called Stop That Ball! We just got another new saloon, which makes thirty-one. I've tried every single one of them, a few times around. Corpus Christi is one of the rowdiest, cutthroatest places I've ever seen. Go out at night and you're liable to get robbed or shot. The only law here is the law of the pistol or the Bowie knife. But I'm pleased to tell you that civilization has found us at last," he ended with a flourish. "Just opened a new theater."

"Amazing! You going?"

"Yup. Tonight they're presenting *Othello*. The theater's opening under the management of Hart and Wells, but the regular company of actors hasn't arrived yet—probably haven't figured out where Corpus Christi is. So they've called for volunteers from the army. I did the one thing an army man should never do—"

"You volunteered."

"Right."

"Don't think you're the right size or color for Othello."

"Nope."

"Iago, then?"

"Nope."

"Who then?"

Sam Grant scuffed his feet. "Say one wrong word and I'm going to throw you back in the Gulf. They're getting me up as Desdemona."

The production was a smashing success, and for his valiant efforts beyond the call of duty, Sam Grant received a bouquet of flowers after the performance.

On February 4, a dispatch from Secretary of War Marcy in Washington reached Taylor. He was ordered to take up a position on the Rio Grande as quickly as possible; the United States claimed that river as the rightful boundary between the two nations.

Chapter 49

IT TOOK a month for General Taylor to get all his supplies and transport ready; on March 2, the army set out for the Rio Grande, almost two hundred miles south.

Bravo had not been inactive during these weeks, going out on forays to scout the land for possible telegraph installations and forwarding this information back to Washington. He'd also heard from Samuel Morse that telegraph lines had been laid to Cincinnati; the network of communications was spreading ever westward.

But now Bravo was glad to be on the move, and most of the 3,554 men in the army felt the same way. Their supplies were drawn by a train of 307 oxen and mules that strung out for 17 miles behind them. They passed farmlands, and lakes fringed with trees in full leaf. Spring had come early to the Gulf Coast, and fireplant, lupin, and phlox grew in colorful profusion. Herds of antelope, spooked by the army, thundered across the plains and faded into the sun-hazed horizon.

Along the line of march, the army men picked up a curious nickname. The dust they kicked up soon covered them with fine white grit, very reminiscent of the adobe houses that were a feature of the countryside. The men were "as white as adobes," which was then shortened to adobes, and from there it was a simple twist of the tongue to call the men "doughboys."

Taylor chose to leave most of his supplies at Point Isabel, near the mouth of the Rio Grande; he posted a small force to guard it, then pressed forward.

On March 20, the army reached the bank of the fast-running river, across from Matamoros. Bravo estimated that the Rio Grande was about two hundred yards across, with banks as high as twenty feet on both sides. "It's going to be a hell of a river to ford," he thought. And they'd have to ford it to reach the Mexican town of Matamoros.

They'd been there less than a day when Jonathan rode into Taylor's camp with a report. Bravo was appalled to see how thin his brother-in-law had grown; his eyes seemed consumed by a burning fire.

"Matamoros is heavily fortified," Jonathan said. "They're gathering boats to make a crossing. General Mariano Arista, commandant of the army, is heading toward Matamoros with six thousand men and a large complement of cannon. He outnumbers us two to one."

Taylor hurriedly began building a fort facing Matamoros. So far, there'd been no real shooting between the two sides; neither wanted the responsibility of firing the first shot and starting a war that might yet be avoided.

By April 20, the American fort was fairly well constructed. That evening, a flourish of trumpets came from the Mexican side of the river. Jonathan said, "That'll be the arrival of General Mariano Arista, commander of the entire Mexican army, come to personally teach us a lesson."

The first thing General Arista did was to offer two hundred acres to every American who'd defect. A goodly percentage of Taylor's army was made up of recent immigrants from Ireland and Germany; the Mexicans played on the fears of these Catholics, insisting that Protestant America was planning to eliminate all Catholics. Two hundred soldiers in Taylor's army swam the Rio Grande to join the Mexicans.

On April 24, General Taylor sent out a party of sixty-three dragoons to patrol the American side of the Rio Grande. Though Jonathan had warned them that General Arista might cross the river in force, the dragoons allowed their Mexican guide to lead them into an ambush. Arista's men killed sixteen dragoons and captured the other forty-seven.

When the news reached Taylor, it plunged him into a somber

mood. He asked his aide, William Bliss, to write to Secretary of War Marcy, describing the action. The last words were, "The hostilities may now be considered to have commenced."

A Mexican attack seemed imminent. The fort was still incomplete, and most of Taylor's supplies were twenty-six miles away at Point Isabel.

On April 30, Jonathan came galloping into the fort and reined up hard at Taylor's tent. His lined face was caked with white dust, and only his eyes looked alive under the ashen mask.

"General, Arista's army has crossed in full force to the American side of the Rio Grande."

"Where are they?" Taylor demanded.

Jonathan leaned on the pommel of his saddle to keep his balance. "Ten miles downstream."

"How many men?"

"A full Mexican brigade, commanded by General Ampudia, Arista's second in command. Their lancers are in the lead. They're moving to cut off our supply lines and capture Point Isabel with all our wagons and supplies."

Taylor shouted to William Bliss, "Pass the order: We march immediately. Leave a detachment here to guard the fort. They'll have to hold out until we get back. The rest of us will march to Point Isabel, secure our position there, then move our supplies and munitions here. On the double!"

Five hundred men of the Seventh Infantry were left to guard the fort with Captain Jacob Brown in command. Jonathan and a detail of Texas Rangers elected to stay with them. Bravo and Sam Grant headed for Point Isabel with Taylor.

Chapter 50

"As A military man, what do you think of General Taylor's plan?" Bravo asked Sam Grant on the forced march back to Point Isabel.

"Don't mean to sound like a second-guesser, but I think he tarried too long. He could have resupplied our fort at the Rio Grande a week ago, before Arista moved up in force and the danger wasn't so threatening."

"Figure it that way myself. Maybe the general is getting a little old."

Taylor's men covered the twenty-six miles to Point Isabel within the day, thwarting the Mexican lancers, and immediately began the tedious and time-consuming task of fortifying their supply depot.

All day on May 2, the Seventh Infantry worked to shore up the weak spots at the Rio Grande fort. The following day a furious duel broke out between the Americans and the Mexicans, with cannonballs flying across the river. A half hour into the battle, a ball from an eighteen-pound American gun struck a Mexican twelve-pound cannon right in the muzzle and the gun exploded. But the cannonade increased in intensity through the following days. The Americans, forced to husband their ammunition, could only grit their teeth and huddle behind their walls.

On the morning of May 6, the Mexican cavalry and infantry successfully forded the Rio Grande and massed in assault positions outside the American fort. Major Brown and General Taylor had arranged a signal, and precisely at 6:30 A.M., Brown ordered all his eighteen-pounders fired at once; that signal meant that the Mexican assault on the fort was imminent. Then the ferocious Mexican cannonade began. Not knowing when Taylor would return, and how long they'd have to hold out, the Americans couldn't fire back for fear of expending all their ammunition, and could only cower under the relentless bombardment.

Just as the Mexicans massed for their frontal assault, Jonathan heard the sound of distant thunder. "That's our men returning from Point Isabel!" he shouted to the others. "The main Mexican army must have gone to intercept them!"

Some ten miles away, at a place called Palo Alto, Bravo climbed as high as he could into a stunted pine tree and put his spyglass to his eye. He called down to Sam Grant, "The Mexican army is just ahead of us, maybe a mile off. Their line looks about a mile long, and one end is anchored in a wood."

General Arista had sent four thousand of his men against Taylor, whose force numbered twenty-two hundred.

"See any cannon?" Sam called.

"Looks like they've got a lot of eight-pound cannon, but they're mounted on massive wooden carriages and drawn by oxen, so that ought to slow them down."

Bravo then trained his spyglass back on the American forces and their supply train which was strung out for miles. "The Mexicans see us, why don't they attack before we can consolidate? One lancer charge and they'd beat the hell out of us."

"Don't look a gift horse in the mouth," Sam called. "Let's just get our men in fighting position."

The terrain between the two opposing armies at Palo Alto was a rolling prairie, with an occasional freshwater pool. Spiny, murderous chaparral covered the ground everywhere, making it impossible for a man to pass through except on the narrow road.

The Mexican artillery opened fire first, but Taylor shouted to his commanders, "The range is still too great. Move our men up a little closer."

The Mexican gunners continued firing, but their powder

was inferior, so their cannonballs hit the ground and rolled; the Americans could see them coming and dodged out of the way.

Taylor formed the American line just beyond musket range, but within range of his cannon. The eighteen-pounders, loaded with grapeshot, opened first, salvo after salvo ripping through the Mexican position. "A little more grape, sir, if you please," Taylor called to his gunners.

Bravo could see the Mexican lancers trying to keep their horses steady under the withering barrage. General Arista was apparently stunned by the force and ferocity of the American artillery attack, and it took him more than an hour to draw up a battle plan. In that hour, the Americans had fully solidified their position. Then Arista played his trump card and ordered his lancers to charge. From the left, eight hundred crack Mexican cavalrymen galloped forward with eight-pound cannon following to support their charge.

American infantrymen of the Fifth Division rushed to meet the Mexican threat, and formed a hollow square, the infantry's traditional defense against cavalry. The first row of soldiers knelt while the second row stood tall, their muskets aimed at the thundering lancers. Rifles and bayonets bristled from the four-sided human fort, ready to deliver their deadly volleys from whichever direction the Mexican cavalry might charge.

"Here they come!" Sam Grant called, as the tide of Mexican lancers in their bright breastplates swept toward them.

A hundred yards from the American square, the lancers fired their muskets, hoping to get the Americans to fire prematurely; before they could reload, the lancers would be upon them. But the infantry, under the steadying hand of the officers from West Point, took the fire. Though some men fell, the square held. Now the lancers were so close that Bravo could make out their faces, and then Sam Grant shouted, "Fire!"

Horses reared, screaming in agony, blood blossomed on the vivid Mexican uniforms, horsemen fell and were dragged through the chaparral by their mounts. The line of lancers faltered, then veered and broke off.

The lancers milled about, just out of rifle range, then rallied as their artillery moved up and prepared to open fire on the Americans, still in their square formation. They might be able to withstand the charge of the lancers, but the Mexican cannon would rip gaping holes in their defenses; then the cavalry would sweep back once more and finish them off.

"Looks like we've got trouble," Bravo shouted to Sam Grant.

At that moment, two six-pound cannon from Battery C of the mobile, well-trained "flying" artillery came hurtling over to assist them. The horses wheeled, the guns turned to face the enemy, the crew dropped off the caissons, and within the minute, they'd unlimbered the cannon, loaded them, rammed, and fired. The very first volley blew the Mexican gunners away from their cannon before they had a chance to fire one round. Within fifteen seconds both American guns were ready to be fired again, and this time they aimed at the lancers, who had re-formed and were hurtling down on the square of men.

The flying artillery fired again and again—Bravo counted five rounds within one minute. The barrage stopped the lancers' charge dead in its tracks, and amid the screams of the wounded and dying, they fell back, their line completely shattered.

As darkness fell, a dense pall of smoke obscured the battlefield and both sides gradually ceased firing. The Mexicans retreated to a new position at the Resaca de la Palma, about a mile away, and some three miles from the Rio Grande.

In the American camp, all agreed that the flying artillery had saved the day. This new weapon would clearly play a formidable part in any future war.

"I'd say this day was a draw. Maybe we came off a little better," Sam Grant said. "But tomorrow may tell the tale. Either we beat them, or they'll overrun us and all our supplies, and this war will be over."

Bravo slept fitfully, wondering what was happening back at the besieged fort, wondering if they would be in time to relieve the trapped men. Visions of blood and gore, of torn limbs and broken bodies haunted him throughout the dark hours, but finally he wakened to a spring morning far too beautiful for the horror of war.

The Resaca de la Palma, where the Mexican army had taken up their defensive positions, was a steep-sided ravine that had once been part of the Rio Grande riverbed. Only one road crossed through the harsh, gullied terrain, and it passed through the Resaca, where the Mexican army lay, bristling with muskets and cannon.

"If we're to relieve our men at the Rio Grande, we're going to have to take the road and the ravine," Grant said to Bravo.

Knowing that he outnumbered the Americans, and convinced that his position was impregnable, General Arista was certain Taylor would never dare attack, and so he retired to his luxurious tent about a mile from the resaca. There he relaxed by sending glowing dispatches to Mexico City describing his victory at Palo Alto.

Confronted with a situation that looked hopeless, and still hearing the distant cannon reverberations of the American fort under attack, General Taylor called a council of war among his officers. Bravo, having distinguished himself in the previous day's fighting, was included.

"Our scouts report that a frontal assault on the resaca would be suicidal," Taylor said. "Arista's cannon are protected, and they command the road. Any suggestions?"

Taylor's officers insisted that he be cautious. Bravo listened until they'd all had their say, and then spoke up. "Suppose we tried to outflank the resaca by crawling through the chaparral?"

"Have you seen that tangle?" one of the senior officers exclaimed. "It's impossible to penetrate."

"General, we have five hundred men back at the fort; surely their lives justify such an attempt." Bravo's thoughts were of Jonathan . . . and of the three children back at the Albright ranch. They'd be orphaned if their father died.

"What would you do?" Taylor asked, fixing him with a dour look.

"We beat them yesterday, and I believe we can beat them today. We've got momentum on our side. They think their position is so solid they've been lulled into a false sense of security. We could take them by surprise."

"That is my opinion also," Taylor said abruptly. He turned to his senior officers. "Gentlemen, prepare your commands to advance." Taylor, impressed with the success of the flying artillery the day before, ordered them to advance up the road and engage the Mexican artillery. At the same time, the American infantry would be inching their way through the chaparral that grew along both sides of the road.

The flying artillery hurtled forward until they came within a hundred yards of the Mexican position. Under heavy fire, the Americans unlimbered their guns, and staring into the flaming maw of the enemy cannon, began to lay down a heavy fire of their own.

To the left of the vital road, the Fifth Infantry crept through the tangle of chaparral, the men cursing as the thorny bush tore at their clothing and ripped their hands and faces. Then the Mexicans spotted them and began shooting.

To the right of the road, Sam Grant, with Bravo crawling beside him, moved the Fourth Infantry forward, slithering this way and that wherever a penetrable place could be found. Once they'd gotten close to the resaca, the balls began to whistle very thickly overhead, cutting the limbs of the chaparral all around them.

"Can you see the Mexicans?" Grant called to Bravo.

"If I lift my head up more than an inch I'll get it blown off!" Bravo shouted back.

"Lie down!" Grant called to his men, "and stay down!" It was an order that didn't have to be enforced.

The flying artillery, fully exposed to the Mexican cannon, was being devastated. One of the officers galloped back to Taylor's command post. "General, those Mexican cannon are just in front of us," he said. "I think they can be taken. Otherwise we're lost."

Taylor immediately ordered the flamboyant dragoons to capture the Mexican cannon. They rode hellbent for leather at the Mexican position and overran it. But the momentum of their charge carried them to the far side of the ravine, and by the time they could wheel their mounts, the Mexicans had recaptured their guns.

Watching this, Taylor thundered, "Take those guns and keep them!"

This task fell to the infantry. Sam Grant and his men had worked their way closer to the resaca; at Grant's signal, they jumped over the lip of the ravine. After firing their first round of ammunition, they engaged the Mexicans in fierce hand-to-hand combat. Bayonets clashed with machetes as both sides battled for the all-important Mexican cannon. Though the Mexicans fought like devils, the Americans fought from the sure knowledge that unless they gained this road, their comrades in the Rio Grande fort were as good as dead. Bravo parried the bayonet thrust of a Mexican soldier and slammed his rifle butt into the man's chin. Gradually the Mexicans began to give ground and the cannon massed in the center of the Mexican line were captured.

Seeing that their principal guns were in the hands of the Americans, the Mexicans began a spirited retreat that soon turned into a full-fledged rout. They fled across the Rio Grande with the Americans in hot pursuit as far as the opposite shore.

Despite his own bumblings, Taylor, through the efforts of the West Point officers and the flying artillery, managed to change a potential disaster into a great victory.

When Bravo and Jonathan were reunited on the Mexican side of the river, Bravo said, "We've won this battle, Jonathan. What do you think will happen now? An armistice?"

Jonathan shook his head. "Those Mexicans will never rest until they've reconquered Texas. We've got to pursue them until we win. Pursue them until there isn't one man left who'll raise his knife or a pistol against any American."

Chapter 51

ON MAY 9, 1846, President Polk received General Taylor's dispatch of April 23, informing him of the Mexican ambush and saying that hostilities had commenced. Polk and the rest of the nation had no idea that by now the battles of Palo Alto and Reseca de la Palma had already been fought and won. Taylor's communiqué gave Polk all the ammunition he needed to ask Congress for a declaration of war.

The news electrified the capital. Rebecca hadn't heard anything from her children in over two months; fretting with worry, she had Tad drive her to Kate's house in Georgetown. "Is there any news from Gunning?" she asked.

Kate, busily making crust for an apple pie, wiped the flour off her hands. "Not a word! And it worries me. With Gunning on the frontier, and now the prospect of war—I tell you, if it were possible, I'd take the children and join him this minute."

"Oh, Kate, do you really feel that way?" She hugged her daughter-in-law. "Come. The Senate's debating Polk's call for war. I think we should be there."

Kate agreed, and the two women hurried to the Capitol, where the debate had flared all day. Rebecca and Kate listened as John C. Calhoun, once more senator from South Carolina, shouted, "I doubt that there is a war in progress in any constitutional sense!"

Then Thomas Hart Benton rose and declared, "I will vote for men and money to defend American soil as far as the Nueces River, the boundary that John Quincy Adams negotiated in 1819, but not one inch further!"

In the House of Representatives, John Quincy Adams held forth: "This demand for a declaration of war is merely Polk's scheme to advance slavery in the United States!"

The debate continued to rage, but when the vote finally came on May 13, the killing of American men by the Mexicans proved to be too strong an argument. The massacres at the Alamo and Goliad a decade before still seethed in America's memory, demanding retribution. And now the new attacks added fuel. The House voted 173 to 14 for war, and the Senate 42 to 2.

Still no word from Gunning, Suzannah, or Bravo. Rebecca, in a growing state of anxiety, busied herself with the war effort. The nation had practically no standing army at all, and the call went out for volunteers, twenty-five thousand to be supplied immediately from the southern states, the areas closest to the conflict, and an additional fifty thousand men to be recruited the following year from the northern states, though nobody believed that the war would last that long.

One afternoon, Rebecca went to Circumstance's house, where the two women began rolling lengths of gauze for bandages. "I wish Suzannah would write and tell me what's going on," Rebecca said to Circumstance. "I haven't heard a word from her in over four months."

Suddenly Jeremy burst in through the door, his young, eager face flushed with excitement. With his turned-up nose, clear brown eyes, and curly hair he still looked like a lad in his teens, though he'd recently turned twenty-one.

"You look like you're bursting with glad tidings," Rebecca said.

"I am! I've just enlisted."

"Oh, Jeremy, no!" Circumstance cried. Not everybody sanctioned this war, and among those who had serious doubts were Circumstance and Wingate.

"Mother, I know the way you feel. Maybe you're right; I don't know. But that's not why I enlisted. Don't you see? Men will be dying. I'm a doctor, and I'm not going to kill, but to save lives."

Circumstance pressed her fingers to her temples, and shook her head sadly. "I don't know why people, why nations can't settle their differences without killing. Sometimes I despair for the whole human race. But if you've enlisted to save lives, then of course you've done the right thing. When do you leave?"

"I don't know. I have to wait for orders. Nobody knows what they're doing. I've never seen such a mix-up as at the War Department. I don't think that President Polk expected the Mexicans to fight."

After their labors were done, Circumstance walked Rebecca home. The spring day was quite balmy, with wispy clouds strewn across a cerulean sky. The city had disagreeable winters and summers that were hellish, but spring and autumn more than made up for them. Almost forty thousand people lived in the capital now, and one no longer had to travel out to Georgetown to shop. After the grim depression, public and private building had commenced again and the Breech-Brand Stone Works were flourishing. Homes and government buildings were sprouting up all along Pennsylvania Avenue. More of the roadway was being paved; the façade of the Treasury Building, with its magnificent marble columns, was almost complete; and there was a grandiose monument being planned for George Washington, to commemorate the fiftieth anniversary of his death.

When Rebecca and Circumstance reached the house on New York Avenue, Tad came running in from his quarters in the carriage house. "A letter for you, Miss Rebecca, all the way from Texas!"

"Oh, thank goodness," Rebecca said. "From Suzannah at last." She looked at the envelope. "This isn't Suzannah's handwriting. I think it's Jonathan's. Something's wrong."

She tore open the envelope and read aloud. "Dear Mother, how can I begin? How can I tell you news so tragic that even now I weep..." The pages fell from Rebecca's fingers and fluttered to the floor. "I don't have to read it. Suzannah's dead."

"That's impossible!" Circumstance cried, scooping up the pages. A Mexican and Indian massacre... Suzannah killed... Becky violated...

Circumstance gulped and read aloud, "Matty and Zeb are old enough to take care of themselves; I don't fear for them at all. But Becky's suffered through something terrible, and we mustn't let it twist her. If anything should happen to me, I know I can count on you to guide Becky over this trying time.

"Suzannah trusted and respected you. After long years of our own misunderstandings, I too have come to love and respect you. So I ask you to do this in Suzannah's name, and in mine. Your loving son Jonathan, who grieves for you in this hour—"

A bloodcurdling scream came from Rebecca. She stood up and stiffened, her limbs trembling, her mouth stretched in a circle of horror as grief tore from her heart. Her daughter, her firstborn, the flower of her womb, the sweet creature who'd never harmed anybody in her life, but who'd given, and given, and always found more to give—why her? "Why?" Rebecca screamed again and again.

Circumstance crushed Rebecca to her bosom, seeing the naked torment in her eyes. Rebecca staggered, words formed on her lips but wouldn't come, then she slipped through Circumstance's arms and fell to the floor in a dead faint.

"Tad! Tad! Go and get Wingate. Tell him it's an emergency. Quickly."

Tad had been listening to the letter, stunned into immobility. Now he pulled himself together and raced off. Circumstance knelt at Rebecca's side. Her face was ashen, her lips blue, and her hands were ice cold. Tenderly Circumstance tried to straighten her crumpled form, careful not to move her too abruptly lest she'd broken any bones.

Soon Wingate arrived and he and Tad moved Rebecca to the downstairs bedroom. While he did a swift examination, Circumstance told him the dreadful news.

"That explains it," he said. "The shock was too much for her. She's had a stroke."

"Serious?"

"One side of her body appears to be paralyzed. I'll know better when she regains consciousness. I want you to get Kate. We'll need people to tend to her round the clock."

Circumstance left immediately for Georgetown. On the way, it came to her in overwhelming waves that Suzannah was dead, the dear friend of childhood, the girl who'd been a sister to her when others had shunned her because of her Indian blood . . . then the tears came, without stop. And Becky violated . . . Having been through that experience herself, she knew what it might do to the girl's soul. Oh, God, but it was a cruel and horrible world.

Within hours of learning the news, Kate had moved herself
and the children to Rebecca's house in Washington. When
Geary started a commotion with Peter, she smacked both boys
soundly. "There's to be no fighting—none, do you hear? And
no noise, and no complaints. Your grandma is sick. We've got
to help her."

Peter rubbed his cheek. "What's the matter with her?"

"She's had a stroke."

"What's that?"

"Well, it's like a part of her has had a terrible shock, and
so she's hiding."

"Don't worry, we'll find her," Peter said resolutely.

Rebecca remained in a coma for two days; on the third, she
opened her eyes to find Peter smiling at her. When she tried
to talk she found that she couldn't get the words out.

Peter reached over and tried to straighten her lips. "Grandma,
you put your lips on crooked today." He ran and got Kate.
"Well, thank the Lord you've opened your eyes. Gave us all
quite a scare, you did, but you'll be around in no time at all."

Rebecca found that she'd lost the use of her right arm and
leg, her right eyelid drooped and her mouth remained pulled
to the side. But with Wingate and Circumstance helping her
exercise, within two weeks the effects of the paralysis had
somewhat diminished. But something had happened to her spirit,
something that couldn't be remedied—not by Kate's coaxing,
nor Circumstance's gentle talks, nor even the grandchildren's
bright interest in her.

One day toward the end of the month, Kate propped Rebecca
up on her chaise and put a light summer blanket on her.

"I killed her," Rebecca mumbled. "It's all my fault. If I
hadn't—"

"Begging your pardon, Rebecca," Kate interrupted, "but
that's exactly what's wrong with you."

"What do you mean?" Rebecca demanded, not expecting
this response at all.

Knowing that desperate measures were necessary or the
woman would remain an invalid the rest of her days, Kate took
a deep breath and plunged in. "You act as if you're the one
who's making the earth spin on its axis, as if you're personally
responsible for everything that happens in this world. Well,
I'm sorry to disappoint you, but you see, there's a God in
heaven who has a say in all that happens, and the sooner you

accept that, the sooner you'll get better."

"Rubbish," Rebecca grumbled.

"It's not rubbish that you lost your daughter, and my heart goes out to you for that—and to myself, for I remember her as a lovely human being. But there are more important things than spending your life mourning, as you once told me when my little girl died. How I cursed you then, for all I wanted was to be left alone in my misery. That's the easiest path to take now, isn't it? Believe me, I know."

"The cases are different," Rebecca muttered. "You're young, you had strength to cope, but I'm in the winter of my life."

"Sure you are, if you want it that way. Oh, wouldn't it be easy just to be an invalid and spend your days feeling sorry for yourself? But think on this. You have a granddaughter. Somebody who's been through a terrible ordeal, somebody who needs all the love and understanding that the women in this family can give her. I'm ready to do that, ready to go to her right now, if that's what it takes. So is Circumstance. Because we know what it means for a woman to be taken against her will."

Tears began to form in Rebecca's eyes, but Kate wouldn't let up.

"The person Becky needs more than anyone else is you, for you've filled her head with strange ideas about all the things that a woman can be... the way you tried to fill my head with them. Well, it's not in me to be like that, but from everything I've heard tell about this girl, she has the will and desire to accomplish it all. You've got the love stored inside you that only a grandmother can give. You owe it to her, you owe it to yourself, but most of all, you owe it to Suzannah."

Rebecca's face trembled and worked itself into a burst of tears, crying from a depth in her that she didn't think possible, crying for the two women of her blood who'd been so savaged—Suzannah killed defending her home and child, her granddaughter ravished... She would have taken their pain, willingly sacrificed her life for them. But since that wasn't possible, all she could do was weep for the cruel cheat that was life itself.

When her pain had dulled and the tears were no more, she lay back gulping, making the small sounds a child makes after the exhaustion of tears. She knew Kate was right; her own misery, her own illness—they were luxuries she couldn't afford. Becky... She lifted her tear-swollen eyes toward Kate and managed the barest glimmer of a smile. At that point, Kate broke down and the two women embraced fiercely, clinging to each other.

From that moment, Rebecca vowed that she'd get better, a little better with each passing day. Exercise was called for, both physical and mental. She read everything printed about the war. When news reached Washington about Taylor's phenomenal successes at Palo Alto, Resaca de la Palma, and Matamoros, his reputation soared.

Polk's administration continued to beat the drums for volunteers, and predicted an early victory. But there was a growing body of dissent, primarily from Massachussetts. That state, to Rebecca, had always represented the conscience of the nation. Added to John Quincy Adams's voice, now came the powerful voices of Ralph Waldo Emerson, who decried the aggressions of the United States, a nation supposedly dedicated to peace and justice. A young, aggressive politician, Charles Sumner, attacked "Polk's War" as little more than a land grab directed against a smaller, weaker nation. Henry David Thoreau, usually the most mild-mannered of men, went to jail rather than pay taxes to support a war he considered immoral. The poet James Russell Lowell branded the trumped-up conflict murder, pure and simple.

Knowing what she did about Andrew Jackson's reasons for wanting the territory, Rebecca found herself hard pressed to determine who was right and who was wrong. Then the horror of Suzannah's death would come over her again, and obliterate every other consideration. For what of the countless parents, American and Mexican, who would lose children in this conflict? Could any amount of land gained balance the life of one child lost?

Rebecca willed herself to hold her pen and she wrote to these New Englanders, trying to fathom what this new pacifist movement might mean to the nation, what it might mean to an entire new concept of human morality. And in her desperate need to know, her body began to heal itself.

The numbness in her lips gradually subsided, her words became distinct again, she swore at her stiff leg when it wouldn't respond fast enough. "I must get well," she insisted to Circumstance and Wingate. "I've got to go to San Antonio, or be in good physical condition when Becky comes to Washington."

Her grandchildren took turns walking with her as she limped along slowly with her cane, down to the Potomac one day, along Pennsylvania Avenue another, each time venturing a little farther than the last. Sharon wove her a crown of wildflowers, and one day Geary and Forrest prepared a picnic lunch that tasted somewhere between sawdust and hay, but Rebecca oohed and ahed over every mouthful. Among her grandchildren, Peter surprised her most; somehow he'd managed to curb his rambunctiousness, and when with her was attentive and gentle. Each day the eleven-year-old boy grew more like Gunning, wide-shouldered, slim-hipped, a thick shock of red-gold hair that couldn't be tamed, and large hazel eyes that could have belonged to a cherub if the Devil hadn't played so merry with them.

But there were times when no matter how hard Rebecca tried to control herself, she would start to cry, tears that streaked her cheeks. Then Peter's own eyes would grow moist, he'd take her hand and whisper, "Does it hurt that much, Grandma?"

"Only for a bit, child, but you're making it better."

Rebecca knew that without her grandchildren she wouldn't have survived Suzannah's death. "The Lord must be saving me for something," she confided to Dolley Madison, who was a frequent visitor.

"I know," Dolley agreed, sadness written on her own face. "When I lost my little boy and my first husband to the fever epidemic in Philadelphia, I too wanted to die; nothing seemed worthwhile anymore. But then I had Payne Todd to care for, and later, the Lord sent me Mr. Madison, and the rest is history. Yes, Rebecca, I do believe you're being saved for something."

Part of it was certainly to help Becky in whatever way she could . . . but there was more . . . much more . . . and Rebecca waited for that event, the reason, to reveal itself.

Chapter 52

AT THE end of May, a courier brought President Polk news from Devroe Connaught in Havana.

"Dear Mr. President," Devroe wrote, "I have the pleasure to report to you that General Santa Anna, if he were to be returned to power, would look favorably on the United States' desire to purchase the territories of New Mexico and California, and to settle the Texas boundary along the Rio Grande River."

Years before, Andrew Jackson had warned Polk that Devroe Connaught was probably a British spy, but Polk found Devroe's news too intriguing to dismiss. Though war had officially been declared on May 13, here was the means for the United States to get what it wanted without a long drawn-out struggle.

Polk continued reading. "General Santa Anna is prepared to return to Mexico immediately, but would naturally have to be slipped through the American blockade at Tampico and Vera Cruz. On your orders, that shouldn't be too difficult to accomplish."

Using his wife Sarah as a sounding board, President Polk weighed and measured the consequences of such an act. He decided to send his own emmissary to Havana to discuss the situation with Santa Anna himself, and if Connaught's information was accurate, to spirit the Mexican general back to Mexico, and to power.

* * *

The June sun baked the Kansas plains, raising shimmering waves of heat from the tall parched grass. Gunning Brand, sitting tall and easy in the saddle, shaded his eyes and saw the hazy outline of Fort Leavenworth straight ahead.

The frontier had weathered Gunning into a lean, tough man. His long full moustache, shoulder-length red-blond hair, and dusty buckskin clothes gave him the look of a mountain man.

He passed through the gates of the rough-hewn timber palisades with his detail of scouts, and reported directly to his commander, Colonel Stephen Watts Kearny. Gunning saluted him smartly—Kearny hewed to strict army regulations. "No activity to report, sir. The Indian tribes are quiet, what with the heat of summer on us."

Colonel Kearny, in his fifties, paced the narrow, airless confines of his log-cabin quarters, his determined stride making the floorboards creak. Gunning respected Kearny enormously. He'd fought in the War of 1812, and for the past thirty years had made a distinguished mark for himself on the frontier. His First Dragoons, stationed at Fort Leavenworth, had the reputation of being the best outfit in the army, and Gunning knew that was a reflection of the man—tough yet fair, and very effective.

Kearny stopped at his desk and glanced at a communiqué, as if to reassure himself that what he'd read before was accurate. "I've just received this directive from the President of the United States," he said. "We're to ready the First Dragoons for travel."

A great smile broke out on Gunning's face, showing his flashing white teeth in his ruddy-tanned face. "To join General Taylor's forces in northern Mexico?" He'd learned about Suzannah's death from Kate, and also learned that Jonathan and Bravo were fighting with Old Zach Taylor. Nothing would please Gunning more than to fight alongside them.

Kearny shook his head. "President Polk has entirely different plans for us. We'll be joined shortly by a thousand volunteers from Missouri. As soon as we've whipped them into shape, we're to move on Santa Fe and take the New Mexico Territory. Once that's secured, we're to strike for California, and take that also for the United States."

Gunning's eyes opened wide. "Take the New Mexico Territory and California with a thousand men?"

"I had somewhat the same reaction as you. But I'm informed

that the California port cities of San Diego, Los Angeles, and San Francisco will have already been occupied by the U.S. Naval forces dispatched there. We're to establish civil governments in both territories."

"Well, we have our work cut out for us, Colonel."

"That we do. Incidentally, in the future, it might be more appropriate if you addressed me as Brigadier General. That promotion has just been conferred on me."

"Congratulations, sir!"

"Thank you, Captain Brand."

"Captain—?" Gunning repeated, and when he saw Kearny grinning and nodding, he forgot all the protocol and pumped his superior's hand.

"Captain Brand, this will be a long and dangerous mission, and I depend on you. Don't fail me—or your country."

"I won't, sir, you can count on it."

Kearny nodded. "Good."

That night, Gunning wrote to Kate and his children. "The news has the whole fort excited, for after months of just sitting, we're finally going to see some action. New Mexico and California! There was a time when I would have jumped at this chance to cover myself with glory, but Suzannah's death has chastened me. I still can't believe it, and remember all the things I should have done, words of kindness I should have shared with her, as she shared everything with those who knew her. My darling Kate, if this teaches us anything, it's that we mustn't delay too long; life can be fleeting, and we must seize it while we can. I wish I could say that I'm a wholly changed and saintly man, but only you can decide that. I love you, Kate. I want us to be together. I want to hold you, want to know the joys of seeing our children grow. We talked about California, and now it seems like Providence is sending me there. I plan to look hard and long at that territory; everything I've heard about it sounds wonderful. Far away from all our old memories and hurts, perhaps, like Suzannah said, we can begin to rebuild. Kate, I love you. Gunning."

Chapter 53

"WELL, WE'RE on the march again," Bravo said as Zachary Taylor's army left Matamoros the first week in June. "Anybody know what Monterrey is like?"

Jonathan, about to ride ahead on a scouting mission, said, "It's the most important city in northern Mexico. Once, during one of those rare peaceful moments between Texas and Mexico, Suzannah and I visited there. She loved Monterrey; it's over two hundred and fifty years old."

"How big?" Sam Grant asked.

"Oh, maybe fifteen thousand. It controls the Rinconda Pass to Saltillo, and if we're to strike at Mexico City, Monterrey will have to be taken."

Where a small rocky trail branched off the main road, Jonathan said, "This is where I leave you. Bravo, take care of yourself. Don't forget to boil all your drinking water—that's a trick we Texans learned long ago." With a wave, he galloped off.

"Never saw a man work as hard as him," Grant said. "You'd think he was aiming to win this war all by himself."

"He is," Bravo said. "Sam, you suppose we'll have to march all the way to Mexico City? That's more than a thousand miles through desert and over mountains."

"Nobody ever said war was fun."

* * *

All through June, Taylor's army marched, swiftly occupying Rynosa and Camargo. At Camargo, despite Jonathan's warnings about the town's unhealthy and unsanitary location, Taylor decided to establish a forward base and camped there for nearly six weeks. The summer sun beat down mercilessly on the fetid town, and the temperature reached 112 degrees. Disease reached epidemic proportions.

Heeding Jonathan's instructions, Bravo boiled all his drinking water and peeled all the fruits he ate; he didn't know the exact reasons for doing that, but those who did seemed to avoid the illnesses. For others in the army, including young Sam Grant, whiskey became a preferred substitute to the water.

One day a group of reinforcements marched into camp, and the regulars crowded around to watch the snappy outfit.

"Who are they?" Bravo asked.

"They're the Mississippi Rifles, six hundred of them, commanded by Colonel Jefferson Davis," Grant said.

Then Bravo recognized Jefferson Davis as he passed and yelled, "Hey, Congressman! Bravo Brand, from Washington."

Davis turned and waved back.

"You know him, then?" Grant asked. "That's one fine-looking soldier."

"Met him in Washington. He was just elected to the Twenty-Ninth Congress, from Mississippi. But I guess he got called up because of the war."

The men of the Mississippi Rifles wore striking uniforms—red shirts with the tails hanging out over their white-duck pants, black broad-brimmed hats—and each man carried a new rifle and an eighteen-inch Bowie knife.

"If you boys can fight as pretty as you look, then we've really got something," one of the deadbeat volunteers called out.

"Oh, they can fight," William "Perfect" Bliss said. "They're the best marksmen in the whole damned army."

Jefferson Davis presented himself to General Taylor and Bravo was somewhat surprised when he saw the old man treat Davis with disdain. Davis started to say something, but Taylor glared at him with a look approaching hatred, turned on his heel abruptly, and left.

"Wonder what's the matter with Old Rough and Ready?"

Bravo said to Sam Grant, who answered, "The old man doesn't like him, that's for sure."

Later that evening, Perfect Bliss told them a story that explained that animosity between the two men. "You see, Taylor and Davis go back a long way. Jeff Davis served under the old man on the frontier and met Taylor's daughter Sarah. Jeff fell in love with her, but Taylor was dead set against his daughter marrying a military man. So Jeff resigned from the army, married Sarah, and they settled down on the Mississippi to become cotton planters. About three months after they were married, they went to visit some relatives downriver, and both of them came down with malaria. Jeff recovered, but Sarah died, and Zachary Taylor's never forgiven him. So now Davis will do anything to prove himself to the old man."

"I'll tell you this, we're all going to come down with fever unless we get out of this pest hole," Bravo said. "There's hardly enough wood left around to make coffins."

Seeing his army being rendered impotent before his eyes, Taylor finally moved from the place that had become a yawning graveyard. In the middle of August, the American army occupied Cerralvo, then moved on to Marín, which they took on the seventeenth of September. Two days later, a little the worse for wear, yet uplifted by the magnificent mountain scenery, the army reached the outskirts of Monterrey.

Bravo peered through his spyglass at the city obscured by mountain fog. Tall church towers pierced the morning mists and reached to snag the clouds. The warming sun gradually dissipated the mists and revealed a white stone city with its proud, colorful pennants flying from every steeple.

"It's a white fortress," Bravo told Sam Grant. "Barricaded, bristling with cannon at every access. It looks like they're waiting to give us hell."

Zachary Taylor chose as his headquarters a pleasant picnic ground three miles from Monterrey called Walnut Grove. The grove was bounded by lush fields of corn and sugar cane. When preliminary scouting reports indicated that the city and its environs appeared impregnable, Taylor scoffed. "We have six thousand hardened troops, ready and willing to use their bayonets, and that's the way we shall take this city, with the bayonet."

"Old Rough and Ready is playing fairly fast and loose with lives, isn't he?" Bravo said wryly. "Ever since the Whig politicians began fawning over him, intent on making him our next President, he thinks he's got to win, no matter what."

"Bitten by the presidential bug, eh?" Sam Grant smiled. "Well, I've heard tell it can give a man a fierce itch."

Jonathan Albright went out on another scouting expedition and at twilight the next day rode back into camp, a dirty bandage wrapped round a gunshot wound in his upper arm. He sought out Bravo and panted, "Ran into a little trouble, and can't rightly draw up the maps and plans that the general expects. Could you do it for me?"

"Not until I've had a look at that wound," Bravo said, and undid the bandage. The bullet had passed cleanly through the upper part of his arm; Bravo doused some whiskey on it—and gave a pull on the bottle to Jonathan—then rebandaged the wound with fresh linen. Afterwards, he helped Jonathan to Taylor's tent where he presented his report.

"The natural setting of Monterrey makes it easy to defend," Jonathan began. "It's nestled in the foothills of the Sierra Madre Range, and it's backed by the Santa Catarina River. On the west, the road that's most important to us, to Saltillo, is guarded by two commanding heights, Federation Hill and Independence Hill."

Taylor listened attentively as Jonathan went on, "The Mexicans built heavy gun emplacements on both hills. The only open approaches to the city are from the north and east, but that's where General Ampudia's massed his greatest concentration of fire."

"What are the possibilities of a frontal assault on the city?" Taylor asked.

"Heavily fortified there also. Ampudia has ten thousand troops, well dug in. They've converted a building into a fortress bristling with cannon. A frontal assault there would cost us dearly. The other approaches are guarded by the Tannery and the Devil's Fort. But even if we were to breach these outer defenses, Monterrey itself is one huge fort. The streets are sandbagged. The houses are stone or adobe, so they'll resist burning or bombardment. What's worse, their flat roofs make them perfect for snipers."

"What do you recommend?" Taylor asked.

"Appears to me that we've got to gain possession of the Saltillo Road. That's the main supply route. If we can capture the road, we can starve the Mexicans out of Monterrey."

"I want Monterrey and I want it quickly. Perhaps a two-pronged attack, a flanking move against the Saltillo Road, and a frontal assault against the city itself."

Bravo glanced at Jonathan. Both knew that such a plan would be in direct violation of everything a commander knew in the field, never to divide the army, making each half become weaker than the enemy's main concentration.

But Taylor, flushed with his victories, was ready to take that risk. On September 20, he sent General William Jenkins Worth with two thousand men on a flanking movement to cut the Saltillo Road. Jonathan insisted on guiding them, saying he could best get them through the unknown, treacherous terrain.

Sam Grant, Bravo, and the remainder of the army, two thousand strong, stayed with Taylor to begin their frontal assault.

Jonathan led General Worth and his men through fields of peas, sugar cane, and corn. By six that evening, they'd gotten close to the Saltillo Road. They were spotted and challenged by Mexican sentries.

"Better back off," Jonathan told Worth. "It'll be dark soon. We'd best wait till morning, or we're going to be shooting at ourselves."

General Worth wisely agreed. A dedicated, professional army man, he'd announced to his staff that the battle for Monterrey would provide him with either a grade or a grave.

During the night, rain began to fall, and though the men complained about the wet and cold, Jonathan told them, "It's a good sign. Ground mist and rain will muffle our approach."

At three in the morning, the Americans began their stealthy advance. Jonathan led them through the gullies and ravines. As first light was breaking, two hundred Mexican lancers rode out against them, supported by two thousand Mexican infantry. But the cavalry charge was met with punishing fire; many of the Americans, though volunteers, were frontiersmen, who had to be good marksmen to earn their food. In the first round of fire, one hundred lancers lay dead or wounded. The charge was broken and the Mexican infantry fell back. By eight that morning, Worth's forces had reached the Saltillo Road.

But they still didn't control it, for the batteries on both

BATTLE OF MONTERREY

TAYLOR'S CAMP

TAYLOR'S FRONTAL ASSAULT

ROUTE OF WORTH'S FLANKING MOVEMENT

CERRALVO ROAD

TANNERY

DEVIL'S FORT

CITADEL

MONTERREY

SANTA CATARINA RIVER

INDEPENDENCE HILL

BISHOP'S PALACE

EL SOLDADO

SALTILLO ROAD

FEDERATION HILL

Federation Hill and Independence Hill opened up, pinning the Americans down.

General Worth hunkered in a ravine, studying the situation. "We'll have to take both those hills, before they murder us with their fire. We'll attack at noon and try to flush them out before dark."

When the sun stood in midheaven, the men forded the Catarina River and overran the Mexican defenses at the base of Federation Hill. Pausing only long enough to reload, squads of men charged up the slopes, pressing flat against the earth to keep from becoming targets to the Mexican sharpshooters on the hilltop. Jonathan stationed a platoon of Texas Rangers at the bottom of the hill, and every time a Mexican stood up to get a better shot at the enemy scaling the hill, a Ranger picked him off.

At last, the Americans reached the crest, and in fierce hand-to-hand combat, drove the defenders off the top and down to a fortress midway on the far slope, called El Soldado. Worth had his men haul up two cannon to the crest, and brought El Soldado under fire. The artillery men hurled round after round into the stone fortress, softening it up, and then the infantry charged with such fury that the Mexicans abandoned Federation Hill completely and fled back to Monterrey.

"We've got the one hill in our hands," Jonathan said to General Worth. "If we take Independence Hill, we'll be in full control of the Saltillo Road."

"The men are too exhausted to fight more tonight," Worth said. "We'll hit them tomorrow at dawn." Then his ears pricked to the distant sound of gunfire coming from Monterrey. "I pray that General Taylor's attack is progressing as well as ours."

But Taylor's move against Monterrey had started badly and was approaching disaster. An inexperienced brevet colonel led the charge with eight hundred men, but blundered right between the enemy's strongest points, the Citadel and the Tannery, and their fire tore gaping holes in his ranks. Bravo and Sam Grant, in the front lines, rushed about, trying to encourage the pinned-down troops, as the cannon fire and the screams of the wounded drowned out their rallying shouts.

Taylor was on the verge of seeing half of his men killed when Colonel Jefferson Davis and his Mississippi Rifles struck back at the Mexicans, allowing hundreds of Americans to escape the deadly crossfire.

Sam Grant poked his head above a wall, then ducked as a bullet whined close and mashed itself against the stone. "General Taylor will kill me if he finds that I've disobeyed his orders. He wanted me to stay in camp and watch out for the supplies," he shouted to Bravo. "But I'm just too curious to see what's going on!"

One-third of the men committed to the frontal assault were killed or wounded in the first few minutes. But Taylor wouldn't give up; too much was at stake. So he poured more men and artillery into the galling fire, only to see them cut down also. The ground was slippery with the blood of the fallen men.

The Americans couldn't hold on to any ground they'd taken and were forced to retire to their only conquest, the Tannery, where they garrisoned that strong point. Night fell, ending the fighting. It had been a serious defeat for Taylor's battle plan. "We've lost nearly four hundred killed or wounded," Sam Grant said solemnly, "and the defenses of the city are still intact. And if it hadn't been for Jefferson Davis, we might all be dead."

Bravo flung himself down on the ground and stared up at the sky, letting the gentle rain bathe his face. "Another day like this and we're done for. I wonder how Jonathan's doing at the Saltillo Road."

"Better than us, I hope," Sam Grant said.

The mild rain continued to fall through the night as General Worth's men huddled in the darkness before Independence Hill. Like Federation Hill, it was essentially a plateau protected by two forts. The one on the crest was little more than a gun emplacement, but midway stood the formidable Bishop's Palace.

"The Bishop's Palace is the key to the western defenses of Monterrey," Jonathan told his Rangers. "Unless we take it, and then storm the city from this end, the battle for Monterrey is lost. We mustn't let that happen, or you know what our families in Texas will suffer."

At three o'clock, reveille sounded in the American camp, and the men began to creep up the slopes of Independence Hill. Bumping into each other in the darkness, sliding on the treacherous incline, they got within a hundred feet of the top before a sentry spotted them. Immediately, a hail of fire swept down on them from the topmost post; the Americans fired back as they scrambled up the remaining distance.

Jonathan reached the top, his Colt revolver blazing, and when that was empty, he slashed about him with his Bowie knife. In short order the ridge was cleared of Mexicans. But as the sun rose, the Mexicans in the Bishop's Palace trained their guns on the American's position.

General Worth ordered a twelve-pound howitzer taken apart, and fifty men carried the components up the hill. They reassembled it and returned the fire coming from the Bishop's Palace. The Mexican infantry counterattacked to recapture the crest, but the Texas Rangers, with Jonathan in the lead, overwhelmed them and the Mexicans fled back to the palace. Worth's men were in such close pursuit that the Mexicans inside the palace couldn't fire for fear of hitting their own men.

With Jonathan shouting, "Remember the Alamo!" they charged over the ruined walls, sweeping everything in their path. The Mexicans abandoned their position and ran pell-mell back to Monterrey.

The Bishop's Palace proved to be the key to the battle. In Monterrey, General Ampudia, seeing that the fortifications guarding his escape route from the city were lost, pulled his soldiers back and willingly gave up ground that Taylor's army hadn't been able to conquer the day before.

American infantrymen slowly worked their way into the city. The streets were covered with a hail of fire from Ampudia's cannon and from snipers on every rooftop. The American artillery men were hit the hardest, for they couldn't maneuver their guns in the narrow streets, and had to stand exposed while they loaded and fired. This gave the Mexican sharpshooters enough time to draw a bead on them.

"Every time we reach a corner, we get pinned down all over again, with more of our men being picked off," Bravo said to Sam Grant. "Instead of running through the streets and exposing ourselves, why don't we go through the *buildings?*"

Grant scratched his head. "What do you mean?"

Bravo kicked open the door of a house, his eyes sweeping the room. It was empty. "Look, this adobe is soft, and in a couple of seconds . . ." He hacked away with his Bowie knife until he'd gouged a hole in the wall. Then he stuffed it with a shell on a three-second fuse. He lit it, and dashed out of the room. A short, muffled explosion left a gaping hole in the wall.

The men went through the wall into the next attached house, blew out another wall, then another, until they'd worked their way down an entire block. In this manner, the Third and Fourth Infantry units managed to get within several blocks of the main plaza where the Mexican army was massed.

As Bravo's unit worked its way toward the plaza from the north and east, General Worth's men advanced from the west. By late afternoon, the American forces had battered their way to within two blocks of the plaza from all sides.

At a lull in the gunfire, a Mexican appeared waving a white flag. A Texas Ranger instantly killed him.

"What in the hell did you do that for?" Grant shouted.

"Because that's what they did to Major Fannin when he surrendered at Goliad. Our men came out under a flag of truce, and Santa Anna had them all shot!"

After a little while, another Mexican waved a white flag, and this one was allowed to present his petition. General Taylor was extremely happy to get it. His troops were exhausted; his ill-planned frontal attack had cost the army sorely. Taylor quickly accepted the terms of Ampudia's truce, and the Mexican army was allowed to march out of Monterrey two days later, with all its men and most of its arms.

Bravo and Sam Grant watched the Mexican soldiers depart marching under flying banners, and to spirited martial music. "What are you thinking?" Bravo asked.

"Same as you, I guess. That we may live to see these men fight against us another day."

Chapter 54

"IT ASTOUNDS me that General Taylor has committed the same blunder again!" Polk exclaimed to the guests in the State Dining Room at the White House.

Dolley Madison was there, her makeup a little too heavy, her yellow gown perhaps a trifle too bright for a woman her age; she was now in her eighties, but still very much the belle of the ball. She had all her mental faculties, and was invited everywhere in Washington. She'd insisted that Rebecca accompany her to the presidential dinner—"As a tonic, my dear"—and Rebecca, eager for the latest news of the war, had accepted.

It was an elegant dinner, five full courses; the Polks did serve wine with the meal, though they themselves abstained.

Polk continued, "Taylor is probably well intentioned enough, but I'm convinced that he lacks the true qualities of a general. First he allowed General Arista to leave Matamoros without pursuing him, and now General Ampudia at Monterrey. This war might have been over now if Taylor had pursued his opportunities and delivered the coup de grace."

Polk slammed a newspaper down on the table. "In spite of his incompetence, all one hears are cries of Taylor for President! Well, I can tell you this hoopla is a sham. The field reports, all of them overly optimistic, are written by his aide William Bliss—and why not? Bliss wants to marry Taylor's daughter. But I have this on good authority, none of the men who fought with Taylor at Monterrey will vote for him. The man has sprouted up like a poisonous mushroom of the bloody battlefield!"

Rebecca had never seen the President this angry. He looked weighted down with cares, and she knew from Wingate that the war had seriously affected his health. All across the country, cries were being raised from dissenters: In Massachusetts, they were calling it "Polk's War," in Congress, John Quincy Adams spoke out daily against the conflict. One might have expected it from Adams, but new voices were also being heard. A gangly young Congressman from Illinois named Abraham Lincoln had stood up in the House of Representatives and denounced the war as immoral.

Polk needed victory, she knew, and needed it quickly, or he'd find he was fighting a war at home as well.

"Despite Taylor's blunders, I am not a vindictive man," Polk was saying. "So in a conciliatory mood, I asked Taylor what his plan was for winning this war. Do you know what he told me? For us to sit in Monterrey and force the Mexicans to push us out of their country. Imbecile! It's precisely what this country daren't have, a war of attrition."

"What do you plan to do?" Rebecca asked.

"Since Taylor had the gall to disclose my plans to certain friends of his, who then leaked the news to the papers, I imagine that all of you know already. I planned to land an expeditionary force at Vera Cruz, then strike inland to the heart of Mexico City. It's only two hundred and forty miles from the coast to the capital, and I'm convinced that unless we force peace on them, we'll never achieve our objectives."

"We hear rumors that General Santa Anna has taken over the command of the entire Mexican army," Rebecca said. "Is it true?"

Polk glowered, it was a subject he didn't care to discuss. Having been instrumental in arranging safe passage for Santa Anna through the American naval blockade, Polk was mortified when Santa Anna dropped all his pretenses of peaceful negotiations and began galvanizing the Mexican population into a full wartime alert. Polk avoided Rebecca's question and said, "This war can't last too much longer. Commander Sloat's captured the port of Los Angeles. General Kearny's occupied Santa Fe. Taylor is in Monterrey, where he'll stay and maintain a defensive posture, according to my orders. The Mexicans know that we're preparing an amphibious assault against Vera Cruz. I think they'll see the light and begin peace negotiations. I'm going to appoint Nicholas Trist to handle our end of the talks."

Rebecca spoke up, "As you know, I had the misfortune of meeting General Santa Anna. I think you seriously misjudge the man if you believe he'll come to the negotiating table that easily. He's crafty and cruel and a consummate politician; he can twist the Mexican people around his finger, as witness the way he's managed to return to power again and again. Even if we do invade at Vera Cruz, can our small army, operating so far from home, win a war in such vast stretches of hostile territory?"

"We must win!" Polk exclaimed. "It's our manifest destiny!"

The President's outburst caused a pall to fall over the table and they finished the meal in silence. Mrs. Polk hadn't planned any entertainments after dinner—the Polks didn't smoke, drink, or dance, and so shortly after dessert, Rebecca excused herself. Though she'd almost fully recovered from her stroke, long evenings tended to tire her, and Wingate had warned her not to overdo things.

Her house lay empty. Kate and the children had moved back to Georgetown, and though Rebecca's life was a whole lot more peaceful, she did miss her grandchildren, whose laughter, tears, and growing pains seemed expansive enough to burst through these old brick walls.

She climbed the steps carefully, taking them one at a time, pausing at the landing so she wouldn't get dizzy. "The last thing in the world I need is to fall and break my hip," she muttered. "I've got to be in the pink of health when and if Becky gets here."

She'd written her granddaughter a number of times, but she'd never responded. Matty and Zeb had, but apparently Becky wasn't yet able to reach out to anyone. Rebecca sat at her desk and wrote.

"My darling Becky, I've just come from a dinner party at President Polk's and he feels certain that the war cannot last much longer. How I wish that were true, so that your father could return to the family. Each night I pray for his safety. But until he does return, I want you to consider coming to Washington. The house is lovely; I've lived here since I got married. When I go, as all of us must some day, and should you decide to stay in Washington and pursue a career, be it law or medicine or whatever you set your mind to, it would ease my heart to know that you'd be living here. That's why I so desperately want you to come to Washington now, I need to see you, need to hold you, need the comfort of your young, fresh face. Becky, my darling, your mother was a woman who knew the true values of life, and who lived by those values. Each day I try to live up to her example, returning bitterness with love, hatred with love, and love with love.

"When she died, I thought my own life was over, and yet I see that I've gone on living. One of the compensating joys of my life is my grandchildren. You above all, Becky, are a reflection of my spirit, my yearnings for what I know all women can achieve in this country. Your mother saw that quality in you, for in one of the rare instances in her life, she cautioned your father not to stand in the way of whatever you wanted to achieve. Deep down in my being I know that there's so much you want to achieve. Let me help you. Let time and distance be the balm of Gilead that heals your spirit. We must do that for your mother, we must do it for ourselves. With so much devotion and love to you, my dear Becky, Grandma."

"Doesn't seem much like Christmas without Ma and Pa here," Zeb said to Matty as they struggled to set the pine tree up in the front room of the ranch.

"We got to do it anyway," Matty said. "Maybe it'll cheer Becky up."

In the year that had passed since their mother's death, both boys had matured greatly. Matty's beard came in heavy enough so that he had to shave every third day, and Zeb was doing his darnedest to grow a moustache, though it had other ideas. Matty, going on eighteen, was beginning to fill out, and promised to have a more substantial physique than his bony father. He stood just under six feet, but when he put on his boots he topped that mark. Fun-loving Zeb, do-anything-for-a-dare Zeb, who liked to laugh better than he liked to work, had been much changed; a deeper, more sensitive part of him had emerged. He did more than his share of the chores; he and Matty not only held the ranch together, but even increased their herd.

"I know Pa's going to be pleased when he gets home," Matty said.

"I can't imagine him here in the house without Mama," Zeb said. "I don't know what he's going to be like."

"He'll be the same as always, our Pa," Matty insisted. But something in him knew that wasn't so. "Where's Becky?"

"Down by the river."

"What's she doing there?"

"Same as usual. Goes there at sunset time and just stares at the water, off somewhere in her own world."

"Zeb, what are we gonna do about her? You're closest to her, you gotta think of something."

Zeb hunched his wide shoulders, then yanked repeatedly on his long black hair. "She's gone away to a place where even I can't follow. Most of the time we move to the same rhythm, things that happen to her, I can sense also. But she's shut herself off. She doesn't want anybody to know what happened, doesn't want to think about it. A week ago she asked me if I thought she should go into a convent."

"Oh, Lord, no!" Matty exclaimed. "I don't have anything against convents, I guess, but not for Becky. She's just trying to escape from the world instead of facing it."

"I better go get her," Zeb said. "Let's light the candles on the tree tonight, that'll cheer us up."

Zeb bundled up in his sheepskin coat and walked through the clear crisp twilight to the river. He found his twin sister standing against a tree; she didn't have any coat on. "Becky, you'll catch your death!"

She gazed at him uncomprehendingly, then shook her head. "I was just trying to feel what the cold was like, just trying to get the feel of anything. But sometimes, I think I'll never be able to feel anything again."

Zeb put his arm around his sister and led her back to the house.

After dinner, Becky took out the three dozen candles that they saved every year for Christmas, lighting them only for a half hour, while they reveled in the glory of the flickering light against the dark needles, and the tangy smell of tallow mingling with pine; then they'd blow out the candles and save them for another year. That way, they got three or four Christmases out of each candle.

"Let's leave them on tonight until they burn down to nothing," Becky whispered. "Oh, please, let's, in memory of Mama. And as a prayer for Papa's safety."

Zeb shot Matty a long glance and his brother nodded. "All right, Becky." Matty put a pail of water near the tree, for though it had been freshly cut, pine tended to be highly flammable.

They sat quietly, watching the tiny auras of candleglow make the tree shimmer with light. A stillness descended over the house as they sat lost in thought.

Then Monday shuffled to the door and whined to be let out. Zeb walked the dog onto the porch. Becky stood up to adjust a drooping candle. Matty turned his head for no more than twenty seconds, but when he looked back at Becky, tallow had dripped on the sleeve of the dress and caught fire. This had ignited the pine needles, and the tree had begun to sputter and crackle as shoots of flame leaped from branch to branch.

"Zeb!" Matty shouted. Matty threw himself onto Becky, who stood immobile, not saying a word, while the fire raced along the sleeve of her dress. Matty wrestled her to the floor and beat the fire out with the skin of a puma.

Zeb ran back inside and dashed the pail of water on the tree, but it kept burning. He grabbed the trunk and hauled it out of the room, leaving a trail of sparking embers on the floor. He dragged the tree across the porch and threw it into the open yard.

Matty put out the fire on Becky's dress, then stomped out all the embers in the house. Then the three of them stood on the porch and watched the tree burn until all that was left was the charred skeleton.

Later that night, after Becky's burns had been tended to and she'd gone to bed, Matty sat up and talked to his brother. "Zeb, she didn't even feel it. Not even when it was burning her skin. I'm scared, Zeb."

"If Pa was here, he'd know what to do."

"But he's not, so we gotta solve it."

"Grandma," Zeb said suddenly. "You read her last letter. Maybe she can help. Because if we don't get Becky to somebody, and quick . . ."

"But all along she said she didn't want to go."

"I'll take her," Zeb said resolutely. "She'll go with me."

"When?"

"Soon as the roads are passable. I'll write Grandma tomorrow and tell her we'll come soon as I've convinced Becky. Don't you fret none, Matty, I'll come back here as soon as

I've delivered her safe and sound. I won't leave you alone. In the meantime, we can get one of the Kelley boys to help out with feeding the livestock and the like. Matty, we just gotta get Becky to Grandma, or we're gonna lose her, and if that happens, then I'm gonna die too."

Chapter 55

"GENTLEMEN, THIS is nothing more than a plot against me by Polk, Marcy, Scott, and company," General Taylor thundered as his officers congregated around his tent. "The President has appointed General Winfield Scott, that pompous fool, to command the Vera Cruz expedition against the Mexicans. Not only that, Scott is taking most of my regular troops and officers, and leaving me with a skeleton staff of volunteers."

Taylor's aides responded with a shout of protest. In the months since the battle for Monterrey, harsh communiqués had traveled between Polk and Taylor, and they'd become hopeless enemies. "Polk's ordered me to stay in Monterrey, but I won't." Taylor declared. "He's hamstringing me because I've won too many battles. He wants all the credit for winning this war himself. Scott wants to meet with me, but you can be sure that when he comes here to gloat over me, I'll be elsewhere!"

When Taylor finished his harangue, the officers drifted away from the tent. Many of them were disgruntled at the news.

"There's more fighting among the big shots in Washington than there is against the enemy," Bravo said to Sam Grant. "But taking away most of Taylor's regulars doesn't make too much sense, especially if it's true that Santa Anna is heading this way with a huge army. I don't know who's right, except

413

that I think Old Rough and Ready is beginning to believe his press notices."

Sam agreed. "I've never seen a man bitten by the White House bug before, but I don't mind telling you that I don't like it."

"Will you be going with Scott to Vera Cruz?"

Grant nodded. "I've already gotten my orders. What about you?"

"Well, lacking any specific rank in this army, I think Taylor will allow me to do what I want. I've a mind to stay here, keep my eye on Jonathan. Taylor's asked him to continue scouting with him, and he's inclined to take such awful chances."

"Your Excellency, the time to strike is now," Devroe Connaught said to General Santa Anna. "Taylor's forces have been halved. It will take General Winfield Scott at least two months, probably more, to consolidate his divisions and attack Vera Cruz. You tell me that the city is impregnable?"

"It is."

"Well then, in that time you can march to Monterrey, annihilate Taylor's entire army, which numbers some four thousand men, then swing down and eliminate Scott. In two brilliant blows you can wipe out the American army in northern Mexico, and then crush their attempt to invade Vera Cruz."

General Santa Anna, reclining on a field bed in his opulent tent, eyed the soft-spoken Englishman.

"Everything depends on speed," Devroe said. "We've made excellent time this far; now strike at Taylor."

Santa Anna had raised a twenty-thousand-man army in Mexico City and marched them to San Luis Potosí. Now he mulled the Englishman's advice. Back in 1836, Connaught had been uncanny in his assessment of the overall battle plan against the rebellious Texans. He hadn't listened to him then, and had fallen into Sam Houston's trap at San Jacinto. Now as Santa Anna studied the map, he became more and more convinced that Devroe Connaught's plan would bring him victory.

Santa Anna strapped on his artificial leg—he'd lost his leg in a battle against the French in 1839. He walked stiff-legged to his tent flap and called to his aide, "Alert the commanders. We march!"

On January 28, General Santa Anna rode out of San Luis Potosí to intercept Taylor. "That old fool has played into our hands," Santa Anna said to Devroe. "My spies tell me that he's left the safety of Monterrey and has moved deeper into our territory. We'll intercept him at Saltillo, or Agua Nueva. As for Vera Cruz, the stupid Americans don't realize that we have a deadly ally, *El Vomito*, the black vomit. Over the centuries, we hardy Mexicans have become inured to it, but the Americans, hah! If we confine them to the coastline, trapped in the fever belt, it will be a miracle if any of them escape alive."

"Nothing would please me more," Devroe said. He stood in his saddle and looked in front and behind him, where the twenty thousand troops were weaving through the countryside like a long black snake. Yes, this could be the turning point in his life-long crusade against the United States.

The march proved difficult. Rain, wind, and cold made the going miserable for the Mexican troops, many of whom were ill-clothed and ill-fed. But Santa Anna suffered no such deprivations. A dozen wagons carried his personal effects; each night he slept in a tent large enough to please an eastern potentate, dined off fine china and silver service, and even had a silver chamber pot.

Despite all his own refined tastes, Devroe looked on this kind of ostentation with a disdainful eye, but Santa Anna told him, "You don't understand the mentality of the peasant. They need somebody to look up to, to adore, and destiny has chosen me for that."

Then why are so many of your men deserting? Devroe burned to ask this piece of pomposity. One would never see such degenerate carryings on in her majesty's army. But that's why the British Empire was the greatest in the world, would grow to be the greatest in all history.

Santa Anna's army straggled into La Encarnación in mid-February. By the time all units had assembled, he discovered that five thousand of his soldiers had died, deserted, or were too ill to fight, leaving only fifteen thousand troops.

"But that's almost four times as many as Taylor has," Devroe Connaught said. "Surely the Napoleon of the West finds that satisfactory odds."

Santa Anna struck a pose and declaimed, "We are very close to victory. Once we defeat Taylor here, we shall ride forward on a crest of optimism, and defeat the Americans everywhere. After we've planted our flag of the serpent and the eagle over the White House, Mexico and I—for I *am*

Mexico—will build a great empire on this continent."

Devroe listened to his ramblings without saying a word.
Sometimes it was necessary for a man to delude himself with
grandiose schemes in order to win a battle.

"Make sure the guards are posted," Santa Anna said to his
aide. "We're getting close to the American lines, and those
damned *norteamericanos*, especially the Texas Rangers, would
give anything to assassinate me."

When news reached General Taylor that Santa Anna was
on the march, he sent out the Second Dragoons to size up the
enemy. But the large patrols always encountered stiff opposition from the Mexican advance guard, and could only report
second-hand information: that Santa Anna had reached La Encarnación and a large army was gathering there.

Taylor then called in Ben McCullough and Jonathan Albright of the Texas Rangers. "I need to know how many men
Santa Anna has, the size of his cavalry units, wagon trains,
number of cannon. Can you do it?"

"We'll do it, sir," Jonathan responded grimly.

At dawn, as Jonathan and Ben McCullough cantered out of
Saltillo, Bravo galloped up behind them and fell into stride.

"No," Jonathan said.

"But you're going to need somebody to watch the horses,
somebody who can ride back in case anything delays you."

"No," Jonathan repeated.

"Maybe Bravo's right," McCullough said. "We've a long
way to go, there and back."

Jonathan finally allowed Bravo to join them, but only if he
confined himself to safe tasks—caring for the horses, acting
as lookout. If anything happened to Jonathan or Ben, he was
to ride back and tell Taylor everything they'd learned.

Several days later, the three men successfully infiltrated the
outer posts of the Mexican army. "Ben, we've got to get closer
to the main camp, count how many divisions Santa Anna has."

Ben McCullough whispered back, "If we get any closer,
we'll practically be in Santa Anna's tent."

"Right," Jonathan said under his breath.

"What?"

"Nothing."

That night, the three of them worked their way deeper through the lines, avoiding the sentries who'd been lulled into complacency by the size of their gathering army. Surely no one would be mad enough to infiltrate here.

By first light, Jonathan, Bravo, and Ben McCullough found themselves on a small rise at the edge of a forest right in the middle of the Mexican encampment. McCullough whistled long and low. "By God, there must be twenty thousand troops here, easy, and every cannon in the Mexican army."

"Fifteen's more like it," Jonathan said. Then he turned to Bravo. "Ride back and tell Taylor."

Bravo hesitated a moment. "It would be safer if Ben went. I don't know the way as well."

Jonathan gritted his jaw, then nodded curtly. "Ben?"

Ben looked at Jonathan keenly. "What are you going to do?"

"Get a little closer, see if I can't find out exactly what Santa Anna has in mind. We're so far inside their lines, nobody even suspects us of being here."

Throughout the day, the men lay in hiding, scanning the encampment with their spyglasses, each time amazed as more and more troops joined Santa Anna's force.

At twilight, Ben McCullough left to go back through the Mexican lines and warn Taylor of the impending attack. Jonathan waited for half an hour until he was sure MuCullough had gotten safely away, then gripped Bravo's shoulder. "Wait here for me. I should be back before dawn. If I'm not, then ride like hell out of here."

"Jonathan—"

"Do as I say," Jonathan commanded. Bravo knew from the tone of his voice that nothing he said could stop him.

Jonathan left the protection of the forest and moved toward the center of camp, his focus always remaining on the small outline of a large, gaily striped tent which he took to be Santa Anna's. He mentally marked the way through thickets and ravines so he could find his way back. At one point he stumbled across a sentry who challenged him, *"Qué pasa?"*

Jonathan kept his head down and answered in Spanish—thank God he'd learned the language—but the sentry remained suspicious. When he came close, Jonathan hit him a blow in the solar plexus that ruptured the man's spleen, killing him.

Jonathan quickly switched clothes, putting on the tattered muslin wraparound pants, the poncho, which some woman had decorated with embroidery, and the tassled sombrero. He knew he was tall for a Mex, but with a slouch and these clothes, he might pass for a soldier. It would get him close to Santa Anna's tent. Once there, one shot from his Colt revolver and the war would be over.

Avoiding the spread-out campfires and the knots of soldiers, he managed to get within a hundred yards of Santa Anna's tent, then saw the cordon of guards. "Damn!" he swore softly. The guards kept the peons way from Santa Anna's quarters, for there'd been some unpleasant incidents of men fighting over the scraps from the general's garbage heaps.

How do I get to him? Jonathan wondered. If he tried to fight his way in, he'd be killed before he ever got close. Then the idea came to him, so simple that it made him smile. Allow himself to be captured! Once he was identified as an American spy, he'd most likely be brought to Santa Anna's tent. He'd be searched, of course . . . He stuck his revolver into the waistband at the back of his pants, then strapped his Bowie knife to the inside of his thigh. And what if they find both these weapons? he thought. No matter, only get into the man's presence and fate would show the way.

He took a deep breath then ambled toward the tent. When a sentry challenged him, he appeared startled, then threw up his hands, shouting, "Don't shoot!"

Guards surrounded him. He was searched, and the revolver was confiscated. With bayonets pricking him from every direction, he was brought to the Mexican intelligence officers, and interrogated. Learning that Jonathan was part of Taylor's army, the exultant officer notified Santa Anna. Then what Jonathan had prayed for happened. Heavily guarded, he was dragged before the general.

Jonathan blinked at the splendor in Santa Anna's tent. A brazier with glowing coals took the chill from the night air. A camp table was set for dinner with crystal, china, and silver service. Santa Anna lay reclining on a couch; he'd unstrapped his artificial leg, and the heavy wooden limb, dressed with a spurred boot, stood leaning against the couch. But no matter what the extent of Jonathan's amazement at the scene, nothing compared to his shock at seeing Devroe Connaught, a shock matched by Devroe's recognition of him.

"Has he been searched?" Santa Anna demanded.

"Yes, your excellency," the aide said. "We confiscated his revolver and this gold English coin."

The officer placed the sovereign on the table. Devroe picked it up and admired it, a sardonic, delighted smile on his face. "Jonathan Albright," Devroe said softly. "How extraordinary, the silken skeins of fate that keep drawing us together." Then he reached into his pocket, and took out an identical coin. He held them both up for Jonathan to see, and very softly said, "Yes."

Jonathan went mad, and his madness gave him the strength of ten as he ripped himself free of his captors and sprang for Devroe's throat. His hands clamped around it with all his strength.

Devroe fell back, gagging for breath, and Jonathan hung onto him. The men fell to the floor. Jonathan continued squeezing, only a few more seconds and Suzannah would be avenged . . . Then a guard hit him on the back of the head with a rifle butt. Even though he'd been knocked unconscious, Jonathan's fingers had to be pried loose from Devroe's throat.

Jonathan regained consciousness to find himself still in Santa Anna's tent. He lay on the floor before the general, his head pounding. Devroe stood alongside him, holding Jonathan's Bowie knife.

"Did you think we were stupid enough not to realize you had some heroic plan in mind? I searched you myself, and found this."

"How many men does your General Taylor have?" Santa Anna demanded.

"Go to hell," Jonathan muttered.

Devroe kicked him sharply in the ribs. "He has four thousand, two hundred, and forty-two volunteers, and perhaps another five hundred of what you call regulars, and maybe seventy-five Rangers," Devroe sneered. "That paltry little force is spread out across all of northern Mexico. You see, we know that much already, thanks to your own loquacious politicians in Washington."

"How many cannon? How many horses? How much matériel at Agua Nueva?" Santa Anna demanded.

When Jonathan didn't answer, Devroe punctuated each question with a punishing kick. Bayonets ringed Jonathan, and every time he tried to move, he felt the prick of cold steel drawing blood.

"Yours is a hopeless cause," Santa Anna said. "You may as well tell me everything you know, or I'll give you to my men. They know of the atrocities that the Texas Rangers have

committed against our people. Parts of your body will be cut
from you before your eyes, and fed to the dogs. I've seen them
disembowel a man and leave him to die; sometimes it takes
days. But if you talk, then I guarantee you a swift death."

"Why don't we commence now?" Devroe asked, and reached
toward Jonathan's groin, the Bowie knife raised.

Jonathan drew up his knees instinctively and cried out, "No!
I'll tell you what you want."

"That's more like it," Devroe said.

Jonathan groveled before the two men, making up figures
as they repeated their earlier questions.

Santa Anna appeared satisfied, and gloated. "You will now
be taken out and hung as a spy. As you twist in the wind, I
want you to reflect on what's about to happen to your army.
Even as we speak, my General Vicente Miñón with his entire
cavalry force is loping around the city of Agua Nueva to cut
the Saltillo Road and encircle Taylor's army. Your army will
be massacred, down to the last man."

Jonathan's mind worked furiously. Vicente Miñón moving
to outflank Taylor? The general didn't know this, nor did Ben
McCullough. Devroe Connaught and General Santa Anna were
the two men he hated most; if he could kill them he'd have
gladly given his own life. But more important was staying alive
and warning General Taylor about the Mexican plan of attack.
But how?

Then he caught sight of Santa Anna's wooden leg with the
spur attached to it, almost within his grasp. Before the startled
guards could stop him he lunged for it. He felt one bayonet
thrusting deep into his gut, but he yanked away from it, and
grabbed the leg. He flailed it about him, catching Devroe a
slashing blow across the face with the spur. Devroe screamed
and Jonathan struck again even as he felt a bullet tear into his
chest.

"Don't shoot!" Santa Anna cried out, immobile and unable
to get out of the line of fire.

With the spur, Jonathan yanked down on the fabric of the
tent and tore it open. Then he hurled the leg at the brazier,
sending the glowing coals flying. He bolted through the tear
in the fabric as the tent began to burn.

Jonathan stumbled out into the darkness. With the tent in
flames, Santa Anna had to be carried out. Much attention was
given to the safety of the general, and this aided Jonathan in

his escape. He dodged through the camp, seeing men running in the darkness, shouting and pointing, hearing the shots that flew all about him. One bullet smashed his elbow and the pain almost made him pass out, but he numbed his mind to pain, numbed his mind to everything save getting back to Bravo. He had to warn General Taylor, had to tell Bravo about Devroe Connaught.

He stumbled and crawled his way toward the glade where he'd left Bravo and the horses. Let me get there before first light, he prayed, before Bravo leaves. He fell and then felt strong hands around him as Bravo drew him into the safety of the forest.

"God, God," Bravo breathed, as he saw the blood all over Jonathan.

Jonathan's dark brown eyes focused on Bravo, words formed on his caked lips, and Bravo put his ear close to Jonathan's mouth.

"The Mexican cavalry . . . circling to cut the Saltillo Road and trap Taylor at Agua Nueva. Santa Anna's got about fifteen thousand men." Then he whispered, "Devroe Connaught."

The hair on the back of Bravo's neck stood up. "What about Devroe Connaught?"

"He's with Santa Anna, advising him. He hired the bandits who killed Suzannah. He boasted about it. Don't let him get away . . ." The words faded on his lips; he looked at Bravo one last time. "Tell my children I loved them . . . You must warn Taylor, our men . . ." And then life left his body.

Bravo crushed the lifeless form of his brother-in-law to his chest, feeling the unutterable sadness of the waste of this life, the waste of this senseless conflict that had brought nothing but destruction to everyone involved in it. But Devroe Connaught, Bravo thought—I'll bring him to justice if it's the last thing I ever do.

He dug a shallow grave and buried Jonathan as quickly as he could, marking the place in his mind. Then he rode hard for Agua Nueva.

Chapter 56

LUCK RODE with Bravo as he galloped hard for Agua Nueva; a number of sentries challenged him, but in the darkness he managed to avoid their fire. A hard day's ride found him within sight of the American encampment and he galloped straight to Taylor's quarters and blurted out the news.

By the morning of February 21, the army was evacuating Agua Nueva, but forced to leave many valuable stores, including wagons and ammunition. Taylor ordered a unit of cavalry to remain behind and destroy everything that hadn't been carted off, and to protect the American retreat.

One of the officers under Taylor's command, General Wool, had long before seen the defensive possibilities of a place called La Angostura, the Narrows. It was a narrow defile about five miles south of Saltillo, and close to the Buena Vista Ranch. Wool established his command post at the ranch while Taylor hurried back to Saltillo to prepare the defenses of the city in the probable event of Santa Anna's superior forces breaking through the Buena Vista line.

Extraordinary, Bravo thought, how Taylor always managed to get himself in trouble, either through oversight, or hasty action, or in this case, willfully disobeying orders. In the past he'd been rescued by his really professional officers, and to them, more than to the doughty old general, belonged the victories at Palo Alto, Resaca de la Palma, and Monterrey. But here at Buena Vista, with fifteen thousand Mexicans pitted against four thousand Americans, it looked as if Taylor had tempted fate once too often.

During the afternoon of February 21, the cavalry saw Santa Anna's army approaching Agua Nueva. They put the torch to everything, then joined the main army deployed in and around the Narrows.

Santa Anna, riding with Devroe Connaught at his side, saw the column of black smoke rising above Agua Nueva. "They have fled!" he cried. When he entered the small town and saw the burning buildings, and the other signs of a frantic departure, Santa Anna was convinced that he'd routed Taylor. "The enemy is demoralized!" he said gleefully. "We shall pursue him and crush him!"

"Your excellency, your men are exhausted, hungry. Perhaps a day's rest—"

"We'll rest when we've slaughtered them all. Forward!"

Bravo gazed at the majestic terrain of Buena Vista. All about him, rugged mountain peaks thrust at the sky, the rock turning pink, mauve, then deep blue with the sunset.

But the troops had little time for the glories of the landscape; they were busily being deployed. At the plateau of La Angostura, the valley on the right, harshly marked with rugged gullies, was impassable for any artillery. On the left, a succession of precipitous ridge and ravines scored the land right to the base of the surrounding mountains. Cavalry could not be used here to any advantage. Because of the Narrows, the Mexican infantry would have to come at the defenders practically single file. The situation reminded Bravo of the ancient Battle of Thermopylae, where a handful of Spartans held off thousands of Persians.

General Wool posted a battery of eight cannon on the road; supporting the artillery were the First and Second Illinois, the Second Kentucky, and a contingent of Texas Rangers. The infantry units took cover on the slopes and spurs to the left and rear of the cannon.

On the extreme left, along the base of the mountain, units from Kentucky and Arkansas dug in to prevent a flanking move by the enemy. Ordinarily these units were mounted, but here the land was so harsh that a man couldn't fight on horseback.

At dawn on February 22, 1847, General Santa Anna, his pennants flying, rode proudly into the valley at Buena Vista. The Americans gawked as the brilliantly dressed cavalry emerged from a cloud of dust.

Bravo had received permission to fight with the flying artillery. "Santa Anna's picked the wrong day for this fight," Bravo said to a gunner standing beside him. "If that Mex general knew anything about our history, he'd realize this was Washington's birthday. Now we can't let old George down, can we?"

The regimental band struck up "Hail Columbia!" Two Tennessee volunteers danced a hoedown to "Yankee Doodle Dandy," while the infantry hooted and hollered at their antics. The watchword of the day was "Honor of Washington," and the password raced from man to man, imbuing them with courage.

The Mexican buglers sounded a halt and Santa Anna deployed his troops. The engineers in each army carefully studied its enemy's moves, alert to gain any advantage. At 11:00 A.M., three Mexican horsemen, under a flag of truce, cantered up. They handed Taylor a note.

"You are surrounded by twenty thousand men and cannot in any human probability avoid suffering a rout and being cut to pieces with your troops; but as you deserve consideration and particular esteem, I wish to save you from a catastrophe, and for that purpose, give you notice in order that you may surrender in discretion, under the assurance that you will be treated with the consideration belonging to the Mexican character; to which end you will be granted an hour's time to make up your mind, to commence from the moment when my flag of truce arrives in your camp."

"Treated with consideration?" Taylor bellowed. "The way he treated the men at the Alamo and shot the Texans who surrendered at Goliad? Major Bliss, tell Santa Anna to go to hell! Put that in Spanish and send it back by this damned courier!"

Major Bliss, ever perfect, translated Taylor's reply: "In reply to your note of this date summoning me to surrender my forces at discretion, I beg leave to say that I decline acceding to your request."

At two in the afternoon, General Pedro de Ampudia, who'd surrendered to Taylor at Monterrey but had been allowed to go free with his men, began a flanking movement with one thousand of his most seasoned troops.

General Taylor sent the flying artillery to that sector. Bravo rode the caissons with the rest of the gun crew. Fire, reload, fire, the cannon volleys echoed across the plateau. But at a crucial moment in the fighting, the Second Indiana Regiment, made up mostly of unseasoned volunteers, panicked at the noise and oncoming Mexicans, and began running away. This exposed the artillery and the men had to withdraw, leaving one cannon behind them.

Ampudia's men reached the upper slopes of the highest mountain commanding the valley, and turned back every American attempt to dislodge them. As the chilling night mists decended on the mountain the Mexicans rejoiced, confident that in the morning, they would sweep down to finish off the Americans.

General Taylor, still concerned with his weak position at Saltillo, took five hundred men from Wool's ranks and raced back to that town to bolster its defenses.

Bravo huddled under his poncho; a cold drizzle began falling, and all he could think of was Jonathan's body lying in an unmarked grave in a foreign country. How would he break the news of his death to the children? He promised himself that if he survived this damned war, he'd go back, find Jonathan's remains, and bury him alongside Suzannah at the ranch. He stared up at the black, starless heavens and whispered, "I swear on my life that Devroe Connaught will be brought to justice."

In the dead of night, fifteen hundred Mexican light infantrymen joined Ampudia's forces on the mountain slopes. Now twenty-five hundred strong, they struck at dawn, Ampudia hurling his forces in a wide sweep to envelop the American left at the base of the mountain. The Kentucky and Arkansas troops, though heavily outnumbered, managed to hold their ground for more than an hour. But it was obvious to Bravo that they couldn't take much more punishment. The American flank and rear was in serious danger of being turned.

Then Sánta Anna ordered his cavalry and infantry units to attack the American left also.

The flying artillery moved forward, supported by the Second Indiana, and Bravo's unit commenced firing with all three guns. The Mexican line wavered under the bombardment, but by sheer weight of numbers their advance continued.

Bravo and the gunners kept up their rapid fire, hoping to halt the Mexicans. "Load them up with double charges of canister!" Bravo yelled.

"We've run out of canister," a rammer answered. "We've run out of everything."

"Then load the cannon with handfuls of stones!"

The barrels of the cannon grew hot and the metal sizzled as the swabbers swabbed them down. The Mexicans surged forward. Bravo kept firing until the last moment, then shouted, "Limber up those two guns and let's get the hell out of here!"

Bravo spurred his mount, racing before the mass of Mexicans that came swarming out of the ravines by the hundreds. The extreme American left, under Ampudia's relentless attack, was almost completely rolled back. The army was a mass of confusion as it retreated toward Buena Vista and Saltillo, pursued by the Mexicans who smelled victory.

At 9:00 A.M., General Taylor finally arrived on the battlefield, back from Saltillo. He was escorted by Colonel Jefferson Davis and his Mississippi Rifles. The presence of Taylor, sitting astride his horse Old Whitey, had an electrifying effect on his men. Some of them even stopped running long enough to take stock of the situation, then began running again.

General Wool galloped up to Taylor. "Sir, we are whipped!"

"That is for me to determine," replied Old Rough and Ready, and took command. "Colonel Davis, move forward with your men." Taylor ordered his former son-in-law.

Davis double-timed into position, all the while pleading with the stragglers streaming by him to return to the battle.

As they rushed to confront the Mexicans, the red-shirted Mississippi Rifles made a stirring sight to the demoralized Americans. Ampudia's cavalry thundered down toward them just as Davis's men gained a portion of flat ground. They steadied themselves, formed ranks, and at Davis's order, fired a volley. The lead cavalrymen tumbled to their deaths. A second volley caught those coming up from behind, and a third volley turned the charge. Bravo watched as the Mississippi Rifles worked in superb unison, their effectiveness reflecting directly on their brilliant commander.

Badly mauled, Ampudia's cavalry fell back to the mountain slopes, where they began to re-form.

* * *

Meanwhile, the Buena Vista Ranch had come under fire from General Torrejón and his lancers: their aim, to cut the Saltillo Road and cut off Taylor's army at the Narrows. But from the ranch house and its outbuildings came bursts of fire from the American marksmen that held the lancers at bay. Another move against Saltillo was barely beaten back by Taylor's skeleton force there. But then part of Torrejón's and Miñon's forces turned toward the Narrows to link up with the rest of Santa Anna's army.

The main threat to Taylor's outnumbered, demoralized men still came from Ampudia and his cavalry, for if they routed Davis's Mississippi Rifles and broke through, and joined Torrejón and Miñon, the American army would be slaughtered.

Once more Ampudia gathered his forces, preparing for the final assault: fifteen hundred lancers against three hundred riflemen. At a signal from Davis, the Mississippians took up positions in a wide V, with the open end facing the oncoming Mexican cavalry.

Bravo watched as the lancers, richly caparisoned, charged forward, and he couldn't help but marvel at their expert horsemanship. Their ranks were beautifully ordered, so close that they looked like one mass of men and horses. Silence prevailed among the Mississippians, as the lancers charged with the gleaming steel of their lances tipped forward.

"Don't fire until I give the order," Colonel Davis shouted to his men. The ground trembled as the lancers thundered closer. But when the Mississippians in their V formation made no move, either to fire or to break and run, the lancers grew confused. When they'd gotten within eighty yards and still nothing happened, their pace slackened. They could see the jaws of the V bristling with rifles, and they stopped dead in their tracks.

"Fire!" Davis shouted, and sheets of flame from the crossfire of the V poured into the ranks of the lancers. Men screamed as they toppled from their saddles, horses reared and went crashing down. The entire head of the lancer column was killed.

The survivors reeled back in confusion and the Mississippians gave chase, firing, reloading, firing until the lancers fled out of range. Bravo couldn't believe what had happened. If the Mexicans hadn't stopped, they would have smashed through the lines. But in the face of the unknown they'd hesitated, and were lost.

428   Evan Rhodes

Once again Jefferson Davis had rescued Zachary Taylor,
literally saving the general's reputation, as well as the lives of
thousands of American soldiers. In all the foolishness associated with war, and the nation's desperate need for a hero, Bravo
knew that lavish praise would be heaped on Taylor. In reality,
his bungling had gotten them into this fix in the first place.

The battle raged on for the rest of the day, its outcome
always in doubt. First one side held the advantage, then the
other, but always Bravo noted that it was the flying artillery
that raced in to shore up a weakened position, or rescue an
impossible situation.

Taylor seemed to be everywhere at once, his disheveled
clothes ripped through by bullets. At one point Bravo heard
Taylor call to an artillery commander, "Double shot your guns
and give them hell!"

The battle continued until dark, with no clear advantage
gained by either side. With twilight, the firing gradually died
down; when the smoke had cleared from the battlefield at Buena
Vista, it was blue with the uniforms of the dead, both Mexicans
and Americans.

Taylor's weary forces bivouacked in the field; the wounded
were carted back to Saltillo. Fresh troops from that base replaced them, but there were precious few reserves. The army
had suffered more than seven hundred dead, missing, or
wounded. Every American soldier knew that another day like
this one and they'd be lost.

Bravo felt so tired that his jaws ached and his body buzzed
with fatigue; every so often his entire frame shuddered with
the recollection of the cannon's roar and recoil. The ringing in
his ears made him think that he might have gone deaf. And
tomorrow would be another day like this one. Was it worth it
for nations to settle their disagreements this way, sacrificing
the absolute cream of their youth? The thought pursued him
through the night, and into the gray mists of morning.

But when the fog lifted, the Americans saw that Santa Anna's army had abandoned their positions and were retreating.
A sound went along the lines that Bravo would never forget,
a single gasp at first, then a murmur that rose and swelled like
a trumpet call, rising to a prolonged and thrilling shout, "Victory! Victory!"

Old Zachary Taylor and General Wool, both stunned with
this unexpected turn, fell into each other's arms and wept.

* * *

General Santa Anna hurried back toward San Luis Potosí, where he claimed a victory for his army. He didn't realize that with another day's fighting he could have defeated the Americans. But his own troops had been exhausted from the forced march, he'd lost more than two thousand men, he was out of food and ammunition, and he didn't dare risk the remainder of his army. For these were the soldiers he'd have to use to fight General Scott in Vera Cruz.

After the battle of Buena Vista, Bravo petitioned General Taylor to be allowed to join General Scott's army. Taylor, who had always believed that Bravo was somehow a spy for Polk, was relieved to see him go.

Bravo's reasons for joining Scott were simple. When Santa Anna engaged Scott, chances were that Devroe Connaught would still be advising him. Bravo was now convinced in his soul that he and Devroe would soon confront each other, a confrontation in which one of them would die.

Chapter 57

BRAVO JOURNEYED back toward Point Isabel on the Gulf Coast. There, he boarded a sail-and-steam ship taking men and supplies to Vera Cruz. The ship unloaded at a beachhead set up ten miles below the port city that Hernando Cortez had founded in 1519.

Several months before, Bravo had learned that Jeremy had joined the army medical staff, and he soon found him working at the hastily built field hospital on the outskirts of Vera Cruz. When the two men saw each other, they gripped each other in a bear hug.

The questions tumbled from Jeremy. He was saddened by the change in Bravo; he looked older, wearier, and pain lingered in his eyes.

Bravo told Jeremy everything that had happened, and of Devroe Connaught's complicity in the murders of Suzannah and Jonathan. "If anything happens to me," Bravo began, "see to it that Devroe Connaught doesn't get away with it."

Grimly Jeremy nodded. "You have my word."

Bravo looked at the dozen or so patients lying in cots, some of them at the point of death.

"Diarrhea, vomiting, dysentery, dehydration," Jeremy said softly. "Our men began coming down with these ailments as soon as we landed. Some swear it's the tainted water, others

say the food is contaminated because everything's fertilized
with night soil. But whatever's doing it, it's as if the land itself
was rejecting us."

As soon as Jeremy was able to get relieved from his duties,
he and Bravo rode toward Vera Cruz to watch the siege under
way. Bravo insisted on knowing all the details of the amphibious landing.

"After some of the most incredible foul-ups, all originating
in Washington—ships sent to the wrong ports, men and munitions never arriving, that kind of thing—General Scott decided that he could delay no longer. We sailed from Lobos
Island on March second. It was ninety-two degrees that day,
so you can imagine what the summer will be like. Scott knew
he had to capture Vera Cruz fast, and get away from the lowlands and into the mountains before the fever season started.
El Vomito, they call it."

"I've heard tell of this fever. How bad is it?" Bravo asked.

"Out of every ten men who come down with it, four die.
So even though Scott wasn't fully prepared, he didn't dare risk
further delay. We were eight weeks late already."

"What's Scott like?"

"Kind of pompous, a stickler for army regulations; the men
call him Old Fuss and Feathers, but I think he's smart, and I
think he's fair."

"How many troops do we have?"

"About eleven thousand at the last count, most of the regulars taken from Taylor's army, as you know. Scott knew that
Vera Cruz was impregnable from the sea, their Fort San Juan
de Ulúa is built out in the harbor on a coral reef, and it's got
a hundred thirty-five cannon, some of them ten-inchers; they
could sink our entire fleet. So he decided to land twelve miles
below Vera Cruz. The actual invasion was a sight to see; when
we headed toward the beach, the whole horizon looked like a
wall of canvas.

"We transferred from army transports to the navy's new
landing boats. Bravo, with your inventing instincts, this should
interest you: the landing boats were designed so one end could
open and the men rush out directly into the surf. We heard
rumors that there were Mexican lancers waiting just beyond
the rise of sand dunes, and as we waded through the surf we
expected them to come charging any second. But they never
did. That's where they made their biggest mistake. If they were

ever going to stop us, it should have been right there at our beach head. We started landing at five that afternoon, and by eleven that night, all eleven thousand of our men were safely ashore, without a single casualty.

"But we didn't count on the sand fleas—never saw so many in my life, and all fighting on the Mexicans' side. Men greased themselves with pork fat, or sewed themselves up tight in canvas bags. Still, in three days, we marched to Vera Cruz, cut their water supply, and formed a ring around the city."

"How many fighting men in the city?"

"Three thousand or so. There's another few hundred in Fort San Juan de Ulúa. We can't take the time to starve them out, because the fever season's almost on us. And a direct assault would cost too many American lives, so Scott's decided to force the city to surrender by bombarding it."

They came upon a team of oxen hauling one of the biggest cannon Bravo had ever seen, a thirty-two-pounder. Behind them other teams dragged two more of the monsters, and behind them came three more teams of horses each hauling an eight-inch cannon.

"Those big ones look like the cannon that blew up on the U.S.S. *Princeton*. Remember?" Bravo asked.

"You're right, they're navy guns. These have been perfected. Commodore Conner agreed to lend them to General Scott, provided navy gunners manned them." Just then, Jeremy waved to a captain in the army corps of engineers in charge of siting the guns.

"Who's that?"

"Real nice man. He's from Virginia, and that's like a kissing cousin to Washington, D.C. So whenever we get time off, we spend it talking about Tidewater Virginia, and the Chesapeake." At a break in the gun crew's labors, Jeremy called, "Hey, Captain, I want you to meet a kin of mine."

The man, about forty, had handsome regular features, dark hair and moustache, and was of medium height and build. When he strode over, Jeremy said, "This here's my cousin, Bravo Brand. And this is Captain Robert E. Lee."

From the moment they shook hands Bravo liked him. Lee's grip was firm, the look in his eye resolute yet gentle. His face and manner reflected consummate intelligence.

"We're about done siting these cannon," Lee said to Bravo. "Our smaller guns didn't make a dent in the walls, but we'll soon see what these guns can do."

General Scott had divided his batteries into four sections, each covering a side of the walled city. By March 22, everything was in place. The cannonade commenced and continued without a pause throughout the day. By evening, the powerful thirty-two-pounders had opened a fifty-foot breech in the wall.

During this time, Bravo had gotten himself assigned to a unit of the flying artillery. One evening, his head echoing with the roar of cannon, he went off on his rest break and stumbled into Sam Grant. Aided by a half-bottle of cognac that Grant had somehow gotten his hands on, they had a rip-roaring reunion. But not even the last of the cognac could hide Grant's despair over the war. "I just want to finish the thing and get home as fast as I can," he said. "Don't care if I never see another gun for the rest of my life."

Throughout that week, the awesome navy guns spewed forth their message of death against the ancient walls of Vera Cruz, while the army's lighter guns shelled the buildings within the city. On March 29, pounded into submission, Vera Cruz surrendered. Since Fort San Juan de Ulúa depended on the city for food and supplies, it had no choice but to surrender also.

"Our casualties are only thirteen killed and fifty-five wounded!" Bravo said in amazement to Sam Grant. "Old Fuss and Feathers may not be as colorful as Old Rough and Ready, but I think he's a damn sight better tactician."

By the first week in April, Jeremy reported the outbreak of several cases of *El Vomito* to General Scott. "Whatever force you leave to garrison Vera Cruz, may I respectfully suggest that you quarter them near the sea. There are fewer cases reported in those areas that are swept by sea breezes."

On April 8, Scott began to move his army inland and into the hills, his immediate objective, the pass at Cerro Gordo. The weather was getting warmer; flies, mosquitoes, scorpions, tarantulas, and every flying and crawling thing plagued the army as they followed the route that Cortez had taken three hundred and fifty years before on his march to conquer the fabled capital of Montezuma's kingdom.

"We will smash them at Cerro Gordo," General Santa Anna said confidently to Devroe Connaught as they rode at the head of the Mexican army. "Cerro Gordo is forty-nine miles from the coast, and controls the road into the mountains. If we can

confine the Americans to the lowlands, *El Vomito* will take
care of the rest. There won't be an American left alive by the
height of summer."

"Let us hope so, your excellency," Devroe said. The general
was sometimes given to the ravings of a madman, yet he couldn't
be dismissed. After the bloodbath at Buena Vista, Devroe had
despaired, yet Santa Anna had returned to Mexico City, convinced the populace that he'd defeated Taylor, then set about
raising a new army. Money was the problem—when was it
not?—but using scare tactics, Santa Anna had "borrowed" two
million pesos from the Catholic Church, persuading them that
if the *norteamericanos* won they'd eliminate all Roman Catholics. With that money, he lured new recruits; now he had an
army of eleven thousand men marching to Cerro Gordo.

As they rode, Santa Anna said bitterly, "Where is the British
intervention that you promised? Did you not tell me that they
would open a second front in the northwest and drain off the
American forces?"

Devroe flushed with embarrassment; he himself had been
caught by surprise by the change in British policy. Her majesty's government had found it more expedient to negotiate the
settlement of the Oregon boundary peacefully, than to go to
war. Devroe also found the news from California very disturbing. The American commanders, Kearny, Stockton, and
Frémont, had decisively beaten the Mexicans there and were
now in complete control of that vast territory. The only way
Mexico could regain it was to defeat Winfield Scott's army,
and force an advantageous peace settlement from the United
States.

As they approached Cerro Gordo, Devroe became more and
more impressed with its defensive possibilities. Commanding
hills overlooked the only narrow road; deep ravines and erratic
boulders could shield the Mexican forces as they lay in wait
for the Americans.

As Devroe set about helping Santa Anna deploy the troops,
he felt a renewed surge of confidence. Their position looked
impregnable; if he could keep Santa Anna from committing
any more blunders, they would most assuredly prevent the
Americans from breaking through the pass and escaping *El
Vomito*.

On April 12, an advance guard of American dragoons encountered the entrenched Mexicans, and sent word to General

Scott. He arrived on the scene two days later. Scott's staff officers wanted an immediate frontal attack. "A glorious frontal charge will impress the folks back home," General Pillow said. But Scott refused to do anything until his scouts had completed a careful reconnaissance of the area.

Bravo asked the commander of one of the scouting units if he could go out with him. "I've had some experience in the field," he said, and told him about Buena Vista. The commander agreed.

When Jeremy found out what Bravo was doing, he shook his head. "Don't you think you're taking too much on? Part of the artillery, and now scouting?"

"I know it," Bravo said. "But I can almost feel Devroe Connaught's presence here, and if there's the slightest chance for me to meet head on with him, I'm going to take it."

Once inside the enemy lines, Bravo left his unit and struck further into the territory. He never did see Devroe Connaught, but he found out enough to make him go rushing back to General Scott. "Mexican cannon control the high ground on both sides of the road. Their defenses go back in depth for a mile. The first position consists of three batteries situated on three promontories. About a mile behind these is another seven-gun battery meant to wipe out any Americans who might have survived the first obstacle. And commanding it all, Santa Anna has fortified Telegrafo Hill; it's six hundred feet high and bristles with another four-gun battery."

"Gentlemen, in the light of what we've just heard, a frontal assault would be suicide."

"Your best plan is to attack the right," Bravo said. "That appears to be their weakest position."

"But there's no road there," Pillow complained, still hell-bent on the glories to be gained via a frontal assault. A man puffed with his own importance, Pillow had received his commission because of his political connections; he'd once been President Polk's law partner.

"Here's a task for the engineering corps," General Scott said. "Let's see what they've taught the men at West Point, let's see if they can solve our dilemma."

"We came to fight a war," Pillow complained, "not build roads."

Nevertheless, Scott called upon Captain Robert E. Lee and two other West Pointers. They set out that night, and pressed deep into enemy territory.

Early the next morning, Jeremy received a hasty summons from Scott's headquarters and went there on the double. When he walked into the general's tent, he saw a man stripped to the waist, his entire torso and face covered with the most gruesome rash of insect bites, scratches, abrasions, and swellings. Bravo barely recognized Captain Lee.

"Can you do anything for this man?" Scott asked.

Jeremy inspected the wounds and huge swellings. "Anything poisonous bite you, captain, like snakes or scorpions?"

Lee shook his head. "But they're about the only things that didn't."

Lee had just returned with his report, but Scott insisted that he be treated first. Jeremy set to work with tweezers and forceps, picking out the burrs, splinters, and insect stingers inbedded all over Lee's body. He dressed the wounds with a salve that his mother Circumstance had made out of aloe and other soothing herbs. Meanwhile, Lee told his tale.

"That first night, I was so busy cutting a path through the jungle growth that I lost contact with my men. I couldn't call to them, for fear of alerting any enemy patrols, so I just kept on. Toughest terrain I've ever seen. Midmorning, I stumbled into a clearing. A small stream meandered through a clearing. Then I noticed the grass was trampled, so I took that to mean that people came there regularly.

"Wish I'd been wrong about that, but suddenly I heard voices; a party of Mexican soldiers were approaching to water their horses. I jumped behind a huge fallen log and squirmed under it. Fortunately, heavy ferns concealed me. The Mexicans filled their canteens, but instead of leaving, they sat down on the log not three feet from where I lay hidden. Every insect in the area began to bite and chew on me—spiders, slugs; I could feel the fire ants stinging me. But I knew that if I moved, I'd be captured or dead, so I just lay there. I thought that I'd found a way to cut the road through that dense jungle that would outflank the Mexicans, so I *had* to get back.

"Finally, the squad of Mexicans prepared to leave, but then another scouting party came in, and then another, and it wasn't until dark that it was safe enough for me to come out of hiding. By that time, every bug within five miles had had its fill of me. Then I made my way back to our lines.

"General, I'm sure that a trail can be cut through that terrain. It will be difficult, parts of it may be impossible, but we're trained to do the impossible. And we'll do it. We can move our men and artillery over this trail, and the woods are so dense that the Mexicans won't even realize it. There's another hill near Telegrafo, called Atalaya, about the same height. If we can move some of our artillery up the back of Atalaya under cover of darkness, we might be able to knock out Santa Anna's position on Telegrafo, and outflank him."

"That sounds excellent, Captain Lee," Scott beamed. "You may be sure that you'll receive a commendation for this."

Scott called a meeting of his senior officers and Lee repeated his report to them. Then Scott said, "In the light of the information Lee's brought us, I propose a two-pronged attack. A brigade commanded by General Pillow will feint an attack on the front position, where Santa Anna expects us. This will only be a diversion, for meanwhile, General Twigg's division of regulars will follow the trail that Lee and his engineers will cut, and then carry his guns to the crest of Atalaya. Captain Lee, when do you think we can have that road?"

"Within ten days, sir. Certainly in two weeks."

"Fine."

Jeremy, who'd just finished dressing Lee's wounds, interrupted, "Begging your pardon, sir, but I think you should know we've come down with two more cases of the black fever. In two weeks...I don't know. Time is essential; we've got to get into the mountains, or half our army may come down with this thing."

Scott looked to Captain Lee.

"Give me three days then," Lee said grimly.

"All right, gentlemen," Scott said. "We'll attack Santa Anna at dawn on April eighteenth."

Though he was running a low-grade fever because of the insect bites, the following morning Lee went out with a working party that included Sam Grant, Bravo, and a few hundred men. They began the arduous task of clearing the most rudimentary path through the underbrush. Horses and mules dragged boulders out of the way, and trees fell to the thwack of axes. Though silence was the order of the day among the working parties, they couldn't help but make a certain amount of noise.

Mexican pickets, alerted by the strange sounds, reported to Santa Anna, "Your excellency, there are noises coming from the forest."

Devroe Connaught, planning strategy, looked up with interest, but Santa Anna dismissed the sentries with a wave of his hand. "Noises, noises—the Mexican peasant always hears noises, the superstitious fool."

"Could there be anything to it?" Devroe asked.

"Impossible. I know this terrain well. Nothing could get through that impenetrable jungle. That's why I, the Napoleon of the West, have chosen this pass to defeat the invaders!"

When the Mexican sentries brought in a second report of unexplained forest noises, an irate Santa Anna accused the soldier of creating trouble and threatened to have him shot. The sentries shrugged and stopped bringing in the reports.

"I can think of a whole lot more things I'd rather be doing than hauling these cannon," Grant said to Bravo. In certain places, the walls of the ravines were so steep that animals couldn't get down into them, so the men had to drag the guns.

Bravo wiped the sweat from his eyes and peered ahead into the jungle. "It looks like we'll never do it, doesn't it? But then I look back to where we came from, and I realize that we are making headway. I tell you, nothing seems to stop that Robert E. Lee."

By twilight of April 17, Lee and the corps of engineers had reached the commanding hill, Atalaya. They prepared for the final assault on it.

"Scott's scheduled this attack for tomorrow at dawn," Lee told his men. "So we've got to get these guns in place by then."

At nine o'clock that night, Bravo, along with five hundred other men, officers and privates alike, put their shoulders into the drag ropes of the three cannon that Lee planned to carry up the mountain—a twenty-four pounder and two howitzers. A fire was kindled at the foot of the hill; and using this as a beacon, they started to climb up in as straight a line as possible, the better to keep out of sight of the Mexican forces on Telegrafo. Additional teams of five hundred men apiece followed Bravo's unit in relays, to relieve the first squad when they dropped from exhaustion. Men fell, cursed, stumbled, lost ground; cannons threatened to fall and crush those hauling them; but inch by inch the men fought their way up the mountainside. By the time the last gun was dragged to the summit, the exhausted men lay sprawled on the mountainside, unable to move. But the three guns were at the crest, ready to fire on Telegrafo Hill.

At seven in the morning, Lee gave the order, "Fire!" The Mexicans were dismayed to discover that the Americans had outflanked them. An artillery duel erupted between the guns on the opposing peaks. The American gunners were more accurate, and scored hit after hit, silencing two of the Mexican guns.

When the firing began, General Pillow began his feint at the Mexican front; it was soon beaten back. But the main American attack at Atalaya progressed quickly. Once the American artillery had knocked out all the guns on Telegrafo, the infantry came streaming down Atalaya, and then up Telegrafo, using their Bowie knives to gain purchase on the steep slopes. At the crest, they vaulted over the ineffective Mexican breast-works—nobody had ever dreamed of an attack from this quarter—and a furious bayonet fight began, cold steel flashing against steel. Disheartened by the audacity and ferocity of the attack, the Mexicans abandoned their hill.

Santa Anna, at last realizing that he'd been outflanked, lit out with Devroe Connaught at his heels, and the two of them disappeared into the countryside. When the Mexicans facing Pillow's division saw that their rear had been lost, they threw down their arms and surrendered.

The battle was over by ten that morning. Three thousand Mexicans were taken prisoner, and another 1,200 killed or wounded. The Americans suffered 431 casualties in all.

"Brilliantly conceived battle," Sam Grant said to Bravo. Both men were sprawled on the ground, limp with exhaustion. "I tell you, General Scott's going to come out of this smelling like a rose."

Bravo barely managed a nod. "I think a hell of a lot of the credit belongs to Robert E. Lee. He's the one who built that path through the jungle."

"Agreed," Sam Grant said. "And Scott thinks so too. Lee's become one of his most trusted field officers. Well, next stop, the halls of Montezuma, just a hundred and eighty miles away. Maybe that will be the end of this damned war!"

Chapter 58

DESPITE THE victory at Cerro Gordo, General Scott's troubles weren't over. Men who'd enlisted for a year in his army were due for a discharge. Scott pleaded with them to reenlist for another year, but most of the volunteers had had enough of the fierce fighting, disease, and deprivation. His army thus reduced to half strength, Scott had no alternative but to set up headquarters at Puebla and wait for new enlistees.

During this period, the regulars found time to make friends, talk about their homes and what they would do when the war was over. But there was no easing up of Jeremy's duties. In the field hospital, beds were filled with men coming down with exotic ailments. More soldiers were dying of these unknown diseases than had been killed on the battlefield. Jeremy was also uneasy about Bravo, for he'd fall into long silent spells, and when he did talk, it was usually about Devroe Connaught.

One evening, Jeremy, Sam Grant, Captain Lee, and Bravo were sitting around their small campfire. Sam stoked his corncob pipe and said, "Captain Lee, in your mind, what's the biggest headache of this war? I mean outside of the men dying."

"Communications," Lee said promptly. "One part of this army never knows what the other part is doing."

Bravo cut in, "All that will change. As soon as we've perfected the telegraph, messages will be sent from one sector to the other as fast as it takes to tap them out."

"That'd be all right if our lines were protected," Lee said. "But what if we were in hostile territory?"

Bravo chewed his lip. "I believe the telegraph is just the first step in marvels we can't even imagine. If we solved this problem, why one day we may even be able to send messages without wires."

"Without wires?" The men laughed aloud at that.

"Laugh if you want, but they laughed when we first began working on the telegraph, and now here it is, a reality."

"Well, Bravo, if you're going to make it a reality, you'd better get back East and work on it," Sam said. "How come you stayed here when the others left?"

"I've got a personal score to settle," Bravo answered softly. "When I meet up with Devroe Connaught, only one of us will be left alive."

"I know you to be a gentle man," Sam mused. "I know you don't like all this killing. Why do you have this passion to kill one man?"

"To me, he's the embodiment of evil. He's caused my family great grief. If I'd killed him ten years ago, as I wanted to, my sister and her husband would still be alive."

"Bravo, you mustn't take that blame on yourself; it's just the way fate deals things out to people," Jeremy said softly.

Bravo shook his head slowly. "You don't understand. Every one of us Brands are in danger if Devroe remains alive, especially the children. Kate's children, and Forrest. There's nothing he won't do to accomplish that end; he's proved that. So I've got to stop him."

Bravo stared into the embers of the fire. Kate—the mention of her name had awakened such memories in him. She was such a fine, wonderful woman, would make such a great mother for Forrest . . . and the boy needed a mother. The more Bravo thought about it, the more attractive the idea became.

General Santa Anna returned to Mexico City on May 19, 1847, only to find that the populace had turned against him. Devroe Connaught grew uneasy as he listened to the shouts of "Coward!" and "Traitor!" hurled at the general as he rode through the streets, shouts which continued even after Santa Anna ensconced himself in the Presidential Palace, a mansion of such grandeur that even Devroe admitted it compared favorably with some of the great palaces of Europe.

Devroe wondered if Santa Anna could survive this political upheaval. Seeing the look of doubt on the Englishman's face, the President said, "I am no stranger to ill fortune. You must understand my people. They have tempers as hot as the jalapeña pepper, and only I know how to control them."

In the next short weeks, Santa Anna amazed Devroe. First he bombarded the public with propaganda, and arrested anybody who dared question his policies. But still the population remained surly. So he issued a proclamation saying, "I am resigning for the good of the country—to prevent an internal revolution, which can only help the enemy."

In the past when he'd tried this ruse, the people had always begged him to stay on. This time, everybody practically applauded. Devroe made hurried plans to leave the country, getting his false passport and papers cleared by the British embassy. For if Santa Anna resigned, he'd have no influence at all with the new regime.

On the verge of having his resignation accepted, Santa Anna did a complete about-face and announced to the Congress, "Due to the overwhelming popular opposition to my terminating my public career, I am withdrawing my resignation."

The Mexican Congress, weak and ineffectual, couldn't unseat him, and so Santa Anna virtually became dictator of Mexico, with unlimited powers to wage war. By mid-July, he'd mobilized more than twenty-five thousand troops.

As Santa Anna mapped strategy with his staff officers, Devroe Connaught studied the maps. Santa Anna said, "Mexico City is perfectly suited for defense. Huge impassable marshes surround us." The marshes had once been vast lakes, and no army could get through them on foot. "The only approaches to the city are by way of these three causeways, and so I've divided my army into three units that can defend these routes."

Santa Anna continued, "Furthermore, General Scott is in hostile territory, miles from his supply depot at Vera Cruz, and he has less than half the men I do. If all else fails, there are two hundred thousand loyal people in this city, who if given the word will fall upon these puny Americans and tear them apart with their bare hands!"

The aides applauded the speech and Santa Anna made a little bow. Devroe spoke up. "It may interest your excellency that you also have a powerful, unexpected ally. I've learned from the British legation that the people of the United States

are disenchanted with this war, crying out against the heavy
casualties you've inflicted with your brilliant strategy. With
just a little luck, you could annihilate Scott's army totally, and
make the United States sue for peace, and under terms that
you'd dictate."

"The battle for Mexico City will determine the future course
of this entire continent!" Santa Anna exclaimed, and in this
instance Devroe knew that the Mexican dictator was right.

During July, reinforcements began to trickle in to Scott's
camp at Puebla, and by the end of the month he was ready to
move again. The second week in August, Scott's army reached
the five-thousand-foot-high plateau on which stood the city of
Mexico.

Bravo gazed around him at the awesome terrain, with huge
black lava beds, malodorous marshes that stretched to the horizon, and rugged mountains that reared their jagged peaks to
a sky wispy with smoke from sleepy volcanoes.

When the American corps of engineers reconnoitered, they
discovered that Santa Anna had prepared well. Lee reported to
Scott, "There are strong outer defenses bristling with cannon.
Within that there are heavily fortified redoubts. And there's
one fearsome barricaded hill called El Peñón, which commands
the main road from the east."

Scott mulled the information over. "Conceivably we could
take them, but at such a great loss of life that it would render
our force useless. We can no longer resupply ourselves with
men or munitions; we must make due with what we have, and
that means as few losses as possible. Captain Lee, find another
way for us to reach Mexico City without coming under the fire
of Santa Anna's outer defenses."

Once more Lee went out, searching, coming upon dead
ends, but at last discovering a possible route along the base of
the mountains south of Lakes Chalco and Xochimilco. "We'd
have to cross some vast lava beds and build some roads across
ravines," Lee told Scott. "But if we were successful, we'd
bypass most of Santa Anna's outer defenses and wind up at
the town of San Augustin."

"Done," Scott said, coming to a quick decision, for by now
he trusted Lee's judgment implicitly.

Horses whinnied, winches creaked as the army marched,
hauling all the artillery and ammunition over the razor-sharp

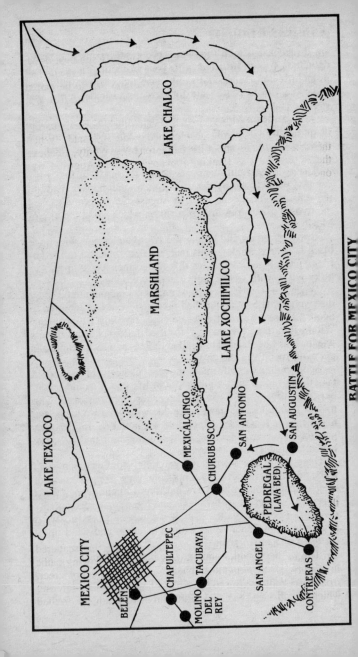

BATTLE FOR MEXICO CITY

stone of the lava beds. The fearsome summer sun beat down
on the black anvil of obsidian. Horses broke their legs and had
to be shot; men collapsed by the score and had to be carted
away in supply wagons. But the resolute army inched forward,
step by step, over the wasteland.

Bravo and Sam Grant walked beside their horses, sparing
them their weight. Grant, face burned by the sun, said, "When
the historians write about the battle for Mexico City, I believe
they'll say that this flanking movement to San Augustin was
one of the most brilliant maneuvers of the entire war."

"This horse doesn't think so," Bravo said as he tried to calm
the skittish animal.

"We've avoided the guns at El Pennón, and now we're in
a position to move against the capital from the south or southwest, which is their weakest point," Grant said. "That Lee's a
military genius."

At last they reached San Augustin, and after quelling the
token resistance offered by the surprised Mexican garrison, the
Americans captured the town and all its supplies. The army
then quickly swung southwest over another lava bed to Con-
treras and took that garrison also after a spirited battle.

Growing desperate because of the steady advances of the
Americans, Santa Anna concentrated a good portion of his army
at Churubusco. Here the battle was hard-fought, primarily because of the resistance put up by the San Patricio Brigade, a
battalion of men who'd deserted the American army way back
at Matamoros, and had fought for the Mexicans since the war
began. When the Mexicans at Churubusco wanted to raise the
white flag, the San Patricio deserters tore it down with their
own hands. At last the town fell. The deserters were court-
martialed and hung for their treason.

"Only three more miles to Mexico City," Grant said to
Bravo. "It's almost within our grasp."

But in the heavy fighting, the Americans had suffered more
than a thousand casualties, and were running out of supplies.
Scott knew he had to give his battle-numbed troops a chance
to rest.

Santa Anna also needed time, time to bring his scattered
forces into one fighting unit, time to quell the growing panic
in the city. He exhorted the citizens to fight from every street,
from every rooftop. But to plan such a house-to-house defense,
which would bleed the American forces to death, he needed

time, and so he sent a peace feeler to General Scott.

Scott, eager to see the carnage ended, suggested an armistice so that they might work out the details of a peaceful settlement.

Santa Anna quickly agreed, but placed the onus of asking for the armistice squarely on Scott's shoulders. On August 14, both sides opened negotiations.

Bravo viewed all this with a skeptical eye. "Scott doesn't realize how wily Santa Anna is," he told Grant and Lee while they were cleaning and oiling their weapons. "He's only playing us for time."

Bravo's assessment proved correct, for two weeks later, after Santa Anna felt that the city's defenses were ready, he rejected every American proposal out of hand. Scott realized that he'd been duped, and ended the armistice.

On September 7, Scott advanced his army to Molino del Rey and fought a bloody battle over the cannon foundry there. The day's casualties were extremely high, and Scott's army was now reduced to about seven thousand effective fighting men.

Undaunted, Scott prepared to storm the bastion of Chapultepec Castle, which guarded the road leading directly to the city. On September 12, the artillery bombarded the thick stone structure. But artillery alone failed to reduce the massive fort, and so the infantry was called in to wrest this key point from the enemy. The fighting there proved the bitterest of the war. The Mexicans fought bravely, but the Americans knew that they *had* to win or they were doomed. Chapultepec fell.

Almost tasting the prize for which they'd hungered since landing at Vera Cruz six months before, the Americans swarmed along the causeways leading to the city, heading toward both the Belén and San Cosmé Gates. Shortly after midday, they captured the Belén Gate. A second arm of the troops reached the San Cosmé Gate about four in the afternoon, only to be stopped by the enfilading fire from Mexican cannon and muskets guarding its approaches.

"Remember what we did in Monterrey?" Bravo said to Grant, who was commanding this unit. "Why not do the same thing here?"

Grant nodded and gave orders for the sappers to blow holes in the walls of the houses along the roadway. The infantrymen dashed through the holes, climbed onto the roofs of the houses and of a church, hauled howitzers up, and attacked the Mexican gunners from the rear. The Mexicans scattered in all directions, and by six o'clock in the evening, the Americans held the San Cosmé Gate.

Though Scott's army now commanded two entrances to the city, the task before them seemed insurmountable, for another thousand Americans had fallen during this day's fighting.

"We've only got six thousand troops to subdue a hostile city of two hundred thousand," Sam Grant said to Bravo, as he lay sprawled on the ground beside him. "If the citizens decide to rise up against us en masse, we're in trouble. They could wipe us out."

"There isn't a soldier in the army who doesn't realize that," Bravo said. "Yet we're willing to press on, risk our lives to the last man."

Grant hiked himself on an elbow. "I think you're right. Wonder why that is?"

Bravo thought for a long moment. "Well, some might say that it's just the dulling of the senses that comes with war. God knows that's part of it."

"Also, we're in too deep to back out." Grant laughed ruefully. "We've got to win, or we're dead."

Bravo grew more serious. "But I think there's more to it than that . . . something akin to a crusade. Our Founding Fathers had a vision of spreading our democracy to its natural borders on this continent, all the land between the oceans—and then, hopefully, to all the world. Maybe in a way we're the advance guard for that. All during the time I was growing up my mother pounded that thought into my head. That Americans somehow had a special destiny, that Fate had chosen us . . . I didn't pay much attention to it then, but now I wonder . . ."

They talked until the first stars appeared in the sky, trying to make some sense out of the carnage all about them. Then Bravo said, "And now, Sam, we'd better get some sleep. Big day ahead of us tomorrow."

"May be our last," Sam agreed.

"Whatever happens, I'm damned glad that I met you. If the good Lord wills that we survive, we'll be friends for life. So at least one good thing's come out of this damned war."

In a few minutes, both men were fast asleep.

Six thousand against two hundred thousand . . . every man weighed those odds as he waited apprehensively for the night to end. But fate was with the Americans. General Antonio López de Santa Anna, crushed by defeat after defeat, and with a civilian population that had totally panicked, gave up any hope of defending the capital. He slipped through the city's far gates with some of his troops and headed for Guadalupe Hidalgo.

Just as the American army prepared for its final assault, a delegation of citizens approached Scott's headquarters and surrendered the city. At eleven that morning, the American flag was raised over the grand plaza.

As Bravo saw the flag flapping in the breeze, he wiped the tears from his eyes, tears of fatigue, tears to wash away all the bloodshed he'd seen, tears of relief that the killing had ended.

General Winfield Scott, Old Fuss and Feathers, exhausted but beaming with pride in his men, rode into the plaza to review the troops. For once, all discipline was lost as the men cheered themselves hoarse for this general who'd led them to do the impossible.

While the celebration was going on, Bravo slipped from the ranks and headed directly for the President's Palace, for if Devroe Connaught was still in the city, that's where he'd most likely be. But he wasn't there. Bravo then went to the British legation, but they claimed that they didn't know anybody of that name, or answering that description. Bravo knew they were lying but there was nothing he could do about it. Devroe had vanished.

The thought that Devroe might go unpunished for his crimes tormented Bravo's soul. With the fighting in Mexico all but over, Bravo felt that he could leave. He said his goodbyes to Jeremy, who was staying with the hospital unit to care for the sick and wounded, then said goodbye to Sam Grant and Robert E. Lee.

Then Bravo struck out for home, intent on only one thing: Devroe Connaught.

CONCLUSION

Chapter 59

BRAVO'S SHIP sailed into the Chesapeake Bay and on up the Potomac in late autumn. His spirits soared as the vast expanse of water sparkling in the sun was gradually reduced as the rolling hills came into view, ablaze with autumn's coloring. As the ship hove toward the quay, Bravo could see the Georgetown docks bustling with morning activity. The sailors tied up the ship and furled the sails, all the while shouting greetings to the eager people on shore. Bravo leaped ashore even before the gangplank was down and as his feet touched the ground he felt a surge of happiness.

"Home! Never again will I take Washington for granted."

With his heart pounding in anticipation, he went directly to Kate's house in Georgetown. He had so much to tell her, so much to declare. On the voyage back home, he'd thought of little else. But as his feet carried him over the cobblestone streets he began to have doubts: Would she listen to him? Would she see the wisdom in what he was about to tell her?

A group of children were playing in front of the house, and Bravo stopped and stood very still, watching them. Though he'd been gone almost two and a half years, and they'd all shot up like saplings, he would have recognized these Brand children anywhere. Kate's children, and his own son Forrest, were laughing and jostling each other, much like a pride of young lions.

"I love them all," Bravo whispered to himself. "I could be a good father to all of them."

Then Forrest caught sight of the man staring at them. The boy circled away from his cousins and came closer, not quite sure . . . But when Bravo grinned at him and extended his arms, Forrest let out a shout and flung himself at his father. The other children recognized him and surrounded him with whoops of welcome. Questions flew back and forth as they followed him into the house.

Kate had been cleaning the upstairs bedrooms and hurried downstairs at the commotion. When she recognized Bravo she let out a great cry and embraced him.

Feeling the warmth of her, his heart surged with desire and hope.

"Oh, it's such a blessing to see you!" she exclaimed. "Every Sunday at church, I lit two candles, so the Lord would keep you and Gunning safe."

"You've heard from him then? He's all right?"

Kate nodded eagerly. "Yes, he's well."

"Thank God for that."

"Does your mother know you're back?"

"Not yet. I came here directly."

"She'll be so thrilled. She's done nothing but worry. You look well. Older. A bit weary . . . You must be starved from your journey. Come sit."

In a short while Kate had food on the table; the children clustered around as Bravo ate. When he finished, he sent them outside with the promise that he'd talk to them in a little while. Then he turned to Kate, and the set of his jaw and the expression in his eyes made her flush.

"Kate, we've a lot to talk about."

"That we have, for this war must have been a dreadful experience for you."

"I don't mean that, Kate. I want to talk about us."

She dropped her gaze, her hands fumbling with the edge of her apron. "This letter I received from Gunning last week," she began hurriedly. "The news is all good. I don't know if you've heard, but the fighting in California is over too. Gunning's planning to stay out West. He's looking for a parcel of land to settle, up around San Francisco way."

He felt a churning in the pit of his stomach as he asked, "Have you decided what you're going to do?"

Her shoulders hunched in a tiny, noncommittal shrug. "I've been asking him to come back East. The children, of course, all want to go West. A three-thousand-mile trek across mountain and desert means little to them, to say nothing of the hostiles, hunger, and disease. I don't know what to do."

"Kate, I love you."

He said it with such simplicity and such feeling that she could only sit there, stunned into silence, while great tears welled in her deep blue eyes. At last she managed to murmur, "Bravo, he's your brother."

He nodded soberly. "I know, and I've thought of little else. If you knew the pain it was causing me, then you'd also know just how much I love you."

"Bravo, don't—"

He reached across the table and grasped her hands. "Kate, you must hear me out. Don't let misguided loyalties keep you from choosing a path that could lead to happiness. If I didn't love you so much I could never speak this way. But I *do* love you. Kate, what I'm talking about is the rest of our lives."

She tried to pull her hands away but he wouldn't release them. "Bravo, think for a moment," she began. "I've heard so much about your family's history. About Zebulon, and Rebecca, and Jeremy. Would you repeat such a star-crossed history? You saw what happened to your mother's life. That anguish has never left her."

"Our life together doesn't have to be that way. Not if you care for me. And that's what I'm really asking you. Do you love me enough to reach out for a new life, a happier life?"

The brimming tears spilled down her cheeks. "Bravo, I don't know how to lie very well. There isn't a person in the world I care about more than you. You know I love you."

"Oh my Kate!" he cried, and kissed her hands.

But this time she did manage to pull her hands free. "Now you must let me finish. When I married Gunning, I stood before God's altar and swore, 'Till death do us part.'" She stared at the worn marriage band on her finger and absently turned it. "I'm just a simple girl, a tavernkeeper's daughter, but I believe in keeping a vow made to God. If I turned my back on such a vow I know I'd suffer such remorse that I'd make both our lives miserable. And then there are the children ... You know how they adore their father. Could I bear making them unhappy just to satisfy my own desires?"

"You know I love your children as if they were my own."

"I think you do; but Bravo, to them it wouldn't be the same. You talk about a happier kind of life, but in our hearts we both know that's a dream, a dream so distant that neither of us will ever grasp it. Somewhere deep within you, you know I'm speaking the truth."

When he didn't answer she pressed his hands fiercely. "I look at your bright, shining face, so tender, so very human, and I know that one day you'll find a woman deserving of your love." He started to protest, all the while knowing that he would never be able to change this woman's mind . . . her constancy, devotion, loyalty, which had drawn him to her in the first place, were the very qualities that ultimately would keep them apart.

"Would you try not to think of me unkindly?" she murmured. "I would die if you did."

He stood up, making a vain effort to hide his own tears. "I could never think of you unkindly. I've been blessed just in knowing you."

They looked at each other for a long moment, a look that whispered of all the things that might have been. Then he cleared his throat. "You'll be joining Gunning in California then?"

She nodded. "I think so. Especially now. It will be easier for everybody."

"If you ever change your mind—"

"Oh stop, or I shall have no heart left," she whispered, her tears now falling uncontrollably.

"You're the last person in the world I ever wanted to hurt. Forgive me . . ." After a long pause he said, "Can Forrest stay with you for a few more days? Until I get settled?"

"Of course."

"Good." With a resigned shrug he smiled and said, "Well, I guess I'd better go and see Mother." He walked out the door, leaving a piece of his heart with her.

Bravo walked three miles into Washington, amazed at all the changes. Trees were being felled, land cleared, houses built. He'd only been gone two and a half years, but he felt like Rip Van Winkle. Every so often the memory of Kate went through him like a knife blade, yet part of him also recognized that she had made the brave decision. At the risk of her own happiness, she would protect everybody else around her, the children, Gunning, yes, even himself.

It was in that melancholy frame of mind that he reached the house on New York Avenue. His heaviness lifted somewhat when Tad greeted him with a joyous shout.

"Ah, Bravo! Welcome home! Your mother's asleep. She usually takes a nap at this hour."

"How is she?"

"Getting older, slowing down a little. Suzannah's death . . ." He shook his head.

Bravo went up the stairs lightly and tiptoed into Rebecca's room. She lay on her chaise, asleep, a book dangling from her fingers. In repose, the worry lines in her face had smoothed. She looked serene and lovely, and only her white hair attested to the fact that she'd recently turned sixty-eight.

Some minutes later she stirred, opened her eyes, and trying to make out the dim form before her, became lost in the confusion of time. Her long fingers reached out hopefully, trembling. "Jeremy?"

"No, Mother, it's Bravo," he said softly.

She sat up, drawing her hand across her forehead. "I was dreaming, I was—Oh, Bravo, Bravo," she whispered, "it's so wonderful to have you back," and she began to sob.

He held her hand until she quieted.

They talked all through tea. For perhaps the first time in his life, he felt she was responding to him not only as somebody of her flesh, but as a human being with a life of his own. With that feeling came a great sense of peace.

He debated long and hard whether to tell her about Devroe Connaught, then decided that she had to know, particularly if anything should happen to him. For he still had much unfinished business.

Her face grew pale when he told her. He thought she might have one of her spells, but she managed to control herself. "What are you going to do?" she asked, terrified of his answer.

"Bring him to justice."

"Oh, Bravo, don't. I've lost one of my children to that monster, I couldn't bear it if . . ." Snatching at anything to keep him from going, she said quickly, "I've heard that he and Véronique are moving to London. Let them go. They'll be out of our lives forever."

Bravo jumped to his feet. "London?"

"Bravo, I beg you, for your own salvation. Don't do anything, or his blood will be on your head for the rest of your life. Think, Bravo! Law and order, *reason*. Those are the marks of a civilized human being; without them, we're nothing but beasts. That's the dream this country was founded on, that's the dream we must have for ourselves."

Before Rebecca could stop him, Bravo bounded down the stairs, checked his Colt revolver, flung on his cloak, and quickly saddled a horse. He galloped through the streets of Washington, the wind belling his cloak behind him. He had no specific plan in mind; he knew simply that he had to confront Devroe before he got away. He'd haul him into a court of law. If he resisted, and doubtless he would, then he'd take him by force.

Night had fallen and the sharp November air had turned hoary with frost when Bravo reached the outskirts of the Connaught estate in the hills overlooking the capital. He avoided the guard at the main gate of the plantation and made a wide circuit that took him to a remote place near the cottonfields.

Halfway there, he came upon the ramshackle slave quarters, and heard the mournful chant of the chained beings lamenting their lot. Someday this too will have to change, Bravo thought.

About a quarter of a mile from the house, he reached a copse and tied his horse there. Silently, he moved toward the house, eyes alert for any guards that might be patrolling. The house looked magnificent in the darkness, with its soaring white columns. Smoke curled lazily from the cluster of brick chimneys; the smell of burning firewood lay pungent on the night air.

Who would ever believe that a scene of such beauty could mask the evil that lay within those walls? Well, this night would see the end of it, the end of the feud that had burned for generations between the Connaughts and the Brands.

Two sentries were patrolling the grounds; Devroe was obviously taking no chances on being surprised. One guard stood near the French doors that looked into the library. Bravo made out the figures of a man and woman in the room, and he took them to be Devroe and Véronique. Thank God they were still there.

He'd have to pass the one sentry to get into the library. He waited until the man began walking again, and when he passed close by, Bravo sprang from behind some boxwood and felled him with his revolver butt. He dragged the man's body into the bushes.

Keeping low, he sprinted toward the house, and flattened himself against the wall. He peered into the room and saw Devroe, wearing maroon velvet evening clothes, arguing with his wife. Véronique, resplendent in bronze satin, nevertheless looked stricken; her dark eyes darted all about in her terror. Bravo could hear their voices.

"Did you really think you could deceive me?" Devroe demanded, his lips thinned into a bloodless line. "Did you think you could lie with every nigger who caught your fancy and not be found out?"

"Lies, all lies!" Véronique cried, fighting for her life.

"While I was away on one of my trips, you had an affair with that mulatto named Tortuga. You became pregnant with his child, so you induced a miscarriage."

Véronique's mind raced like a fox before the hounds. How had he found out? And why had he waited so long to confront her? It had been years ago. Then it came to her. That Haitian witch! The filthy creature hadn't died after all and must have told Devroe.

Devroe went on, "When Gunning Brand came back to Washington, you threw yourself at him. When he rejected you, you sent an anonymous letter to his wife. That much my own informants told me. I have no love for Gunning Brand; I'd as soon see the whole family in Hell, and will, before I'm finished. As I shall see you in Hell."

"What are you going to do?" she whispered.

"I've been busy this week," he said. "First, I've seen my solicitors. Cut you off without a cent. There's not a store or hotel in Washington that will give you credit. Then I've had you declared an unfit mother; you're forbidden to see the children, on pain of imprisonment."

She straightened and said with an air of triumph, "Have you forgotten that I still have papers implicating you in the entire British spy network in the United States?"

"I haven't forgotten, and that's why *I'm* leaving for London, shortly. And taking the children with me. The authorities here are uncomfortably close on my trail anyway. So you may use your information as you like."

"Devroe, please, I am the mother of your—"

He cut her short with an abrupt wave of his hand. "I plan

to leave you in this foul, benighted country to suffer the fate you dread most of all. That's right, my dear—poverty. I'm throwing you back in the gutter where I found you."

Outside, Bravo could wait no longer. He pushed on the door handle, but found it locked. He lifted his foot and kicked in the door, sending the glass crashing. Véronique screamed and after an instant of shock, Devroe started for the gun cabinet on the wall.

Before he could reach it, Bravo fired, splintering the door of the cabinet and forcing Devroe away from it.

Drawn by the commotion, the second sentry ran through the French doors, but as he entered, Bravo pistol-whipped him and he crumpled to the floor.

In that moment of distraction, Devroe picked up a silver stiletto that he used as a letter opener and slipped it into his pocket. Véronique saw his move. Her glance flashed one way then another, trying to determine how all this might serve her.

"You're coming with me," Bravo said to Devroe.

"And just where are we going?" Devroe spat.

"To the authorities."

"On what charges?"

"Spying. You claim to be an American citizen, yet you were in the employ of General Santa Anna. That's treason, and punishable by hanging."

Devroe paled and stammered, "You've no proof; it's your word against mine."

"There's enough suspicion about you in Washington already. My evidence will complete the picture."

"You'll never get me off my property. I have sentries posted everywhere."

"Devroe, I'd prefer killing you myself, so don't push me." He strode to the man and put his revolver against his head. "There are five bullets left in this chamber, and all of them will be in your brain if you make one false move."

At that moment, a guard who'd been posted in another part of the house blundered into the library, his gun drawn. Bravo whirled Devroe around so that his body faced the sentry.

"Don't shoot!" Devroe shouted.

"Tell him to bring your carriage to the door—the two-seater."

When Devroe didn't respond quickly enough, Bravo cocked the gun. Devroe called out, "Do as he says, man!"

The guard bounded from the room. A stillness settled in the library, broken only by the sounds of heavy breathing.

"You won't get away with this," Devroe said. "I'll have you arrested on charges of breaking and entering. Everybody in the capital knows you bear me a personal grudge. Your own mother had you jailed when you attacked me in the White House."

"I should have killed you then. My sister would still be alive."

"What do you mean?" Véronique demanded, and when Bravo told her, she cried out, "Alors! How horrible. You know I had nothing to do with that, nothing!"

"Save your sympathy, Véronique. You're as much a part of this as he is."

The guard poked his head back into the library. "The carriage is ready out front."

"Tell him to get away from that door or you're dead," Bravo ordered.

Devroe did as he was told. As they started out the door he winced with pain and whined, "I can't move my crippled hand without the other. Is it all right if I put it in my pocket?"

"Go ahead, then," Bravo said.

Devroe reached over with his left hand and tucked the crippled arm into his pocket. As he withdrew his good hand, he pulled out the stiletto and lunged at Bravo. Bravo fired. The bullet caught Devroe in his crippled arm. Since he had no feeling there, he continued the downswing with his knife, aiming it at Bravo's heart.

Reacting with animal instinct, Bravo whirled aside, but the knife plunged deep into his right shoulder. His gun clattered to the floor. Devroe bent to scoop it up. Bravo tackled him and the two men went flying across the room, Devroe's stiletto skittering into a darkened corner.

"Véronique, get his gun!" Devroe shouted, as he and Bravo fought.

Véronique ran and picked up the gun. Before the guard could come back into the room, she closed and locked the door. She held the revolver with both hands and tried to aim it. It was heavy, and she'd never fired anything like this before. The forms of the two men wrestling on the floor blurred before her eyes; she aimed first at one, then the other, never sure which was which, but knowing that what she did now would affect the rest of her life. There were only three of them in the room . . . then the conviction of what she must do came to her. Terrible, yes, but she was fighting for her life. Both of them must die, and she would be able to say they'd killed each other.

Bravo was punching Devroe with his one good arm, but he was losing blood and felt himself weakening. Unless he finished him off quickly, got the gun back . . .

He saw Véronique coming close, her satin skirts whispering as she moved to stand over them. Then she fired. The bullet splintered the floorboard. Devroe looked up, and when he saw that she had the gun, relief lit his eyes. But the relief turned to terror when he realized that she was aiming at him.

"Véronique, don't!" he cried out, then the cry strangled in his throat as her second shot caught him under the jaw, the bullet smashing up through his mouth, and lodging in his brain.

Devroe went limp in Bravo's hands. He stared at him, stunned, then looked to Véronique, who was preparing to fire again. He rolled across the Aubusson carpet as she pulled the trigger; the bullet grazed his thigh.

He sprang to his feet, grabbed the legs of the Louis XVI writing table and upended it, holding it in front of him like a shield. She fired again and he felt the force of the fifth bullet thud into the wood. One more bullet—she had only one more bullet. But now he heard pounding at the door as the guard tried to kick it in.

Still holding the table in front of him, Bravo rushed at Véronique and bowled her over as she tried to fire the last shot. She screamed as he grabbed her wrist and bent it backwards until she dropped the gun. He grabbed the revolver and leveled it at her. "You murdered him."

"It was an accident!" she whimpered.

"No, Véronique. It was murder. I was at the window. I heard everything Devroe said to you. It won't be too hard to convince the jury that you had motive enough. And I'm going to make damned sure that you stand trial."

Another guard burst into the room and Véronique's eyes flashed with hope. But Bravo cocked his pistol and held it to her head. He said to the guard, "Your master's dead, and your mistress will be too, if you so much as make a move."

Thrusting Véronique before him, Bravo said, "And now, Véronique, you and I will take the carriage to the city."

Chapter 60

REBECCA WAITED anxiously at the Washington train station amid the light fall of January snow. She almost dreaded this moment, wondering how Becky and Zeb would be, what they'd look like. She wondered also whether she'd be able to retain her composure and not break down in front of them. That would be the worst thing of all.

Because of the telegraph lines that had been laid between the railway stations, Zeb had been able to telegraph ahead and tell Rebecca they'd be arriving. All the Brands had decided that they must be at the station to greet them.

"Now don't stand too close to me," Rebecca admonished the children, who kept crowding around her skirts. "And don't swamp Becky either. We mustn't frighten her off."

"Well, she's my cousin," Peter said belligerently, "and I've got a right to be here."

"Me too," Geary seconded.

"If you two don't behave yourselves I'm going to tan your backsides in front of everybody," Kate told her obstreperous sons. "Better yet, I'll just take you both home so you won't get to see them at all."

Both boys had heard the no-nonsense tone in their mother's voice and quieted down. Peter, Geary, Sharon, and Forrest had been scrubbed, combed, and polished until they fairly shone.

461

Kate had also taken special pains with herself, she so wanted her niece to like her, so much wanted to help the poor child.

Circumstance and Wingate rolled up in their new carriage; Wingate's practice was prosperous enough so he could now afford such amenities. Doe bounded out of the carriage, carrying a bouquet of dried flowers she'd made. Bravo was with them, fully recovered from his wounds.

"Well anyway, my father conquered California," Peter whispered to Forrest, who shot right back, "But my father conquered Mexico City and ended the war."

That stymied Peter for a moment, but he was saved by the distant wail of the train whistle. The children shouted, "Here it comes!"

The great puffing engine became visible, coming toward the city at the astonishing speed of twenty miles an hour. With clanks and groans the train slowed, eased into the station, and ground to a halt.

Rebecca searched the window, thinking maybe they had decided not to come, maybe they'd missed the train, maybe . . . Then she saw a tall youth leap to the platform—Zeb! He reached up and helped Becky down.

Rebecca had told herself that she wouldn't get excited, that she wouldn't start crying, but there she was, waving furiously while the tears rolled down her face. She rushed to Becky and embraced her fiercely. She held the girl to her heart, murmuring, "It's all right, you're home and you're safe." But she felt Becky stiffen slightly under her touch, and released her.

Then all the Brands and the Granges and the Albrights piled into the carriages and headed for Rebecca's house, where a large meal was waiting. As they drove along Pennsylvania Avenue, Rebecca stole glances at her granddaughter. Her heart shriveled at the remote, lusterless look on Becky's face . . . she who'd been so full of life, reduced to this. I will save her, I *will!* Rebecca swore to herself.

"Don't you think those poplars are lovely?" she asked, pointing to the tall, elegant trees. "Thomas Jefferson planted them almost fifty years ago, and I was here when he ordered it done."

Becky managed a smile and nodded politely.

"There's the White House," Rebecca said, as they approached the President's House.

For the first time a glimmer of interest sparked Becky's eyes. She twisted her head as their carriage rolled by. "I had no idea it was so beautiful," she said.

Rebecca patted her granddaughter's hand. "It's even more beautiful inside. Would you like to see it? I'm sure Mrs. Polk would invite us to tea."

Becky blinked her eyes, once more unresponsive. To gloss over the uncomfortable moment, Rebecca turned to Wingate. "How is the President these days?"

"Still wearing himself out. I wouldn't be surprised if he worked himself to death."

"Has he changed his mind about running for a second term?"

"Definitely not," Wingate said. "Even if he wanted to, I don't think he'd have the strength to campaign. And Sarah Polk is adamant that he not run. He's just not well enough."

"Well then, from the sentiments one hears in Washington, and from what I read is happening in the rest of the country, I'll wager that Zachary Taylor will be our next President."

Bravo frowned.

When they reached the house, Becky's remoteness seemed to lift somewhat, and she wandered around the rooms, touching things. "It's just as mother described it to me," she murmured.

During dinner she warmed a little more, for it was almost impossible for anybody to remain withdrawn with five eager young cousins asking questions at once, and promising to take the new arrivals to see absolutely everything in Washington.

When the meal and the talk was finally over, the others went home, and Becky, Zeb, and Rebecca settled down for the night. Rebecca tossed fitfully, alert to any sounds in the house. Finally she decided that sleep wouldn't come that night, so she lit the whale-oil lamp and padded down the hallway. She stopped first at Zeb's room. His door stood open and he lay sleeping peacefully. In the drifting radiance of the lamp, his fiercely handsome face looked so much like his grandfather Zebulon's that for a moment she was cast back through the years.

Then she went to Becky's room and opened the door quietly, gazing at her granddaughter. But Becky reacted to the light and bolted upright, terror contorting her face.

Rebecca quickly sat on the edge of the bed and held the trembling girl, rocking her back and forth. "I need you here, Becky," she whispered. "I need you all the more with Suzannah gone. The only thing that makes my life bearable is having you here. I look back on my life and all I see are my failures, all the things that I should have done. But then when I hold you in my arms I think, Becky will do them, she'll pick up the torch of righteousness and carry it, shedding its glorious light all around her, knowing that the higher it's held, the more people will see its light.

"Becky, this is a monstrous world we live in, a world of deceit, and hate, and war, a world that might be better if women had a greater voice, if they could bring their influence to bear. We must bring the qualities of gentleness and kindness to all men, so that the killing will stop. We must do it because it's in our nature to do it. For too many centuries we've been silent, allowing men to hold sway. Becky, for the future and salvation of the world, our voices *must* be heard.

"I know what an impossible thing that must seem to you in this time of sorrow, yet if your mother were here beside us, she'd say the same thing, for her whole life was lived with those gentle precepts. Becky, I'm old, and getting tired. Sometimes I wish I could lay this burden down, but it appears that the good Lord has other plans for me. But I can't do it alone.

"I need your help. You must give me my immortality—for that's what you represent, with your young hopes and young dreams for a different kind of world."

But Becky still didn't respond; Rebecca loosened her grip on the girl. She gazed at her, the long red-gold hair so rich and alive in the lamplight, the enormous hazel eyes reflecting twin pinpoints of light. Behind the mask of terror, Rebecca saw such an intelligent face, shining with idealism, emboldened with the dream of new worlds to explore, a face animated with all the good things that a woman could be.

But what was the use if she couldn't reach her?

As Rebecca rose to go, Becky reached out tentatively. "I'll try, Grandma," she whispered almost inaudibly. "I don't know if I can do it, but I'll try."

And Rebecca's heart sang.

They sat by the window and watched the dark night give way to first light. Rebecca rose suddenly. "Come, there's something I must show you."

She led the way to the musty attic, then opened the trapdoor leading to the roof and climbed up. Her weary bones complained with each step, but she pressed on. When she reached the top, she gave Becky her hand and helped her onto the roof.

The promise of dawn had just begun to color the billowing

masses of clouds that raced across the winter sky. They stood bundled in their blankets, their arms around each other, and watched as the glowing light revealed the landscape.

Far in the distance, Rebecca could make out the hazy outline of the Capitol building . . . closer, the silver-gray thread of the Potomac . . . the surrounding hills. Washington was no longer a little village set in a miasmic, snake-infested swamp, but had grown into a real capital, one that Americans could be proud of.

"A long time ago—oh, I think it was in 1814—I stood on this very roof and doused it with pails of water to keep it from catching fire when the British were burning Washington. They set fire to the Capitol building, and to the White House, and as I watched both buildings burn, I thought that it was not only the end of my world, but the end of our nation.

"But we persevered. And we rebuilt. And eventually we won. I believe with all my heart that that's the secret to anyone's life—to have the strength to take the blows of fate, and the perseverance to rebuild. Now as I look about me on this beloved land, as I see the sun burnishing the dome of the Capitol, I thank the Lord he gave us all the strength to persevere . . . to grow from a loose confederacy of thirteen states, to a great nation that extends from sea to shining sea.

"Becky, it's a new year. The future is ours. It will always be ours. All we need do is recognize it, seize it, honor it."

The great orb of the sun rose, casting its roseate light on the Capitol, and the pristine stone of the White House took the lifting light of dawn.

Selected Bibliography

For a more complete biography on Washington, D.C., the White House, and the earlier Presidents, please see the listings in earlier volumes of this series, *The American Palace*.

The Presidents

Borden, Morton. *America's Ten Greatest Presidents*. Chicago: Rand McNally, 1961.

Frank, Sid, and Arden Davis Melick. *The Presidents: Tidbits and Trivia*. Maplewood, N.J.: Hammond, 1982.

Lorant, Stephan. *The Glorious Burden*. Lennox, Mass.: Author's Editions, 1976.

Jackson

Coke, Fletch. *Andrew Jackson's Hermitage*. Hermitage, Tenn.: The Ladies' Hermitage Assoc., 1979.

Davis, Burke. *Old Hickory*. New York: Dial Press, 1977.

Remini, Robert, V. *Andrew Jackson and the Course of American Freedom 1822–1832*. New York.: Harper and Row, 1981.

Van Buren

Fitzpatrick, John C. (ed.). *Autobiography of Martin Van Buren*. Washington, D.C.: (American Historical Association, Government Printing Office) 1920.

Polk

Nevins, Alan (ed.). *Polk, the Diary of a President 1845–1849*. New York: Longmans, Green, 1952.

Washington, D.C.

Ewing, Charles. *Yesterday's Washington, D.C.* Miami, Fla.: E. A. Seemann, 1976.

Froncek, Thomas. *The City of Washington*. New York: Knopf, 1981.

The Mexican War

Connor, Seymour V., and Odie B. Faulk. *North America Divided*. New York: Oxford University Press, 1971.

Dufour, Charles, L. *The Mexican War*. New York: Hawthorne Books, 1968.

Eaton, Clement. *Jefferson Davis*. New York: Free Press, 1977.

Freeman, Douglas S. *Robert E. Lee: A Biography*. 4 Vols. New York: Charles Scribner and Sons, 1934.

Grant, Ulysses, S. *Personal Memoirs of U.S. Grant*. Charles Webster, 1894.

McIntosh, James T. *The Papers of Jefferson Davis*. Baton Rouge: Louisiana State University Press, 1981.

Nevin, David. *The Mexican War*. Alexandria, Va.: Time-Life, 1978.

Nichols, Edward, J. *Zach Taylor's Little Army*. New York: Doubleday, 1963.

Singletary, Otis. *The Mexican War*. Chicago: University of Chicago Press, 1960.

Miscellaneous

DeVoto, Bernard. *The Year of Decision, 1846*. Boston: Houghton Mifflin, 1943.

Frank, Beryl. *The Pictorial History of the Democratic Party*. Secaucus,
    N.J.: Castle Books, 1980.

Ganoe, William A. *The History of the United States Army*. Ashton, Md.:
    Eric Lundberg, 1964.

Goode, James M. *Capital Losses: A Cultural History of Washington's
    Destroyed Buildings*. Washington, D.C.: Smithsonian Institute
    Press, 1979.

Josephy, Alvin M., Jr. *History of the Congress of the United States*. New
    York: American Heritage, 1975.

Linton, Calvin D. *The Bicentennial Almanac*. Nashville, Tenn.: Thomas
    Nelson, 1975.

Smith, Marie, and Louise Durbin. *White House Brides*. Washington, D.C.:
    Acropolis, 1966.

Urdang, Laurence (ed.). *The Timetable of American History*. New York:
    Simon and Schuster, 1981.